The
Darkness
at Dawn

Pamela Roberts Lee

outskirts
press

Outskirts Press, Inc.
http://www.outskirtspress.com

Paperback ISBN: 978-1-9772-1285-6
Hardback ISBN: 978-1-9772-1286-3

Cover Photo © 2019 Matthew M. Grinberg. All rights reserved - used with permission.

Outskirts Press and the "OP" logo are trademarks belonging to Outskirts Press, Inc.

PRINTED IN THE UNITED STATES OF AMERICA

PART ONE
1634 - 1636

Chapter 1

Lightning banished the darkness around John Lee, a boy of thirteen. He and the other passengers cowered, sitting on the ship's 'tween deck, below the ship's main deck and above its hold, praying they'd survive the storm. John thought he saw movement to his left, but by the time he looked, the darkness had returned. Seconds later, thunder roared through the void. The *Francis* was forty-eight days out of Ipswich, England, bound for Massachusetts Bay. John was traveling with his Guardian William Westwood, his wife Bridget and their other ward, thirteen-year-old Grace Newell. But for the moment, he was alone.

Gradually, John's sight readjusted to the dark and the ship's deck and passengers' baggage reappeared. He heard the wailing wind, the sea pounding against the hull, and the screams of frightened children younger than himself. Above them, the ship's master and helmsman battled to keep the ship afloat. Through the dim light from the candle in the steerage cabin overhead he could see the helmsman pulling hard on the pole-like wooden whipstaff controlling the ship's rudder.

The storm had struck suddenly in the afternoon, its rolling dark clouds low on the northwestern horizon. Like the other passengers, John assumed God's blessing would ensure their safe passage to Massachusetts Bay. He felt certain the storm was God's challenge, and he prayed they'd all be strong enough to meet it. But whatever fate might befall them, he would accept it as God's will.

A second lightning bolt seared the night, the inevitable thunderclap almost instantaneous. In the brief light, John saw a man standing above one of William Westwood's bags, clutching William's gold-inlaid silver chalice. John was shocked that one of his Puritan brothers would try to steal it. The chalice had been rescued from a Puritan church sacked by Anglicans and was to be the centerpiece of Reverend Thomas Hooker's Puritan church in Massachusetts Bay. Almost all the *Francis's* passengers were members of Hooker's congregation.

The next lighting flash was blinding, the thunder simultaneous, and so loud John thought the ship's hull would split open. In that instant of light, he was surprised to see the man with the chalice only four feet away, looking right at him. The man's eyes were as black as the pit of his father's well in Colchester, and as cold as the north wind that swept over his father's farm in January. But when lightning flashed next, the man was gone.

Though the crew had secured the ship's canons and equipment on the 'tween deck, and the passengers had tied down their baggage and supplies, many smaller items slipped free during the storm. John heard them sliding back and forth in the darkness, as the storm pitched the ship in all directions and made the *Francis's* timbers groan all around him.

He called into the darkness. "Master William are you all right?"

Only the wailing wind replied.

The storm now controlled all conversation, its voice the only sound John heard. Its force pushed the ship from side to side. The storm's spray provided his only smells and tastes. It rolled over him through the hatch above, forcing its way into his mouth and nose. He gagged on its salt as he was thrust about on the floor. Frequent bursts of lightning were his only source of light, providing short still-life bursts of chaos.

He braced himself against the ship's hull, waiting for the storm's fury to pass. He hoped it would leave as swiftly as it came and prayed the crew's preparations were adequate. When they'd first sighted the storm, senior helmsman Ben Mapes told John the ship's master had two options. He could run before the wind, thereby reducing the wind's strength passing before the ship. This would require that all sails but the foresail at the ship's bow be furled. In this way the ship might be able to make some headway toward its destination.

The second option was to lie to by sailing angled into the wind, while preventing the ship from turning broadside to it. This would allow little headway and require all sails but the main course, or lower main sail, to be furled. The ship's master elected to lie to because night was approaching, and it would be impossible to alter options later by changing sails on a stormy night.

As the storm approached, and wind lashed the ship's decks, John watched the crew furl all the sails but the main course. The afternoon sky grew darker with clouds rolling above them. The *Francis* and its traveling companion, the *Elizabeth*, moved farther apart to avoid colliding. Before darkness fell, the *Elizabeth* was but a distant shape when the passengers went below to ride out the storm.

With the storm's full fury upon them, it was Mapes's task to keep the main course full and bellied forward. He could do this by pulling the whipstaff, so the rudder was angled into the wind, allowing the main course to partially fill from the stern. Their salvation depended upon Mapes keeping the *Francis* from being struck broadside by the waves crashing against it, while also preventing the main course filling from the bow.

Since Mapes had the rudder hard over, angled toward the wind, allowing the ship to barely edge into the wind, the rudder was more exposed to the waves. A sudden wind shift or the main course filling from the bow could tear the rudder away when the waves struck at full force. A rudderless ship could easily be capsized by a broadside wave. Therefore, if John was upright, he felt confident Mapes was in control.

The wind howled at a still higher pitch, and water flowed under John's outstretched legs. The creaking masts and moaning bulkheads were louder than ever. Had the hull been breached?

Without warning, John was thrust onto his left side. Had the

Francis been hit on its broadside? Seconds later, he was upright again. The wind screamed outside, while an irregular hammering sounded above; at times it came in rapid spurts, at other times it struck once every few seconds. The steerage cabin's candle was now out. He worried Mapes would be unable to keep the whipstaff at the proper angle in the dark.

Sheets of rain splashed through the ship's hull, soaking John's breeches and doublet. As he wiped the water from his face, he was struck on the head by something bulky and soft. He heard it hit the deck's floor then slide towards the bow. He braced his hands against the hull. Someone gripped his right hand.

"Is that you John?" came Grace Newell's childlike voice.

"Yes, it's me," he answered. "Are you alright?"

"I'm scared. Master William and Bridget disappeared. Are we going to die?"

He felt Grace's trembling, and squeezed her hand, forcing away his fear. "No. God is with us. The storm will end soon."

Grace moved her body against his, "I pray you're right. But what of Master William and Bridget?"

John placed an arm around Grace's shoulders as they leaned against the ship's hull. "Don't worry about Master William. He knows what to do. He and Bridget were just moved by the storm."

They sat together for the next hour. Finally, the storm's fury weakened. Eventually, the morning sunlight seeped into the 'tween deck and Grace fell asleep in his arms. John wondered how his fellow passengers had fared during the night. Then he remembered the chalice and the man with the black eyes. He wasn't ready to conclude the man had stolen the chalice. Perhaps it came free of its bag in the storm and he was simply returning it. Or it could be that he'd taken it from the bag to secure it. But even as he had these thoughts, he realized that theft was the most likely explanation.

John's eyes were heavy. With Grace still in his arms, they began to close. Without warning, the man's black eyes stared at him again, and this time he was smiling. John lunged at the man to reclaim the chalice, but he laughed and disappeared as John woke. He was against the bulkhead again, with Grace in his lap. Just a dream, he thought, and fell back to sleep.

Chapter 2

The *Francis* moved silently through the white-tipped waves, a stiff breeze at her stern. Nearly all the passengers were asleep on the 'tween deck. John was not among them. He and a few others woke at ten in the morning. The first thing John saw was sunlight streaming through the hatch grate to the steerage cabin above him.

He looked towards the ship's bow. The dim light from the open bow hatch and gun ports revealed bodies sprawled amid rumpled bedding, clothing, wooden plates and utensils. Earlier, small family areas had been separated by drapes, obstructing his view of the 'tween deck. Now the drapes lay heaped on the deck, and he could see all the way to the bow. The 'tween deck was a dark musty tunnel, dominated by the capstan's heavy oak base ten feet in front of him, the main mast twenty feet beyond that, and the windlass at the bow.

The capstan's heavy oak timber rose above him and disappeared into the main deck. He glanced back down to the capstan's wooden cylinder. Weeks earlier, the crew had pushed wooden poles into the cylinder to winch barrels of beer, dried beef and other supplies onto the ship. Small drops of water flowed down the capstan, picking up other drops as all made their way to a pool of water at its base.

A score of sleeping men, women and children lay on the floor around the capstan. Among them were John's guardian William Westwood and his wife Bridget. William's back was propped against the capstan with Bridget's head resting in his lap. William's long, wheat-colored hair was wet and matted, and looked nearly black. A little farther down the 'tween deck, towards the bow, William's friend Joseph Barnard and his wife Katherine slept on wet, dirty bedding. Sleeping beside them was the Barnards' ward, seven-year-old

Henry Hayward.

The main mast was drenched. John assumed this was because the mast extended far above the upper deck and collected more rain during the storm. It then flowed down the mast into the 'tween deck. He felt certain this was the source of the water that washed over him during the night. Water pooled at the mast's base, where a handful of passengers slept. The rest slept against the hull.

His view of the windlass was less clear. It was a heavy wooden winch built low to the 'tween deck's floor and used to raise and lower the anchor. He knew it was at the bow, and when he saw a low dark shape there, he realized he'd found it.

A large, multicolored pile of clothes and bedding rested near the main hatch, between the main mast and the windlass. The pile climbed up the hull's side and included a handful of storage bags. He was certain the soft object that struck his head during the storm would now be in that pile. He decided to check the pile for William's bag. Hopefully, the chalice was still in the bag.

He slipped off his doublet and placed it in his lap under Grace's head. He slid his legs away and lowered the makeshift pillow with Grace's head on it to the floor. Grace half-opened her eyes and smiled before falling back to sleep.

John rose and walked toward the pile, taking care not to step on any sleeping passengers. The deck was slick with water, so he braced himself against the hull to keep from slipping, while ducking his head under the main deck's support beams.

Once at the pile, he sorted through the bags, coats, blankets and other items. So many things had found their way to this spot, it might be impossible to quickly find William's bag, even if it was there. Several nearby passengers began to rustle. Finally, one of them grunted, "Stop rummaging through those things."

John turned to see a pudgy young man in his late teens squatting on the deck in a heap of wet blankets. His face was full and fleshy, and his stringy brown hair hung below his shoulders.

"I'm looking for my master's bag," John announced. "It was lost in the storm."

"I don't believe you. If it's true, let your master come look for it."

The pudgy man stood and tied the cord to his dirty wet shirt. He was about John's height, five and a half feet tall, but looked to be half again as heavy. John recognized him as one of the older boys who'd hung together and bullied the younger children on the voyage. John had taken pains to avoid them.

Several passengers were now watching the confrontation. John decided not to press too hard. "I will stop," he said, "if you promise to keep others from going through the pile until we can do it together."

"I can't do that."

"Why not?" John demanded.

"It's not my job."

"Well, in that case you can watch me look for my master's bag."

The pudgy man sighed and squatted back on the wet blanket. John climbed back on the pile and the passengers lost interest. He rummaged through the heap for several minutes. The pudgy man watched him all the while. Finally, convinced William's bag must be elsewhere, he made his way back to the stern. While moving past William and Bridget, he spotted the gray wool bag in which William kept the chalice, his diary and other personal items. He concluded William must have found the bag after the storm passed. John was both disappointed and relieved. He wouldn't be able to search the bag for the chalice until William woke, so —for the moment at least— he could focus on something else.

John sat against the bulkhead next to Grace, who slept peacefully with her head on his doublet. He looked up through the hatch into the steerage cabin, watching Ben Mapes's hands on the whipstaff until he fell asleep.

John woke to the sound of several men sopping up the pool of water by the main mast. It was mid-afternoon. He watched the men sweep water through the leather-flapped scuppers covering drainage openings along the deck until his head cleared from sleep. The smell of wet wood filled his nostrils, and he shivered in the penetrating cold. He rose to his feet and climbed the ladder toward the warmth above.

At the top of the ladder he called out, "Please open the hatch."

"Is that you John?" a familiar gravelly voice replied.

"Yes Ben. Please open the hatch."

The hatch lifted, and John saw the weathered face of Ben Mapes smiling down at him. "How are my Puritan friends on this fine sunny afternoon?" Mapes asked.

"Sleepy," John replied. "What are you doing at the helm? Why aren't you sleeping now?"

Mapes laughed, "How can I give up the helm when we're chasing the *Elizabeth* and running under full sail before the wind?"

"Aren't your arms tired?"

"A little, but I was relieved for a few hours this morning after the storm passed."

As Mapes held the whipstaff steady, John watched the compass in the binnacle cabinet in front of them. The *Francis* was still on course. The candle beside the compass was now lit.

"How did you keep our course when the candle went out last night?" John asked.

"You operate the whipstaff by feel in a storm," Mapes explained. "My problem was the steerage cabin's damned door. Once it flew open, it kept flying back and forth. I thought it would come off its hinges and knock me senseless."

"I heard it pound," John said. "Lightning lit the 'tween deck when the door slammed open. I thought we were going to founder when we were on our side."

"Think you were afraid? Up here water poured over the deck

through the open steerage cabin door. It was like a waterfall."

After several minutes of silence, Mapes asked, "Would you like to handle the whipstaff?"

"Yes." John took the whipstaff, as he had many times before on their journey.

"Stay on the compass setting. I just pegged the direction and speed on the traverse board for our last half hour. Peg it again when the hourglass empties."

Mapes moved forward of the whipstaff and organized several ropes tangled during the storm.

John looked behind him at the traverse board, which hung on the wall between the steerage and master cabins. Four pegs were in it, with strings marking their heading and speed for each half hour. There would be eight pegs in the board when Mapes's watch was done.

After thirty minutes, John turned to Mapes and asked, "Can you take the whipstaff again? I want to go onto the main deck for some sun."

"Tired already?" Mapes chuckled. "I'll be right there." Mapes was still forward organizing the tangled ropes. He stood just as the ship's Master, Martin Cutting, emerged from the master's cabin. Cutting was tall and broad-shouldered, the sort of man John expected to find running a cross-Atlantic voyage. Cutting smiled at John when he saw him at the whipstaff.

"Good day, Master Cutting," Mapes said.

"I'm glad you left the whipstaff in good hands Ben," Cutting replied, looking at John. "Did Ben tell you we're chasing the *Elizabeth*?"

"Yes sir," John answered. "When will we catch her?"

"If we're on course, we should see her within the hour. I'm going on deck now. Come with me"

John followed Cutting through the steerage cabin doors, past the capstan's upper half and onto the main deck, which was now awash in sunlight. His body warmed quickly, and fresh air filled his lungs.

Above him, the ship's sails blossomed before a stiff breeze. Most crewmen were aloft, in the ropes below the fore and main mast's spars.

"They want to be the first to sight the *Elizabeth*," Cutting said.

"What's the reward?" John asked.

"My gratitude." Cutting smiled before walking toward the ship's bow.

John stood alone at the rail below the forecastle deck, the sun at his back, and the sky's deep blue reflected in the rushing sea below him. He watched the droplets in the white mist of the wave crests. He breathed in the salty air while the ocean swells rose and fell.

A crewman shouted to another in a voice deep with the twang of John's hometown of Colchester. It sounded like his father's voice, causing John's mind to wander back to the room where his father had spent more than a month in bed with an unending cough. The last time John had seen him there, his father wasn't coughing, nor was he in his bedclothes. He didn't understand why his father was propped up on the bed in his finest suit. He looked from his father to his mother, seeking an explanation. His mother's gaze dropped to the floor.

His father was pale and emaciated, but his voice was calm, "I am too sick to make the crossing. You must go with William and Bridget Westwood to avoid getting my illness. Your mother and I will come later."

John said nothing in response. He didn't want to go without his father, so why hadn't he complained? But that was what his father wanted, and he did as he was told. To this day he wondered why his father was wearing his finest suit while sitting in bed. He rarely wore that suit. Just the day before, the bed had been drenched with fever-sweat.

A shout from above brought him back to the moment. He looked up at the ship's main topmast. The crewman yelled again, "It's the *Elizabeth!*"

Several passengers rushed past John and up the ladder to the forecastle deck, hoping to spot the *Elizabeth*. Other passengers emerged from the steerage cabin and crowded against the ship's railing.

John leaned over the rail and looked ahead. At first, he saw nothing, but when the waves dropped lower, he saw the *Elizabeth* downwind in the distance. Ben Mapes turned the *Francis* to gather more wind in her sails.

John watched the distance between the two ships close for the next hour. The crew resumed their normal duties and many passengers lost interest and went below deck. John turned away from the *Elizabeth* and glanced up at the stern's half deck behind him. He saw Master Cutting calling directions to Mapes, who was in the steerage cabin below him. Except for John and a handful of other passengers, the main deck was empty.

He leaned against the rail, staring at the waves rolling and swelling in the distance. The sun was dipping lower and the air was quickly getting cold.

He pulled his doublet tightly around his chest and thought of the cold night he and his father had mounted horses at their farm for the six-mile ride to see Reverend Hooker preach in Dedham. It was dark as they passed through Colchester's narrow streets. He'd kept his horse close to his father's for safety until they were in the countryside again.

Dedham's church was crowded when they arrived. It was hard to breathe while pressed together with the others. All were excitedly awaiting Reverend Hooker's arrival. All hushed when Hooker entered the room and climbed the pulpit high above them. Hooker stood behind the lectern and looked upon the people without speaking. Then he stood ramrod straight and thrust his head forward. As he did, his height and frame appeared to grow. His face was full, his hair cut just above his shoulders, and his eyes dark and piercing. He began to speak: softly at first, but his volume rising with each word.

The depth of Hooker's voice was unlike anything John had ever heard. It reached into him as if Hooker's hand had grabbed his heart.

Much of what Hooker said that morning John neither heard nor understood, so moved was he by the experience. He remembered Hooker's message though. It was simple and direct: the people must never break their covenant of obedience with God but remain sincere and faithful to Him.

When Hooker spoke, the people breathed as one, and stared at him as if entranced. When he finished, many sat exhausted, while others rose and prayed aloud. As John stared up at Hooker, he knew there was nothing more important to him than following the reverend wherever he went.

John's recollection was interrupted by the sound of heavy footfalls approaching from behind.

"Good day, John Lee," a man whispered.

John turned and looked up into his face. The sun was behind him, casting John in shadow. The man's eyes were dead and black. "I need but a moment of your time," he continued with a cold smile.

A shiver slid up John's spine. This was the same man he'd seen the previous night with William's chalice.

Chapter 3

John's chest tightened and his breathing quickened. He tore his gaze from the man's dead-black eyes and assessed their owner. He was young, and perhaps four inches taller than John. His long coal-black hair and narrow beard and moustache did little to hide the deep scar running between his left earlobe and collarbone.

The black-eyed man was flanked by two other young men. One was tall with a broad nose, pockmarked face and missing front teeth. The other was the same pudgy youth who'd confronted John earlier during his search for William's bag.

"How do you know my name?" John asked.

"I know much about you. I know you are traveling with your guardian William Westwood and you care as deeply for his other ward, Grace Newell, as you would for a sister."

It was then that John recognized the man. He was Richard Hawkes. He looked older than his 19 years and had formed a following among the teenage boys during the voyage.

"You saw me take a chalice from your guardian's bag last night," Hawkes declared in a hoarse whisper. "We still have a long way to go and it would be easy for someone to fall into the sea, with no one to know until the ship traveled far ahead. It would be tragic if Grace were to meet such a fate." Hawkes raised his chin and stared down at John.

"What do you want?" John demanded, straining to hide his fear.

"A simple thing. You are a pious Puritan to whom an oath is sacred. Swear you will never tell anyone what you saw last night, and no harm will come to Grace. Refuse and she'll not survive this voyage."

John scanned the main deck. More than a score of passengers were milling around. Master Cutting stood on the half deck near the stern, directing the crew. John considered yelling for help but realized it would be useless. Hawkes had doubtless hidden the chalice by now and would deny he'd stolen it. Alerting passengers and crew would only place Grace in even greater danger. Instead, he met Hawkes's stare. The raised chin and broad black hat made Hawkes appear even taller than he was. The man with the pockmarked face stared blankly at John, while the pudgy man smirked.

John hesitated, fearful an oath to cover-up a crime might itself be a sin. Still, he had no choice. But perhaps he could get something in return. In as firm a voice as he could muster, he said, "I will agree to this, but only if you agree to return the chalice."

Hawkes's mouth dropped open, and he moved so close John could smell the salted pork he'd eaten at noon. "The hell you say," Hawkes growled. "What makes you think you can spout demands at me?"

Hawkes's answer was a question, not a refusal. More passengers were on deck, and Hawkes must know his time to extract an oath was dwindling. "You made a request," John announced. "I will agree to it. What I ask for in return is simple. Return the chalice and your theft will remain undetected."

Hawkes shifted slightly, and his eyes narrowed. He glanced toward the passengers, some of whom were moving toward them. He looked at John with a brittle smile, "All right, I will return the chalice. Now give me your oath."

John didn't hesitate. "I agree. I swear in God's name that if you return the chalice to William Westwood, I won't disclose your theft."

With that, Hawkes nodded and turned away, followed by his cohorts.

John took a deep breath, filling his nose with the scent of wet wood and salt spray. The deck around him was alive again with the sounds of passengers and crew, and the sun caressed his skin. He felt overwhelming and joyful relief at Grace's safety. But this proved short-lived when he realized that he'd just sworn an oath to a thief. An oath forever silencing him, while allowing an evil man to live in his community, undiscovered and unpunished. The oath seemed a mortal sin and a wave of nausea engulfed him. The voice of his guardian pulled him from these thoughts.

"John, have you seen my chalice? It's not in my bag."

John's heart skipped a beat. William Westwood's blue-gray eyes pierced his soul as he waited for an answer. How could he lie to his master? He swallowed hard. "When did you first discover it was missing?" he asked.

"When I reached into my bag for my journal."

William faced the stern and announced, "There is Master Cutting. I will ask him to order a search."

The alarm spread in minutes, and the *Francis* was abuzz with the search. John was embarrassed as he watched Master Cutting assign the passengers and crew to search areas of the ship. How stupid this whole thing was, he thought. But he'd sworn an oath, and there was nothing he could do. His throat tightened when he saw most searchers head to the 'tween deck below. He and the other searchers were told to search the forecastle, half, and poop decks. He moved about with the others, pretending to look for something he knew was not there. He'd been evasive and ignored William's question. Now his pretend-search was furthering the lie.

A man's muffled cry sounded from below decks, "We found it! We found the chalice!"

The cry was echoed by those on the main deck. A crewman emerged from the 'tween deck with the chalice cradled in his hands. Directly behind him was Richard Hawkes. William hurried to meet them. John plowed his way through the passengers to William's side.

Everyone cheered as William held the chalice high above his head. A broad smile filled Richard Hawkes's face as William singled him out for attention, "Richard Hawkes found it!"

As the crowd grew quiet, John heard a voice rising over all others. It was Hawkes, "I will tell you how I found it." His voice was strong and deep, nothing like the hoarse whisper John heard earlier. The crowd grew silent with anticipation.

"It was only through God's grace I found it," Hawkes told them. "I knew a pile of loose clothing, bags and equipment was near the bow, as my friend James Eastman had been guarding it since this morning." Hawkes pointed to the pudgy man who'd accompanied him earlier.

"This told me," Hawkes continued, "any loose items, including the chalice, were likely at the bow. I moved forward beyond the pile to the windlass. There I saw a glint of light behind a vertical beam by the forward wall. When I looked, I found the chalice behind the beam."

The crowd cheered again as William placed his arm on Hawkes's shoulder, "Reverend Hooker's congregation is grateful to you Richard. You did us a great service today."

William moved to John's side, a broad smile filling his face. "Thanks be to God, John. We would not have found the chalice without Richard Hawkes' cleverness. Its value is great, but the spirit of faith it will bring to our congregation is priceless."

John's chest felt hollow as he stared down at the deck. He barely noticed when the *Francis* pulled abreast of the *Elizabeth*. He tried to forget the day's events and tell himself it wasn't his fault. But his mind screamed that a thief became a hero because of him—and he'd let that thief escape.

That night, John lay fitfully in the 'tween deck's darkness unable to sleep. It was too late, he thought. There's nothing to be done about it now. But even that thought made his stomach turn. He felt the deck's gentle rolling beneath him as the sea swelled and rolled in the night's calm. A few old men snored in the darkness. Several young men, still wide awake, talked about the wolves near the settlements surrounding Boston.

"Their packs pluck women and children who wander far enough

away from their villages to make them easy prey," one of them declared.

Across the darkness John heard a baby cry, its mother whispering "shhh, shhh," to silence it.

He drifted aimlessly toward sleep, but his mind jerked him awake many times before sleep finally captured him.

John found himself standing alone on the half deck, where the ship's master usually stood. A blood-red sun sat low on the horizon as passengers and crew moved about on the main deck below him. He wondered what they were doing. Some gazed at the places where the deck met the railing, while others looked at the spaces around the hatch, and still others seemed to be examining the area beneath the forecastle deck.

Three wolves emerged from the steerage cabin. Two were gray, the largest was black. The wolves gazed up at him briefly and he turned his gaze to the sea. He heard a scream and turned back. The black wolf growled at a woman on the main deck, while its companions bared their teeth. As one, passengers and crew turned their eyes to John - as did the black wolf.

He gazed back dispassionately.

The black wolf launched itself at the woman's throat as the gray wolves bounded after the other passengers.

John snapped awake drenched in sweat, his heart beating furiously.

Chapter 4

Nine days after the storm, heavy fog forced the *Francis* and the *Elizabeth* to sail farther apart. John made his way to the main deck at dawn and stayed there all morning. It was damp and cold on deck, and most of the passengers remained below. Several crew members were above in the ratlines.

"They climb faster now," Ben Mapes said to John, who stood by the port-side rail. "We're nearing Cape Sable, and they know the voyage will be over soon."

John nodded absently, still troubled by his oath to Richard Hawkes.

"And it's time to scrub the 'tween deck again," Mapes told him. "So, you'll be looking livelier too."

Within minutes, John and his shipboard friend Edmund Aldburgh had organized a group of younger boys to scrub the 'tween deck. Henry Hayward was among them, trailing behind as John and Edmund led the way to the bow.

"Let me carry the bucket, John," Henry pleaded.

"It's full of water and too heavy," John answered.

"I carried it last time."

"That was when we were done, and it was nearly empty. You can carry it when we're done."

"Let me do something now."

"All right. Help me clear the passengers from the deck so we can scrub it."

Soon they were at the 'tween deck's stern. John knew the people there, so it would be easy to move them. "We're here to scrub the deck," he announced. "Please move your belongings so we can work."

His announcement was met by a chorus of groans, but soon the passengers, including William and Bridget, picked up their belongings and moved forward.

A short time later, the boys had finished scrubbing all but the bow. Most of the passengers there had already moved their belongings and gone to the main deck. Only a handful remained. Richard Hawkes was one. He sat on the 'tween deck with the pockmarked man and the pudgy man, who John now knew to be James Eastman. The three gave no indication they intended to move.

"Would all of you remove your belongings so we can scrub the deck?" John asked.

The others quietly obliged, but not Hawkes's group. John felt the eyes of nearby passengers upon him. He knew they were waiting to see what he would do. "Would the rest of you move so we can finish scrubbing the deck?" he asked again.

Hawkes scowled at John, "I don't take orders from boys. Come back when my friends Edward Roach, James Eastman and I are not sitting here."

"I can't do that," John said. "It's my job to scrub the deck now and return the buckets when I'm done."

Hawkes neither spoke nor moved. John turned to Edmund and, in a voice loud enough for all around them to hear, ordered, "Get Ben Mapes."

Moments later, Edmund arrived with Mapes, who scowled at Hawkes and his companions. "Get up, gather your belongings, and move to the stern so these boys can scrub the deck. You may find it fine to live in squalor, but I'm sure the other passengers don't."

Hawkes slowly rose and bent his tall sinewy body over to pick up his things. Eastman and Roach did likewise and all three walked to the stern, where Hawkes turned and glared back at John.

Later in the day, John ate supper on the 'tween deck with William and Bridget Westwood, Joseph and Katherine Barnard and the two couple's wards, Grace Newell and Henry Hayward. The women and men spoke separately as the women passed out pea porridge. John moved closer to the men so he could hear their conversation.

"Why not Boston?" Joseph Barnard asked.

"The farmland is poor and there's little of it left," William replied.

"Is the soil in Newe Towne much better?"

"A little, but there's also more farmland."

"Yes," Joseph said, "I heard there was little land left on the Shawmut Peninsula and Boston is getting its wood from the bay islands. What of Newe Towne? Will we have such problems there?

"Some think so. They would like to move to better farmland, saying the soil in Newe Towne is too sandy."

"Where would that be?" Joseph asked.

"Winthrop wants us to find better farmland in Massachusetts Bay and to stay there, but most of the congregation wants to move west to land along the Connecticut River. The Indians call the place Suckiaug. It means black earth. The Dutch already have a fort there and others in the congregation fear if we move there we'll have to fight them."

"What about the Indians?" John asked.

"There are many tribes," William answered. "They call their leaders sachems. They're constantly at war with each other but the most feared tribe is the Pequots. Before I left Boston for East Anglia to bring Bridget over, one of their allied tribes killed John Stone, an English trader, and his men. They refused to turn the murderers over to Massachusetts Bay for punishment. War with them is sure to come, if it hasn't already. "

Katherine turned from the other women and interrupted the men, "Enough about Indians William, tell us about the church."

"The congregation is strong," William answered. "Reverend Hooker preaches with passion, and his assistant Reverend Stone is an expert on the Puritan church's tenets."

"How many have converted to full membership in the church since moving to Newe Towne?" Katherine asked.

"A few testified to the congregation that God had selected them for His grace," William answered. "They were converted by the congregation before I returned to East Anglia."

John had no idea what William was talking about. He looked at the others, who nodded and smiled. He blurted out, "What do you mean by 'converted' and 'grace'?"

Katherine gasped, Bridget's mouth dropped open, and Joseph sat up straight. John wished he'd kept his mouth shut. His face was warm and his heart pounded.

"John, I'm surprised," William said. "I thought you would have learned this. Our faith teaches that God has chosen which of us shall receive the gift of everlasting life in heaven. Those God has chosen to have received His grace. The souls of those not given His grace are sent to hell. We can't change God's decision by anything we do during our lifetimes since His decision is made before we're born. We must spend our lives searching for evidence we have been selected. When we're convinced God has chosen us, we present our evidence to the congregation. If the evidence is strong, we're converted to full membership in our church and can receive the holy sacrament."

John felt the others staring at him when William finished. *Why did father not tell me this?* He asked himself.

"Thank you," he said, and sat quietly on the deck as the conversation moved on to other topics. But John was no longer listening. He trusted William and didn't doubt the truth of what he'd said, but William's view was not what his father had taught him, or what he believed. Could God really ignore a person's deeds when passing judgment? Hadn't Christ taught that whoever believed in Him would have everlasting life? He needed some fresh air. "Excuse me," he said. "I'm going to the main deck."

He quickly climbed the ladder to the steerage cabin. He was disappointed when Ben Mapes wasn't there. Henry shouted from behind, "John, John, wait for me. I want to come with you!"

"Be sure you're dressed warmly," John declared. "It's cold on deck." He'd barely spoken the words when Henry bounded past him through the capstan cabin in front of the steerage cabin, then out onto the main deck in a linen shirt and breeches. By the time John reached the main deck, Henry was chasing after two of his friends.

John walked to the ship's rail. Sea, sky and clouds were gray, making it hard to see the horizon. He watched a crewman climb the ropes on the foremast and crawl into one of its working tops. Nearby, passengers milled about.

He turned when the ship's bell struck. He saw Richard Hawkes approaching. John stared coolly at Hawkes until he stopped before him.

"Good day, John Lee. I trust Grace Newell is well."

John cared little for anything at that moment; he was still shocked knowing that God may have already marked him for hell. "What's the point of your question?" he asked. "You know she's well for you passed her on the way here. How did she look to you?"

"I asked about Grace to remind you that her life depends on you keeping our bargain. Because if you break it, I swear I'll kill you both."

John held Hawkes's glare and said, "I told you I would honor my oath. Don't threaten me again."

Hawkes took a half step back. "I've said all I need to say to you for now. Remember it." He turned and walked back to the 'tween deck.

Chapter 5

Three days later, John stood on the main deck with the other passengers, shifting from one foot to the other to better see the shoreline. The sails fore and aft were full, rolling and swelling at right angles in the swift westerly breeze. Nearly all the crew was aloft; some working, but most looking to the west towards land. Scores of gulls trailed the ship, diving into its spray and soaring high above the stern and mizzen sails. The fragrance of burning wood mixed with the sea's brisk scent, while the taste of salt danced across John's tongue.

They first sighted land four days earlier. Since then the two ships had tacked several miles off the coast on their way south to Boston. The early morning sky was still gray, and the sun had yet to rise. The two ships sailed closer to the shoreline, but not so close as to run aground. Here and there, John saw smoke rising from the heavily wooded shoreline. He was told this came from Indian encampments.

The sun was barely above the horizon when Ben Mapes pulled hard on the whipstaff, turning the rudder and swinging the *Francis* to the west. The *Elizabeth* followed and the two ships began their run between the forested islands of Massachusetts Bay, heading for Boston while the passengers cheered.

John moved to the bow and climbed onto the forecastle deck, which was higher than the main deck, to get a better view. William, Bridget and Grace joined him there. "We just passed between Long Island and Deer Island," William announced. "Ahead to the left is Spectacle Island."

The islands were surrounded by small sandy beaches, beyond which rose forests of oak, ash, maple, and pine. Several small boats, called shallops, were moored at Long Island, which was the largest of the islands. Felled and stripped trees lay stacked on the beach.

"That lumber is going to Boston," William said.

"Look ahead," Grace said. "There are houses at the base of those hills on the mainland."

"That's Boston," William announced.

William stretched out his arm and began pointing. "The hills you see are Fort Hill to the south, the Tramount at the center, and Copps Hill to the north. The Tramount is the largest hill. It has three peaks. The peak closest to the city is Cotton Hill, next is Sentry Hill, and farthest away is West Hill, which rises over the bay behind the city. The tallest peak is Sentry Hill, at one hundred fifty feet high."

The *Francis* and the *Elizabeth* tacked into a westerly breeze and entered the harbor, anchoring a few hundred yards from shore. Many other ships were in the bay, among them two full-rigged oceangoing pinnaces and a score of shallops and other smaller vessels.

Soon shallops would ferry the passengers to shore, but John lingered for a last look at the town as William and the others went to get their belongings. To his left, below Fort Hill, he saw heavy green marshland along the bay, ending near the seaside houses. Beyond the marshland was a large field of what William called Indian corn. Boston's center lay directly ahead, consisting of two rows of weathered gray clapboard houses flanking a dirt road. The houses and the road followed a gentle slope up from the bay to the town square at the base of the Tramount.

Almost everything before him was gray and barren, including the unpainted fences lining the roads and dividing the homes' and buildings' lots. This provided a stark contrast to the bright blue sky and colorful gardens of radishes and squash, along with orchards of apples and pears. The only other trees were clumps of pine, ash and birch, south of Fort Hill near the peninsula's narrow neck.

To the north of Fort Hill was a large cove containing many wharfs. Within the cove and up the slope above it, fences and buildings spread along two roads. Farther up the slope, the road to the left split around a marketplace. To the right, the town spread north along a road that ran parallel to the bay for as far as John could see. Another hill loomed in the distant north.

"John," William yelled, interrupting his sightseeing, "get your belongings, we're going ashore soon."

William had already laid most of their possessions on the main deck. The other passengers were busy doing the same. After John brought up the last of the family's belongings, he stood with William, Bridget and Grace on the main deck. Joseph Barnard and his family were close by. Henry stayed by John. Bridget, Grace and Katherine Barnard looked proper in their colorful linen waistcoats, skirts and woolen cloaks.

The two families shuffled across the deck with the others, toward the shallops. John saw Ben Mapes helping the passengers onto the shallops and walked over to him. "I'll miss you Ben," John said. "What are your plans? Will you be living in Massachusetts Bay someday?"

Mapes frowned. "No John. I'm not cut out to be a Puritan farmer. I'll stay at sea where I belong."

"Maybe we will see each other again," John said.

"Perhaps," Mapes smiled.

John followed the Westwoods and Barnards down the ladder onto the next shallop. It bobbed up and down as the passengers stacked their belongings and took seats at the stern, in front of the young man operating the rudder. "Welcome to Boston," the young man announced. "I'm Israel Turner. Where are you from?"

John relaxed when he heard the familiar high-pitched nasal twang of East Anglia. "Colchester," he said. "And you?"

"Norwich. I came over on the *Elizabeth Bonaventure* sailing from Yarmouth last year."

"Have things changed much since you arrived?"

"Quite a bit. There are so many people, towns have sprouted up all along the bay, and there are too few trees to build homes. A favored few were given the right to take lumber from the bay islands and are rich because of it."

"That's to be expected." John said.

Richard Hawkes interrupted the conversation, "Who's been given the right to take trees from the islands?"

"Robert Rose," Turner said. "He's friends with Governor Winthrop."

"Where does he live?" Hawkes asked.

"It's easy to find him. His house is across from the Governor's."

John turned away from the conversation. Soon they were at the wharf. While waiting for the passengers ahead of him to disembark, John listened to Hawkes's questions about Robert Rose and his operations.

The Barnards climbed from the shallop ahead of the Westwoods, saying their goodbyes before entering the town to report their arrival and seeking transportation to Newe Towne. William left the shallop to report their arrival to the Puritan authorities, as required of all passengers, while John remained to help Grace and Bridget get their bags onto the wharf.

William returned a few minutes later with a short young man. The man's clothes were clean, but his doublet was frayed at sleeves and collar. He was about John's height, a good half a head shorter than William. The man had a ruddy, freckled face, a light mustache, and scraggly reddish-brown hair.

"This is Sam Pierce," William said. "He's brought a cart and will help load our belongings."

"Good day," Sam Pierce said in a reedy voice. "Leave your things on the wharf. I'll put 'em on the cart and bring 'em to you in town."

"Let me help you load the cart," John offered.

"No sir," Sam said. "It's my job. Best you rest with your family 'til I've loaded the cart."

"Sam's right," William said. "We'll wait in town."

John nodded and followed the others from the wharf. He looked back as they walked the road into town. Sam, who weighed no more than John, effortlessly slung their three largest bags onto his back and loaded them into the cart.

John turned back to William. "Why didn't he let me help him with the bags?"

"Sam's my servant. I paid for his passage. He must work for me for seven years to repay it. He's proud and refuses any help for the work I give him."

At that moment Sam called out, "I've loaded the cart. Come, I'll help you climb on."

Sam helped Bridget and Grace onto the cart's bench. William climbed on last and grabbed the ox's reigns. "John," he instructed, "follow behind the cart with Sam."

The cart moved slowly up the main road's slope, John and Sam walking silently behind. The Tramount loomed before them. Gray clapboard houses lined the dusty road. While the houses near the wharf were two stories high, those farther ahead were single-story homes. No dwelling was as impressive as the best John had seen in Colchester.

They'd gone 100 yards when a middle-aged man stepped from a house and stood by the road staring at them. He was William's height, but much thinner. Coupled with his narrow face, long brown beard and narrow mustache, he looked emaciated. "Good day William," he said. "Welcome back. I just received the *Francis's* passenger list and discovered you were on it. I need to speak with you. Come inside, it won't take long."

"Good morning Governor," William replied.

"Just Mister now," the man said. "Thomas Dudley is governor now."

"Well, you're still Governor to me," William replied.

John had seen this man before. His face was sketched on flyers in Colchester, advertising God's new land in Massachusetts Bay. John's heart pounded as he watched William climb down from the cart.

"Bring your family inside with you," Winthrop said.

"Governor, this is my wife Bridget, and my wards Grace and John," William announced, before turning to the others. "This is Governor John Winthrop."

Winthrop smiled and nodded to Bridget and held the house door open. John trailed behind Bridget and Grace as they followed the men into the house. The two-story house was larger than those surrounding it, but the interior was unpretentious. The furnishings were of simple pine and maple, the wooden floor mostly bare, with a few woven rugs scattered here and there. A lobby separated the first floor's parlor and hall room. William and Winthrop went into the hall, which was the first floor's main room, while John sat with Bridget and Grace in the parlor. John listened to the men as they spoke in the hall room.

"I'm glad you're back," Winthrop said. "I need to talk to you about Newe Towne. What's happening there worries me."

"What do you mean?"

"Most of your congregation wants to leave Massachusetts Bay and settle more than a hundred miles to the southwest along what the Mohegans call the Quinetucket River or Great River."

"We call it the Connecticut," William said. "The possible move has been discussed for a long time. What's changed since I left?"

"They're through discussing it. Now they've started planning their move."

"Who's pushing hardest?"

"Your congregation's elder, William Goodwin. Also, John Steele, Newe Towne's deputy on the General Court. But most pressure now comes from Deacon Stephen Hart. I'm afraid Reverend Hooker agrees."

"Why are you telling me this?" William asked.

"You are your congregation's legal counsel. Its leaders listen to you. Convince them to stay in Newe Towne."

"I doubt I can change their minds."

"For mercy's sake, there's a Dutch fort there," Winthrop snapped. "Do they want to fight the Dutch?"

"I'm sure they've thought about that. The land is richer there, and there's more of it than in Newe Towne. That's all that matters to them."

"Listen," Winthrop said, "I'll help you find more land here along the bay. I'm afraid if your congregation leaves, many others will follow."

"I'll tell our leaders of your offer," William said. "But we've looked for land in Massachusetts Bay before. The land along the Connecticut is much richer."

"Carefully consider my offer," Winthrop said. "I don't want to have to oppose your congregation's request to move. As you know, Massachusetts Bay claims the land along the Connecticut River and your move would be illegal without its approval."

"Others have valid claims to those lands as well, and we can seek their approval."

"You mean Lord Saye and Sele along with Lord Brooke under their grant from the Earl of Warwick he received from the King?"

"Yes," William answered.

"Massachusetts Bay's claim is stronger," Winthrop said. "The Warwick grantees have never set foot in New England and no one has even seen the grant."

William nodded, "I'll tell Reverend Hooker what you said."

It was warmer when they left Winthrop's house. John sweat in the rising sun's heat and tugged down the brim of his hat to shield his eyes. Sam walked beside him behind William's cart.

The marketplace was in the center of the road atop the slope leading up from the bay. It was nearly empty when they reached it.

"Why's the marketplace empty?" John asked Sam.

"Market day's Thursday," Sam explained. "The square was filled yesterday."

John stopped and looked back at the ships in the bay. Three small pinnaces sailed towards the wharf, where several shallops were being unloaded. Two larger ships sailed towards the bay islands.

"Quite a sight, huh?" Sam asked. "I like guessin' where they're goin'. Those ships headin' out are too small for the crossing. Probably just takin' trade goods to coastal settlements."

After watching several other ships in the cove, John nodded to Sam and turned back to the cart. It was now more than 50 yards ahead of them and nearing the narrow neck connecting the peninsula with the mainland to the south. Small clapboard homes on half-acre lots lined the road, their vegetable gardens packed with radishes, squash, pumpkins, and beans.

There was a common to the west where land had been set aside. In time, it would be parceled out to the townspeople for crops. In a few months, there would be corn here, ready for harvest, but for now the view was unhindered. Beyond the common, marshes extended for a half mile, eventually merging into the expansive bay beyond the peninsula. The small white sails of a dozen shallops, ketches and barks dotted the bay's deep blue waters. Farther off, rose the dark green and brown mainland coast. A blue river sliced it down the middle.

"That's the Charles River," Sam said. "Newe Towne's upriver. We'll be there before sunset. The ferry will take you, Grace, Bridget and William across the river to Newe Towne after you've skirted the bay and river until you reach it. The ferry is too small for the cart and ox. I'll take the cart farther upriver and cross where there is a ford at Watertowne."

They reached the ferry in late afternoon. It was little more than a small weathered shallop, with barely enough room for Grace, John,

Bridget and William. A squat muscular man in his early thirties sat on the dock near the ferry. His broad-brimmed hat covered most of his face. "Good day sir," he said to William in a nasal twang. "I'll take you across."

Soon they were halfway across the river. John glanced back and watched Sam at the cart's reins, moving slowly along the river's opposite shoreline.

The ferryman seemed pleased to have company and began to talk almost as soon as the shallop started moving. "I'm Thomas Greene," the man announced. "Newe Towne is a fine place. Most of its people are well-to-do. There are marshes at the river's edge, and the town center is less than a quarter mile from the river. Almost all live in the middle of town and grow corn in the surrounding fields. Oxen, cattle and hogs are kept outside town; the cattle in the Cow Common to the northwest; and, the oxen in the Ox Pasture to the northeast."

John was getting used to Greene's voice. Soon he stopped listening and watched the shoreline grow closer. It was marshland, and the line between river and marsh was blurred. In some places he saw more river than marsh, with blue water topped by strands of thin grass. In other places he saw more marsh than river, with no water visible at all. A high, circular palisade of vertical logs surrounded the town on three sides.

Greene was still talking as he tied the shallop to the town's wooden pier, "I assume you are followers of Reverend Hooker?" he ventured.

William smiled, "Yes, we are. I am William Westwood, and this is my family."

Greene's calm smile disappeared. Shocked embarrassment spread across his face. He spoke without raising his eyes from the post to which he'd tied the shallop. "I'm sorry sir. I didn't recognize you with your family. I assumed you were new."

"Think nothing of it. I could see you were excited about Newe Towne and didn't wish to interrupt since this place is new to my companions."

They walked toward town, the evening sun just above the horizon. John guessed it was an hour before dusk. The dirt road from the dock to the town rose above the marshes, and the pungent smell of marsh mud and decaying plants filled John's nose as they walked along. Marsh grasses of different shades reached out of the blue water, merging here and there with low, brownish-green shrubs. Where there was no water, there was mud. The cackling of geese, the rattling churr of wrens, and the conversation of frogs filled the air.

Gradually the marsh melted away and they saw a small orderly maze of similarly constructed houses fronted by vegetable gardens. The homes lined the unbending main road for a half-mile. The road itself was intersected by three equally straight roads, each of which was also lined with houses and gardens. The homes were framed with light brown, unweathered clapboard, which gave the town a fresher feel than the gray of Boston.

A handful of people worked gardens in the distance, but closer in there was no one about. A pounding sound filled the air. It seemed to come from nowhere in particular and everywhere at once.

William stopped before a house at the second cross street. "Our home is near. This is Deacon Stephen Hart's house. I need to speak to him."

"What's that pounding sound?" John asked.

"Samp mortars. They're hollowed out tree stumps where women and children grind corn into corn meal by pounding a block of oak into the stump. After you've been here for a few days, you won't hear it."

William knocked on the door while John, Bridget, and Grace stood behind him. The door opened, revealing a barrel-chested man of about thirty, with long brown hair dropping to his shoulders. The man's face brightened. "Well, William," he said in a deep voice. "Good to have you back. Bridget, you look beautiful. And who are these young people? All of you are dressed so fine and it's not even the Sabbath."

"Good evening, Stephen." William said. "I'm glad to be home, and ready to get back to God's work. These are my wards Grace Newell and John Lee. He's John Lee's son."

"It's good to meet you Grace. And John, when I last saw you in Braintree you were at least a foot shorter. You now have your father's square shoulders, green eyes and honest smile. Everyone, come into our house and Sarah will make something to eat."

Before they went inside, a woman burst through the door. Her face was dewy and framed by blond hair tied up under a linen cap. Thin framed with a svelte figure, she looked tiny beside her broad-shouldered husband.

"I knew I heard your voice, William," Sarah Hart said. "And Bridget, it's been too long since we last sat together. And this is John Lee. Aren't you a handsome young man?"

Sarah continued before anyone could reply, "It's good to meet you, Grace. Come with me and Bridget to the parlor and we'll prepare food."

After the women left, John sat with William and Deacon Hart near the fireplace. John watched the flames caressing the logs and listened to the two men talk.

"Governor Winthrop spoke to me today," William said.

"Your first day back? What on earth for?"

"He opposes our move and wants me to convince you and the others to find more land here, rather than moving. He offered to help us find it."

"I'm not surprised." Hart said. "Since you left, he's pushed us hard to do that. Sometimes I think he loves what he's created here more than he does God. Well, those of us who came later didn't get as much of his dream. It's time for us to make our own dream real with Reverend Hooker along the Connecticut River."

"You're bitter. How can you speak against Governor Winthrop when he's done so much for our Puritan faith?"

"Don't be a fool. He cares no more for us than he cares for the settlers in Roxbury, Salem or Charlestowne. What he cares about is Massachusetts Bay and that we stay here to strengthen his City of God. If we stay, our crops will be smaller each year and our congregation will fail to grow. If he won't agree to our move, we should move without approval and rely on the Warwick Patent."

"I've never seen the Patent," William answered. "I doubt it exists in any form other than rumor. It's better to receive authorization from Massachusetts Bay. Several other towns are seeking this. We should too."

"I'll leave this decision to you and Reverend Hooker," Hart said. "But if our request is denied we should leave anyway and sort things out later."

John looked out into the house's entryway, where Grace played with a younger girl. He guessed she was about five. They sat on the floor, making dandelion necklaces. He was about to turn away, but something about the girl demanded his attention. She looked toward him, smiling sweetly as their eyes met. He smiled back. It lasted only a few seconds, but the girl's pale blue eyes seemed intelligent beyond her years. Then she turned away and resumed playing with Grace.

"That's my daughter Mary," Hart said. "She was born before we crossed on the *Lyon*."

John turned back to the fire. The men's conversation was merely background noise as he focused on the sounds of Grace and Mary playing. Mary's infectious laughter could easily have been that of someone years older.

The fire exploded in a cloud of sparks. John's gaze snapped to a boy about eight, who'd just thrown a log on the fire. He added another log.

"That's my oldest son Daniel," Hart said with a smile.

By the time they left Hart's house, the sky was the gray of early nightfall. They walked to William's house as the distant howl of wolves rose over the log palisade to the north. Sam greeted them when they entered the house.

"You'll sleep in the attic with Sam," William told John. "Bridget will prepare a bed in the parlor for Grace."

Half an hour later, John lay on the attic floor with his hands clasped behind his head, gazing up into the darkness and listening to Sam snore. Then reality sank in. He wanted to be here, but here was not how he'd imagined it. He was alone, without his father or mother, who'd sent him ahead to escape getting his father's illness, and in a church which had a strange belief that God saves only a favored few, making the decision before they're born without considering the good they did with their lives. He took a deep breath, tucked his head under his pillow, and fell asleep.

Chapter 6

It was 10:00 A.M. when Richard Hawkes, James Eastman and Edward Roach left the wharf. Hawkes decided to avoid the Puritan greeting party and spend the morning surveying the town for a storage building that would fit in with the buildings around it and where he could store what he stole undetected. He knew three strange men loose in the town would eventually draw the attention of its constable and the men assigned to greet the *Francis's* passengers. He calculated it would be mid-afternoon before anyone would be concerned by their absence.

He studied the town's layout from the *Francis's* deck before boarding the shallop taking them to the wharf. The town was built around a large cove. To the south was a fort on a large hill on the promontory jutting into the bay. Beyond that was a marsh and a maze of houses and gardens. To the north, along the shoreline, there were fewer houses and more vacant land. Small wharfs were interspersed among the buildings. Ketches and shallops were moored at several wharfs and farther inland there were warehouses. *This is the town's working underside*, he concluded. *I will find my warehouse there.*

After gathering as much information about Robert Rose's business as he could from the shallop's pilot, Hawkes led Eastman and Roach north along the bay's shoreline. He glanced up the main street's slope as they passed it. William Westwood's cart was rolling toward the marketplace with John Lee and a short wiry man trailing behind it.

Hawkes's body tensed as he watched Lee walk up the slope. Who could think this boy would be the one to discover him, he thought. He'd planned well, but never imagined that lightning would reveal him. But for the boy, he would have sold the chalice to the Dutch and had enough wealth to start a business; now he had little. Westwood was a fool. Even on a ship of Puritans there are thieves. *That damned boy*, he cursed to himself; now he had to worry whether he would keep his silence.

He led his men north on the dusty road lining the bay. *Maybe it was a good thing*, he thought. A chalice, even one as valuable as William's, had a finite value. If he worked for Robert Rose, he could be worth much more; not only more in wealth but also in power. He knew Rose couldn't keep an eye on everything happening in his business. Many things probably disappeared without his ever knowing. The thought made him smile. Perhaps he should find more warehouse space than he'd planned on.

The road swung to the west around a small cove. Gray clapboard homes lined the road as it turned back north. Several small wharfs jutted into the bay. Some looked well built, others as if they would collapse under their own weight. The workmanship was inferior to what he saw in Colchester while working as an apprentice carpenter.

The sound of saws ripping into wood filled the air. Here and there he noticed saw pits with men using saws to slash squared timbers into planking for floors and walls. *Soon there will be sawmills and only the poor will cut timber this way*, he thought. *Whoever owns the first sawmills will become a wealthy man.*

Ahead, the road crossed a marsh that spread to the northwest. In the distance to the north was a large hill. This was not good, he thought, they were almost beyond the town and hadn't found a space substantial and discreet enough to serve his purpose. Then, below the hill, he saw the outline of more clapboard houses beyond which were several large buildings. Encouraged, he picked up his pace. Eastman and Roach extended their strides to keep up.

"Those buildings ahead, past where the bay road forks into two roads, one staying along the Bay and the other heading inland, appear large enough for my purpose." Neither Eastman nor Roach replied as Hawkes's pace quickened yet again and they struggled to keep up.

Soon they were on the road's inland branch. The houses were spaced widely and there were cornfields running toward the hill now dominating the view to the northwest. Near the men there were several large barns interspersed among large buildings used for storage.

"We will store our merchandise here," Hawkes said. "James, find if any buildings are for lease or purchase. I want one by week's end."

Eastman belched and asked, "What are we going to store here?"

Hawkes's piercing black eyes froze Eastman where he stood, "I said we will store merchandise there. Isn't that enough?"

"But we have no merchandise," Eastman said.

"Let me worry about that. Soon we will have enough to fill two buildings."

Hawkes turned back towards the town's center. He reached the point where the interior road merged with the bay road. He heard men's voices to his left, down a section of the bay road they hadn't traveled. The sound was familiar. As he moved closer the voices grew louder and he heard laughter. *It's a tavern*, he thought.

The tavern was smaller than the one he'd waited outside of for his father that night in Colchester. He remembered the mist gathering on his forehead as he crouched in the alley, watching his father through the tavern's open door. It slid down his face, mixed with his blood, and tasted salty as it dripped into his mouth. *Damn him,* he thought. *I can still feel my face burning from his fists.*

His father was laughing. It was a deep rolling laugh. A big man's laugh. There was a bloody bandage tied over his father's right-hand knuckles. It moved with his noggin of beer. His father's dingy brown doublet was open, with its ties loosely swinging. His dirty wet linen shirt hung haphazardly over his soiled tan breeches. Blood blended with the dirt staining them.

Hawkes remembered the faces of the other boys who waited with him in the alley that night. It was strange he couldn't remember their names. *That bastard,* he cursed under his breath.

It was early afternoon when Hawkes and his men returned to the wharf. The Puritan greeting party was waiting for them. There were three of them, all old. *They look unhappy*, Hawkes thought, *but they'll get over it.*

"We were about to contact the constable," a craggy faced man announced.

"I'm glad you didn't," Hawkes said. "We wanted to see the town."

"You should have come to see us first."

"Can you direct me to Robert Rose's house?" Hawkes asked.

The old man frowned and shook his head while muttering softly to himself. He pointed to a two-story house with diamond paneled window casements fifty feet away.

Hawkes smiled as he stared at the house. It stood out among those surrounding it. Its garden was not filled with turnips and squash but rather a colorful array of flowers and plants. A house whose owner is worthy of my service, Hawkes thought. I will introduce myself to him this afternoon. In the meantime, my men and I will wait in the marketplace

It was late afternoon when Hawkes strode from the marketplace to Rose's house. His black hair hung loosely to his shoulders, partially covering the long scar on his neck. His head was topped by a black, broad brimmed "capotain" hat. He had only one presentable doublet. It was black and packed for such occasions. The sun was hot, and he removed the doublet's sleeves to keep cooler. His white linen shirt sleeves rippled in the breeze blowing from the bay.

Rose's house was at the street's low point, close to the town's main wharf. The shallop's pilot told Hawkes that Rose used the house as both his office and residence, so he expected Rose to be there when he called. A servant girl led him into the first-floor parlor room, where he sat at a rectangular table. The room was simply decorated. He guessed it was reserved for meetings with Rose's Puritan business associates, who favored simplicity and assumed that Rose's private

THE DARKNESS AT DAWN

rooms were more ornate.

He waited only a few minutes before a tall middle-aged man strode into the room. His gray flecked hair dropped to just above his shoulders and his face was dominated by a bulbous nose. He stiffened and folded his arms in front of himself when he saw Hawkes sitting at the table. "What do you want?" he asked, his nasal twang giving evidence that he was also from East Anglia.

"I came with a business proposal. You will find it attractive."

"Well, let's hear it quickly. I'm on my way to the meetinghouse and already late."

"I'm Richard Hawkes from Colchester. I arrived in Boston this morning. The town has granted you a license to cut and sell timber on Long and Hog Islands. My proposal involves Deer Island, for which you just received a license."

"Yes, I know. Get to the point."

"Hire me to manage your lumber operations on Deer Island rather than have your manager on Long and Hog islands do it. Assign him Long Island for the competition and me Deer Island. If so, you will get competition between both of us because each of us will know that the one who produces the most lumber will be placed in charge of the lumber operations on all of your islands."

"I like my current manager. I see no reason to use a new manager for Deer Island."

"I offer more than competition," Hawkes replied. "As I walked about town this morning, I noticed saw pits everywhere. Many pits were surrounded by inferior wood. Soon Boston will have a sawmill. When that happens more wood can be cut, and people will demand it be of superior quality."

"That's not news to me," Rose said.

"But is your current manager a skilled carpenter?"

"No, what does it matter?"

"Well, I am a skilled carpenter who understands milling. I know how to tell good wood from bad, how to select the best trees for timber and how to prepare felled trees to ensure their wood does not crack before being milled. Your profit will increase, not just from greater volume, but also from an increase in the quality of wood you produce. I will produce more and better-quality wood than your current manager."

Rose took a seat across from Hawkes.

"So, my wood is inferior?" Rose asked.

"Some I saw today was. Have you received complaints about dried and decayed lumber?"

"Some."

"There will be none if you hire me"

"You are a confident man, Mr. Hawkes," Rose said. "What would you do differently?"

"For one thing, I wouldn't leave felled lumber on the ground as long," Hawkes answered. "I will also seal the ends of the logs with wax as soon as they're cut."

"Why can't I just have my current manager do these things?"

"You could. But if he doesn't already know these things, I doubt he would ever discover the other things I plan on doing."

"What other things?" Rose asked.

Hawkes smiled at Rose. *Suddenly, getting to his meeting is not so important*, he thought. "Hire me and I will tell you."

Rose leaned back and laughed. When he stopped laughing, he leaned forward and said, "I like a confident man. You are certainly one. You remind me of myself when I was young. Listen carefully. I don't need another manager, but I will take a risk on you because you have the potential to help me now and in the future. For now, you can have Deer Island in a four-month competition with my current manager, who will have Long Island. If you win, you can have all my islands."

"Fair enough," Hawkes answered with a smile.

Hawkes walked back up the road past the marketplace. He was

confident that he could produce more lumber for Rose on Deer Island than Rose's other manager could on Long Island and probably produce enough that Rose wouldn't notice if he took some for himself.

He found Eastman and Roach under a maple tree near the marketplace. He heard Eastman snoring thirty feet away. Roach sat in the brown grass beside him, his legs pulled up to his chest and his arms wrapped around them. He stared indifferently at Hawkes.

"Rose hired me," Hawkes announced. "He likes me. It will be easy to steal from him."

Roach stood. Eastman snored as the two men stood facing each other. Roach was two inches taller. He looked directly at Hawkes. "What did he hire you to do?" he asked.

"To manage his lumber business on Deer Island and to compete against his current manager who will have Long Island."

"What do we know about lumber production? It's good to be hired but another thing to do the work. How will we produce more lumber than the other manager?"

The question surprised Hawkes. He was not used to being challenged, but realized he couldn't dismiss the question since he needed Roach to help run his new business. Roach was strong and scared people when he looked at them. He'd help keep the workers in line.

"You're right," Hawkes told him. "None of us has produced lumber. But that's not what we're hired to do. Our job won't be to fell trees. Rose has indentured servants to do that. Our job will be to lead them, and those Rose assigns to transport the lumber to his markets. If you've learned anything about me, you know that I can plan how to get a job done and how to direct the men doing it. For what other reason did you choose to follow me? As a carpenter, I learned how to select wood and protect it. I will use those skills in our effort. Who could do a better job than me in running Rose's lumber operation?"

Roach said nothing. He looked at Hawkes with a slight smile, but a smile still wide enough to show the gap where he'd once had front teeth.

"We have four months to prove ourselves," Hawkes said. "Rose will lend me a dozen of his servants. You'll need to control them. He will challenge me and his other manager to out produce each other on the island each is assigned. Whoever is ahead at four months will be given the job of managing his lumber operation on all the bay islands."

Roach's expression softened. He nodded and sat under the tree while Eastman snored on.

Chapter 7

John Lee woke before dawn in William's attic. Sam snored in the darkness. Below him he heard pots and pans clanging. When it was silent, he heard a woman's footfalls. The smell of cornbread filled the attic. He rolled over and went back to sleep.

When he woke again a faint light came up through the attic's floorboards.

"John, Sam, come to breakfast." Bridget yelled from below.

John quickly dressed and rushed down the ladder with Sam following him. As he stepped from the ladder's last rung, Bridget grabbed his arm and led him across the bare wooden floor to a table near the fire. Grace sat at its hearth. The room was dim, its only light coming from the fire, two candles sitting on the table, and the room's two small diamond paned windows. William sat at the end of the table farthest from the fire. The fire's smoke stung John's eyes. He picked a seat at the table near William. Sam nodded at William before turning to leave the house.

"He needs to feed the hogs and chickens," William said. "He usually feeds them much earlier, but we were late getting to bed last night. He'll get breakfast later."

John sat at the table eating the samp porridge and cornbread Grace brought him. He glanced around the room as he ate. The walls were made of flat boards molded at the edges with the space between filled with clay and chopped straw. The room's floor boards were large and merged together unevenly. *If simple lives bring us closer to God*, he thought, *I'm closer to God here than in Colchester.*

"It's a modest house." William said. "Do you like it?"

John's chest tightened. William was staring at him as he carefully considered his answer. "It's a nice house," he replied. "I'm happy to be here."

William laughed, "A cautious answer. You will make a good apprentice assistant."

"What do you mean?" John asked.

"I'm on Newe Towne's Board of Townsmen and am meeting with Reverend Hooker today. You're coming with me to learn how things are done here."

Suddenly, John was no longer hungry. He swallowed the porridge in his mouth and took a sip of beer from the leather noggin Grace served him. He tried to smile but his upper lip quivered as he did.

William smiled, "Fear not, Reverend Hooker is only intimidating when he's on a pulpit. He'll be pleased when he learns you are the son of John Lee of Colchester. Besides, you will be too tired to be nervous after you finish working in the garden with Sam after breakfast."

After eating, John found Sam in the garden digging a mound to use for planting squash, peas and pumpkin. The moist scent of freshly turned soil filled the air. A half dozen marsh wrens gurgled as they circled looking for insects and snails. He continued looking at the town while Sam dug in the dirt.

"Ya gonna help?" Sam asked.

"Sorry," John answered. "I was looking at the town."

Sam stood up and moved to John's side. He pointed to the road to his right.

"I'll show ya some things," Sam said. "That's Crooked Street. It runs to Water Street, which you came in on last night. Both roads run into Braintree Street."

"Braintree, that's the town in East Anglia where my father took me when he went to meet with Elder Goodwin, Deacon Hart, John Steele and William to plan our congregation's move to New England."

"I know nothin' bout that," Sam said. "Takin' Braintree Road east leads to the plantin' field. Takin' it west leads to the West Field near the Great Swamp. But ya must cross through the palisade. It's on all sides of town except along the river."

"Are there other towns near us?"

"Two. Menotomy's west and Charlestowne's east."

"How many houses are in town," John asked.

"Enough," Sam said. "Best we get started. William wants us to plant this garden by noon. I'll show ya how to do it."

Sam dropped to his knees and dug his hands into the small mound he built.

"We're plantin' squash and corn in this mound," Sam said. "I put manure in the mound and now I'm plantin' seeds over the manure. Get down and help."

After they planted a dozen more mounds, Sam looked at John while both were on their knees with their hands in separate mounds. When John looked back Sam was smiling.

"There's sixty," Sam said.

"What did you say?"

"There's sixty houses in town," Sam said with a smile.

William found John at noon. John brushed the dirt from his hands and went inside the house to change into a clean doublet and breeches. He walked north up Crooked Street with William towards Reverend Hooker's house. It was slow going because many townspeople were working in their vegetable gardens and stopped them to welcome William back from East Anglia. Two men, guiding carts headed east towards the planting field outside town, also greeted William.

When they finally reached the top of the slope, John looked back at the bay he walked around the day before following William's cart. Down the slope near the bay, he saw the high thin grass, green foliage and brown mud of the marsh they crossed walking into town. Across the Bay, the Tramount dominated the view as it climbed high above the Back Bay's deep blue water. Delicate white clouds hung motionless in the sky above it.

John let the sun fall on his face, closed his eyes and breathed in deeply. The smells of freshly laid manure and newly cut wood mixed with the sweet scent of daffodils. The sounds of saws cutting lumber and the pounding of samp mortars mixed with the chirping of sparrows and wrens feeding in the newly turned soil.

William led John off the road onto the dusty path leading to Reverend Hooker's house. Vegetable gardens grew on each side. John found it hard to think of this great man with his hand in the dirt. That was until he looked closer at his gardens. It seemed as if no one had worked in them for some time. The soil was hard, and most plants withered.

William's knock was answered by a middle-aged man wearing a loose linen shirt hanging over his purple breaches with gray flecked brown hair hanging to his ears. John recognized Reverend Hooker at once. His face was heavily lined, square jawed, and capped with bushy gray eyebrows. He was no taller than William, but his thick chest gave the impression he was stronger.

The man's face brightened when he opened the door. He instantly grabbed William's right arm.

"Welcome home William," Hooker announced. "I missed you. How was your passage? Did you bring Bridget back with you?"

"Our passage was uneventful. Bridget is with me. Sadly, I bring bad news from England,"

"We'll talk about this later. First, tell me who this young man is."

"He's John Lee, the son of John Lee of Colchester."

"Ah, John Lee's son." Hooker said. "It's good to see you. Your father did much to get us here. Will he be joining us soon?"

John froze when he realized both William and Hooker were staring at him. He fought to speak while looking at Hooker's feet, "He was ill when I left. I don't know when he'll make the passage."

William put his hand on John's shoulder and smiled, "His father sent John to Newe Towne with me. He promised when he was well, he and John's mother would make the passage. I agreed to be John's guardian until then."

"Bless you William," Hooker said. "Come inside."

John followed the two men into the house. The three of them sat together in the hall near its fireplace.

"Tell me of England." Hooker asked, leaning over the fireplace's hearth.

"Things are bad. Bishop Laud's persecution of our Puritan ministers continues and now that he's Archbishop the church's full power is behind him. His agents infiltrated many congregations and our people have been whipped and fined. Early this year he ordered ship captains not to take passengers to New England unless they give oaths of allegiance to the Anglican Church. He has also ordered that all shipboard services be conducted with the Book of Common Prayer."

"I'm not surprised. It was clear to me things would get worse."

"One more thing Reverend, Governor Winthrop met me when I arrived. He's unhappy we're close to moving to the Connecticut River. He threatened to fight any request we make to the General Court and Court of Assistants to do so. He asked me to convince you and our other leaders not to make such a move and to look for other land in Massachusetts Bay."

"What did you say to him?" Hooker asked.

"I told him when I left for England many of our leaders were in favor of moving because there was no longer good farm land in Massachusetts Bay. Is this still the case?"

"Yes. If anything, our resolve to move is stronger. So strong, Deacon Hart is taking five men to a place on the river the Indians call Suckiaug to determine if it is suitable. These Indians are the Suckiaug and they have sought an English settlement there to protect them against the Pequots."

William chuckled, "Of course it would be Stephen who would lead such an expedition. No one in Newe Towne wanted to move to Connecticut more. Should I prepare our argument to the General Court and the Court of Assistants?"

"Yes, do so at once."

John Lee was now two hours into his first lesson with Reverend Stone who was Reverend Hooker's assistant and the congregation's teacher of Puritan doctrine. William arranged for John to study with Stone and while John was excited by the prospect at first, he no longer was. His lesson had gone poorly, and he wanted it to end.

He'd hoped Reverend Stone would warm up to him. Just the opposite happened. Dressed in black, Stone glared at him across the meetinghouse table, his dark brown eyes, sharp nose, and pointed chin giving him a bird-like quality.

"Have you been trained in the scriptures?" Stone asked in a reedy voice.

"My father read scripture to me and we discussed what he read. After I learned to read, we would read scripture together."

Stone's face tightened. He rose from his chair and looked down at John as John sat on a bench with four other students.

"You weren't trained by a Puritan cleric?" Stone asked.

"No sir," he answered.

"Your father didn't take you to such a cleric for training?"

"No sir."

"Why not?"

John was struck dumb by the question. As he looked into Stone's icy stare, he fought to control his anger. Stone had attacked his father and he wanted to fight back. *Christ help me*, John thought. *His sunken cheeks make him look like a dead man.*

"I don't know why my father didn't send me to a Puritan cleric," John said. "I only know that until we became followers of Reverend Hooker we didn't attend church regularly, but we did study the Bible together. Reverend Hooker awoke our spirit in ways other ministers never did."

"What do you know of the Covenant of Grace and the process of conversion?"

"My father didn't teach me about them as they weren't in the Bible I read with my father. Where do these ideas come from?"

Stone's brow furled as he spit out his answer, "Don't be insolent. Every Puritan knows these things for they're at the core of our faith."

"I'm sorry sir. My father taught me of the loving God Christ spoke of. A God who caresses each of us and that Christ's sacrifice has saved those who believe in him. I don't mean to challenge you or our church. I only want to learn from you what I don't know."

Stone stepped back from John's bench and smiled for the first time.

"Very well," Stone said. "I have a great deal to teach you."

For the next two hours Stone continued to question John about his education. John spoke of his love of history, particularly the stories of King Arthur, medieval knights, crusaders, and Greek myths his father taught him. But when he recounted his study of the classics, particularly Aristotle's teaching the world was created by an unmoved mover, Stone's face turned red with anger.

"The history you speak of comes from the worship of pagan gods," Stone admonished. "These stories are useless for they don't represent God's truth. That truth is found in the Bible and in the words of our savior. The Greek philosophers don't speak of our God or our Christ. If they speak of a god at all it is a false god. We won't study these philosophers for nothing can be learned from them."

John was puzzled for he grew up with the legends and philosophers he spoke of and he and his father discussed them often. Was Reverend Stone saying they couldn't teach him anything at all? He stammered, "Sir, can't we learn of heroism by studying the heroes of ancient Greece, England's Knights of the Roundtable, and the crusaders?"

"You've missed my point!" Stone raged. "We learn little of heroism from these stories compared to what we learn from our Savior's sacrifice. His death on the cross was an act of courage and sacrifice all can learn from. Mythical stories or legends can never come close to what Christ's sacrifice teaches us of heroism. Heroes are those who persevere when times are most difficult, not those who quickly dispatch an overmatched foe."

Finally, Reverend Stone announced, "We shall resume your studies the day after tomorrow. You are dismissed for today."

As he left the meetinghouse, John glanced back at the table used for communion. The chalice Richard Hawkes had stolen sat on it. It was always there, reminding him of Hawkes's unpunished crime.

Four weeks later, John saw Richard Hawkes for the first time since they left the *Francis*. Hawkes was mounted on a jet-black stallion looking down at him from a low rise fifty yards from where John was removing weeds in William's cornfield. John had seen few horses since he arrived in Newe Towne. There were only a handful in New England and they were expensive. Instead of horses, William bought animals to pull a plow or feed a family. However, now that the fields were full of sheep and cattle and there were enough oxen to pull their carts, more and more settlers were bringing horses to Massachusetts Bay.

That still didn't explain where Hawkes got his black stallion, nor why he was sitting on it watching him. John watched Hawkes guide his stallion across the field to where he was. He wished he'd taken the cart back to town to get more manure instead of asking Sam to do it.

As Hawkes came closer, John saw Hawkes had also found the money to buy a new black doublet, black breeches and a broad brimmed black capotain hat.

"Good day John Lee," Hawkes sneered. "Beautiful day isn't it?"

John wiped the dirt from his face with a coarse rag and stared up at Hawkes sitting astride his stallion. The day was not beautiful. The sky's solid gray clouds gave no promise sunlight would grace the fields of Newe Towne that day.

"I suppose it's a beautiful day for a worm who wants to show his head in the daylight without shriveling up," John said. "It's not a beautiful day for a bird flying in the sky."

Hawkes's smile disappeared. *What an impudent child*, he thought.

Hawkes's pulse quickened. He fought to control his rage. He, not his rage, must control this moment. Still, he couldn't let this boy compare him to a worm. He would address the matter that brought him from Boston after that. His smile reappeared.

"Can I assume you didn't mean to compare me to a worm but only to comment on the weather?" Hawkes asked.

"I spoke of the weather," John answered. "A worm would find itself to be lacking many of your qualities."

Damn him, Hawkes thought, as he again fought to control his rage. He wanted to jump from his stallion and strangle this petulant boy. He decided to move on to the issue bringing him and let the slight go unanswered.

"I came to see how you fared since our passage," Hawkes said. "As you can see, I've done well in Massachusetts Bay. I'm employed by Robert Rose, a wealthy merchant, to run his lumber business and have twelve of his indentured servants working for me. My success has given me enough money to buy this stallion. What have you and your guardian done in Newe Towne?"

Why is he here? John thought. He hoped Sam would return soon. Meanwhile, he would keep Hawkes busy.

"William has been about the town's business." John answered. "I spend most of my days working in his fields with his indentured servant. He'll be back from town soon."

Hawkes leaned over on his stallion and looked into John's eyes.

"How is Grace?" Hawkes asked. "I trust she has come to no harm."

John's throat tightened and his pulse quickened. It was at last clear why Hawkes came to see him. Hawkes wanted to ensure he remembered his oath and that he would keep it. The oath was a curse to him now and he didn't need to be reminded of it.

"Grace is fine and continues to be so." John declared. "You don't need to issue threats against her, and you don't need to remind me of my oath. I think of it every day. I am through talking with you. Leave William Westwood's field now."

"I won't leave until I'm certain you'll honor your oath." Hawkes spit. "Besides you're too weak to force me to leave."

John looked into Hawkes's eyes, "I swore an oath not to disclose your theft. Whether I honor the oath is between God and me. I don't fear you, or what you might do to Grace or me, as much as I do the punishment God would inflict on me should I violate the oath."

"You have yet to tell me you will honor the oath. I won't leave until you do."

"I promised you under oath. I answered this same question on the *Francis*. Will you ask me this question every day? If so, know the answer will be the same. My oath was given in God's name. That should be enough for you. I am bound to God to obey it, not you. Now crawl back into the hole you came from before the sun breaks through the clouds and you shrivel up like the other worms crawling up from the ground today."

Instantly, Hawkes jumped from his horse and drove his right shoulder into John's chest. Both hit the ground hard, but John harder as Hawkes landed on top of him. As he lay on the ground, John gasped for breath. Quickly Hawkes kneeled over him and began pounding John's face with his fists. John tried to curl up in a ball but was only able to get his forearms up to his face to fend off Hawkes's blows. Unable to get through Lee's forearms with his blows, Hawkes redirected them to John's stomach.

Sam saw them fighting as he approached with a cart of manure.

While he didn't know who John was fighting, Sam could tell the man was getting the best of the fight. He jumped from the cart and ran towards the fight.

Meanwhile, Hawkes's fury was spent. No longer angry with John, he was angry with himself for losing control. Beating John was never his goal and he was frustrated he lost his focus. He needed to reassert control and make this boy think he never lost it. By the time Sam reached them Hawkes was standing over John.

Sam looked at John and breathlessly asked, "What happened? Ya alright?"

John raised himself onto his elbows and looked up at Sam while spitting blood from his mouth, "We've had a dispute. This man is Richard Hawkes, a fellow passenger from the *Francis*. He's about to leave."

Sam looked quizzically at Hawkes. Hawkes ignored him and continued looking down at John.

"I'm confident I can trust you," Hawkes announced. "Choose your words more carefully next time we meet. Grace's well-being is in your hands."

Sam looked at John after Hawkes left. John was standing with dirt, grass and corn flax on his breeches and heavy work shirt and still wiping blood from his mouth and nose.

"What was you two fightin' bout?" Sam asked.

"Just a misunderstanding." John answered.

"What did he mean Grace's well-being was in your hands?"

"Nothing."

"What ya mean nothin'?" Sam asked.

"It's between him and me." John said.

"Sounded like a threat to me. What ya gonna' do?"

"I don't know."

"Let me know when ya do. I'll help."

John smiled at Sam before turning and walking toward the cart of fresh manure.

Chapter 8

"I have to leave," John announced to Sam as they worked in William's field three weeks after Richard Hawkes thrashed him.

"What?" Sam said with a puzzled look. "It's barely afternoon and we got weeds to clear from this corn patch."

"I'll see you tonight."

"Where're ya goin'?"

John didn't answer. Instead, he turned and walked through the standing corn towards the path to Newe Towne.

"What do I tell William?" Sam pleaded.

John ignored Sam and kept walking. He bent down into the cornfield and pulled Bridget Westwood's carving knife from the soil where he left it early that morning. He wrapped a linen rag around it and tucked into his breeches before turning onto the path. As he strode forward, he thought of the crusaders. Like them he was on a mission – a mission to save Grace's life and the church's purity by eliminating the threat of Richard Hawkes.

He reached the ferry within an hour. Thomas Greene, the ferryman, lay under a rough barked tree ten feet from the small wooden wharf where his shallop was tied. John had made many trips across the bay to Boston and knew Greene well. He bent over Greene.

"Thomas, wake up," John barked.

"Is that you John?" Greene mumbled.

"Yes Thomas. Can you take me to Boston?"

They were three quarters of the way across the bay when the sun slipped under the tree line behind them in the west. John didn't notice. He was also oblivious to the waves beating against the shallop's hull as it sliced through the water, and he cared little about the

Tramount ahead of them. He stared vacantly at the bay's soft swells as he focused on his mission.

"You're quiet John," Greene said while pulling the shallop's oars. "What's bothering you?"

John turned to Greene, "What?"

Greene let out a hearty laugh, "You're in a dream today."

"It's nothing. I'm just tired."

John jumped from the shallop as soon as Greene tied it to the Shawmut Peninsula's wharf. He immediately started north on the path to Boston. He moved between the fields of corn, leaning forward at a brisk pace. The green, yellow and brown of ripening corn surrounded him but there were touches of gray and black where the sun's light no longer fell as it set in the west. He knew he had to do it but not how and where. It would have to be after sunset when Boston's streets were empty. Before Hawkes beat him, he said he worked for Robert Rose. He would wait for him at Rose's house.

Rose's three-story house cast a shadow across the town's main wharf when he reached it. Several adolescent boys played below the house in front of the wharf. They chased each other and wrestled in the dirt. He ignored them until one boy yelled, "Your dead, I stabbed you." The boy's cry snapped John from his trance, and he pulled his eyes from the dirt and stared at the boys.

As he waited, he shifted his eyes from Rose's house across the street to the street in front of it and then to the wharf, repeating the process for nearly an hour. Still there was no sign of Hawkes; just a few sailors on shallops and barks at the wharf repairing fittings and inspecting lines and sails along with an occasional passerby on the street. In the enveloping dusk he became certain his effort was not only futile but also foolish. He would wait only until dark.

A few minutes later he saw a thirty-foot shallop gliding towards the wharf through the fog that came with dusk. Its two sails were furled, and four men beat a constant rhythm with their oars. A fifth man stood at the stern, his eyes fixed on the wharf.

"Enough," the man at the stern yelled. "We can glide in now."

John stiffened and peered through the fog at the man who yelled. The voice was Richard Hawkes's. His hands trembled as the time to act was near. He hid behind a pile of wooden barrels on the wharf.

Hawkes jumped onto the wharf before the head line was wrapped around a mooring post. He turned back to the shallop and said, "I'm going to visit Rose. I'll be at the warehouse in an hour."

Hawkes crossed the street to Rose's door. The shallop was in the light of the wharf's oil lamps now and John saw one man had broad hips and a protruding belly. He was certain he was James Eastman. Edward Roach stood beside Eastman watching the other two men tie the shallop to the front mooring while Eastman tied it to the rear. After the shallop was secure the men left the dock. Two men walked south on the bay path while Eastman and Roach walked in the opposite direction.

John ducked farther behind the barrels as the two men passed. One man stated, "Not wise to cross him. He's cunning and cruel."

Hawkes was at Rose's house when John turned back to him. A short chunky woman greeted Hawkes before the house swallowed him. The street and wharf were now abandoned, and the night's chill spread through John like ice water. The wharf floated above the fog which wrapped itself around the supporting posts, making them invisible. He shivered in the cold, moving closer to the wall of a darkened warehouse farther from the wharf. He leaned against the wall's aged wood and massaged the handle of Bridget's knife while watching Rose's door across the road.

Within moments he was bathed by light pouring from Rose's open door. He ducked and backed along the warehouse's wall. Hawkes tipped his head to the chunky woman and walked onto the road, turning north along the bay path Eastman and Roach took earlier. John waited until Hawkes disappeared up the path before he began following him.

It was black along the bay. Behind him the light of the wharf's oil lamps fell onto the fog where it disappeared as if the life was sucked out of it. There was no light to his right where the bay spread into a deep impenetrable darkness. He heard Hawkes's steady footfalls ahead of him. Away from the oil lamps his eyes were able to penetrate the darkness and he saw the ghostlike image of Hawkes walking on the path. He silently began closing the gap between them.

After a few minutes Hawkes turned up a side street. They were now alone among darkened warehouses. It was time. John picked up his pace, less fearful he might be discovered. With every step he felt Bridget's knife slide along his hip. As he continued closing the distance between himself and Hawkes, he grabbed the knife's handle and pulled it from his breeches. He breathed deeply. Before he could take another step, he was engulfed by coldness as he felt someone grab his right forearm. He turned. Sam Pierce's face was no more than two feet from his. Neither he nor Sam spoke. The only sound was Hawkes's footfalls moving ahead of them up the road.

"Ya really think you can kill him with that knife?" Sam whispered. "He's nineteen and fully grown. You're a boy. He beat you to a pulp three weeks ago. This time he'll kill ya."

"I have to do something"

"Why?"

"I can't tell you."

"Why not?"

Without answering, John turned from Sam and looked up the road in the direction Hawkes was walking. Hawkes's footfalls sounded softer now. Above the footfalls he heard the faint sound of men's voices. Gradually the volume of the voices increased, and he knew the men were moving towards Hawkes.

"It's about time you came to meet me," Hawkes yelled.

In the darkness John saw the hazy images of Hawkes and two men standing next to him: one tall and broad shouldered, who John assumed was Roach, and the other much shorter and fat, who he assumed was Eastman.

"You plan on killin' these men too?" Sam whispered. "Seems ya gonna need another way to get revenge."

"It's not about revenge," John whispered.

"What then? When we was in William's field Hawkes said Grace's well-being was in your hands. He threatened to kill Grace? You tryin' to kill him to protect Grace?"

"I can't tell you."

"I can't help ya if ya don't."

"I haven't asked for your help Sam."

"Thought we was friends?"

"We are, but I still can't tell you."

William's house was dark as John and Sam walked towards it along Crooked Street well after midnight. John's pulse quickened as they passed Deacon Hart's house. Perhaps he could enter the house undiscovered, John thought; but he knew that was not likely. He and Sam missed supper and that would not go unnoticed.

John and Sam had spoken little on their return to Newe Towne and they weren't speaking now. They knew the ferry would not be operating so they crossed the Charles River at a ford three miles west of Newe Towne where it narrowed at Watertowne. It was a long trip and John was exhausted.

They'd just left Crooked Street onto the path to William's house when the door to the house opened. In the darkness, John saw the shape of a man at the door. The man waited as they walked towards him. It was William.

"Quiet," William said. "Bridget finally fell asleep. She's sick with worry."

John stared at William while Sam fixed his eyes on the ground at William's feet.

"Where have you been?" William grumbled. "Neither of you were in the cornfield when I went there this afternoon."

"I went to Boston," John answered. "I didn't mean to worry Bridget."

"And you Sam?" William asked.

"I followed him when he left the field."

"Why did you go to Boston John?" William asked.

John dropped his eyes and shifted his weight to his right foot, uncertain what to say. "To find Richard Hawkes," he answered.

"Why?"

Again, he hesitated before answering, "A personal matter."

"What do you mean a personal matter?"

"I can't tell you."

William stared at John through the darkness. John's heart pounded and his cheeks burned as he stared back at William. He dropped his chin to his chest. William turned to Sam.

"What do you know about this Sam?" William asked.

"Nothin'."

William slowly shook his head and sighed, "I'm disappointed in you John. You ignored your responsibilities and violated my trust. Now both of you get to sleep. You only have an hour before you must start working in the garden."

John slipped past William into the house with Sam trailing him. Before William entered the house behind them John pulled Bridget's carving knife from his breeches and set it on the small table near the fireplace where Bridget kept her knives. Sam smiled at John and whispered, "Lucky for you they had porridge tonight and not pork. They woulda' needed Bridget's knife for that."

John lay awake in the attic staring into the darkness above him wondering what would have happened if Sam hadn't grabbed his arm. The possibilities were endless, but none seemed good. Still he feared if he did nothing Hawkes would attack him again, or even worse, attack Grace. He heard Sam roll over on his bed of straw.

"I don't think ya coulda done it," Sam whispered. "You's not one to stab someone in the back."

John breathed in the attic's musty air before answering, "Killing is sometimes justified."

"When?" Sam asked.

"In war . . . and sometimes to save a life."

"What ya know of war?"

"My father and I spoke about the crusades to save the Holy Land from the infidels all the time. Killing them was justified. We also read the stories of King Arthur and the roundtable in Thomas Malory's *Le Morte de Arthur*."

"So what," Sam laughed. "You's not at war with Richard Hawkes."

After a moment of silence Sam spoke again, this time without laughing, "So ya was protecting Grace?"

John hesitated. He knew he was bound by his oath and said nothing.

They both lay quietly for several minutes. John knew Sam was still awake because he didn't hear deep breathing.

"So, who's this Thomas Malory anyway?" Sam asked through the darkness.

"He wrote of King Arthur and his knights," John answered.

"Why do ya care about that?"

"They were heroic and chivalrous."

"Chiv a what?"

"Chivalrous. It means they were courageous and fair."

They lay quietly in the dark for several minutes before Sam asked, "What's it ya wanna do in Massachusetts Bay?"

John thought about the question while staring into the darkness above him.

"I want to fight for Reverend Hooker and our church," He answered finally. "It's here in this new land we can build God's world. I want to fight to see it happens."

"So ya wanna be a soldier?"

"If God wills," John answered.

"A crusader!" Sam laughed. "Well in less than an hour you'll be back on your knees in William's garden."

After several minutes of silence John asked, "Do you believe in the Covenant of Grace?"

Sam laughed, "It's Puritan hogwash used to keep the faithful in line."

"Careful what you say," John replied.

John paused before continuing, "Why are you in New England if you don't believe in Puritan teachings?

"Ya don't have to believe in everything they do to like the people you's with," Sam answered. "I like William and Bridget, don't you?"

"Of course." John answered. "Do you believe God brought a plague upon the Indians to free land for us to settle as we've been taught?"

Sam laughed, "If that's true, why's God not built us houses and fed us?"

The attic was silent for several minutes before John answered, "I suppose believing and acting on a belief are two different things."

Sam's snoring was the only response.

Chapter 9

"**D**amn it to hell," Richard Hawkes yelled. "This is the second month in a row Elisha Lyman has out produced us. It's our forester Andrew Elliot's fault."

James Eastman and Edward Roach said nothing. They watched Hawkes pace back and forth in the roughhewed storehouse he was leasing in Boston.

"We need to motivate him," Hawkes announced. "If we do our production will increase."

Until that moment Hawkes never doubted he could keep his promise to Robert Rose to produce more timber than Rose's current manager, Elisha Lyman. Rose loaned him twelve indentured servants to fell trees and remove timber as well as six woodsmen and five timber handlers. But he also loaned him a forester named Andrew Elliot and it was Elliot who Hawkes depended upon to select the trees to be felled and to manage the teams of woodsmen cutting them down. *What a lazy obstinate man*, he thought.

"How do we do that?" Eastman asked.

"I'm thinking," Hawkes said. "All I know is I won't be bested by that ox."

Hawkes smiled to himself when he remembered the shock on the tall burly Lyman's face when Rose told them both the competition's rules. Lyman would work on Long Island and he would work on Deer Island. The competition would last four months. At the end of that period the man producing the most timber would be awarded the job of harvesting the trees on all of Rose's islands.

Hawkes thought it would be easy to beat Lyman until the first month ended and he learned Lyman out produced him. Each day, he watched as shallops and barks plowed through the bay to Long Island and returned to Boston loaded with timber. Elliot's response to Hawkes's efforts to cajole him into increasing Deer Island's production was always the same. He could hear it now, "The men are working as hard as they can." *Enough*, Hawkes thought, *it's time Elliot learned his place.*

"Bring Elliot to me this afternoon," Hawkes barked.

Roach looked at him with a blank stare and nodded while rising from his chair. Eastman leaned forward in his chair.

"Why don't you just go with us to Deer Island and talk with him there?" Eastman asked.

"I said to bring him here."

"What will you do?" Eastman asked.

"I'll give him two options: one pleasant and one not. Now, go get him!"

Hawkes sat alone in the storehouse after Eastman and Roach left. The window's light struck his face, making the room even dimmer around him. He wondered why he waited so long to deal with Elliot. Whatever the reason, he was prepared to deal with him now.

He rose and stood before the window looking back at the chair. *This is where I'll stand*, he thought. *Elliot will sit where I was sitting, but there will be only one chair in the room.* He pushed the three other chairs to the room's side against the wall, satisfied Elliot would not be able to see them. He placed a small pine table next to the chair. On the table he laid a large hunting knife and small flaying knife. Finally, he wrapped a rope around the chair.

He was waiting at the window when Eastman and Roach brought Elliot into the storehouse. It was noon.

"Put him in the chair," Hawkes ordered.

Elliot blinked while staring into the window's light behind Hawkes. Roach grabbed Elliot's arms and dragged him across the room to the chair. Elliot strained to free his thin frame from Roach's unforgiving grasp.

"What are you doing?" Elliot asked. "Why have you dragged me here like a common criminal?"

"Sit down in the chair and shut up!" Hawkes yelled. "I have questions about your lumber production on Deer Island."

"You didn't need to haul me here for that."

"Yes, I did," Hawkes said. "I will find the solution to my problem much quicker here."

"I won't sit in that chair," Elliot protested.

Suddenly, Elliot broke free from Roach's grip and screamed at the top of his lungs. Roach slammed Elliot to the floor, knocking the breath out of him. Elliot gasped for air while Roach held him down.

"Put him in the chair Edward," Hawkes ordered.

Elliot's face was ashen when Roach pushed him into the chair. It creaked as if it were about to collapse when Elliot's back slammed into it. Dust flew in the rays of sunlight streaming through the window. Hawkes calmly walked through the glowing dust towards the chair.

"Tie his chest to the chair Edward," Hawkes ordered.

Hawkes leaned down and looked into Elliot's eyes while Roach wrapped the rope around him.

"I'm sorry, but I want your full attention this time," Hawkes said. "I don't think you gave it to me when we talked before."

Eliot squirmed against the rope, gasping for air. His eyes bulged as he stared up at Hawkes.

"Slacken the ropes Edward so Andrew is more relaxed," he said. "Also take the knives off the table. We don't need them now."

Elliot was breathing unevenly and drops of perspiration slid down his cheeks as Hawkes approached him.

"You failed to increase production," Hawkes said starring down at Eliot. "Instead, Lyman is further ahead of us. Rather than challenge the men as I ordered, you gave me excuses. Now challenge the men! You have four weeks to out produce Lyman. If you do, I will ask Robert Rose to end your indenture. If you don't, I will tell Rose your laziness led to our failure. I will also tell him you slandered him as well as the Governor and Court of Assistants. I will enjoy watching you whipped and cropped. What do you choose?"

Elliot's lips trembled as he stared up at Hawkes.

"That's a lie," Elliot said. "I never slandered them."

"You know I'll do it and you know they'll believe me," Hawkes said. "So, you don't agree to my proposal?"

Elliot was trembling as he answered, "I didn't say that."

"You wouldn't say that of course." Hawkes answered softly. "I would have no choice but to tell of your slander. It would be better to wait and see if you earn your freedom first, don't you think?"

Hawkes leaned down and stared into Elliot's eyes. "Now give me your answer," he barked.

"I'll try," Elliot answered.

"You'll do it," Hawkes answered. "All you needed was motivation. Now you have it."

Hawkes smiled and placed his hand on Elliot's shoulder.

"Go back to Deer Island," Hawkes said. "I'll be there tomorrow morning. Then we will go about besting Lyman."

Hawkes slumped into the chair after Roach and Eastman left for Deer Island with Elliot. The light from the window blinded him and he closed his eyes. He knew it would take more than Elliot's commitment to defeat Lyman. He would also need to motivate the other men. He decided to offer them a share of his pay for the four-month competition plus any bonus Rose paid him if he won. He would lose little by making this offer. If he lost, they would get nothing. If he won, he would be running timber operations on all of Rose's islands. He could easily share part of any bonus Rose might award him. *What would be the smallest amount I could offer that would be enough,* he asked himself. *Thirty percent to be shared among them all should be enough.*

The bark cut through the waves three hundred yards from Deer

Island's beach when Hawkes saw the men gathered just inside the woods' tree line. The morning sun seared his eyes, making it impossible to tell how many men were there. To the men's left the ground was barren and dotted with tree stumps for several hundred yards. Above the beach before the tree line was a one room hut. Outside the hut smoke from a fire rose into the clear blue sky. Fifty yards before the hut a wooden pier jutted out over the sand and one hundred feet into the island's small bay. Scores of logs were piled near the pier. A handful of men stood near them.

"Andrew Elliot is in the brown doublet at the trees' edge." Eastman said.

"He called a meeting," Hawkes said.

"Well, it's over now," Eastman said. "They've seen our bark."

The men walked from the trees across the sand towards the pier with Elliot trailing them.

Hawkes walked onto the pier when the bark was secured. Eastman and Roach followed him.

"Good day Richard," Elliot said. "I just spoke to the men."

"What about?" Hawkes asked.

"I told them they would need to work harder if they wanted to win the competition."

Hawkes glared at Elliot. "Gather the men," Hawkes spat. "I will speak to them now."

Within fifteen minutes the men were standing in the trees. Hawkes stood with his face towards the bay and the men in front of him.

"Andrew announced that you will need to work harder if we are going to win the competition with Lyman," Hawkes said. "Why do we need to win this competition?"

No one spoke. Most men stared at Hawkes with blank faces, while the rest shifted back and forth. Finally, a man behind the others yelled, "So you can take control of Rose's islands."

"That's part of it," Hawkes said smiling. "But now each of you will have a reason as well."

The men leaned forward.

"If we win, Rose may give me a bonus in addition to control of his islands," Hawkes said. "In that event, I will give thirty percent of my pay and any bonus to you to share."

Several men smiled; others whispered among themselves; but, most just looked at Hawkes with open mouths.

"I mean it!" Hawkes yelled.

"You mean we get to share your reward?" a tall man yelled.

"Yes," Hawkes shouted. "Now let's beat Elisha Lyman!"

Hawkes turned and led Elliot towards the small hut where they planned each day's work. Behind him the men cheered.

There was a penetrating rain when Hawkes reached Robert Rose's house two months after meeting with his men. His black boots were covered with mud, but his black cape kept the rain off his doublet and his broad brimmed capotain hat shielded his black hair. Before knocking, he looked through the rain at the town's wharf. A tall broad-shouldered man climbed from a bark. The man looked up the road. Hawkes smiled at the man when their eyes met. The man didn't return his smile. Hawkes knew he wouldn't smile either if he were Elisha Lyman.

Hawkes was sitting at the hall table when Rose's servant brought Lyman into the room. It was four months since they last met in this room with Robert Rose.

"Good day Elisha," Hawkes announced, rising from his chair.

"Good day Richard," Lyman replied, his eyes riveted to the table.

Hawkes sat next to Lyman. Across the table, an empty chair faced them. Neither man spoke. They sat silently for nearly an hour staring into the fire beyond the table before Rose entered. Rose smiled and sat in the chair facing them.

"Sorry I'm late," Rose said. "My meeting with the Governor lasted longer than planned. Your competition was spirited. My forests produced more timber than ever. Production was so great I'm giving each of you a bonus. This bonus will be on top of what I already agreed to pay you for the competition."

Hawkes smiled and nodded at Rose. *I won't tell the men about the amount of the bonus*, he thought. He leaned forward in his chair.

"Unfortunately, only one of you can win," Rose said. "While timber production on each island was great, the timber production on Deer Island was greatest. Congratulations Richard, you won and will now manage timber production on all my islands."

Hawkes nodded at Rose. Lyman was slumped in his chair staring at the table. Suddenly, Lyman stood up. His hands trembled as he stared at Rose.

"Damn it Robert, you can't do this," Lyman pleaded. "I managed your timber production on Long and Hog islands for almost a year. I made you a good profit. How can you turn over all your timber operations to one so young and inexperienced?"

"Calm yourself Elisha," Rose said. "There are many opportunities for a forester with your skill in the new settlements west of Boston. Come see me in six months. I plan to begin producing timber there."

Lyman's eyes dropped.

"That's better," Rose said. "Leave us now. I need to talk to Richard about the islands."

After Lyman left, Rose turned to Hawkes with a good-natured smile, "So, tell me how you did it. You were far behind after the first two months."

"I motivated the men," Hawkes answered.

"Well, keep motivating them," Rose laughed. "You now have Lyman's team, plus another team to work on Hog Island. What are your plans?"

"Along with the team on Deer Island, I will place the three teams in competition among themselves," Hawkes said. "These islands will soon be bare of trees. You should plan what you will do when they are."

"Do you have ideas?"

"Start growing corn where trees were felled. The demand is high and it's now legal tender."

"Good idea. Do it right away. Anything else?"

"Yes. I promised Andrew Elliot I would recommend you release him from six months of his indenture if we won the competition. He'll still have five years to serve."

"Tell Andrew I have done this," Rose said.

Rose pulled a cloth pouch full of coins from his doublet. He opened it and poured the coins on the table. They twisted and turned as they fell.

"Here is what I owe you," Rose said. "It's ten pounds twelve schillings. Eight pounds twelve schillings for four months work and a two-pound bonus. Now, come sit with me at the fire in my study."

Rose led Hawkes down a corridor through a heavy oak door into a maple paneled room. They sat in two oak chairs before a small fire. The servant girl who first greeted Hawkes entered the room.

"Margaret, bring each of us a beer," Rose ordered.

Rose turned and looked at Hawkes, "Beer's fine isn't it Richard?"

"Of course."

Rose laughed, "Poor Elisha. He was shocked with the amount of timber you produced. I was too. I like you Richard. You're bright, confident, plan well and get the most from the men working for you. How did you acquire these skills?"

Hawkes sipped his beer and looked into the fire. *The truth would shock him*, he thought. *Thievery and murder don't mix well with his type.*

"I was an apprentice carpenter in Colchester making ends meet the best I could," Hawkes answered. "I found four lads needing coin willing to follow my lead. I scouted the neighborhoods for homes receptive to our talent to perform odd jobs. I quickly found a leader serves his men best when he gets them work. I have that knack."

"Well you got my work and now you have more," Rose said. "I hope you will continue to work for me long after you finish work on the islands. What do you say?"

"I like working for you," Hawkes said. "You're a good man. But I want to build what you built for yourself. I want my own business. To do that I must find a new town with new opportunities."

"Do you know of Newe Towne and its people's plans?"

"I know the town but not its plans."

"They want to move south along the Connecticut River," Rose said. "Former Governor Winthrop and others in Massachusetts Bay oppose this. If they succeed in moving it could be the opportunity you seek."

"When will they leave?"

"Not for at least a year. It would give you time to clear my islands of timber and make a tidy sum for yourself."

"Sounds interesting," Hawkes said.

"Good. I'll introduce you to Stephen Hart, a business associate of mine who is one of their leaders."

Rose faced the door, "Margaret bring two more beers."

The men were waiting just inside the tree line when Hawkes's bark reached the island's pier. He knew they were watching him, but as he walked towards shore on the pier whenever he looked towards them, they acted busy with work. Eastman and Roach met him as he stepped off the pier onto the wet sand.

"Get Elliot," Hawkes ordered. "Bring him to the hut. I'll wait for him there."

Roach turned and headed into the trees while Eastman followed Hawkes to the hut.

"How was the meeting?" Eastman asked.

"Fine," Hawkes said. "We have more pounds to spend and two more islands to manage. I promised the men thirty percent of my pay for the last four months plus any bonus I received. Bring the men to the beach. Give them their shares after I speak to them."

Hawkes closed the door to the hut after Eastman left. He decided if he gave the men thirty percent of what Rose paid him, as promised, they would get three pounds three schillings to share among themselves. He concluded this was too much especially since he bore the risk and created the competition. They didn't know how much Rose paid him so he would give them less.

There was a knock at the hut's open door.

"I've brought Andrew Elliot," Roach grunted.

Hawkes walked from the hut and greeted Elliot, "Congratulations Andrew," Hawkes said. "We won the competition."

Elliot dropped to his knees in the sand and muttered, "Thank God, thank God."

"Stand Andrew," Hawkes said. "It's time to tell the men."

The men were gathered on the beach by the time Elliot stood. Hawkes smiled as he and Elliot walked towards them. The men's weary looks were replaced by laughter when they saw Hawkes's smile.

"We won the competition!" Hawkes exclaimed.

Cheers erupted and several men slapped each other on their backs. Hawkes waited for the celebration to end before speaking.

"Your thirty percent share of my pay and bonus is one pound twelve schillings," Hawkes said. "James Eastman will give you your share of this amount this afternoon."

The men cheered again. When the cheering stopped Hawkes motioned to Elliot and pointed to a tree just inside the tree line. Elliot waited for Hawkes at the tree. Hawkes stared at Elliot with his hands clasped behind his back.

"Bad news," Hawkes said. "Rose refused to grant you a complete release from your indenture."

Elliot's jaw dropped before he asked, "How much time did he release me from?"

"Six months."

Elliot squeezed his eyes shut and rocked back and forth before crumpling to his knees.

"No, no," Elliot moaned. "I was to be free today. This can't be, this can't be."

Hawkes grasped Elliot's shoulder with his right hand.

"Get up Andrew," he said. "Have faith. God has another plan for you. Serve me as I oversee Rose's timber production. If you continue as forester on Deer Island and do well, I will ask Rose to reduce your indenture again next year."

Elliot pulled himself up from the wet ground. The knees of his breeches were soaked and his eyes bloodshot.

"So, there's hope my indenture might end next year?" Elliot asked.

"If you obey my orders and we succeed."

"I will. I will."

For the first time in the eight months that Hawkes had worked for Rose, Deer Island was more sand than trees. He sat in the hut staring across a small table at Eastman.

"We need to find a way to increase our wealth," Hawkes said.

"How do we do it?" Eastman asked.

"These trees will be gone soon," Hawkes said. "When they are, we will only have what Rose paid us while we harvested them. Unless . . . ."

"Unless what?"

"Unless we take some timber for ourselves. Rose relies on me to keep the records," Hawkes said. "We will have every fifteenth bark deliver timber to the mill at Roxbury. We will sell it to the mill's manager for corn at a discount. He'll make his profit when he sells it at market price later."

Hawkes looked out the hut's door at the cove. He turned back to Eastman and scowled, "Where is Edward? He always disappears when we talk business."

"Somewhere in the woods no doubt."

"I'll tell him my plan later."

What will we do with the corn?" Eastman asked.

"Keep it in our warehouse and use it to pay our bills until we've enough to sell on the open market."

They were quiet for several minutes. Eastman stepped outside the hut. When he returned, Roach was with him.

"I want to move next year," Hawkes announced.

"Why?" Eastman asked.

"We were late to Boston," Hawkes said. "There are no opportunities for us here. We need to find a place where we are among the first settlers."

"Where would that be?" Eastman asked.

"Reverend Hooker's congregation is planning to move west to the Connecticut River."

"Winthrop will never let them leave," Eastman protested.

"He can't keep them from leaving," Hawkes answered.

"But we don't have friends in Hooker's congregation," Eastman said.

"Rose does business with one," Hawkes said. "I spoke to him and he said he wants to build saw mills and grist mills when they move."

"Doesn't John Lee live with Hooker's congregation?"

"He won't be a problem," Hawkes said. "If he is, Edward will make sure he's not for long."

Roach stared out the door and said nothing. His face was lit by the sun, highlighting the scars and crevasses randomly roaming across it. Hawkes was certain Roach hadn't heard a word he and Eastman had said.

Chapter 10

"**H**urry John, the meeting starts soon," William announced. John looked up from the garden's dirt at William who stood above him framed by a bright September sun. It was two months since William scolded John for his nighttime trip to Boston. William hadn't forgiven John, but now he was focused on winning approval for their congregation's move to Suckiaug.

"Clean up," William ordered. "Sam can finish."

John looked at Sam. They'd been weeding the garden since before sunrise.

"Sorry Sam," John said.

Sam shrugged his shoulders.

The meetinghouse was full when William led John down the center aisle to the front row. John sat while William talked with Elder Goodwin and Reverend Hooker. The members of their congregation sat to John's left. Facing him were chairs reserved for the General Court Deputies of each Massachusetts Bay town. Together these Deputies formed the colony's General Court. A few Deputies sat, but most milled about talking. To the General Court's left were two rows of chairs reserved for the Court of Assistants who served as the Governor's closest advisors. It would take a majority vote by each body for the congregation to prevail.

John's chest tightened when he spotted former Governor John Winthrop seated in the Court of Assistants' first row. To Winthrop's left sat Governor Thomas Dudley, a broad-shouldered man with a full face framed by long dark hair.

"Sit everyone," Dudley ordered. "The meeting's starting."

"The General Court and Court of Assistants will now consider the application of Reverend Hooker's congregation for approval to move from Newe Towne to the Connecticut River." Dudley announced. "Who speaks for the application?"

William stood and announced, "I am William Westwood and I speak for the application."

"Proceed," Dudley ordered.

William strode to a spot near the chairs of the Assistants and the General Court's Deputies. He gazed at each Assistant and Deputy as he passed, finally fixing his eyes on Governor Dudley.

"Governor, Deputies of the General Court and Assistants of the Court of Assistants," William announced. "We ask for permission to move to Connecticut for several reasons. I will present them today."

John's nervousness evaporated as he listened to the smooth cadence of William's voice. *William has done this before*, he thought. John leaned back and listened as William continued.

"Our most important reason is tied to our location's geography," William continued. "Everyone knows the towns of Massachusetts Bay are too close together and farmland is limited. Each ship from England compounds this. The situation in Newe Towne is worse. We are like an hour glass, pressed by Charlestowne to the northeast and Watertowne to the southwest. With the Charles River to our south, we can only spread north, but the distance to our neighbors would be too great."

As he listened, John realized why their congregation's leaders asked William to come to New England with them on their first trip even though it would mean he would have to return for Bridget, who stayed behind to care for her dying mother. Building a church was more than laying stones and raising walls. It also required the subtle skills of persuasion William possessed. "If we stay in Newe Towne we will have no room to grow and no room for our friends and families still in England," William continued. "Our congregation would eventually wither away as it ages and is unable to secure the services of ministers of the stature of Reverend Hooker. We might even find it difficult to keep our ministers."

William was interrupted by Deputy Governor Robert Ludlow, a tall thin man seated next to Dudley.

"Your argument is hollow," Ludlow protested. "Everyone knows we offered your congregation more land near the bay. You rejected the offer. I won't vote to approve your move based on this argument."

John's heart raced as he watched William turn and take a step towards Ludlow. The room was hushed as he spoke, "Deputy Governor Ludlow, we're grateful for your offer but there's not suitable land in Massachusetts Bay. The best land is taken and what is left is sandy and dry. But land along the Connecticut River is moist and dark."

"There's still good land along the bay," Ludlow countered. "You didn't find it because you didn't look for it and you didn't look for it because you didn't want to find it. The truth is your congregation's move has nothing to do with land. It has to do with power: the power that comes from being your own colony."

Behind John, some of the men in Hooker's congregation shouted in protest. William turned to the congregation and motioned for silence. The shouting was replaced by mumbling and finally silence. William turned back to Governor Dudley.

"Governor, I object to the Deputy Governor's claim. There's no evidence to support it. It is untrue. I ask you to direct him to withdraw it."

Dudley leaned forward and looked at William, "Your congregation's request is controversial. Those on both sides have strongly held positions. If I ordered what you ask, I would spend all my time considering similar requests from both sides. Proceed."

"We all know that Indians along the Connecticut have tried for years to get us to settle near their villages," William said. "Their reason is selfish: they want us to protect them from the Pequots. Two months ago, six members of our congregation sailed up the river to a place the Indians call Suckiaug. It means black soil. The Suckiaug tribe's village is there and to the south there's a small Dutch fort. We will move there if our request is approved."

"Massachusetts Bay will benefit by our move," William continued. "Its people, not the Dutch, nor the people of Plymouth, will have settled Suckiaug. This will give Massachusetts Bay greater influence over the area and a loyal ally."

The Deputies of the General Court and Assistants of the Court of Assistants peppered William with questions the rest of the day. John's mind wandered when the questions became repetitive. He and Sam were going to clear weeds from William's cornfield that afternoon. They also needed to cut off the beetle infested leaves. He wondered how Sam was doing. There was so much work to do, but William wanted him here to learn how to argue a point and work within the government's structure.

"That concludes today's session," Dudley announced. "We will continue tomorrow morning."

"It's time to go," William said.

John trailed William from the meetinghouse. Their shadows were long as they walked to William's house.

"What do you think about today's session?" William asked.

"We did well," John answered. "What do you think?"

"It went as I expected. Most Deputies of the General Court and members of the Court of Assistants have made up their minds. It's hard to change minds. Fortunately, most General Court Deputies have decided to vote with us."

"What about the Court of Assistants?"

"They're close to former Governor Winthrop. We can expect few votes from them."

"Then what's the point of a week of hearings?" John asked.

"It's a process John. People need a process before they feel right about a decision, even if they already know what they want."

When they were within a hundred feet of William's house, John saw Sam working in the garden where he left him that morning.

"Tomorrow's session will start an hour earlier than today," William said. "Finish your chores so you can go with me."

John stopped on the road. William took two steps before turning back to look at him.

"Can I stay and work with Sam tomorrow?" John asked. "We need to weed and trim the pest infected corn stalks and finish the garden."

"Sam can do it."

"But you gave me these chores to do with him. I should help him."

"Sam is my servant. He'll understand."

"But he's also my friend."

William paused. He stared at John and smiled. "I suppose you won't miss much. Go ahead and finish your work but be done by Thursday. The hearing's last day is Friday. It will be the hearing's most important day and I want you there."

William and John reached the meetinghouse at sunrise on the hearing's last day. William was quiet as they walked from his house. It was cold and the sky was gray. John followed William and the congregation's other men to their seats. William remained standing as the Governor, Deputy Governor, Deputies and Assistants filed down the hall and took their seats. John stood at the front bench next to William. As soon as Governor Dudley was seated, they both sat.

"You may speak Deputy Governor Ludlow," Dudley announced.

Ludlow stood before Dudley. He turned back and scanned the spectators behind him, fixing his eyes on William for several seconds before turning back to Dudley.

"God sent us to Massachusetts Bay to create a pious community to be a beacon of light to everyone," Ludlow began. "He has blessed us. But now the seeds of our destruction are being sown as more and more of our people seek to leave. We're now debating whether the congregation of one of our most revered ministers should be allowed to leave. I fear if this thread is loosened the fabric of our community will unravel."

Ludlow was doing well, John thought - too well. He saw a few heads nod agreement among the General Court and the Assistants.

"To permit the Newe Towne congregation to leave our colony will undermine its strength and weaken its ability to serve God," Ludlow continued. "Our once unified City of God will be divided and weakened."

Ludlow pointed his right hand at William and the congregation seated behind him.

"Don't let these people tear apart what we've worked so hard to build. If you do, you will have to answer to God for allowing his kingdom on Earth to collapse."

A few men opposing the congregation's application sitting across the aisle and some General Court Deputies nodded.

"Reverend Hooker is a magnet attracting people to his ministry like flakes of metal," Ludlow continued. "Just as he's drawn people to Newe Towne from East Anglia and from other parts of Massachusetts Bay, he'll draw others to Connecticut who would have otherwise stayed in Massachusetts Bay."

Ludlow paused and looked at William and their congregation. He turned back to the Deputies and Assistants and pointed to the congregation.

"Whether they care or not, we must care that they would be in constant danger from the Indian tribes in the region, particularly the Pequots," Ludlow continued. "They would also face the risk of attack from the Dutch fort. These threats would not just put their congregation at risk; they would also entangle those of us in Massachusetts Bay for we will be forced to come to their aid. For this reason alone, they're selfish to ask us to allow them to leave."

Ludlow held his head high as he strode back to his chair. A few men across the aisle mumbled their agreement but it seemed to John that the opponents were just as exhausted as his congregation with the five-day ordeal.

"We will now vote on the application," Dudley announced.

John and the rest of Hooker's congregation knew what they needed. There were twenty-five Deputies on the General Court. They needed the votes of thirteen. They would also need the votes of six of the ten Assistants.

The vote of the Deputies of the General Court was taken first. The meeting room was quiet as one by one Governor Dudley asked for each Deputy's vote. Halfway through the vote, the count stood at six Deputies for the congregation's application and six Deputies opposed. John glanced at William who was studying a sheet of paper listing the General Court's Deputies.

The vote continued for several minutes. Suddenly, William gripped John's forearm and announced, "We've enough votes from the General Court. The case is now in the hands of the Assistants."

"The vote of the Deputies of the General Court is fifteen in favor of the application and ten opposed," Governor Dudley announced.

Behind him John heard the excited whispers of his congregation. His mouth was dry as Dudley began to take the votes of the ten Assistants, the Governor, and the Deputy Governor. Dudley announced he was voting in favor of the application.

Not surprisingly, Lieutenant Governor Ludlow voted against the application. Next Dudley called upon each of the ten Assistants. When former Governor Winthrop voted against the application, it was clear it would not be approved.

"The application has not received a majority vote of the Assistants," Dudley announced. "Therefore, it's denied."

Jeers erupted from John's congregation. Across the aisle, those opposed to the application cheered. As the cheers of the victors died, the jeers of the congregation continued. Dudley pounded his gavel until the room was silent. The people of John's congregation stared furiously at Dudley.

The silence was broken by the voice of an Assistant who voted against the application, "I move to reconsider the vote."

The meeting room was again alive with the congregation's voices. John looked at William who held his index finger over his lips.

Dudley announced, "This has been a difficult week. It's not the time to consider this motion. We will recess and take a day of humiliation to seek guidance from the Lord."

John watched William talk with Reverend Hooker while the meetinghouse cleared. Elder Goodwin, Deacon Hart and Reverend Stone joined William and Reverend Hooker. After briefly speaking, William left the congregation's leaders and walked across the room to Governor Dudley and former Governor Winthrop who were still seated in their chairs. Their discussion was brief. At the end of it, all three men were smiling.

John continued watching as William walked back across the room to the congregation's leaders. They talked briefly. When they were done all of them were smiling.

It was dark and the temperature was dropping when John and William walked home. John expected William to be sullen. Instead, William walked at a brisk pace.

"What do we do now?" John asked.

"We already did it," William answered.

"What do you mean?"

"We decided not to force another vote after the day of humiliation declared by Governor Dudley," William continued.

"Why not?"

"We might lose."

"So, we stay in Newe Towne?" John asked.

"No. Our congregation decided on a different approach. Other towns are anxious to leave Massachusetts Bay for Connecticut and Governor Dudley does not want to create a precedent for their move by approving our application. He and the Assistants have agreed if we don't renew our application after the day of prayer our congregation can leave without formal approval. We also agreed to recognize Governor Winthrop's son as the first Governor of all the new settlements in what will be called Connecticut."

John knew William taught him an important political lesson: Victory can often be earned without winning it.

"I want you to go with me today John," William announced.

It was two days after the congregation's hearing and John had entered William's house for breakfast after completing his morning chores. Bridget had already placed a bowl of corn porridge and a piece of boiled pork where John normally sat.

"Where're we going?" John asked.

"Boston, to train with the militia," William answered. "When we move to Suckiaug you will need training if we have to fight the Pequots.

John knew William was right. It was only because of their fear of the Pequots that the Suckiaugs and other river tribes wanted the English to move to their lands. War with the Pequots was unavoidable. But if there was a war Connecticut would be in the middle of it and Massachusetts Bay over a hundred miles away.

Gray clouds hung low as they climbed into the Newe Towne ferry later that morning. As the ferry slid across the river William announced, "You've told me you wanted to be a soldier. I want you to meet Lieutenant Thomas Bull when we reach Boston's Common. He'll lead the militia's training. He was a lieutenant in the war in the Netherlands. He'll train you."

It was noon when they reached the Common. There were at least eighty men in the field. One man towered over them. His burnished pike helmet made him seem even taller. He wore a metal breastplate over his buff leather coat. Around his neck an orange scarf flowed in the wind as he gave instructions to a group of men.

The man smiled at William, "Good day William. So, this is your ward."

"Yes Thomas," William said. "He's John Lee of Colchester."

"He's a strong young man." Bull said. "He'll make a fine soldier."

Bull turned to John, "Your guardian says you want to be a soldier. Is that true?"

"Yes sir," John answered. "I want to fight for our people and church."

"Well by God's will you came to the right place. Sharpen your blade for I'm training the best militia in New England."

John nodded, uncertain if he should respond.

"William, you and John join the men to the south and practice with pikes. I will be there when I finish with these men."

John followed William across the field to the men Bull pointed to. He'd never handled a pike and was nervous. Several men watched John and William as they approached. A short barrel-chested man wearing a weathered gray cloak stepped forward.

"Did Lieutenant Bull send you?" the man asked.

"He did," William said.

The man pointed to a pile of pikes lying in the field.

"Each of you take a pike," the man said. "If you know the pike drills you can join us, if not, you can watch us until Lieutenant Bull arrives."

The pike was heavier than it looked when John lifted it from the pile. He felt out of place as he held it at his side. When William joined the other men, he felt awkward standing alone away from the men watching them move as they drilled with their pikes. *William moves through the pike's positions effortlessly*, he thought. Then he felt a hand on his shoulder.

"Fear not, after my training, you will flawlessly perform this drill," a deep voice to his right announced.

He turned into the heavily lined face of Lieutenant Bull. Bull continued, "The thing about a pike is you don't have to load it. Once you learn to use it you can fight with it alone or in line with others. I was a pikeman in most of my battles and only trained as a musketeer later. Line up with the others and I will take you through the positions."

John stood next to William in a line of six men. To their left was another line of six men.

"We have a new man," Bull said. "I will demonstrate the pike positions for him. Watch as I do."

Bull moved through the pike's positions by shouting each command and effortlessly moving into the position commanded. When he ordered "charge your pike," Bull swiftly brought his pike to shoulder level pointing ahead with his left hand on the pike ahead of his left shoulder and his right hand at the pike's base behind his head. He next ordered "push your pike" at which point from the same position he thrust the pike forward with such great speed it penetrated the armor on the scarecrow being used as a target. John doubted he would ever acquire such speed.

"When you are trained you will charge your pikes in unison sweeping the enemy from the field and defending the musketeers behind you whose fire will open gaps in the enemy's formation you can exploit," Bull said.

By the end of his first day of training, John knew the basic pike positions and his nervousness was gone.

"We will perform these pike positions when we train," Bull announced. "After that we will perform musket drills. When the time comes, you won't think, you will do things instinctively."

As the men left the Common, John heard Deacon Hart's voice from across the field.

"William," Hart yelled. "There's someone I want you to meet."

John and William turned to Hart. Walking across the field to-wards them were Hart and Richard Hawkes. Hawkes's coal black hair and black eyes screamed at John as he crossed the field.

"William, this is Richard Hawkes," Hart said. "He manages my friend Robert Rose's lumber business on the bay islands. Richard is to be Reverend Stone's assistant."

John felt Hawkes's cold stare while Hart spoke. He warded off Hawkes's stare by keeping his eyes on Hart.

"I know Richard from our crossing on the *Francis*," William said. "It sounds like you've done well since you arrived, Richard. Will you be coming to Suckiaug?"

Hart and William turned to Hawkes. It was now impossible for John not to look at him too. Hawkes was smiling.

"Yes, after I finish my work with Robert Rose," Hawkes said.

John's mind screamed "*no*" when he heard Hawkes's words. His face felt flush and his stomach turned. Hawkes was looking at him.

"Good day John Lee," Hawkes said.

"Good day," John answered.

"I guess we will be seeing more of each other in the future," Hawkes said.

John didn't answer.

"It's good to see you again Richard," William said. "John and I need to meet Lieutenant Bull now."

Hawkes nodded at William.

"I will see you on our next training day," Hart said

"By all means," Hawkes replied. "I am pleased to serve in the militia.

Most men were gone when John and William met Lieutenant Bull. Bull took them to a spot at the Common's edge near a strand of trees.

"Thank you for staying to talk about more training for John," William said.

"We will work for a few hours after every training day and three days every other week," Bull said. "Today we will practice hand to hand fighting."

John thought he knew how to fight, but as he worked with Bull, he realized he knew little. Bull was strong, swift, and experienced. John quickly learned he was no match for him. Bull would first demonstrate a technique, convincing John of its effectiveness by putting him on his back. Bull next explained the steps he took and helped John apply them. The technique John liked best was using an attacking opponent's momentum to throw him to the ground. Bull assured John in battle this would be a technique he would use often.

Chapter 11

It was late December and the first of Reverend Hooker's congregation had been in Suckiaug, which they named Newtown, for nearly two months. John and Sam hiked the one hundred miles from Massachusetts Bay with William and Bridget Westwood and two dozen other families. But Bridget was sad because Grace Newell decided not to go with them but to stay in Massachusetts Bay with a family in Roxbury. Their trip was uneventful. The weather was fair, and they reached Newtown in fourteen days.

Once in Newtown, the men built temporary lean-to thatch roofed shelters to protect them from the coming winter's cold and snow. Their huts were carved into the side of a hill, giving them three sides of earth to insulate them from the cold. They finished the last hut just as the bright days of October were replaced by November's slate gray skies.

They brought enough food for three months and counted on shipments of more food to be brought up the Connecticut River for their needs during the winter. They now knew this was a false hope. Very little food made it up the river and their hunger cast a pall over their feeble settlement.

Then, they began coming down with the fever.

John first saw Henry Hayward coughing when they went outside to get firewood for their families' huts. By the time they brought in wood, little Henry's face was beet red, his forehead burning, and the whites of his eyes filled with red veins.

When Bridget laid Henry in bed, Henry begged John to take him with him when he went out for firewood the next day. While John promised he would, he was worried as he walked to William's hut.

He'd never seen anyone become so sick as fast as Henry.

By the next morning Katherine Barnard also had the fever. Sarah Hart and Bridget took turns caring for Katherine and Henry. Joseph Barnard spent the morning pacing in his hut while the two women tried every method they knew to fight the fever. But by mid-afternoon, it was clear both Katherine and Henry were deathly sick.

Bridget could stand in no longer. She rushed through the hut's door and fought her way through the blowing snow to William's hut. She burst into the hut with a torrent of snow swirling in behind her.

"Mary and Henry are worse," Bridget yelled. "Nothing has worked. They'll die unless we get help. Go to the Suckiaugs and see if they have a cure."

William and John put on their heavy wool breeches, doublets and capes, and sped through the door. They trudged through the snow to the Suckiaug village two miles north. Smoke poured from the bark covered long houses and wigwams. A dog was tied to the nearest long house. It barked as they walked past. Within minutes, a man emerged from the long house to which the dog was tied. The man was slightly taller than William and appeared to be near forty. His deer skin mantle was draped over his left shoulder with the fur turned against his bronze skin. The muscles of his uncovered right shoulder gave evidence of a lean muscular body. He walked towards them.

In broken English he announced that he was Huritt, a sub-sachem of his tribe, as he led William and John into the long house.

The long house's inside was framed with saplings and heavy bark strips lashed to the saplings to make its roof and walls. The only light came from the two openings in the roof which released smoke from the two fires burning inside. A bench made of saplings covered with deer and bearskin ran along the length of each wall.

A woman and young man sat on the bench. The woman was about Huritt's age and the young man about twenty. They exchanged smiles with William while Huritt introduced them as his wife Kimi and son

Chogan. Huritt retrieved a pipe, lit it, and motioned for everyone to sit on the bench.

William waved his hand before the pipe, slowly stating in English that there was no time to smoke the pipe as he needed medicine for two people with fever. When Huritt understood, he turned to Kimi and, speaking Algonquin, asked her to prepare a potion to cure the fever.

Kimi prepared a potion from wild berries, roots, and leaves. She placed it in a clay pot which she gave to Huritt. Huritt turned to William and told him there was enough for both their sick people and each should drink half of what was in the pot.

"John, you are the swiftest," William said. "Take the potion to Joseph Barnard's hut as fast as you can."

John grabbed the pot from Huritt and sprinted from the long house. When he reached the Barnards' hut he gave the pot to Bridget and repeated Huritt's instructions. Bridget stared blankly at him. Her face was drawn and her eyes bloodshot. John knew she didn't understand.

"Give this potion to Henry and Katherine," he repeated.

Bridget's jaw tightened and she waved her finger at him, "Not unless you tell me what's in it."

John was shocked. How could Bridget refuse to give the potion to two people so sick?

"Please give this to them," John pleaded. "It's from the Suckiaug."

Bridget shook her head. Joseph Barnard jumped from his seat and stood above Bridget.

"Bridget, use the potion!" Barnard exclaimed. "Henry will die without it. Look at him!"

Bridget and John turned to Henry. His eyes were closed, his face ashen, his bedclothes soaked in perspiration, and his hair wet and matted. John saw little to reveal this was the same seven-year-old boy who followed him everywhere since they were on the *Francis*.

Bridget took the pot to Henry's bed. She divided the potion in half by measuring it into two small cups. She gently lifted Henry's head and poured the potion into his mouth. She laid Henry's head back on his pillow and brushed his wet hair off his forehead before bending over to kiss him. Then she slumped to the floor and began crying. John fought back tears while he watched Joseph hold his wife's hand as she lay unconscious in their bed.

William had not returned from the Suckiaug village and Deacon Hart was nowhere to be seen. John knew he had to act. He took the cup containing the rest of the potion to Katherine's bed and, as her husband held her hand, poured the potion down her throat. When he was done, John sat silently on the hard dirt floor.

Within minutes William opened the hut's door. There was not enough room for everyone, so William went to his own hut, promising to return in the morning. John walked out with him. The sky was clear and the air freezing. After William left, John watched his breath pour out as he exhaled into the cold night. Each fragile breath quickly scattered and disappeared. He took a long breath and held it before reentering Joseph Barnard's hut.

By the early morning darkness Henry Hayward was dead. John and Bridget were with Henry when he took his last breath. As soon as Henry died Joseph Barnard fell to his knees and prayed. Tears slid from Bridget's eyes as she shivered next to Henry's bed.

John said nothing. He stared at Henry, refusing to accept he was dead. As he thought of the once lively little boy who no longer was, he struggled to find meaning in his death. His Puritan faith taught him no man could understand God's ways, but he prayed just this time God would reveal the meaning of His ways to him. God did not answer. As he thanked God for letting Katherine live, outside the hut the wolves surrounding the tiny village howled.

Chapter 12

It was a bright blue April morning four months after the fever lifted and the Connecticut River sparkled below John and Sam. They had just plowed four rows of soil in the planting field the settlers had set aside for the spring planting. The two oxen stood in the brown grass they were plowing, and John was ankle deep in the freshly turned furrow behind the plow. Sam was ahead on John's right holding the oxen's harness. John pulled the check line from his neck and turned to Sam.

"That was a hard winter," John said. "I miss Henry."

"Me too," Sam answered.

"Thank God Katherine survived and only five died after Henry," John said. "It can't be said whether she was saved by the Suckiaug's potion or by providence. What matters is she's healthy and her husband Joseph was not touched by the fever."

"When ya next goin' to the Suckiaug village," Sam asked.

"Tomorrow."

"You go often. Ya must like 'em a lot."

"We owe them for saving us this winter," John said. "I've helped Huritt, Chogan and Chogan's friend Etchemin, carve canoes from trees. We also hunt deer together."

"Ya speak their language now?"

"Passably."

William interrupted them, "Come with me John. It's time for the meeting."

They walked south on the path to the Little River. A dense pine and maple forest ran along the path on their right. To the left, one hundred feet down the slope to the river, were the settlers' huts.

They had traveled halfway to the Little River when to their left a large field full of tree stumps spread down the slope to the settlers' dug out huts. In the center of the field was a rectangular building made of roughly squared logs with gaps filled with clay and hay. Its roof was thatched and its windows open aired with pine boards to close them.

"Elder Goodwin's triumph," William said. "It will serve as our meetinghouse until we build a larger one."

By now the five men clearing the tree stumps from the field spotted them. Deacon Hart waived at William and John as they walked down the slope into the field.

"Good day William," Hart said. "A great day for the first meeting of our General Court."

"Yes, it is Stephen," William said. "Where is Elder Goodwin?"

"In the meetinghouse making last minute preparations," Hart answered. "He drove the men hard to finish the meetinghouse today."

"God has blessed us," Hart said. "It's time to get on with it."

"Are the Deputies from Dorchester and Watertowne here?" William asked.

"They're in the meetinghouse."

John followed William to the meetinghouse. Several men and women standing outside greeted William as he made his way through them into the meetinghouse.

"God be with you William," a tall thin man yelled as they walked through the door.

The room was much smaller than Newe Towne's meetinghouse. The benches were pushed closer together, making it impossible to move to the central aisle without forcing those sitting on the bench to stand.

John squeezed himself into the third row while William moved ahead to the oak table reserved for the General Court's Deputies. John was amused to see Roger Ludlow, his congregation's former opponent, seated next to William. Having moved to Windsor, which was several miles north on the river, Ludlow was now its Deputy to

Connecticut's General Court and the Court's Chairman. Three other men sat with Ludlow and William at the table, including John Steele, a member of their congregation.

Ludlow announced, "The first meeting of Connecticut's General Court is called to order. The first matter involves Henry Stiles."

Ludlow stared ahead at a short thin faced man who stood facing him and announced, "Goodman Stiles, you are accused of trading a musket to the Indians for corn. Do you deny this?"

"I don't deny it," Stiles said. "My family needed food."

"What shall we do about this, Deputies?" Ludlow asked.

"While trading muskets to the Indians isn't yet a crime, its consequences are dangerous," William said. "I move we order Goodman Stiles to recover the musket from the Indians in a fair and legal way before the General Court's next session. The court should also make it a misdemeanor to trade muskets, powder and musket balls to the Indians in the future."

After a short discussion, the deputies agreed to William's motions, stating it would now be a misdemeanor, the punishment for which would be severe, to trade muskets, pistols, powder or shot to the Indians. Meanwhile, Stiles promised to recover the musket.

The next two matters weren't as interesting. John watched half asleep as the Court announced that loose swine would either be returned to their owner for a fee, or the town could sell the swine at a public auction. The court next approved establishment of the new church in Watertown southwest of Newtown. He listened as Watertown's men told of the hardships they endured and announced their former church in Massachusetts approved of their new church.

When the session was complete, the other men of the General Court rose from the table while William motioned John to come forward.

"We have another meeting," William said. "Deacon Hart, John Steele, Elder Goodwin and I are discussing plans for bringing Reverend

Hooker and the rest of our congregation to Newtown next month."

The four men sat around the same oak table used by the General Court while John sat alone on the Meetinghouse's first row bench.

"We need guides," Hart announced.

"Indians would be best," Goodwin said. "What about the Suckiaugs?"

"William, you know them," Steele said. "You should ask them."

William turned to John and then back to the men at the table while pointing to John, "John knows several Suckiaugs. Who should we ask to guide our congregation John?"

John was struck dumb. He was never asked to say anything at the meetings he attended with William. But William was right, he knew the Suckiaugs better than anyone else in town. He visited their village many times to see Huritt, his son Chogan and Chogan's friend Etchemin. Still, he wondered if this alone qualified him to recommend guides for Reverend Hooker and the congregation.

"Who should we pick John?" William said, now with urgency in his voice.

"Yes John, tell us," Hart echoed.

"I would pick three Suckiaugs," John said. "They're Huritt, the Suckiaug village's leader, his son Chogan, and Chogan's friend Etchemin. I will go with them to Newe Towne and help them bring our people here."

"William, do you know these men?" Goodwin asked.

"I do," William answered. "They'll be good guides."

"One of us should go with John and the Suckiaugs to guide our congregation here," Goodwin said. "While John's strong and mature for his age, he's still young. Who would like to lead them?"

Immediately, Hart spoke, "I will lead them. We will take John Winthrop's pinnace, *The Blessing*, to Boston and meet Reverend Hooker in Newe Towne in May when they're ready to travel."

"It's settled," Goodwin said, "William, you and John ask the Suckiaugs if they'll help lead our congregation here. Stephen, make your preparations immediately."

John was nervous and said nothing as he and William walked back to William's house. He didn't fear the danger ahead of him. What he feared was he would fail in what he was asked to do. Never was such great responsibility thrust upon him. He was always protected and guided by his father or William. Neither would be with him now.

William sensed John's concern and turned to him. "I know you are worried about what you've been asked to do. I am not. In the two years since we arrived on the *Francis*, you have done all I asked as well as I could myself. Trust in God and he'll guide you."

After eating Bridget's evening meal, John and Sam sat together on the grass outside of Sam's small hut looking down the slope at the Connecticut River. The light of the full moon struck the river at an angle making each wave shimmer and the white bark of each birch tree lining the river glow. Several bats flew across the moonlit sky while along the river's shoreline owls hooted.

"So, they want you to lead Reverend Hooker here?" Sam asked.

"Yes."

"Take me with you."

"William needs you here."

"No, he don't," Sam said. "He'll do fine without me."

"I'll ask him."

"It's a considerable distance," Sam said. "You'll need me. Tell him that."

There was a long silence as both John and Sam stared at the river. Finally, Sam stood and looked down at John.

"Funny isn't it?" Sam said.

"What's funny?"

"We's not just takin' Reverend Hooker's folks here but also Richard Hawkes."

John's mouth opened as he looked up at Sam and stammered, "I suppose that's true."

"You bet it's true," Sam laughed.

Chapter 13

The *Blessing* arrived in Boston on May 30th. Deacon Hart, John Lee, Sam Pierce, and their Suckiaug guides Huritt, Chogan and Etchemin disembarked in the morning. Hart took the Suckiaugs with him while John and Sam stayed in Boston to buy three horses for William. John traded for two saddles and three horses with the wampum and beaver pelts William provided him for that purpose. One horse was a black gelding, the second a chestnut stallion, and the third a gray mare. They rode south on the Shawmut Peninsula towards Newe Towne. John sat atop the black gelding while Sam followed him on the gray mare with the chestnut stallion tied to the mare.

A light breeze flowed through John's hair as he sat above the path on the gelding. He breathed in the earthy scent of the mudflats and salt marshes spreading out hundreds of yards west until they merged with the Back Bay. But soon his exhilaration turned to sadness when he remembered days spent with his mother and father. He wondered how they were and prayed to see them again soon. He stopped asking William about them after his first year in Newe Towne for William's answer was always the same: "I've heard nothing."

Within an hour they were off the peninsula and entering the modest farms surrounding Roxbury.

"Grace lives hereabouts," Sam said. "Let's stop and see her."

"We don't have time," John answered. "She probably doesn't want to see us anyway."

"How ya know?"

"Because she didn't want to move to Newtown with us and argued with Bridget about it. She wouldn't even listen to me when I told her how exciting our life in Newtown would be. She now has what she wants - a new life with a new guardian."

Sam stopped his mare. In response, John reined in his gelding and looked back at Sam and said, "Why did you stop?"

"I get it now," Sam said with a broad smile. "You was protecting Grace when you stalked Hawkes that night. But now you don't worry since she's here in Roxbury and Hawkes is still in Boston and will soon be in Newtown."

John stared at Sam without speaking before wheeling his gelding around and pushing it forward. Sam laughed as he followed John south out of Roxbury. They rode along the Back Bay for three-quarters of an hour without speaking before crossing at a ford three miles upriver from Newe Towne.

The sun was midway to the horizon when Sam broke the silence, "Think William's gonna let you keep a horse?"

"Are you mad?" John laughed. "William doesn't give things away."

Sam stopped his mare. In response, John reined in his gelding and looked back at Sam.

"How ya think Hawkes was able to buy the stallion he rode to William's field last year?" Sam asked.

John shrugged.

"Must've stole what he used to buy it."

"Careful when you make such claims Sam - even if you've proof. Richard Hawkes isn't one to ignore such accusations."

They reached Newe Towne in late afternoon. The streets were lined with carts loaded with all manner of belongings needed on the trip and once the settlers got to Newtown. John and Sam guided their horses towards the meetinghouse between the carts, cooking utensils, and sacks of seed, plows, axes, clothing and candles piled on carts and on the ground ready to be loaded. Previously, the congregation had loaded other belongings on the barks, shallops and pinnaces set to sail to the town of Saybrook at the mouth of the Connecticut and then up river to Newtown.

The meetinghouse was dark, and John stiffened when he saw Reverend Hooker along with Reverend Stone, Lieutenant Bull and Deacon Hart seated at a large oak table at the front of the meeting-house. A few other men were seated on benches facing the table listening as the leaders discussed the trip's details.

"Ah, John Lee, you're just in time, Deacon Hart is about to tell us how he'll use you and our other scouts on the trail," Hooker said. "Come sit at the table."

John nodded at Hooker and walked briskly towards the table. He had nearly reached the table when Richard Hawkes turned and faced him from his seat on the front row bench. Hawkes raised his chin and smiled smugly. John glanced at Hawkes without expression as he walked by him and took a seat on Hart's right.

"Our scouts will move far ahead of the cattle and the main company following them." Hart said. "They'll mark the path for the cattle train which in turn will mark it still clearer when Lieutenant Bull, Richard Hawkes, and their men bring the cattle through behind them. The scouts will return to the cattle train in late afternoon and both will find a suitable place for the main company to camp for the night and prepare the site for their arrival."

"How many cattle do you have Thomas?" Hooker asked.

"A hundred and sixty," Bull answered. "Plus, six cows, a steer and a bull I'm taking to Saybrook for the new governor, John Winthrop the younger."

John listened while the men discussed the wagons' order, the Indian villages they would encounter and the meals to be prepared on the trip. Finally, Hooker stood and smiled.

"We're ready!" Hooker announced. "With God's help we will reach Newtown in a fortnight."

While the discussion at the table continued, Hawkes focused on other matters. He was grateful to Robert Rose for hiring him and for being so inattentive during the two years he worked for him. He now possessed a small fortune in wampum and beaver pelts from the sale of timber and corn he stole from Rose. But in Boston he would always be Rose's man. Connecticut was where he could build his own empire. Deacon Hart would be his path to wealth and Reverend Stone his path to power. He smiled to himself when he thought of how much Stone listened to him already and how Hart spoke of how they would operate gristmills together. But there was still the matter of John Lee. He had said nothing about the chalice in two years. Hawkes wondered whether this would continue. Lee was an enigma. Hell, he himself would not hesitate to tell of the theft under similar circumstances if it was advantageous for him. Lee said he would honor his oath, but he wondered how he could be certain. *There's only one way*, Hawkes concluded.

John woke on the Meeting House Common's grass an hour before sunrise. He blinked his eyes open and looked above into Sam's broad smile.

"Thought ya was gonna sleep all mornin'," Sam said. "I saddled the horses. Load your things so we can leave."

John lifted his buff coat from the dew-covered grass, thrust his arms into it, tucked his brown breeches into his black boots, and threw the bag with his belongings onto his gelding before climbing onto it. The congregation would not wake for an hour, so John and Sam moved forward quietly.

The sky was bright with stars. Soon, a faint glow worked its way across the sky from the east. Low on the eastern horizon a small crescent moon continued to rise with the spreading light. The faint smell of manure wafted in the air as they passed through the Cow Common and turned west through the marsh towards Watertowne.

Huritt, Chogan and Etchemin were waiting for them when they entered the woods between the two towns. As John directed, the three

Suckiaug traveled far to the west beyond the towns of Watertowne and Waltham during the night. He climbed from his gelding and approached Huritt.

"Did you find a place to camp for tonight?" John asked.

"Yes," Huritt answered. "I will take you to it."

John and Sam followed Huritt west on the Indian path. Behind them the sun rose over the trees. John knew the congregation was now awake and imagined their excitement as they threw their possessions into their carts and tied them to their backs. *They're now on their way to the assembly point west of town*, he thought. *Lieutenant Bull and the cattle have already been on the path for an hour and are stirring up dust in Watertowne.*

Two hours later, Huritt and John reached the meadow Huritt picked for the congregation. Its lush grass sloped down to a small languid stream across which an impenetrable tree line grew into the stream on the opposite shore. The path they took was covered with a black canopy of trees, while above the meadow the sky was open, and the sun shone down on them. John took a deep breath and allowed the odor of pine and cedar to fill his nose before he turned to Huritt and announced, "Perfect."

"I will take Chogan and Etchemin farther west to set up our own camp," Huritt said. "We will each take turns scouting farther west tonight to guard against attack."

By day's end, the serpentine train of carts and men, women and children began spilling into the meadow. Lieutenant Bull, along with Hawkes, Eastman and Roach, had arrived less than a half hour before and had set the cattle to graze. After a supper of beef stew and fried fish, Reverend Hooker blessed the congregation.

As the campfires blazed, John slipped away from the camp and found a place in the field of cattle where he could sleep under the stars. He woke in the darkness of morning and stared at the Milky Way rising from the southern horizon while a full moon poured light on the field of cattle around him. He lay in the field staring at the unchanging panorama of stars. He prayed they shined on his mother and father that night as well.

Chapter 14

Richard Hawkes whipped his black stallion up the steep pine covered hill. It was the sixth day of the congregation's journey. Behind him, Eastman and Roach pulled their spent horses up the same hill. They had left the cattle train early that morning and were now ten miles ahead of the congregation.

Hawkes was moving fast to the northwest to meet with the three Nipmucs he traded with in Boston. Through their trading he found there was greater profit selling muskets to Indians than in selling the corn and timber he was able to siphon away from Rose's operations. Soon his musket trade would extend far beyond his trade with the Nipmucs. From Newtown he could trade with all the Connecticut tribes.

Hawkes wheeled his stallion around at the hill's summit and looked down the slope at Eastman and Roach making the climb. Roach was first. He climbed effortlessly, his tall muscular frame moving smoothly through the underbrush and boulders lying in front of him. Eastman was fifty feet behind Roach and his short pudgy body stumbled over the boulders and shrubs. Finally, Eastman completed the climb. Hawkes looked down from his stallion at Eastman who was bent over catching his breath. He turned to Roach who was astride his horse next to him.

"The Nipmucs said to meet them on the highest hill on this ridge," Hawkes said. "This is it. We'll wait here."

Immediately, three Nipmucs emerged from the trees. Their brown skin glistened with sweat. Breech clouts covered their midsections while deerskin sandals and leggings their feet and legs. Hawkes recognized them immediately and raised his right hand.

"Welcome Hassun," Hawkes said. "Who are you taking me to meet?"

"Young Pocumtuc warriors who live near the Agawam village," Hassun said. "They're eager for wealth and power. They've neither now."

"Good, they're hungry," Hawkes said. "Who's their leader?"

"Megedaqik. It means 'kills many'."

Hawkes pointed to the other Nipmucs, "Find a meeting place two days west and have Achak and Aranck bring me there to meet this Megedaqik."

By late afternoon, Hawkes, Eastman and Roach were back on the trail the congregation was traveling.

"The congregation is three miles east," Hawkes said. "We will meet them."

Hawkes reined his stallion to the east and led Eastman and Roach forward. At that moment, two miles ahead, John Lee and Sam Pierce rode in the opposite direction towards them.

"Where's the Suckiaugs?" Sam asked. "They was to meet us by now."

"Don't worry," John said. "They'll be here soon."

At that moment, Huritt, Chogan and Etchemin were in the woods just off the path between the two groups of Englishmen. They were on foot and moving quickly ahead of John and Sam, looking for threats to the congregation. When Huritt heard the heavy hoofbeats of horses he turned and ordered Chogan and Etchemin to follow him deeper into the woods along the trail. Once there, they crouched under the branches of two pine trees waiting to see who was coming. Huritt listened as the hoofbeats grew louder. There were at least three horses moving towards them.

Huritt heard the hoofbeats of two horses coming from the opposite direction. He crawled closer to the trail where he saw John and Sam riding towards him. Still uncertain who the three riders coming in the opposite direction were, Huritt held his hand up motioning Chogan and Etchemin to stay in the trees.

Huritt glanced back down the path in the opposite direction. Three riders emerged from the trees' darkness onto the path. He instantly recognized Richard Hawkes and his men. He crouched lower while watching the two groups converge before reining their horses to a stop 60 feet from each other on the path.

"Why are you so far ahead of the cattle?" John asked. "Lieutenant Bull has been looking for you. He needs your help herding the cattle to tonight's camp."

"We've been scouting for hazards and possible ambushes," Hawkes answered.

"By whose order?" John demanded. "We're the congregation's scouts, not you. You are assigned to help Lieutenant Bull with the cattle. We don't need your help scouting."

Hawkes's face turned red. He stared coldly at John. He clicked his tongue as he slapped the side of his black stallion with its reins pushing it forward. Eastman and Roach nudged their horses forward alongside Hawkes. As they moved forward, Hawkes figured the odds of three to two favored him. Especially, since one was a 15-year-old boy and the other a short small framed man.

"I see the beating I gave you last year taught you nothing," Hawkes said. "It's time I teach you another lesson."

John frowned and pressed his legs into his gelding's sides and began riding at a trot towards Hawkes with Sam riding next to him. As the groups closed, Hawkes drew his sword while Eastman pulled a knife from his belt and Roach reached into his bag for his hatchet. The pace of the horses quickened as John and Sam drew hatchets from their belts.

Huritt, Chogan and Etchemin stepped from the trees just before the groups merged and stood on the path next to John and Sam. Each held a hatchet and stared at Hawkes and his men. Hawkes pulled his stallion to a halt while Eastman and Roach stopped alongside him. Hawkes scowled and shook his head.

"I won't fight savages," Hawkes spit. "There will be another day John Lee. Now we need to take care of the congregation."

"Agreed," John said. "Go to Lieutenant Bull. He needs your help."

John stared at Hawkes as the two groups warily passed through each other going in opposite directions. *So, even Richard Hawkes is afraid in the face of superior numbers*, John thought.

John smiled at Huritt after the groups passed and said, "Thank you."

Huritt nodded.

Chapter 15

The next day John and Huritt led Sam, Chogan and Etchemin through a heavy forest into a broad meadow along the north shore of a long dark blue pond. It was the journey's seventh day and they were four miles ahead of the cattle and five miles ahead of the congregation.

"We will build the camp here," John proclaimed.

"This is a good place," Huritt confirmed.

Sam moved to John's side as John looked south down the length of the pond. While narrow, the pond's dark blue revealed it was deep. Pine, maple and birch trees spread beyond the pond.

"It's noon," Sam said. "We'll set up the camp for the congregation."

John glanced at Huritt, who with Chogan and Etchemin looked at the meadow to find a place for the congregation's camp.

"Can we trust the Wappaquasset?" John asked.

"Yes," Huritt answered. "Their sachem was the first to ask the English to move west. I will take you to him."

Huritt led John into the woods near the pond. They walked on the main trail until it met another, narrower, trail.

"We leave the main trail here," Huritt said. "The village is at the other end of the pond."

Huritt strode ahead of John, his muscles rippling with sweat. The heat of day was upon them. The trees lining the path allowed little sunlight to reach them. Huritt strode ahead with no apparent concern of ambush. John turned from side to side peering into the woods.

Suddenly, Huritt stopped and turned to John, "Stop looking about. Enemies approach quietly while a friend approaches loudly to announce his coming. We come as friends. Do not look into the woods so much. Walk forward without fear and make noise. The Wappaquasset have been watching us all day."

John's eyes dropped. After a moment he raised them and looked at Huritt. Huritt smiled before moving forward again. John followed, this time keeping pace with Huritt while looking straight ahead.

After a half hour the path opened into a dark green meadow. The pond was beyond the meadow. Along it were bark covered wigwams and long houses. Three Indians approached from the woods: two were in their late teens; the other man's hair was gray.

"They are Wappaquassets," Huritt said. "They followed us here."

The gray haired Wappaquasset greeted Huritt. The two men spoke briefly before Huritt turned to John, "This is Acquittanug, the Wappaquasset's Sachem. They have tracked the congregation for two days and gathered corn and fish for us."

"Thank you Acquittanug," John said. "Reverend Hooker and his people are grateful."

John and Huritt returned to the congregation's meadow at mid-afternoon. Sam, Chogan and Etchemin were building dozens of campfires and clearing the tall grass near the pond.

"It'll make it easier for our cattle to get to water," Sam announced.

The cattle began streaming out of the woods within half an hour. Deacon Hart was with them along with two other men. Hart road his horse towards John.

"The camp is in good order," Hart announced. "What about food?"

"The Wappaquassets are bringing corn and fish," John replied.

Scores of cattle flooded into the camp and the once quiet meadow was filled with their bellowing as Hart and the two other men, who were assigned to Lieutenant Bull, herded them to the pond. Lieutenant Bull walked out of the trees as the last of the cattle passed John. He strode across the meadow, slapping his right thigh with his right hand. He stared at John with bulging eyes when they met.

"Have you seen Richard Hawkes and his men today?" Bull asked.

"They abandoned the cattle early this morning and Deacon Hart and I, along with the rest of my men, have struggled to control them all day."

"No sir." John answered.

Bull's heavily creased face relaxed as he smiled, "It would be best if you're not near him when I find him."

An hour later, when it was clear the congregation would not be arriving for a while, John searched for Bull. He found him sitting in the grass near the pond with Deacon Hart.

"Sit with us," Hart ordered. "Lieutenant Bull is talking about his military service."

John nodded at Bull and sat in the grass with the two men. The sun was setting and the three of them moved closer to the fire.

"Where did you first fight after your training?" Hart asked.

"In local skirmishes in Scotland and Ireland. Later, I fought in the Netherlands for the protestant cause against the Spanish and Catholics. During the years just before I came to New England, I served under Thomas Fairfax in Sir Horace Vere's expedition to the Netherlands. I was a pikeman at first but later a musketeer. I still favor the pike, especially the half pike."

Lieutenant Bull's words were met with silence. John waited for Hart to say something, but Hart simply stared into the fire. He wondered whether Hart was rude or simply disinterested. He wanted to know about Bull's battles but felt it would be presumptuous to ask about them. Finally, he broke the silence, "Can you tell us about your battles?"

"My battles were never glorious," Bull replied. "What I remember most were the banners waving us into battle and the dead and dying lying in the field when the battle was over. I lost many friends. I never enjoyed battle."

"If you found battle horrible, why did you continue being a soldier?" John asked.

Hart spun his head away from the fire and stared at John, "God have mercy on you. That was a rude question John. Don't pick at a man's wounds."

John dropped his head and stared into the fire. Before he could apologize, Bull spoke, "It's alright Stephen. A fair question John. I'm pleased to answer it."

Both John and Hart leaned closer to Bull. John's breathing was shallow, and his heart beat furiously as he waited for Bull to speak.

"I always believed in our cause when I fought; but believed in the men I served with far more," Bull said. "They were my brothers and like brothers we fought for each other, sharing both happiness and sorrow."

Bull pulled an eight-inch leather handled knife from a sheath hanging from his belt. The knife glistened as Bull pulled it through the fire's glow and held it in front of John and Hart.

"This knife belonged to my friend Martin Sherman," Bull said. "We fought together in the Netherlands. I had run a Papist through with my pike when I turned and saw Martin's throat slashed by another Papist who came up behind him. I knocked Martin's killer to the ground and slashed his throat from ear to ear with Martin's knife which I pulled from Martin's hand. I carry Martin's knife to honor his memory."

John stared at Bull, his hand covering his mouth, while Hart turned away and looked into the fire. The fire's hissing and popping filled the silence. Bull looked into the fire for a moment before turning back to John.

"Truth be told, battle brings me to life," Bull confided.

"How is it you're leading cattle to Newtown?" John asked, desperate to change the subject.

"Governor Winthrop sought me out when I landed in Boston on the *Hopewell* last year," Bull said. "He needed a military adviser. Later, when he learned I was going to Connecticut with Reverend Hooker's congregation, he asked me to take six cattle to his son in Saybrook. When Reverend Hooker learned this, he asked if I would guide all the cattle going to Newtown with the congregation."

Bull paused for a moment. He leaned towards John. They were so close to the fire its smoke stung John's eyes.

"You've trained with me for eight months," Bull said. "During that time, you said you wanted to be a soldier. Is this still true?"

"It is," John answered.

"There's little glory in battle," Bull said. "But if you have a sense of honor and duty, military service can fill a void."

"Can you kill a man, John?" Bull asked. "I don't mean when firing in a line of muskets or when you are cornered by a foe with no other option. What I mean is can you kill a man with stealth when he's unaware or when you disarm him in battle?"

The fire's crackle screamed in John's ears as he thought about the question. But his answer was never given, for before he answered, horses entered the meadow, their riders' voices filling the air. Immediately, Bull and Hart rose from the fire and began walking up the slope to the camp. John followed a few paces behind them. Suddenly, Bull bolted ahead towards three men entering the meadow from the trees. As Bull continued to race towards the men, John realized they were Hawkes, Eastman and Roach. Leaving Hart behind, John ran to catch Bull. He was twenty feet behind Bull when he saw Bull rip the ladle Hawkes was drinking from out of his hand and throw it to the ground.

"Have you no shame," Bull yelled. "This water is for those who earned it today and you didn't."

Hawkes's mouth dropped open and he backed-up two steps.

"What are you doing?" Hawkes complained.

"You know what I'm doing. Reverend Hooker assigned you and your men to help me herd the cattle. You disappeared today; leaving those you abandoned to herd the cattle alone. This isn't the first time you and your men have done this."

"Listen, I have other tasks than herding cattle on this trip," Hawkes countered. "I've also been asked by Governor Winthrop to scout ahead and contact the Indian tribes along our route. We were doing that today."

"I know of no such assignment," Bull said. "I doubt Governor Winthrop gave it to you. All I know is Reverend Hooker assigned you to herd the cattle with me."

"I didn't think my absence on Governor Winthrop's assignment would create a hardship for you," Hawkes said. "I'll make certain at least one of my men is with you at all times."

"That's unacceptable. All your men are assigned to me. I'll bring this matter to Reverend Hooker when he arrives."

As the sun set and the meadow darkened, the congregation finally began entering the meadow. Sam Pierce and Deacon Hart led them to the campsite. At the same time, Acquittanug and his warriors brought the fish and corn he promised. Reverend Hooker thanked Acquittanug for his kindness and the congregation's people began to carry the fish and corn to the campfires Sam prepared for them.

Soon the odor of charred fish filled the camp. John ate with Sam, Huritt, Chogan and Etchemin along the pond while in the meadow above them Bull and Hawkes met with Reverend Hooker.

"By his absence, this man put our people at risk today Reverend," Bull asserted. "Order him and his men to stay with the cattle from now on."

"I have to honor my pledge to Governor Winthrop," Hawkes said. "I promised Lieutenant Bull to always leave one of my men."

"He has no mission from Governor Winthrop," Bull said. "I need his help. Order him to stay with the cattle."

"Richard, I accept your word you have this mission, but one man isn't enough." Hooker announced. "Leave at least two men with the cattle during the day unless Lieutenant Bull gives you permission for more of your men to be away."

Hawkes smiled at Bull as the two men walked back to the fires.

"I'm glad we resolved this problem." Hawkes said.

"We resolved nothing," Bull said. "Whatever you've been doing in the woods has nothing to do with Governor Winthrop."

Hawkes smiled at Bull before walking to the fire he shared with Eastman and Roach.

Chapter 16

Hawkes was on the move again two days later. He slipped away from the congregation at midnight, leaving Eastman and Roach behind as Reverend Hooker directed. He rode west away from the deep blue lake the Indians called Shenipsit, where the congregation had camped that afternoon. He was ten miles beyond the congregation when his Nipmuc followers came out of the trees. He didn't know they were there until Hassun grabbed the reins to his black stallion.

"The path is dark tonight," Hassun said. "It is fortunate we found you."

"How far to the meeting place?" Hawkes asked.

"We will reach it before sunrise."

"Did you bring the muskets?"

"Yes," Hassun answered. "A matchlock and a snaphaunce for you to show him. They will be on your horse in leather sheaths near your own musket."

Hawkes dismounted and began walking along the path with Hassun. Achak and Aranck trailed them with Hawkes's stallion. Within an hour they moved out of the trees into a broad grassland. They turned north towards where they would meet Megedaqik.

"Tell me about Megedaqik," Hawkes said.

"His eyes are angry," Hassun answered.

"Why is he angry?"

"Who can say," Hassun replied. "Men become angry for many reasons. He wanted to be his tribe's sachem. He's not. Perhaps this is the reason."

Hawkes said nothing. He was pleased Megedaqik was frustrated. It would make him hungry.

They were on a narrow path amidst the heavy grassland. Hawkes's mind was on only one thing — how he would convince Megedaqik to work for him building a fur trade along the Connecticut. His success depended on Megedaqik and Megedaqik's ability to find more angry men like himself within the other western tribes to work for him.

As the sky lightened in the east, Hawkes and the three Nipmucs crossed a shallow stream in a large open field. They slid into the forest where they hid while waiting for Megedaqik.

The sun was still below the tree line when the three Pocumtucs strode into the field from the trees. They glanced about furtively for a few seconds. Hawkes turned to Hassun. Hassun nodded.

"I will greet Megedaqik," Hassun whispered.

"Not yet," Hawkes replied. "I'll tell you when."

Hawkes knelt in the dew-covered grass and stared at the three Pocumtucs. They walked to a small stream seventy-five yards from where Hawkes was. At first, there was little to tell Hawkes which of the men was Megedaqik. Soon, Hawkes focused on the shortest of the men. Like the other two, the man was well muscled with broad shoulders, but there was something different about him. Finally, Hawkes realized what it was. Whenever he talked to either of the other men he leaned forward. Forward so far, the other man stepped back.

"You can greet Megedaqik now Hassun," Hawkes said.

Hawkes stood and reached for his musket while Hassun entered the field and walked towards the Pocumtucs. The three Pocumtucs rose. Hassun continued walking towards them. Megedaqik raised his right hand. Hassun did the same. Within minutes Hassun was walking towards Hawkes with Megedaqik at his side and the two other Pocumtucs trailing. Hawkes examined Megedaqik's weathered face and broad nose as Hassun extended his right arm towards Megedaqik.

"This is Megedaqik," Hassun said.

Megedaqik stared at Hawkes impassively, his lips tightly drawn. The two men studied each other. *How right Hassun was,* Hawkes thought. *Megedaqik's eyes are angry.*

"Greetings Megedaqik," Hawkes said. "Hassun praises you."

After Hassun translated what Hawkes said, Megedaqik grunted, "He barely knows me."

"What did he say Hassun?" Hawkes asked.

"He said thank you," Hassun lied.

Hawkes smiled and pointed to a small clearing among the trees where Aranck and Achak built a fire.

"Sit with me Megedaqik," Hawkes said.

They sat at the fire while the other men hovered about them. Hawkes motioned for the other men to sit. None did. He kept his eyes on Megedaqik. Megedaqik sat rigidly.

"Hassun, bring the leather bag from my horse," Hawkes ordered.

As soon as Hassun handed him the bag, Hawkes pulled out two strands of wampum and an eight-inch knife with a curved antler handle.

"I bring you gifts of friendship," Hawkes said. "Together, I hope we will build a prosperous beaver trade along the Connecticut River."

"Thank you for your gifts," Megedaqik said. "You are too late though. An Englishman named Pynchon has already built a trading post on the river near our village. Tribes from both north and south bring their beaver pelts to the trading post."

After Hassun translated, Hawkes smiled and leaned towards Megedaqik.

"I'm no fool," Hawkes proclaimed. "I know of the trading post. My trading post will be northeast of your village and deep in the forest. I will use Indian and Dutch agents so Pynchon will believe the Dutch are the traders. If you work for me, you will run my post. Hassun and my Nipmuc followers will bring you trade goods and bring me the beaver pelts you receive in trade. As payment for your service, I will let you keep some of the trade goods Hassun brings you."

"Why should I not just trade for beaver pelts myself and take them to Pynchon?" Megedaqik asked. "I would earn more this way than working for you."

"What would you trade for the pelts?" Hawkes asked.

Megedaqik stared back at him without speaking.

"I can tell you," Hawkes barked. "Nothing! You'd have nothing to trade. Nothing of value."

"I will get trade goods from the new settlers for the beaver pelts I take them," Megedaqik said.

"Ah, but how will you get the pelts? Trap them yourself? Even if you do the English will never give you the types of trade goods I will. They'll give you metal pots and pans for beaver pelts, just like Pynchon does. I will bring you muskets to trade."

Megedaqik sat up, "Do you have one of these muskets with you?"

Hawkes smiled and stood up, "I do."

He walked to his stallion and pulled a five-foot-long matchlock musket from a dark brown leather sheath hanging from its saddle. He handed the musket to Megedaqik who ran his hands up and down it for several minutes before shaking his head.

"It's heavy," Megedaqik said. "It would be hard to kill a deer with it."

"I will show you how to use it," Hawkes said. "You'll have more respect for it when you know how to fire it."

Hawkes took the musket from Megedaqik and stuck a twig into the fire. When it was burning, he touched the twig to the rope-like match dangling from the musket near its trigger. As the match burned, he blew on the musket's firing pan.

"The musket is ready for loading," he said.

With the match still burning, he bit off the end of a paper wadded cartridge containing powder and poured the powder into the firing pan before he poured the rest of the cartridge's powder down the musket's barrel along with the lead ball also in the cartridge. He dropped the wadded paper from the cartridge down the barrel and rammed the matchlock's scouring stick down the barrel pushing everything tightly together.

"The musket is loaded," Hawkes said. "I'll fire it."

He set the musket on an oak tree's branch and aimed it at a pine tree twenty feet away. He blew on the burning match before attaching it in the trigger's jaws and opening the firing pan. He pulled the trigger driving the burning match into the firing pan. There was a pop followed by a loud explosion as the firing pan lit the powder in the musket's barrel. The pine's base exploded in a spray of shattered bark and splinters of wood.

A loud cheer rose from all the Indians except Megedaqik. He sat stoically as both the Nipmucs and Pocumtucs stomped about yelling a war cry. When the celebrating stopped Megedaqik stared at Hawkes from across the fire.

"I have seen weapons like this before." Megedaqik said. "They're slow firing, heavy and have a match that must always be lit. They're useless in hunting deer and in wet weather. They'll not get many pelts in trade."

The other Indians were silent. Hawkes smiled at Megedaqik after Hassun translated.

"You're wise," Hawkes said. "I know the matchlock's weaknesses. That's why I brought you a musket even most Englishmen don't have."

Hawkes walked to his stallion where he pulled a longer musket from its sheath. He held it before Megedaqik. Its deep burgundy butt and new metal barrel glistened in the sunlight.

"This is a snaphaunce," Hawkes said. "It's lighter and can be fired without a match."

Megedaqik smiled, "I saw a weapon like this once. Fire it."

Hawkes took the musket in his left hand, filled its priming pan with gunpowder, and closed the pan. He loaded powder and a lead ball into the muzzle with a primer rod. He aimed the snaphaunce at another tree. This time without resting it on the oak's limb. He pulled the trigger. A popping sound came from the firing pan followed by the explosion of gunpowder in the musket's barrel. A second later a branch of the tree shattered. Megedaqik smiled when he looked across the fire after the shards of wood finished falling to the ground.

They struck a deal within an hour. Megedaqik agreed to have the surrounding tribes bring beaver pelts to the clearing near a cave in the forest each month. Hassun and his Nipmuc warriors, along with Dutch traders known to Megedaqik, would meet the Indians there and give them trade goods, including matchlocks and a few snaphaunces. Hawkes agreed he would give Megedaqik three snaphaunces each month as payment for his services.

After the meeting, Hawkes's notified his partner, Robert Rose, that a deal had been struck and that Rose should send Hawkes his first shipment of muskets by ship up the Connecticut River as soon as Hawkes sent word to him that he was settled in Newtown.

Chapter 17

John and Huritt stood on a bluff overlooking a wide river two thousand feet to the west. To their right, a small stream wound through the grass into the trees along the river. The morning fog above the river languidly melted away as the sun rose behind them.

"The river is narrowest here," Huritt said. "There's a ferry pulled by a rope, but it is too small to take everyone across. The cattle will have to swim."

"We will get help from the town," John said. "Sam and I will go there when he returns with Chogan and Etchemin."

John sat in the grass while Huritt walked down the bluff towards the river for a better view. *This is the moment*, John thought. The river was much wider than he imagined. It would be hard to cross. He knelt in the grass and prayed for God's help. He was certain God heard him. He was just not certain of God's plan. He hoped it was the same as his.

He rose to his feet when he heard branches moving on the path he and Huritt followed climbing to the bluff. Sam was the first to emerge. Chogan and Etchemin trailed him. They were out of breath.

"There's a path to the river north of here," Sam gasped. "It runs to a small ferry."

"We will need more than a small ferry to cross," John answered. "Huritt is looking for another way across. We will use the ferry for as many people as we can. The cattle will swim. You and I will get help from the Dorchester settlement down river."

"Chogan, when Huritt returns take him and Etchemin to meet Deacon Hart and bring him and his other scouts here," John continued. "Once here, help him guide the cattle and congregation to the ferry. Sam and I will meet you there. With luck, we will bring men and boats from Dorchester to help us cross."

John and Sam reached the Dorchester settlement at mid-morning. It was little more than several dugout huts. Its people named it after the Massachusetts Bay town they came from. They moved to Connecticut at the same time as Reverend Hooker's congregation and, aside from Roger Ludlow, John knew none of them.

John and Sam were one hundred feet along the dry path through the village when two men approached on foot. Both men were short; one was bald.

"We were expecting you," the bald man said. "Our ferryman sent his son with word of your arrival after he took you across the river. I am William Brown, and this is Gregory Belcher"

Good day," John said. "We're scouts for Reverend Hooker's congregation on our way to Newtown."

"Ah, the Newtown people," Brown said. "How many?"

"Around three hundred and one hundred sixty cattle."

"Well you're almost there." Brown said. "How do you plan on crossing?"

"We will bring as many as we can across on the ferry," John said. "The cattle will swim. Do you have men who can help us?"

"Gregory and I will help you," Brown said. "We can get more men to help; probably a few boats as well."

By now six more men had gathered around them. Ahead, a tall lean man walked towards them with several others trailing him.

"That's Constable Warner," Brown said.

John and Sam dismounted their horses to greet the constable.

"Welcome to Dorchester," the constable said. "Word spread fast of your arrival. It's time we get some boats up river."

The constable motioned to the men around him. Immediately, more than a dozen men strode to a small wharf jutting into the river.

"Thank you, sir," John said. "We'll ride north to meet the congregation at the ferry on the other side of the river. They should arrive by early afternoon."

John and Sam travelled two miles upriver before looking back. Near Dorchester the river was filled with over a dozen shallops, barks and flatboats, all heading north.

"You did it!" Sam shouted.

"Not yet," John cautioned.

While John was meeting Dorchester's constable, Richard Hawkes slipped across the river two miles south of Dorchester with Hassun, Achak and Aranck. Hawkes was worried and he didn't like being worried. Time was running out. If he was to eliminate the threat posed by John Lee on the trip it must be now.

Hawkes's breeches and boots were still drying long after his stallion shook off the water from their swim across the river. But being wet was of little concern to him. He followed Hassun who lead him on the path to be used by Hooker's congregation the next day. The path was more worn than the Indian trail they followed from Newe Towne. Its width was greater but the forest surrounding the path was just as deep.

They were on the trail for only a few minutes when Hassun spoke, "We built a trap to kill your enemy. See the leaves on the path in front of us? Under the leaves is a pit into which your enemy will fall onto a bed of sharpened tree branches when he passes tomorrow."

Hawkes liked Hassun's plan. It was simple and relied on the consistent practice followed by Lee when leading his scouts. He had the Suckiaugs move parallel to the road to check for ambushes and to protect him on the trail while he kept Sam Pierce several hundred feet behind him. Hawkes had only one concern.

"How will you keep animals or other people from falling into the trap," Hawkes asked. "If that happens it won't be ready to kill Lee in the morning."

"Achak, Aranck and I will watch the trap through the night to keep out animals or people who might stumble into it," Hassun said.

"The trap is just off the main path on a separate path we built. It is covered with a blanket over which we placed shrubs and tree limbs. We placed small trees at the entrance to the path with the pit. We will remove these in the morning and place them before the main path making the pit's path appear to be the main trail."

"A good plan," Hawkes said.

Hawkes immediately spun his stallion around, leaving Hassun and his men behind as he rode away. He rode to meet the cattle before his absence angered Lieutenant Bull again. As he approached the river he smiled while pushing his stallion to a gallop. Lee's death would look like an accidental fall into one of many Indian hunting pits in the area. The trees along the path flew past him as he imagined the next morning's events.

The first cattle reached the river at mid-afternoon. John met Deacon Hart and Lieutenant Bull at the river's edge amidst the cattle's deafening moos and bellows.

"So, we cross here," Bull shouted over the clamor. "All my men except Richard Hawkes are with me. He disappeared again this morning. We will take the cattle across in the order they reach the river. Be alert, for once the crossing starts there will be little time to think."

With that, Lieutenant Bull and four of his men began herding the cattle into the river. Bull sat high in his horse above the swimming cattle. He and his men stayed downstream from the cattle, keeping stragglers from floating past them with the current.

The first of Dorchester's shallops, barks and flatboats arrived soon after the cattle began their swim. At the same time, the small ferry was pulled up on to the slip below where John and Deacon Hart stood. James Eastman and Edward Roach stood next to them.

"James, Edward, put four cattle on a flatboat and stay with them until it's crossed the river," Hart ordered.

John was curious as he watched Eastman and Roach push the flatboat away from the slip with their polls. John planned for the cattle to swim because he doubted they could keep their balance on the flatboats' bobbing decks, but Deacon Hart disagreed. Soon the flatboat was halfway across the river without incident. This fact did not go unnoticed by Bull who stood next to John, having returned from across the river.

"That settles it," Bull announced. "We'll load as many cattle as we can on the flatboats and the rest will swim over."

Soon the river was ablaze with motion. The ferry, which once floated alone, was now surrounded by flatboats carrying cattle across the river and returning with men from Dorchester who volunteered to help the congregation cross the river. The river glistened in the mid-afternoon sun's rays, dotted with scores of cattle swimming across it with only their heads above the water. Men on horses swam alongside them fighting to stay mounted. Meanwhile, the ferry made its way back and forth across the river carrying the congregation's members.

As John watched the activity from a ridge above the river, he began to worry as the river's shoreline became overcrowded with cattle and the congregation. Certain the cattle and people waiting near the river would soon be pushed into it by the press of those now arriving, John ran to the river to meet Lieutenant Bull who was returning on a flat boat from his latest crossing. As he stood on the shore waiting for Bull, a sea of baying cattle and scores of men, women and children from the congregation pushed against John forcing him closer to the river while all around him the pungent odor of manure filled the air.

"The shore is filled with people and cattle," John yelled as Bull jumped onto the shore from the flatboat. "We must move people back to the bluff and keep them there until the cattle cross."

"I can't deal with that now," Bull said, his jaw clenched, "Find Deacon Hart and get some men to help the two of you do it."

Bull immediately turned back to the river. Suddenly loud screams rose from the people on the shore.

"A flatboat capsized," a man yelled. "Three men fell into the river.

Two have surfaced but Thaddeus Learned is missing."

As men dove into the water looking for Learned, Lieutenant Bull shouted above the fray, "Don't take anymore cattle across on the flat boats. Make them swim."

John gathered Sam and Deacon Hart and the three of them led the congregation away from the river to a bluff above it. But the people coming up from behind needed to be stopped so they would not add to the pressure at the river. He needed to find Reverend Hooker. He drove his gelding over the bluff, leaving Hart and Sam behind to keep the people in front from pushing towards the river.

Reverend Hooker was just reaching the bluff when John saw him. He dismounted and raced through the people between them.

"Sir, the people and cattle are bunching up at the river," John said between gulps of air. "Speak to them and stop them from moving forward."

"I will John," Hooker said calmly.

The people parted before Hooker as he strode through them to a higher bluff overlooking the river. When he was atop the bluff, he raised his arms and looked down at the congregation bunched along the river. A few people saw Hooker standing on the bluff. Word spread and within moments all the people were turned to the bluff where Hooker stood.

"It is here," Hooker announced in a booming voice. "It is here we face our last test. Never forget God is with us as we face this test. No power can stop us when He's among us. Each of you must cross the river peacefully when you are called. Until called sit quietly. When you do, He will sit beside you."

Within minutes the congregation was seated at the river's edge and along the road to the river. As the congregation sat, Lieutenant Bull stood at the river's edge directing the men herding the cattle.

After Bull pushed the last cattle across the river, he ordered his men to load the people onto the flatboats and the small ferry.

Suddenly, a man yelled from across the river, "We found him. We found Thaddeus Learned. He's alive."

At first there was confused silence, but when the congregation understood the announcement a buzz arose along the river. In an instant the buzz was replaced by cheers.

Reverend Hooker appeared again on the bluff. He spread his arms above him allowing the wind to open his black cape.

"This is evidence of God's grace," Hooker boomed. "All of us will soon be across the river and tomorrow we shall sleep in Newtown!"

The congregation cheered again as they gazed above at Hooker who smiled down from the bluff. During this shared adoration, a young man appeared at Hooker's side. The young man's hair was long and black and a pointed black beard with a thin black mustache decorated his face. His round broad brimmed black hat was pulled up on one side where a bright red feather was pinned. The few seeing him took little notice.

John recognized the young man at once. It was Richard Hawkes. He stared at Hawkes as Hawkes looked down at him. A chill passed up his spine when Hawkes nodded at him.

It was sunrise the next day when John, Sam, Huritt, Chogan and Etchemin left Dorchester for Newtown. The congregation stayed up late the night before celebrating their river crossing with the people of Dorchester. They would not start the journey's last leg until mid-morning.

As always, John rode his gelding down the center of the path with Huritt, Chogan and Etchemin moving parallel to him in the forest and Sam trailing several hundred yards behind. The low gray clouds provided little light and the path was dark. A misty rain began falling on the trees. Soon the accumulated rain on the leaves slid onto the ground, dampening the path ahead of him.

By mid-morning John realized he'd lost contact with Huritt, Chogan and Etchemin. He was not concerned since on the journey they often ranged away from the path to discover threats lurking deeper in the forest. Now alone, the path became monotonous and John found it difficult to keep from dozing as his gelding made slow but steady progress.

John's boredom was broken when the path made a right turn. As his gelding walked to the right on the turn, he noticed a large pile of tree limbs to his left. From his vantage point high on his gelding, he saw what appeared to be a path beyond the fallen tree limbs. While he found this other path curious, he'd seen such "false" paths elsewhere on the journey and was not concerned.

As soon as he moved forward again, John saw that the path in front of him was covered with wet leaves. He assumed the leaves fell from the trees in the misty rain. He considered moving off the path to avoid getting his gelding's feet and legs wet walking through the leaves but decided to go through them when he saw there was mud lining the trail's edge.

Suddenly, his gelding dropped from beneath him. He sat in mid-air as it plummeted down before his butt slammed into the gelding's back when it stopped falling. He slid off the gelding's back and down a wall of damp earth. As he lay face down against the wall, he felt a searing pain in his left shoulder. His gelding was not breathing.

The pain in his shoulder increased as he continued to lie against the wall. Wherever he was, it was dark, and he was upside down and unable to right himself. Using his good right arm, he felt across his body to determine what pinned him to the wall. As he grabbed what pinned him, he felt splinters from it fall off in his hand. It was a tree limb. He felt two more tree limbs as he fumbled about trying to discover where he was. Finally, realizing he couldn't free himself, he began to yell.

Two hundred yards behind, Sam heard John's cries. He whipped his horse forward. Shortly after his horse made a right turn, he reined it in just before plummeting into a deep pit. He dismounted and peered into the pit. What he saw shocked him. There below him spread across the pit's center was the back of John's gelding. Its body was pierced in four places by sharply pointed pikes driven into the pit's base. He heard John's cry again and looked to the horse's side and saw John's legs and boots. Several feet below, was the back of John's head and shoulders. There was a pike running vertically from the pit's base resting along John's left shoulder. It had torn away part of his doublet.

"Ya hurt?" Sam yelled into the pit.

"I'm upside down and can't move," John said. "My left shoulder feels like it's burned with a hot poker. Where am I?"

"In a pit of stakes," Sam answered. "One stake grazed your shoulder."

"How's my horse?"

"Dead. Four stakes through it. Don't squirm or ya' ll slide deeper into the pit."

Hassun heard John's cries. He and the other two Nipmucs now knew John's fall, which they watched, was not fatal.

"Let's kill him now," Achak barked.

"It must look like an accident," Hassun replied. "Let me think."

But before Hassun could devise a plan, they heard the hooves of Sam's horse.

"There's no time," Achak said. "We must kill both Englishmen now.

"Alright, but it has to look like an accident," Hassun answered. "We will surprise the other man and throw him into the pit. If either survives, we will kill him with wooden stakes."

Hassun led his men through the trees towards the pit. They were stunned when Huritt, Chogan and Etchemin emerged from the trees on the opposite side of it. Outnumbered and with no chance to make

John's death look like an accident, Hassun ordered the other two Nipmucs to retreat into the woods.

Bridget Westwood's broad smile told John all he needed to know. Bridget hugged John while William beamed beside them as scores of men, women and children from Reverend Hooker's congregation walked by them on the main road through Newtown.

"You've done it John," William crowed.

"What happened to your shoulder?" Bridget asked. "You're bleeding. Come into the hut and I'll wrap it."

"I'm fine Bridget," John said. "It's just dried blood. I fell in a trapping pit. Sam pulled me out."

He turned to William and cleared his throat, "I'm sorry, but one of your horses was killed in the fall. I'll pay you for its loss when I've saved enough corn to do so."

"We'll discuss it later," William answered with a smile.

The congregation continued pouring past William's lean-to hut, and the other log huts built the previous autumn, on their way to the Little Meadow where they would camp with the cattle. "Come inside," William said. "Bridget will fix supper."

As they turned to enter William's hut, the people standing near them turned and looked behind them. John and William turned to see as well. In the distance, Richard Hawkes rode towards them on his black stallion.

"Richard Hawkes," William said. "Always dramatic."

William's words went unheard for John's focus was on Hawkes. He crossed his arms in front of him when Hawkes saw him. Hawkes leered down at him as he rode by. John glared back until Hawkes passed him.

It was dark inside William's hut, the only light coming through the open door, the narrow chimney and the two small candles sitting on the small wooden table near the door. John forgot how small the hut was. It was always cold during that first winter but now John was hot. He hung his buff coat on a wooden peg on the wall before sitting at the table with William. He glanced at the fireplace.

"I will cook supper at the pit outside," Bridget said.

John and William stared at each other across the table. For the first time in three weeks John was exhausted. His head dropped to his chest as soon as he closed his eyes. William was staring at him when he opened them again.

"Sleep on the bed," William said. "When you wake Bridget will have supper ready."

It was much darker in the hut when John woke. A cool breeze flowed through the partially open door. It was gray outside and the low murmur of hundreds of distant voices flowed in with the evening breeze. He heard Bridget whisper.

"We can't keep this from John," Bridget said.

"It can wait until tomorrow," William answered. "Let him enjoy tonight first."

"It will be harder to tell him later. Tell him now."

John opened his eyes and sat up in the bed. Both Bridget and William turned and looked at him with open mouths. *There's something wrong*, John thought.

"Tell me what?" John asked.

Bridget's eyes dropped. William cleared his throat. Neither answered.

"Tell me what?" John demanded.

William sighed and turned his chair to John. A tear slid down Bridget's cheek as she watched John from behind William. William's chair was now three feet from John. John turned and sat on the edge of the bed facing William. William leaned forward and took a deep breath.

"I have sad news," William said.

"Tell me," John said.

"Alright," William replied. "After you sailed for Boston to bring the congregation here, I received a letter from a friend in Saybrook. The letter said he just returned from Colchester and that while there he learned your father and mother died two years ago from the same illness. They asked Bridget and I to take you with us to New England so you would not catch it."

John's heart beat furiously as he stared at William. Bridget sobbed. John was too stunned to say anything. He fought to breathe but was only able to take short shallow breaths. His eyes dropped to the floor. He prayed that Bridget would stop sobbing. Finally, he looked at William and said, "How do you know what your friend said is true?"

"I trust my friend," William said. "He would not give me such tragic news unless he knew it to be true."

John felt helpless. He asked himself how they could be dead. His father promised he would come the day he told him to go with William. The room was silent as John stood and put on his buff coat.

"I'm going outside," he said.

William nodded.

"Supper is ready," Bridget said. "We will eat when you come in."

It was cold now and John pulled his coat's collar around his neck as he looked at the scores of campfires burning in the dark meadow below him. Sadness welled up inside him as he thought of his father's strength and his mother's grace. He thought of his father's love of God and how he told John that God loved John as much as he did. Finally, John remembered how his father wore his best suit the day he told John he must go with William and Bridget to New England. Now he knew why his father wore it that day. It was his father's way of being the courageous warrior of God he told John he should become. Despite his pain, his father wore his suit and propped himself up in his bed so John would remember his strength and not the weakness of a dying man.

After a few minutes, John walked back into the hut.

PART TWO
1636 - 1637

Chapter 18

That September, tension between the Pequots and the English finally exploded when Niantic Indians, allied with the Narragansett, killed the English trader John Oldham and several of his men on Block Island off the Connecticut coast. Believing the killers sought refuge with the Pequots, Massachusetts Bay demanded they give them up. When the Pequots refused, Massachusetts Bay's soldiers burned several Pequot homes and their crops. In response, the Pequots laid siege to the English town of Saybrook at the mouth of the Connecticut River.

By mid-December John knew they needed help from the Suckiaugs. The siege of Saybrook made it impossible for Newtown and the river towns of Dorchester (soon renamed Windsor) and Wethersfield to receive enough food and supplies from boats traveling up the river.

Heavy snow blew into their faces as John, Lieutenant Bull and Sam Pierce trudged through the snow drifts blanketing the road to the Suckiaug village. Bundled in heavy wool clothes, bear skin coats and fur hats, they hiked from Newtown's meetinghouse, past the town's most northerly homes, and into the woods beyond the town. Lieutenant Bull was on John's right and Sam on his left as they leaned into the howling wind. John turned to Bull and announced, "Thanks to God, we were able to store enough firewood for the winter."

"At least we'll die warm," Bull said with a wry smile.

Sam laughed. *Humor is good now,* John thought, *It's a sign of confidence. We'll survive if we keep it.*

The Suckiaugs' wigwams and long houses were shrouded in a white mist as they entered their village. They saw nothing living until a man emerged from the snow. He was wrapped in a black bear fur and heavy deerskin leggings and moved effortlessly through the snow.

He pulled the heavy fur from his head and smiled. John smiled back when he recognized his friend Huritt.

"Good day friends," Huritt said. "Come into our long house. Kimi and Chogan will be pleased to see you."

The long house's inside was dark, lit only by a fire near its entrance. John's eyes weren't adjusted to the darkness when he heard Chogan's voice, "It is good to see all of you."

"Kwe kwe," Kimi said.

"Kwe kwe, Kimi," John answered.

The Englishmen sat near the fire along an interior wall of hanging reed mats. Kimi ground corn in a clay bowl while Chogan strung a bow in the firelight.

"How can I help you," Huritt asked.

"Winter's come and we don't have enough corn to feed the new people who arrived this year," Lieutenant Bull answered. "Can you share some of your corn with us? We'll repay you with corn from our next harvest."

"Our harvest was good, and we can share corn with you," Huritt said. "Our Sachem Sequassen needs to approve. We'll go to his long house."

The snow tapered to flurries and the sky brightened as they walked through the village to Sequassen's long house. Sequassen was alone when they arrived. The lines of his weathered face showed as he listened while Huritt told of Bull's request.

Huritt translated Sequassen's answer, "We will share our corn with you. We're happy you came to our lands and we know you will help us fight the Pequots when the time comes."

"Thank you Sequassen," Lieutenant Bull said. "We will remember your kindness."

"I have another matter to discuss," Sequassen said. "My warriors tell me both Dutch traders from the south and French traders from the north are trading muskets for wampum and beaver pelts with the northern tribes. It is rumored an Englishman is offering to trade many more muskets. Few have seen him as he uses Dutch and Nipmucs to trade his muskets. He is said to have deep black eyes and hair."

"I will report this to our leaders," Bull replied.

The snow stopped as they walked back to Newtown. The late afternoon sun's rays struck the fresh snow revealing each rut and deer track. John looked to his right at Bull as they walked along the path.

"We're lucky to have these neighbors," John said. "I can't believe an Englishman would trade muskets to the tribes."

"It doesn't surprise me," Bull exclaimed. "Not everyone is as forthright as you. Many men put greed ahead of everything else."

That night, as he was about to fall asleep on the floor of William's hut, John heard wolves howling. He was used to the sound and hardly noticed it now, but tonight he did. His heart raced when he thought of Sequassen's description of the Englishman trading muskets. *Could the dark eyed man be Richard Hawkes*, he asked himself.

Hours later, in the darkness of early dawn, he awoke drenched in sweat from a horrifying dream. In it, three large wolves were loose in Newtown. They were led by a coal black wolf. One by one the wolves tore apart the townspeople fleeing before them. John was alone, running before the wolves with the townspeople's bodies lying in the road behind him when he woke.

Chapter 19

Richard Hawkes woke in good spirits. The winter sun's rays caressed his face as he lay in bed in the large dugout James Eastman and Edward Roach built for him. He smiled as he imagined the house he would own by year's end. It would have three times the space of his dugout, at least two floors, and overlook the Connecticut River. It would, of course, be in the north part of town with the founders.

As he ate breakfast, Hawkes thought of the success he'd enjoyed since arriving in New England. His work with Robert Rose earned him a small fortune. He was now finding success trading muskets to the Indians for beaver pelts. He partnered with Rose who'd shipped him muskets for a commission on the beaver pelts Hawkes received in trade. Eastman and Roach were delivering the muskets to Hassun, Hawkes's Nipmuc partner. In turn, Hassun and Dutch traders working for Hawkes, took the muskets to Megedaqik to trade with the western tribes. He now had an imposing cache of wampum and beaver pelts from this trade. He stayed away from the actual deliveries, leaving this to the Indians and Dutch to avoid detection as it was now a crime to trade guns to the Indians. Because only he offered the Indians muskets, including the new snaphaunce, his trade for beaver pelts now equaled Pynchon's, who offered only English utensils, knives and cookware.

After breakfast Hawkes walked to the small roughhewn hut where he kept his black stallion. It was cold in the hut, but the cold didn't bother him today. After rubbing down his stallion with a flat wooden comb, he pulled a brush from the hut's wall. He was brushing his stallion when Eastman and Roach found him.

"We just delivered muskets to Hassun and the Dutchmen,"

Eastman said. "Hassun gave us the beaver pelts and wampum he received from Megedaqik for last month's shipment of muskets."

Hawkes ignored both men while continuing to brush his stallion as they spoke. He turned to Eastman and announced, "Good. Robert Rose will have more muskets for me soon. They'll be stored in my Boston warehouse until he puts them on the next pinnace coming here. Put enough beaver pelts and wampum on the pinnace to pay him for them."

Eastman cleared his throat, "We need to talk about something else."

Hawkes stopped brushing his stallion and turned to Eastman, angry Eastman was about to spoil his day.

"What is it?" Hawkes spit.

"Hassun believes Megedaqik betrayed you."

"What?" Hawkes barked

"Hassun claims Megedaqik has stolen beaver pelts he received in trade for the muskets we provided him rather than delivering them to Hassun and the Dutchmen for transport to you," Eastman said.

"What's his evidence?"

"He didn't say. He wants to talk to you about it. He's camped north of Newtown."

Hawkes's muscles were tight, and his face flushed. He glared at Eastman without speaking. *So Megedaqik's cheated me*, he thought. *I shouldn't be surprised. He asked too many questions. Make an example of him.* A brittle smile came to his face.

"I will consider Hassun's accusation," Hawkes said. "If it is true, I will punish Megedaqik so severely no one will dare steal from me again."

Eastman shuffled about nervously before stating, "I understand."

"We leave this morning," Hawkes ordered. "Wait for me while I change."

Hawkes decided to dress to impress the Indians he was meeting.

After dressing in a cream-colored linen jerkin, black leather breaches, and a three-quarter length buff leather coat, he hung an eight-inch black bone handled knife on his belt. Over his right shoulder and across his chest he wore a bandolier on which hung twelve small wooden tubes containing gunpowder and paper wadding for ramming down his snaphaunce with a lead ball. He pulled a black cape over his shoulders and walked to his stallion.

The Little River flowed before Hawkes as he mounted his stallion. Eastman hung Hawkes's sword and snaphaunce on the stallion. Hawkes adjusted the red plume of feathers in his broad brimmed black hat and nudged his stallion west along the Little River with Eastman and Roach trailing him. Once out of town they turned north towards Hassun's camp.

They reached Hassun's camp at noon. It was in a secluded patch of grass along a small creek in a thick strand of massive old trees more than one hundred feet off the ancient Indian path they traveled on. Hassun greeted them. Achak and Aranck were with him. Aranck appeared calm but Achak's eyes moved about anxiously.

"So, you think Megedaqik betrayed me," Hawkes said as he dismounted. "Tell me about it."

Hassun's mouth opened. Hawkes knew the abruptness of his question and the lack of normal greeting pleasantries had the effect he intended. The Nipmucs must be convinced of his decisiveness and know future acts of disloyalty would be dealt with as swiftly as he was dealing with this one.

Hassun closed his eyes before answering, "I discovered Megedaqik's treachery last week when Achak, Aranck and I took your beaver pelts from him at our cave near Agawam. I asked him why the number of pelts was less than before. He said it was because fewer tribes came to trade. Later, a Pocumtuc warrior, who didn't know I worked for you, told me I should trade the pelts at Pynchon's trading post. I decided to visit the post because I had not seen it yet. I left Achak and Aranck with your pelts."

A loud rustling sound rose from deep in the woods. Hassun stopped talking. The other men stared into the woods towards the sound. A doe and two fawns emerged from the woods, glanced at the men, and scampered back into the woods.

It's good the men are nervous, Hawkes thought.

Hassun turned to Hawkes and continued, "I saw Megedaqik enter the trading post as I approached it. He led three horses with many beaver pelts strung over them. Later he led his horses from the trading post. They were no longer loaded with pelts."

Hawkes interrupted, "Perhaps the pelts were traded to him for the muskets I pay him for working for me? What makes you think he stole the pelts from me?"

"I thought this might be possible until I talked to Megedaqik at the Agawam village later that day. He claimed he never traded pelts at the trading post and never traded any muskets you gave him for his service. He showed me where he stored the muskets you gave him. He claimed the only pelts he had were those he received in trade for your muskets."

Enough, Hawkes thought. *That damn bastard will pay for this. Keep your head and stay in control. They'll remember what you do.*

Hawkes looked at Hassun and ordered, "Find Megedaqik's assistants Rowtag and Matunaaqd. Bring them to me at the cave. I will give them the chance to save their lives if they agree to serve as my agents. Tell Megedaqik I want to meet him at the same place."

Hawkes reached the cave with Eastman and Roach at noon. Immediately, they began preparations. Eastman and Roach moved the small trees hiding the cave's entrance. They strung a rope over a log they braced seven feet above the cave's floor across two tall rocks. They brought a wooden table used for the monthly rendezvous into the cave and placed it under the rope. Hawkes set his knife, sword and musket on the table while Eastman started a fire near the cave's entrance. Hawkes stared into the fire, sitting on a boulder. Eastman and Roach knew not to disturb him when he was so intense, and they quietly walked from the cave.

An hour later, Hassun reached the cave with Matunaaqd and Rowtag. Hawkes strode from the cave to meet them. He nodded at Matunaaqd and Rowtag before turning to Hassun and bellowing, "Now get Megedaqik!"

Hawkes turned to Matunaaqd and Rowtag after Hassun left. He smiled at them. They looked back at him with ashen faces. Beads of sweat gathered on Rowtag's forehead while Matunaaqd's tongue lightly flicked across the bottom of his upper lip.

"Your leader is a traitor, but I want you to keep working for me," Hawkes said. "Do you want to do that?"

After an awkward silence, Rowtag answered, "We want to keep working for you."

"Good," Hawkes said. "I have one more question." Both men looked at the ground as he continued, "What do you do to your tribe's traitors?"

Matunaaqd lifted his eyes, "This is a most serious crime," Matunaaqd said. "First, we torture traitors and then we kill them."

"Megedaqik has stolen beaver pelts from us and traded them for wampum at Pynchon's trading post," Hawkes announced. "Today you will participate in the punishment of this traitor. Tomorrow you will start to run my business here."

The late afternoon sun's rays glanced off the large oak trees' trunks, and a fine dust on the forest's floor glowed like rising dew, when Hassun brought Megedaqik to the clearing outside the cave.

Hawkes's walked to Megedaqik, his black cape flowing in the light breeze. Achak and Aranck followed him. Their faces were painted black on one side and red on the other. Megedaqik knew this was war paint. Matunaaqd and Rowtag followed two feet behind them.

As they approached him, Megedaqik's eyes narrowed before he

bolted into the woods behind him. Achak flew after Megedaqik and tackled him just inside the woods. Within seconds, Hassun joined the fray and Megedaqik was quickly subdued.

"Bring him to me," Hawkes ordered.

Hawkes's pulse raced as Achak and Hassun dragged Megedaqik to him. Hawkes stared into Megedaqik's eyes as the two Nipmuc held him before him.

"Why are you doing this?" Megedaqik asked.

Hawkes answered in a soft voice rising in volume, "Because you violated my trust."

"No, never."

"You sold my pelts to Pynchon."

"No, no I didn't."

"It's useless to deny this," Hawkes replied.

Hawkes looked at Hassun and nodded, "Bring him into the cave."

Megedaqik dug his heels into the dirt, kicking up dust, as Achak and Hassun dragged him towards the cave. Roach lifted Megedaqik's legs and the three men quickly carried him into the cave. They stripped Megedaqik's mantel from his back and his leggings from his legs. They tied his wrists to the ropes Eastman and Roach hung earlier and pulled him up before the fire.

Hawkes stepped to the table in front of Megedaqik. He removed his cape, buff coat and jerkin, leaving his chest and upper body bare. His muscled torso glistened with sweat in the firelight. He picked up the musket lying on the table. Megedaqik stared at him with his arms stretched above him by the ropes. Hawkes rammed powder and shot down the snaphaunce's barrel, pointed it at Megedaqik's right knee and fired. Megedaqik's knee erupted in a spray of bone, flesh and blood. Megedaqik recoiled in pain but did not scream.

Hawkes walked forward until he was no more than two feet in front of Megedaqik. He stared into Megedaqik's eyes and smiled.

"That was just the beginning of your punishment," he exclaimed.

Megedaqik spit in his face. Hawkes ignored the wad of spit slowly sliding down his left cheek. Hawkes returned to the table and reloaded the musket. Beads of sweat slid down Megedaqik's face. Matunaaqd and Rowtag looked away.

"Look at him," Hawkes shouted. "Watch everything I do to him so you can tell everyone the punishment they'll receive if they betray me."

Hawkes fired the musket into Megedaqik's other knee. Blood sprayed across the cave coating Hawkes's chest and face. He casually wiped Megedaqik's blood from his lips. Megedaqik slumped as he hung from the ropes with neither leg now able to support his weight. Achak moved closer to Hawkes, a broad smile on his face. Hassun and Aranck stepped back briefly but quickly resumed their original positions. Roach's impassive expression didn't change. Eastman rocked back and forth, his eyes bulging, as he watched. Nearly unconscious, Megedaqik began to moan with his head resting on his chest.

"Throw water in his face James," Hawkes ordered. "I don't want him to pass out."

The splash of water brought Megedaqik's head off his chest and he stared at Hawkes again. Hawkes took his sword from the table. Its razor-sharp blade glistened in the firelight as he raised it and pointed it at Megedaqik. Without a word, he thrust it into Megedaqik's abdomen. Now in shock, Megedaqik's head slumped to his chest while blood poured from the wound. Megedaqik's silence infuriated Hawkes. He swung the sword and sliced Megedaqik's left foot off at the ankle.

As his life poured out of him, Megedaqik began to scream. Finally, Hawkes felt the pleasure of triumph. Except for Achak, the other men recoiled from the bloody scene. Achak smiled and asked Hawkes, "Let me help you kill this traitor."

"Yes," Hawkes whispered.

Achak pulled his knife from his belt and walked towards the screaming Pocumtuc. In one swift motion he slit Megedaqik's throat from ear to ear, nearly decapitating him. The cave fell silent.

Hawkes turned to Matunaaqd and Rowtag and ordered, "Select a well-traveled place and mount Megedaqik's head on a pike. It will serve as a warning not to betray me."

"But what about revenge from his tribe," Eastman asked.

"There will be no revenge," Hassun said. "He's so feared by his tribe's leaders they'll do nothing."

After cleaning Megedaqik's blood from his chest and face, Hawkes pulled on his tunic, tied the stays to his buff leather coat and fastened his black cape over his shoulders. He ordered Hassun and Achak to burn Megedaqik's body and clean the cave. When they did this, he led Eastman and Roach to their horses. *I'm finished here*, he thought as he mounted his stallion.

Chapter 20

It was a pale gray morning in late February 1637 and John was cold. He and Sam were finishing their chores on William's farm and the sun was finally rising. Two weeks before, the town received its new name when the General Court announced from henceforth the town of Newtown would be known as Hartford. It was said the new name came from Reverend Stone's home town of Herford, England. But John didn't care where the name came from, only that there was no longer confusion between their former town of Newe Towne in Massachusetts Bay and their new town of Newtown along the Connecticut.

The rising sun failed to warm them as they repaired the fence between William's and Joseph Barnard's fields. Snow had fallen for three days and the nights had been moonless, bright with stars, and bitterly cold since it first fell. It was now crusty and the ground frozen forcing them to limit the fence's repairs to replacing its rails above ground.

As he lifted a fresh rail into place, John announced, "William says our militia has a new captain. He's John Mason. He served with Lieutenant Bull under Lord Fairfax in the Netherlands fighting Papists."

"New commander, same result," Sam said.

"How's that Sam?" Joseph Barnard asked as he walked to the fence from across his field.

"The Pequots' siege of Saybrook won't stop," Sam said. "They run when the militia's there and return when it's not. That's not gonna change with a new captain."

"You're a cynic Sam," Barnard smiled. "But this time you're right. We won't defeat the Pequots unless we destroy their forts and villages."

Within an hour the sun was above the river below them. Hanging in a deep blue sky, it contrasted with the leafless trees lining the river. The temperature continued to drop for the first hour after sunrise and John was glad when it was finally time for breakfast. He and Sam plodded through the crusty snow up the slope to William's new house along the town's main road.

The congregation built William's new house in a house raising party the previous fall. John was disappointed though, for while William could have chosen to build a two-story house like Reverend Hooker's, he chose a simple house. That meant John and Sam would continue to sleep in the attic.

As soon as John and Sam entered the house, Sam took his breakfast from Bridget and walked outside to eat while John sat at a heavy oak table close to the fireplace. He was starved and immediately after William said grace he bit into the pumpkin bread and spooned down the pea soup Bridget prepared, washing everything down with beer from the leather noggin she poured it into.

William sat back in his chair and asked, "How go your lessons with Lieutenant Bull?"

"Well," John answered. "I'm a good shot with a matchlock and even better with the new snaphaunce. Lieutenant Bull says I'm good fighting in close quarters with pike, sword and knife."

"Whatever Lieutenant Bull is doing you're much stronger," Bridget said. "You're now as tall as William and almost as broad."

"What about your lessons with Reverend Stone?" William asked

"We studied English and Puritan history the last few weeks," John said staring at the lines in the oak table by William's wooden bowl. "Always the scriptures."

"What scriptures?" William asked.

"Yesterday Leviticus and the punishment for witches."

"What does Reverend Stone say about witches," William asked.

"He says they must die," John answered.

"What do you think?"

"It's what Leviticus teaches."

"Has he said we should avoid hanging innocent people accused of witchcraft?" William asked.

"No."

"What do you think?" William asked.

"Only witches should be hanged," John answered and after a pause continued, "Should I ask Reverend Stone what he thinks about this at this afternoon's lesson?"

"That's for you to decide," William said.

John reached the meetinghouse before Reverend Stone's other students. He sat in the first row of benches. The room was musty from the damp hay stuffed between its roughly hewn logs. The small shuttered windows provided the only light. Even in the damp cold he felt God's presence. He bowed his head and let God's warmth flow through him until the other three students entered.

The students were sons of the town's most prominent families and treated John like the ward he was by sitting at the other end of the bench. He smiled at the boy closest to him. The boy nodded and dropped his eyes to the floor. John turned back to the pulpit. Below it, on the communion table, as it always did, rested the chalice Richard Hawkes stole on the *Francis*. John cursed the night he saw it happen.

Stone finally arrived after John and the other students had been waiting in the cold room for nearly an hour. As always, Stone dressed in black. He ignored the students while he climbed to the pulpit. Once there, he peered down at John and the other students. Finally, he looked down at John and commanded, "Sit with the others."

John nodded at Stone and shuffled ten feet to where the other students sat. They ignored him and continued staring at Stone.

"Today, I will discuss the Covenant of Grace," Stone said in a reedy voice.

John was disappointed Stone chose not to continue his discussion of witchcraft from their last session. His question would have to wait. Still, he might finally understand the Covenant of Grace.

"Before Man's fall, God promised salvation to Adam and Eve if they obeyed His laws," started Stone, his dark brown eyes darting from student to student. "When Adam disobeyed God's law and ate the forbidden fruit Eve gave him, Adam violated this covenant thereby ending Man's right to be saved by his good works. But out of his mercy God offered man a new covenant. A covenant He alone controlled. We call this covenant the Covenant of Grace."

The room was silent except for the steady drip of melting snow from the roof onto an open window's sill.

"In this covenant God gave salvation, not for obedience to his law, since this was part of the original covenant which was violated, but for a special faith God gives to those He grants salvation."

Stone's voice grew louder, and the vapor of his breath flowed like fog into the frigid room, "Only through a faith implanted by God Himself can we be saved. Those chosen will display God's election through their pious behavior."

Stone lowered his voice to a whisper, "But those chosen are hard to tell from those who follow God's laws but who are not chosen. Each group's reason for following God's law is different. Those not chosen follow God's laws because they're taught to follow them, while those who are chosen follow God's laws because the Holy Spirit has touched them. So, while evil deeds are evidence of damnation, a pious life isn't proof one is chosen."

John was stunned. If what Stone said was true, he could never know he was chosen.

With these words Stone paused briefly. Then, he concluded, "Each of you must look for evidence God chose you. This evidence will come from study and reflection, or, if you are fortunate, it will come through the Holy Spirit's revelation. Only if you find this evidence can you seek to become a full member of our church by presenting it to our congregation.

Now finished, Stone stared down from the pulpit at the four young men. While John met his gaze, the others lowered their heads.

"Why would love for God not be sufficient to save us?" John asked. "If God has preselected those to be saved, why does it matter how the preselected lead their lives?"

Stone's face tightened. The other students shifted in their seats.

"Be careful John," Stone said. "Your questions border on heresy. Our Puritan beliefs are not to be challenged."

Stone looked down at the four students. His face was flushed. "This lesson is over," Stone announced. "You are dismissed."

As John turned to leave, he noticed a man in the shadows near the entrance to the meetinghouse. When he reached the entrance, the man emerged from the shadows. John's pulse quickened when he recognized Richard Hawkes. Hawkes greeted John with a self-satisfied smile. Neither spoke as they passed each other: John on his way out of the meetinghouse and Hawkes walking to the pulpit to meet Stone.

"I'm here to talk about the Pequot menace," Hawkes said to Stone when he reached the pulpit. "We have to find a way to deal with it."

"I agree," Stone said. We'll discuss it soon."

"I heard John Lee's heretical questions," Hawkes said. "This isn't his first heretical behavior."

"I know how to deal with my students Richard," Stone said. "I don't need your help. John is my brightest student and like a stallion he'll eventually bend to my will."

Chapter 21

"It's a cold March day for rolling in mud," Deacon Hart asserted with a broad smile. "After drilling with matchlocks, Lieutenant Bull wants us to wrestle."

Hart's barrel chest looked even larger under his heavy buff coat as he and John Lee stood together on the meetinghouse porch. Below them thirty militiamen lunged and parried in the damp meetinghouse yard practicing with pikes. Some were in groups of three or four while others were paired together. John's right toe tapped on the porch as he watched the men while in his mind, he critiqued each thrust, deflection and recovery.

"I would rather have snow on the ground for wrestling," John answered.

"Either way we're going to get wet," Hart said.

They turned when the meetinghouse door opened. Lieutenant Bull strode through the door, his head held high and his breastplate and helmet shining in the afternoon sun. Bull nodded at them before looking down from the porch at the militiamen who were turned to face him.

"Gather around men," Bull announced stepping down from the porch.

When the men were all standing before him, Bull commanded, "Each of you take a matchlock from the meetinghouse and assemble with your units for musket drills."

John lined up with the other men at the meetinghouse door. One by one they entered the meetinghouse where Bull opened the three large oak cabinets containing the town's matchlocks, powder and shot. John took a matchlock, a matchlock rest, musket balls, and twelve cartridges of gunpowder from the cabinet. As he did, he kept a good distance between himself and Richard Hawkes who trained in the meetinghouse yard earlier with Eastman and Roach.

The men formed into the militia's four companies. John carried the heavy matchlock over his shoulders and grasped its rest in his left hand as he raced across the yard to his company. The sound of clanking metal breastplates, matchlocks and swords filled the air as the other men simultaneously jogged toward their companies.

"Form four firing lines," Lieutenant Bull roared. "We will train to shorten our firing sequence to a count of thirty. I will call out the commands on a pace to complete the entire sequence in that time. Stop if you fall behind. Those who keep up with me will finish."

Lieutenant Bull stood to the right of John's company when he thundered, "Recover!"

In unison, the men pushed their matchlocks forward and held them parallel to the ground.

"Secure your match," Bull yelled.

The men responded by ensuring their musket's match was lit.

"Pick"

The men picked out any gunpowder still in their matchlock's firing pan.

On the order "Shake out your pan," the men blew loose gunpowder from their matchlock's firing pan.

Next Bull called out "Handle your primers, prime your pan, close your pan and blow off your pan" to which the men responded by taking a wooden bottle containing a paper cartridge containing gunpowder from their belts or bandoliers and poured a small amount of powder into the firing pan, closed the pan and blew off excess powder from around it.

By this time, several men in John's company were behind the sequence called out by Bull.

Bull next commanded, "Cast about your piece, charge your piece, draw out your scouring stick, put them in the barrels, ram down your charge, withdraw your scouring sticks, return your scouring stick." The men responded by placing their matchlocks on the ground with their barrels up, pouring gunpowder and a ball down the barrel, ramming them down the barrel with their scouring sticks and replacing the scouring sticks in their holders along their matchlocks' barrels.

By this time only John and one other man were keeping up with Bull's commands. The other men stopped and held their matchlocks at their sides.

Bull completed the firing sequence, "take up your piece, blow off your match, cock your match, present your piece, open your pan, fire." In response John picked up his matchlock, blew on his match making it glow, cocked the hammer, placed his matchlock on its rest, opened the firing pan and pulled the trigger ramming the hammer with the match into the firing pan. The gun exploded firing the lead ball to its target.

Bull glanced at John and smiled before ordering John and the other man completing the sequence on time to wait on the meetinghouse porch while he drilled the other companies.

By the time Bull finished drilling all four companies there were eight men waiting on the porch. Among them were Deacon Hart, Richard Hawkes and Edward Roach. Bull stood on the dirt below the porch looking up at them.

"Well done," Bull said. "You finished the firing sequence on time. Now gird your loins for close quarter fighting. I will return to watch any remaining fights after I take the other men through the firing drill again. Deacon Hart will pair you and supervise your fights until I return."

John and the other men followed Hart to a damp patch of grass. They gathered around Hart. Hawkes stood with Roach directly across the circle sneering at John. He glanced at Hawkes briefly. His heart was racing, and he found it difficult to concentrate on what Hart was saying. He felt Hawkes's eyes on him and turned back to him, this time meeting his sneer with a tight-lipped smile.

Hart announced, "Here are the pairings. I will fight Matthew Spence in the first match. The second match will be Edward Roach against Robert Glenn."

Only four men remained to be paired. John's heart felt as if it would burst as he stared at Hart, refusing to glance back at Hawkes whose eyes bored into him.

Hart continued, "The third match will be between James Smith and Robert Hargrove and the last match between Richard Hawkes and John Lee."

John felt his heart stop. He tried to swallow but his mouth was too dry. He forced himself to look at Hawkes. Hawkes nodded at him with a broad smile. He forced himself to nod back.

"I'll give each of you a stick," Hart said. "This stick is your knife. To win you must either physically disable your opponent, take his stick while keeping yours, or use your stick to make a move that would kill him if it were a knife."

After he gave each man a stick, Bull announced, "Matthew Spence and I will fight now."

Matthew Spence was as large as Hart. The two big men stepped into the small patch of grass while John and the other men backed away into the mud surrounding it. The two big men were instantly on each other. Both dropped their sticks and wrapped their arms around the other trying to bring him to the ground. Each breathed heavily after pushing each other for over a minute. Then Hart groaned and pushed hard enough to drive Spence off the grass into the mud while the men watching scattered to get out of their way. Both men lost their footing in the mud and soon slipped and fell. On their knees they resumed their struggle, but the mud kept both from getting footing sure enough to gain an advantage. Finally, Hart threw back his head and let out a hearty laugh. When his opponent began to laugh as well, both men stood up with mud dripping from their breeches and shook hands.

"The match is a draw," Hart laughed.

The other men laughed as the two muddy warriors moved from the muck and back onto the grass. John was not one of them. His stomach tightened and all he could think of was how soundly Hawkes beat him when they fought before. He knew he was bigger and stronger than he was then. He also knew he was now trained to fight. Still, he questioned whether the result would be different. Hawkes was twenty pounds heavier and trained with the militia.

The next two fights were shorter. Roach easily dispatched the large muscled man he was paired with. As the big man lumbered after Roach, trying to wrap him in a bear hug, Roach repeatedly slammed his fists into the man's face until it was a bloody pulp. Blinded by blood, the big man tripped and fell forward. Roach instantly jumped on the man's back and drove his fists into his kidneys until Hart pulled him off.

John's stomach tightened still more as he watched the fight before his. Unknowingly, he was beating his right hand against his thigh. Suddenly, a hand grabbed his beating hand. He looked to his right and saw Lieutenant Bull.

"It's alright to be nervous," Bull said. "It means you're ready. Forget about your last fight with him. You weren't trained. Now you are. Let your training take over and your body will move as it is trained to. Your quickness will allow you to overcome him by using his strength against him."

The fight before John's ended inconclusively. Having finished their matchlock drills, the remaining militiamen were now gathered with the earlier combatants to watch the last fight.

Deacon Hart moved to the grassy area's center while the excited militiamen shuffled for a better view.

"The last match is between Richard Hawkes and John Lee," Hart announced.

A roar of excitement rose from the militiamen as John and Hawkes entered the grassy area and began circling each other with their sticks in their right hands. John knew Hawkes would try to use his superior strength to overpower him, so he waited for Hawkes's attack before making his countermove.

Suddenly, Hawkes charged him, slamming his shoulder into John's chest. John's back crashed into the ground driving the air from his lungs. He gasped for air as Hawkes slammed his fists into his sides. *What an idiot*, John thought as he fought off Hawkes's blows. He didn't slip Hawkes's attack, instead he froze. *Stop thinking*, John thought. *Let your training take over.*

John swiftly struck Hawkes under his chin with the heel of his right palm. Hawkes recoiled from the blow and released his grip around John's waist. He pushed Hawkes away from him with his hands and while Hawkes was above him John drove his right knee into Hawkes's groin. Hawkes screamed and rolled into the grass writhing in pain. The militiamen's cheers rang in John's ears. He grabbed the stick that fell from his hand, rolled Hawkes onto his stomach and pulled up his head by his long black hair with his left hand while simultaneously pulling the stick across Hawkes's unprotected throat.

The men cheered as Hart made his way to the grassy area's center, separated John from Hawkes, and yelled, "John Lee is the winner."

Lieutenant Bull grabbed John's shoulder. A dozen men slapped him on the back. Spontaneously, Hawkes climbed through the men and screamed in John's face, "I will be prepared for your tricks next time."

John stared back at Hawkes impassively while inside he felt like screaming with joy. Gradually, the militiamen left for their homes. John and Lieutenant Bull stayed behind for a separate training session. After an hour of sword play, they sat together on the meetinghouse porch watching the setting sun.

"I'm proud of you," Bull said. "You handled your earlier setback and took the fight to your foe using your training. In a fight it's easy to over think and ignore your training."

"Yes sir."

Lieutenant Bull put his hand on John's shoulder, looked squarely into his eyes, and said, "Soon we will be in a real fight with the Pequots. It will be far different from what you are used to. After our first volley there will be a melee as we charge their line and they try to repel us. In the melee you may be attacked from any direction. Especially if you are occupied fighting an enemy in front of you. While I can prepare you for the confusion of a melee only your experience will enable you to successfully fight in one."

Bull paused briefly before continuing, "I think of my first battle often. I was so cocky and thought I knew everything. But I was not ready for the battle's speed. I was told of it, but until you experience it yourself, warnings are just words. The enemy was coming from all sides. Even though we knew we needed to stay in formation to defend each other, several green soldiers left formation to fight alone and were immediately cut down by the enemy. I myself fought outside our formation and while I was killing an enemy in front of me, I was struck from the side with another enemy's sword. It took me many battles before the action of battle slowed down in my mind enough for me to understand what was going on."

For the first time John saw worry on Lieutenant Bull's face. Bull continued, "In the coming battle stay on my right shoulder at all times when we're closely engaged with the enemy. If our men are behind us, you will only need to worry about an attack from your right as you fight to the front. I will protect your left as you protect my right."

"I will," John answered.

"Now, about Richard Hawkes," Bull said. "I've known many men like him. They must control all situations and humiliate all foes. For whatever reason, he has marked you as his foe and now that you've humiliated him today, he will seek revenge. He will seek his revenge at a time and place of his choosing when he knows you are least pre-pared. He will have no timetable for doing this. It might not happen for years. All you need to do is ask me and I will help you deal with this man.

It was frigid now. Neither man spoke for several moments. Finally, John looked at Bull. "Thank you for your offer sir," he said. "But I must deal with Richard Hawkes alone."

"I understand John, but remember courage is also shown when one is unashamed to ask for help. My offer will always remain open."

Chapter 22

Richard Hawkes fumed about his loss to John Lee for two days. At first, he wanted to strike back; but killing Lee now was out of the question for he would be the likely suspect this close to his defeat. Challenging Lee to another fight was also a bad option for Lieutenant Bull's training made Lee a formidable foe. There would be another time. Until then he would build his power and wealth. Today's meeting with Reverend Stone was designed to do that.

As he waited for Stone in the front row of the meetinghouse, he thought of how weak-willed Stone was. Stone worked with Reverend Hooker in East Anglia and followed him to Massachusetts Bay like a puppy, but when it came time to select his assistant, Hooker ignored him and offered the position to Reverend John Cotton of Boston. Stone meekly accepted the position after Cotton refused it.

Notwithstanding his title of teacher to the congregation, Stone was a loner and socially isolated within the congregation. He would fill this gap in Stone's life by becoming his friend and confidant. Stone was an insecure man whose ego required constant stroking and he would stroke that ego. So far, he was successful. Stone now believed the Pequots must be destroyed so their land would be open to English settlement and the spread of God's word. Hawkes would get much of this land when it happened. He convinced Stone to be more assertive in his dealings with Hooker and, in response to Stone's request, Hooker made Stone chaplain of Connecticut's militia.

Hawkes heard the meetinghouse door open behind him. He turned and in the dim light saw the familiar bony black clad figure of Reverend Stone walking up the meetinghouse aisle towards him.

"Good day Richard," Stone said after sitting on the bench next to

Hawkes. "Sorry mess, this Pequot situation."

"Our army is poorly led," Hawkes said. "The only way we can end the war is by attacking their settlements and forts."

"Captain Mason is planning that now," Stone asserted.

"But will he be ruthless enough?" Hawkes asked. "Ruthlessness is a trait he hasn't shown in his game of chase with the Pequots around Saybrook. When the Pequots are destroyed two things will happen. First, we will take their land which will give us the ability to parcel it out to both English settlers and Indian allies. This will expand the scope of our influence. Second, many Indian tribes in Massachusetts Bay have seen the power of God and some tribes' members have converted. This can also happen here once the Connecticut tribes watch the Pequots destroyed by our God."

"Commendable goals," Stone said. "But what about the lives lost in such a war? Can't we achieve the same without killing so many?"

"Only war can lead to this. Don't support half measures."

"I will consider it, but I don't have the ability to control how this war will be fought," Stone replied.

"As the newly appointed militia chaplain you have more power than you imagine," Hawkes answered. "At a crucial moment Captain Mason will seek God's guidance and you will be asked to provide it. Your voice will be the only one he hears. Place me at your side so I can help you give him guidance."

"I'll bring you with me when the militia moves," Stone said.

"A good decision," Hawkes affirmed.

Stone abruptly stood and walked towards the meetinghouse door. Hawkes quickly rose and followed Stone down the aisle. When they reached the last row of benches, he grabbed Stone's arm.

"I have another matter," Hawkes declared. "Let's sit together for a bit longer?"

"I guess I can spare more time," Stone said with a quizzical look.

They sat together in the last row of benches. Stone waited for

Hawkes to speak.

"Have you noticed how powerful Elder Goodwin has become since we moved to Suckiaug?" Hawkes asked.

"What do you mean?" Stone said.

"Who takes charge when Reverend Hooker is in Boston?"

"I haven't noticed."

"That's my point," Hawkes said. "You haven't paid attention to what's happening here."

"I have too."

"No, you haven't. Who runs our meetings when Reverend Hooker is gone? Do you?"

"Well, no," Stone said. "That's the job of our elder."

"Only because you let it be. Goodwin increases his power with each meeting he runs. Who do the people listen to about the growth of our town? Do they come to you?"

"No," Stone answered.

"They go to Goodwin now," Hawkes said. "Pay attention and you will see you are being replaced by Goodwin. When the time comes do you think Goodwin and his supporters will let you replace Hooker?"

"I haven't thought about it."

"Don't you think it's time you did? Hooker won't live forever."

Stone pulled away from Hawkes and silently moved his head from side to side before saying, "I can't believe this is true."

"Open your eyes and you will see it is."

Stone dropped his head and stared at the meetinghouse floor for several moments. He lifted his head, looked back at Hawkes and asked, "What should I do?"

"Take charge at meetings and start building a following you can call on when the crisis comes."

"Who should I start with?" Stone asked.

Excitement coursed through Hawkes's veins. Stone had nibbled at the bait, now it was time to hook him.

"Deacon Hart," Hawkes answered. "He's threatened by Goodwin's increasing power as much as you. He and Goodwin have been rivals since they planned the congregation's move to New England three years ago. Hart had to passively watch as Goodwin made the decisions and issued the orders. Even now Hart blames Goodwin for giving him less land than the other founders."

"Will you speak to him for me." Stone asked.

"I will."

Hawkes watched Stone walk from the meetinghouse. He sat at the bench for several more moments before standing and striding towards the meetinghouse door. His smile broadened with each step until his teeth shone brightly in the sun when he pulled the door open.

Richard Hawkes thought of how much he admired the man he was about to meet as he walked to Deacon Hart's house two weeks after his meeting with Reverend Stone. Hart was a powerful force within the congregation and a forward-thinking land speculator and entrepreneur. Hart was not like the other Puritans in another way Hawkes appreciated: he was not afraid to live in a large home and to own valuable furniture, houseware and clothes. From the moment Robert Rose introduced him to Hart, Hawkes knew Hart could provide him with business opportunities and power. He found it easy to ingratiate himself with Hart. Hart's pride was immense, and he beamed whenever Hawkes showed interest in one of Hart's many businesses. On such occasions a single question or compliment would lead to hours of conversation.

Hart's house was north of William Westwood's house on Hartford's main road, but the two homes were vastly different. While Westwood built a simple one-story home, Hart built a home more reflective of his status. It was two stories with a large lean-to kitchen on the first floor built onto the parlor on the other side of the stone chimney.

Rain poured on Hawkes as he rode north along the town's main road to Hart's house. Except for two hogs and three cows wandering aimlessly along the road, he saw no signs of life. He turned off the road onto a path Hart carved through the massive oaks and maples hiding his house from the road and followed the path's gentle slope towards the Connecticut River. Two hundred yards above the river he stopped at the house and tied his stallion to a post before the house's burnt red oak door.

Before Hawkes knocked, Hart opened the door and announced, "Welcome Richard. Come in. Let's discuss my grist mill operation."

"Thank you for inviting me," Hawkes replied as he followed Hart into the house.

"You're drenched," Hart said. "Come to the hall where you can dry while we sit by the fire."

The two men walked into the hall where they sat at the fire's hearth. Hawkes gazed about the room at the handcrafted oak table, chairs and shelves. A finely detailed oak cabinet filled with pewter, wooden serving ware and linen lined the wall, while a table large enough to seat a dozen people filled the center of the room.

Hart looked at him and smiled, "I'm glad we're finally able to talk about my grist mills. Robert Rose praised the job you did for him. I hope our relationship proves to be as successful."

"I'm sure it will," Hawkes answered with a smile.

Hart poked the fire, bringing it to a blaze. He turned back to Hawkes and said, "Matthew Allyn operates the only grist mill in Hartford. I financed its construction and am the mill's primary share-holder. Matthew insists on operating the mill, but he's a poor miller. He's inefficient and keeps shabby records. Much of the cornmeal he makes is lost, which reduces my profits. That's why I want you to take over the mill's operation."

"I would be pleased to do so."

"Excellent," Hart said. "I will show you the mill."

The rain had stopped, and yellow and orange streaks were breaking through the clouds when Hawkes and Hart reached Allyn's grist mill. It was on the Little River's north side three miles upriver from its confluence with the Connecticut. They tied their horses to posts outside the mill and walked along a muddy path downstream to where Hart said they could get the best view of the mill. From there, they watched the mill's large wheel turning just below a small dam on a brook entering the Little River.

"Allyn built the mill shortly after our congregation arrived," Hart said. "The mill is adequate now, but too small for the town's future."

"How will you handle the situation?" Hawkes asked.

Hart pointed downstream from the mill to two small tree covered islands and said, "I will build a larger mill on the river's other side next to the smallest island. The power to turn the wheel will come from a dam built between the island and the shore."

"When do you want me to begin operating the mill?" Hawkes asked.

"Allyn is a crusty old man who thinks he has to do everything himself," Hart said. "I will convince him it is in his best interest to let you run the mill."

"Tell me if you need help convincing him. Meanwhile, I'll find a miller to operate this mill and the others you build."

They walked on the path along the Little River on their way back to their horses when Hawkes stopped. Hart stopped and looked back at him.

"We need to talk about something else," Hawkes said.

"What is it?"

"Reverend Stone believes Elder Goodwin is attempting to gain control of our congregation. He needs your help to stop it."

"Why does he think this?" Hart asked.

"Goodwin dominates every meeting when Reverend Hooker is gone." Hawkes answered

"I noticed this."

"Shouldn't our assistant pastor run these meetings?" Hawkes asked.

"Yes," Hart said. "Why would Goodwin want control of the congregation? Reverend Hooker seems healthy."

"There will be a time when he's not. Then every vote will matter."

Hart rubbed his chin while staring at the location for the new mill. He turned back to Hawkes, "Tell Reverend Stone I will support him and watch for evidence Goodwin is challenging his authority. William and I have a long history between us, and I don't doubt what Reverend Stone says."

"I'll tell him."

Chapter 23

John Lee stood with the other militiamen. It was a May morning and a mist hung over the Connecticut River, climbing up the slope from the river until it touched the meadow beneath them. Within a few minutes the sun climbed above the trees and the mist disappeared. Red, blue and white banners waived in the sun and the breastplates and helmets of the veterans of the fight in the Netherlands shined brightly. John wondered how many of them were watching Hartford's sunrise for the last time.

He couldn't remember when he first knew this day was inevitable. It may have been when Massachusetts Bay soldiers attacked and burned Pequot homes and crops in December; or when the Pequots laid siege to Saybrook in reprisal for it; or the day Wethersfield was attacked in May by the Wongunk, who were Pequot allies. It didn't matter. Now he was standing in the meetinghouse yard with ninety militiamen from Hartford, Wethersfield and Windsor (formerly Dorchester). Everyone knew while Massachusetts Bay started the war, Connecticut would wage it.

John stood in the center of Hartford's four companies. The men of Wethersfield and Windsor stood on each wing. All companies were spread out facing the meetinghouse's porch. Lieutenant Bull stood in front of John. Wethersfield's and Windsor's commanders stood before their contingents.

Earlier, Bull told John he would be his aid during the coming battle. John didn't know what an aid was supposed to do and wished he could remain hidden in his company. Like most of the men, John carried a matchlock musket and rest. He wore a bandolier across his chest where twelve wooden powder bottles hung. The other men carried pikes.

Uncas, the Mohegan's sachem, and sixty of his warriors stood in the trees next to the militiamen. The Mohegan army was a beautiful sight with colorful feathers, shells and beads worn by its warriors in their hair and clothing. Uncas was a stocky six feet tall. His shoulder length hair was straight, glossy and jet black. It shone in the morning sun from the bear fat he dressed it with. Its blackness was accentuated by the soot he worked into his hair to further darken it.

Captain Mason and Reverend Hooker walked through the meetinghouse door and onto the porch facing the army. Somewhat portly with a broad face, Mason wore his black hair to his shoulders. He strode to the porch's front and looked down at Lieutenant Bull and the commanders of the Wethersfield and Windsor militias.

"Bring your men to attention," Mason ordered.

In turn, Lieutenant Bull and the other militia commanders ordered their militia's to attention. Instantly, the militiamen snapped to attention.

Reverend Hooker stepped forward. His ankle length cape flowed in the breeze. When he reached the porch's edge, Hooker stopped and stood until all the militiamen were staring up at him.

"Men of Connecticut, you are taking a journey with an end known only by God. Only one thing is certain. God will be with you on this journey. The battle's outcome will decide our future. A loss may mean our people's destruction. A victory will preserve our way of life for generations. Fight courageously and don't do the work of the Lord's revenge with half measures. Do so boldly and completely."

"All right men," Mason shouted. "To the ships!"

John cheered with the other men as they broke ranks. Lieutenant Bull led them to the landing where the ships waited. John was surprised how different they were from each other. The largest was a three masted two deck pinnace like the *Francis*. The expedition's leaders and the militiamen boarded it. After boarding, Captain Mason, his deputy Lieutenant Robert Seeley, Lieutenant Bull and Reverend Stone moved to ship master's cabin where they would be quartered.

John stood alone with Richard Hawkes, who boarded the ship with Reverend Stone.

"It seems we will be together on this ship," Hawkes smirked.

John said nothing, but merely continued to stare at Hawkes. Finally, he turned and walked towards the bow where he, Hawkes and several others were assigned hammocks in the forecastle. Almost immediately, Hawkes grabbed John's shoulder and spun him around.

"Don't ignore me when I talk to you," Hawkes yelled.

John pulled Hawkes's hand from his shoulder and announced, "We're going to war and your complaint isn't among my priorities now."

Several men stopped to watch their confrontation. Hawkes pushed his face into John's. John didn't budge.

"Someday we will be alone, and you won't be able to ignore me by claiming military duties," Hawkes said.

The pinnace pulled up anchor and within an hour it was sailing down the river followed by the two smaller ships. The largest of the other two ships was a flat bottom pink. Earlier the Mohegans climbed aboard it. Most were on deck and John noticed nearly all were pale and sickly looking.

The smallest of the other ships was a shallop used for coastal trading. Its single mast billowed in the north wind pushing all three ships along. Ten mariners, most of whom were used for rowing, manned the shallop which carried food and supplies.

The three ships sailed south past the Dutch fort into a forest lining the river. Later in the afternoon, as they passed through a narrow stretch of the river, John heard a loud scrapping sound behind them.

"The pink has run aground!" the pinnace's lookout yelled.

The pinnace's Captain swung it hard to starboard to maintain contact with the pink.

"They'll have to unload her before they can move her from the rocks and mud," a seaman standing near John declared.

Immediately, the pinnace's crew dropped its shallop into the river to take the Mohegans to shore so the pink's crew could free it. The shallop's men tied ropes to the pink and began to row towards the river's center with it in tow while, waist deep in water, other seamen pushed the pink from the mud. The soldiers on John's ship cheered and laughed as the pink floated back into the river's channel. Meanwhile, on shore, Uncas glowered.

Lieutenant Bull announced, "Satan be damned. Uncas and his warriors will never get back on that boat. They didn't want on it in the first place."

Bull's prediction proved true. When the pink moved close enough for the Mohegans to wade to it, Uncas waived his arms back and forth and yelled for it to pull away from the shoreline. John watched with Bull as the Mohegans disappeared into the trees.

"They'll be at Fort Saybrook before we get there," Bull said. "Uncas knows when we defeat the Pequots he'll be the most powerful sachem in Connecticut. He'll have no power if he doesn't help us."

It took the ships two days to reach Fort Saybrook which protected the town of Saybrook. The fort's palisade loomed above them as John waited on the pinnace's deck to board the shallop taking the militia to shore. He followed Lieutenant Bull onto the shallop where they sat next to Captain Mason and Lieutenant Seeley. Two rows ahead, Reverend Stone and Richard Hawkes sat together.

The shallop made its way across the bay towards a cove just north of where the fort stood. The town of Saybrook was a half mile from the bay's opening. Heavy black smoke rose above the trees on the other side of the town.

"What's happening?" John asked the shallop's operator. "I thought we lifted the Pequots' siege."

The operator shrugged, "That's what we thought until a bunch of them attacked this morning. Luckily, the Mohegans arrived in time to capture one and chase the rest away. He's now in the stockade. A few Pequots came back to rescue him this afternoon. They burned down a farm house before the militia drove them off."

"Take heart, we will soon wreak vengeance on them in their own village," Hawkes roared. "They'll receive no quarter when we do."

John and Bull glared at Hawkes.

"Do you plan on fighting by yourself?" Bull asked.

"We will fight together." Hawkes answered.

"Well, in that case, Captain Mason will decide if and when quarter is given," Bull asserted.

Mason stared at Hawkes without speaking.

They walked on a road from the wharf around the bay. The road rose gradually until they neared the peninsula's tip where it jutted into the river's mouth. Here the road was steeper as it climbed towards the fort's vertical timbers. John shielded his eyes from the sun with his hand as he hiked up the hill towards the fort alongside Lieutenant Bull with Mason leading and Hawkes trailing behind.

"Awesome, isn't it?" Bull said.

"Yes," John answered.

"The Pequots' fort is just as impressive," Bull said.

John's chest tightened.

"That's why we'll strike hard without warning," Bull said.

A guard met them at the fort's gate. He led them through the inner courtyard to a small log hut consisting of a single room dimly lit by a handful of candles and a small fire. Two men sat silently at the table in the center of the room. One man, who John didn't know, was English. The other man was Uncas.

Captain Mason stepped forward and announced, "Uncas, John, it's good to see both of you."

"I am glad to see you my friend," Uncas said. "We chased off the Pequots and captured one of their warriors."

The Englishman stood up from the table and glared at Uncas.

"Where is he now?" Mason asked. "If he's alive, I would like my men to question him about the enemy's size, location and plans."

"He's in my custody," the Englishman answered in a coolly efficient voice. "He revealed nothing when questioned."

Mason turned to Bull, "Thomas, this is Captain John Underhill. We fought together in the Netherlands. He's brought men from Massachusetts Bay."

"He tells only half truths," Uncas said. "The Pequot would have told us what we wanted if this man let us keep him."

"I condemn torture," Underhill said.

"Do you object if two of my men question the Pequot?" Mason asked.

"No, but they'll learn nothing from him," Underhill said.

"You may be right, but I want to try." Mason declared.

Mason ordered the two militiamen he had brought from Windsor to follow Underhill to where the Pequot was being held. Underhill was leading them from the hut when Hawkes stepped forward.

"Captain Mason, let me assist these men," Hawkes said. "I have experience with interrogations."

Reverend Stone spoke before Mason could answer, "Richard has persuasive skills. He'll help your men get the Pequot to talk."

Mason hesitated for a moment before announcing, "I don't have time to inquire into your experience Mr. Hawkes. I will let you help my men if you agree to let them lead the questioning."

"Thank you, sir," Hawkes said.

Hawkes's pulse beat in his ears as he followed Captain Underhill and Mason's two men across the fort's courtyard into the log hut where the Pequot was held. Two prison cells were at the end of the hut's single room. The Pequot stared at Hawkes through the door of his cell. Hawkes sneered at the Pequot who glared back at him. *Perfect*, Hawkes thought. *He'll not break easily.*

Underhill pointed to the Pequot and said, "That's him. If you need me, I'll be in the other hut."

Underhill pointed to the Mohegan sitting at a table in the room's center and announced, "I will leave him to translate."

Hawkes pulled down the board used to lock the door as soon as Underhill and his men left. He smiled at the Pequot. The Pequot glared back.

Mason's men pushed the Pequot into a chair near the table's bench. The bloody slash marks inflicted by the Mohegan interrogation oozed blood. Hawkes moved to the chair. The Pequot's face was covered with blood, his nose flattened, his lips split open, and one of his eyes swollen shut. Hawkes was impressed with the Mohegans' work. Their interrogation was methodical. His would be too.

Mason's men stripped the Pequot of his leggings and moccasins, leaving only the breech clout covering his mid-section. They threw a rope over a beam. Hawkes watched approvingly as they tied the Pequot's wrists to the rope's ends and pulled him up until his feet were off the floor. One man took two more ropes and tied each to the Pequot's ankles and tightened each rope to the room's pillars. The Pequot was now fully suspended with both his arms and legs pulled tightly apart by the ropes.

The Mohegan interpreter watched as Mason's men went about their work. He had nothing to do for the Pequot was silent. Finally, one of Mason's men drew a whip from his bag and announced, as the Mohegan translated, "You will be whipped until you agree to cooperate."

The Pequot remained silent while Mason's man drew back the whip and drove it into his back ten times. After watching Mason's man whip the Pequot ten more times without breaking his silence, Hawkes could stand no more. Mason's man was leaning against the table gasping for breath when Hawkes approached him.

"Whipping won't get you what you want," Hawkes said. "It's

possible this man will die before he gives us what we want, we won't know this unless we take him to the edge of death. Let me question him. I can do that."

Mason's man was still breathing heavily when he answered, "You might be right. Go ahead."

Hawkes nodded at Mason's man before removing his sword and knife from his belt and taking off his buff jacket and jerkin. After removing all clothing above his waist, Hawkes turned to the Mohegan translator and said, "Remove any clothing you don't want bloodied and approach the prisoner."

The Mohegan moved closer to the Pequot.

Hawkes pounded his fist on the table and yelled, "No, not there. Get closer. I want him to smell your breath when you talk to him."

Mason's men, who were sitting dejectedly on the table's bench, jumped up when Hawkes yelled and moved farther away from the prisoner.

"Come back here," Hawkes yelled. "I need your help to break him."

Awakened by Hawkes's yelling, the Pequot prisoner raised his head and looked directly at him. Hawkes moved towards the Pequot while motioning the Mohegan to do the same. When all three faces were no more than two feet apart Hawkes stared into the Pequot's eyes and smiled.

"You've shown courage," Hawkes whispered while the Mohegan translated. "I'm now going to see if you are a warrior. Prove to me you can bear torture without telling us what we ask or crying out in pain. Do you have anything to say before I start?"

The Pequot dropped his head to his chest without speaking.

"Very well, let it begin," Hawkes announced.

Hawkes pulled the Pequot's head up by his matted bloody hair and looked directly into his swollen eyes. He released the Pequot's head which again fell forward onto his chest. He turned to Mason's man who whipped the prisoner.

"Hand me your whip," Hawkes commanded.

"What makes you think he'll speak if you whip him again?" Mason's man said.

"I don't expect him to speak after I whip him again. It will only be the beginning of my interrogation."

Mason's man shrugged his shoulders and handed his whip to Hawkes who turned to the Pequot and cracked the whip three times. The Pequot slowly lifted his head from his chest and looked at Hawkes.

"Your back is flayed from the Mohegan and English lashes," Hawkes said as the Mohegan translated. "Each lash I give you will dig deeper until your bones will cry in pain. Endure this if you can. Tell us what we want to know if you can't."

Hawkes walked behind the prisoner. He glanced at Mason's men. Their ashen faces looked at the floor. The Mohegan moved away from the Pequot while Hawkes stood behind the Pequot. Without warning, Hawkes struck the first blow. After his third blow, blood flew across the room every time he pulled the whip back to strike the next blow. All the while not even a moan passed over the Pequot's swollen lips.

Hawkes stopped. The room exhaled when he did. Mason's men, who looked away halfway through the whipping, looked back. They breathed unevenly.

Hawkes glared at Mason's men and ordered, "Take the prisoner down and tie him to the table on his back."

The Pequot fell to the ground like a pile of loose rags as soon as Mason's men released him from the ropes suspending him. They dragged him across the floor on his bloody feet to the table and lay him on his back.

"Pull his arms and legs out and tie them to the table," Hawkes demanded.

With the prisoner laying stretched out before him on the table, Hawkes reached down to the floor and lifted his sword. He drew it from its scabbard.

"Move away from the prisoner," he ordered.

Sweat poured down Mason's mens' faces as they backed away from the table."

"Before you start you should ask him if he's willing to tell us what we want to know?" the taller of Mason's men whispered across the silent room.

Hawkes turned and leered at the man, "What did you say?"

"I said you should ask the Pequot if he'll tell us what we want before you torture him again?"

"This man won't talk," Hawkes scowled. "But he will die."

In a move so sudden it was over before perceived, Hawkes lifted his sword above his head and brought it down on the Pequot's right wrist making a dull thud as it cut through the wrist's flesh and partially through its bone. Blood shot across the room and for the first time the Pequot screamed. Hawkes lifted the sword again and brought it down on the Pequot's wrist. This time the cut was clean and the tight rope stretching the Pequot's arm pulled his hand away from his arm.

Mason's men backed against the room's wall while the translator turned away, knowing his service was no longer needed. The Pequot's screams filled the room as Hawkes walked to the table's other side and stood above the Pequot's left arm. Across the table the Pequot's right arm spurted blood with each of his heartbeats. Before Hawkes continued, there was a loud banging at the door. Captain Underhill strode into the room when one of Mason's men opened it.

After surveying the bloody scene, Underhill glared at Hawkes as the Pequot screamed.

"What are you doing?" Underhill yelled.

"Questioning the prisoner," Hawkes answered.

"Without success it seems."

"I'll do better next time."

"There will be no next time," Underwood spat.

Underhill glared at Mason's men and said, "Load and prime one of your matchlocks and give it to me with a lit match. I will do what you didn't. I will save this man from further pain and suffering."

Within seconds the tallest of Mason's men handed Underhill a loaded and primed matchlock with a lighted match. Underwood calmly attached the lighted match to the matchlock's firing hammer, pointed it at the screaming Pequot's head and pulled the trigger. The room was deathly silent as Captain Underwood dropped the matchlock to the floor. The sound of it hitting the floor echoed throughout the room. Underhill turned and glared at Hawkes.

"You disgust me," Underhill said. "I will report your actions to Captain Mason and recommend you are punished for what you did."

Hawkes smiled at Underhill, washed the Pequot's blood off himself and casually began to put his clothes back on. He was not worried about Underhill's threat for Mason would not punish him. They were at war with the Pequots and punishing him for killing one would hurt the men's morale. Underhill's sense of honor was quaint but had no place in a war against savages.

Word of Hawke's torture of the Pequot quickly spread among the militiamen. Most thought Hawkes's actions were justified. Captain Underhill's complaint was acknowledged by Captain Mason, but, as Hawkes predicted, Mason had neither desire nor time to deal with it. Mason was leading men into battle and assured Underhill he would consider the matter after they defeated the Pequots. Underhill felt he did his duty when he reported the matter and was satisfied to leave it to Mason to decide what, if any, action to take.

Mason's two men told the other militiamen what they witnessed in graphic detail. John Lee was disgusted when he heard the details. His disgust grew during the next two days as the ships lay wind bound in Saybrook's bay. Each day he watched Hawkes stride about the fort as if nothing happened. Finally, when he could take it no longer, he complained to Lieutenant Bull. Bull placed his arm around him and assured John he would have severely punished Hawkes were it within his power, but Captain Mason was their commander and they must accept his decision.

On the delay's second day, Captain Mason directed Reverend Stone and Richard Hawkes to move into quarters on the pink to make room for Mason's officers on the pinnace. At first, Stone was upset, but Hawkes convinced him the move was favorable as they would have more room and because Stone was the militia's chaplain, Captain Mason would have to consult him about any major decision regardless of which ship Stone was on.

That afternoon, Mason called a meeting of officers in the master's cabin on the pinnace. Lieutenant Bull, Lieutenant Seeley, the Windsor and Wethersfield militia commanders and Captain Underhill were present. John and the officers' aides stood against the steerage cabin door while the officers sat at the small table used for the ship's master's charts.

"I'm troubled by the orders we received from the General Court," Captain Mason said. "The Court ordered us to attack the Pequots at the Pequot River's mouth in the western part of their territory. Their numbers are much greater than ours, so our attack's success depends on surprise. But surprise will be lost if we attack where ordered, for they will see our ships coming and challenge our landing. I have an alternate plan."

"We can't violate the Court's orders," Wethersfield's commander declared. "We must first ask the Court for permission to vary from them."

"Hear me out," Mason answered. "I believe my plan meets the requirements of our orders. We will still attack the Pequots, but not precisely as the orders state. Rather than attack them first at the Pequot River's mouth, we will sail past it and land in the Narragansetts' land east of it. From there we will march back east into the Pequots' land and attack them. This will keep the element of surprise."

"I like your plan," Lieutenant Bull said.

"We still need the Court's permission to vary from its order no matter how good your plan is," Wethersfield's commander protested.

"Sir, we're in a war and about to engage the enemy," Mason declared. "It will take days to get the Court's approval and we will lose the element of surprise. I will ask Reverend Stone for God's guidance. We will attack as I propose if he approves. Do you agree?"

Everyone in the room knew the Wethersfield commander would need to agree with Captain Mason's proposal. None were surprised when he did so immediately. But now, Captain Mason had placed the decision in the hands of Reverend Stone. John knew Stone's decision would depend on what Richard Hawkes said to Stone and Hawkes's advice would be tied to whatever gain Hawkes felt he could obtain from Stone's decision.

It was mid-afternoon by the time the messenger reached Reverend Stone with Captain Mason's request. The messenger asked if he should wait for Stone's guidance. Before Stone could reply, Hawkes intervened, "Tell Captain Mason Reverend Stone needs time to consider the matter before he can determine what God wills."

After the messenger left Stone asked, "Why did you send him away?"

"Captain Mason transferred you to a lesser vessel. If he wanted your advice immediately, he should have kept you on the pinnace."

Reverend Stone smiled, "There's irony in Mason's predicament. I will let him wait for my answer until tomorrow. What do you think I should tell him?"

"You have two options," Hawkes said. "You can tell him it would be best to seek the General Court's approval, or you can tell him you believe God wants him to proceed with his plan without delaying getting the Court's approval. You will only benefit by advising to attack without consulting with the General Court. If so, you will be lauded as the man who authorized the attack destroying the Pequots."

John Lee was pressed against the small hut's wall used as Captain Mason's headquarters with the other aides and advisors. Mason, Lieutenant Bull, Lieutenant Seeley and Captain Underwood were seated at the room's table. The room was silent as Mason waited for Reverend Stone's arrival.

After several minutes, the hut's door sprung open and Reverend Stone entered with Richard Hawkes trailing him. Stone walked to the end of the table opposite Mason while Hawkes squeezed against the wall with the other aides. Stone's eyes were ablaze, and his hair disheveled as he stared at the men at the table.

"The Holy Spirit revealed God's will to me," Stone said.

"What is it?" Mason asked.

"We must attack the Pequots before they prepare their defenses. It isn't necessary to seek the General Court's approval before doing so."

Mason nodded at Stone and looked around the table. No one spoke.

"It's settled," Mason announced. "Tomorrow we sail to the Narragansetts' lands. From there we will march west to attack the Pequots."

Wethersfield's commander nodded his approval.

Chapter 24

John Lee lay in a hammock along the forecastle's wall watching rain slide down the foremast through the forecastle deck above him. The army had been anchored near the Narragansetts' village for two days. Throughout that time, sheets of rain blew across the bay, making it impossible to stay above deck or to bring the army ashore without risking shallop's capsizing. John went on deck when he heard men talking outside the forecastle. The rain had stopped, and Captain Mason, Lieutenant Bull and Captain Underwood were looking at the shoreline from the ship's rail.

"Sharpen your blade John," Bull announced. "We go ashore this morning. You and I go in the first group."

Within an hour, all the militiamen were on deck with their muskets, pikes and bags. The rain had returned, but this time it was a misty rain and not the pounding rain that kept them from landing. It would still be cold and wet when they were ashore.

John boarded the pinnace's shallop with Lieutenant Bull. They sat together at the bow as men took seats behind them. Bull turned to John and asked, "Nervous?"

"Just the cold," John said. "It makes me shiver."

"Nerves do that too," Bull responded, fingering his dead friend's knife hanging from his belt. "Too early to be nervous anyway. It will take two days to march to the Pequots' fort."

It was raining when they stepped onto the muddy beach. John's boots slid as Bull led them across the beach into the ferns under the birch trees. John looked back and watched the shallop reach the pinnace to bring the second group of militiamen ashore.

"Build a shelter here," Bull said. "I will get the other men."

John chopped several branches from the birch trees, stripped them of leaves, and bent them across the branches he earlier had driven into the ground. After building a frame, he covered it with several leaf covered branches. The other militiamen built similar shelters. He climbed into his shelter and sat on the wet grass, watching the rain fall through the shelter's narrow opening. The smell of damp leather and wet wool filled the air.

Bull returned to the clearing in early afternoon. It was too wet to start a fire. The men hunkered down in the rough shelters they built. Bull climbed into John's shelter and sat next to him. The rain slid through the leaves onto their heads and ran down their faces.

"Forgive us our trespasses," Bull said. "This infernal rain is more than annoying. We will need to stay here tonight."

John shared a piece of dried beef with Bull and lay back in the wet grass with his hands behind his head.

"God willing, it will clear up tomorrow," Bull said.

Bull shook John out of a deep sleep. John felt the drenching cold and remembered where he was.

"Gird your loins John," Lieutenant Bull boomed. "It's stopped raining and we're moving. Go ahead with Uncas's scouts and find a dry path for us. Get back before dawn so we can start our march."

John raised himself from the wet grass, pulled his bandolier over his shoulder, and picked up his matchlock. Two Mohegans waited outside his shelter. He led them west through the sleeping camp into the trees above the meadow. He knew they needed to find an Indian path and that such a path would be far enough away from the shore so it could be used in all weather. They found a path a mile and a half west. He sent a Mohegan back to tell Lieutenant Bull the route the militia should take, while he and the other Mohegan moved along the path toward the Narragansetts' village.

He rejoined the army as it approached one of the Narragansett forts in early afternoon. The sky was clear, and a bright sun shone on the vertical timbers of the fort's palisade. The militia formed with its red, blue and white banners waiving outside the fort while the Mohegans waited in the woods behind it. When there was no sign the Narragansett sachem would send an emissary, Mason, Bull and three other officers hiked to the fort's entrance. John and the other militiamen waited in formation.

Four Narragansett warriors came out to meet Mason. Mason and the Narragansett leader spoke briefly before the leader went back to the fort, leaving the other Narragansett outside with Captain Mason and his officers. Moments later, the Narragansett leader returned and spoke to Mason. Almost immediately, Mason and his officers returned to the militia.

"What happened," John asked Bull.

"We won't get help from this sachem," Bull said. "He's afraid of both us and the Pequots and won't get involved.

"Can we defeat the Pequots without the Narragansetts' help?"

"We will have to if we can't get the sachem at the next fort to join us. That fort is twenty miles west. We will march until dark and arrive at the fort at noon tomorrow."

At noon the next day, they were near the border between the Pequots and Narragansetts. John scouted ahead of the militia with two Mohegans and reached the fifteen-foot palisade of the second Narragansett fort just ahead of the rest of the militia. A few Narragansett women were working in the vegetable garden outside the fort but were quickly whisked into the fort by several Narragansett warriors.

By the time the militia reached the fort, its entrance was secured and there were no Narragansetts outside its walls. Mason and Bull led several officers to the fort's gate, leaving the militiamen in formation one hundred yards behind them. Mason yelled at the Narragansetts staring through the gaps in the palisade used for firing arrows. *Curious* John thought. *They say nothing.* Captain Mason and his officers returned to the militia after standing before the fort for several minutes without a response.

When Bull reached John's side he announced, "Our army will sleep near the fort tonight. Hartford's militia will guard the fort's rear."

The foliage was heavy where John was posted near the fort's rear. Throughout his watch briar bush thorns cut into his arms and legs. When his watch was done, he found a dry plot of grass and lay on his back. He took a breath and gazed at the blazing stars above him.

The sky was gray when he awoke. The gray disappeared as streams of light from the rising sun scattered through the sky, replacing the gray with a deep blue.

"Come meet the Narragansetts," Lieutenant Bull said. "They asked for a meeting with Captain Mason and he wants his officers and aides with him."

With his musket slung over his right shoulder, his sword and knife hanging at his belt, and his musket's rest in hand, John followed Bull to Mason's camp beyond the tree line near the entrance to the fort. When they arrived, two of Mason's officers brought twelve Narragansetts into the camp. Each Narragansett carried a knife, axe, bow and arrows. Their faces were painted for battle. A Mohegan translated.

"We were sent by our sachem Miantinomo," the Narragansetts' leader announced. "The Pequots are our enemy and our sachem wants to help you destroy them with four hundred of our warriors. He sent us to prove we have the courage to fight the Pequots with you."

The twelve Narragansetts formed a half ring facing Mason and his officers. The Narragansetts' warlike appearance seemed odd for a peaceful meeting until a Narragansett stepped forward into the half ring and stood before Mason. The warrior stared into Mason's eyes. The warriors behind him chanted in unison. With each refrain the chant's volume increased until the single warrior began to step forward and back while thrusting his spear forward to the chant's rhythm.

Suddenly, the chant stopped, and the warrior thrust his spear into the ground in front of Mason. In the silence, the warrior declared his hatred of the Pequots and swore his allegiance to the English. When the warrior was finished the other warriors stepped forward and performed the same dance while swearing the same oath.

Within an hour, the militia was on the march again. This time it was trailed by ninety Mohegan and four hundred Narragansett warriors. By noon, the sky was a cauldron as a furious sun beat down on the sweat drenched column of men moving along the narrow Indian path amid giant oak, maple, birch, and elm trees. The path they followed was narrower, causing the train of men to stretch out for over a mile. John was at the train's front and was unaware the Narragansetts behind him were slipping away and returning to their fort.

They were well into Pequot territory when the army reached a river the Narragansetts called the Pawtucket. Mason sent Mohegan scouts ahead to search for Pequot ambushes. The river's ford was near a Pequot fishing spot but today no one was there. While the army rested at the ford, what had been a trickle of Narragansett deserters turned into a flood. Soon the Narragansetts' contingent was reduced by more than half.

After a brief rest, the army resumed its march, arriving at a large Pequot cornfield at mid-afternoon. No longer ahead of the column, John walked alongside Lieutenant Bull in front of the Connecticut militia behind Captain Mason, Captain Seeley, Reverend Stone and Richard Hawkes.

Assured by Mohegan scouts that there were no Pequots in the area, Captain Mason called a meeting of officers to discuss their attack. They met under a stand of maple trees at the edge of the cornfield. The officers and Reverend Stone sat in a circle while John, Hawkes and the other assistants stood against the trees.

Mason announced, "We will attack the small Pequot fort at dawn. Their main fort, where their chief sachem, Sassacus, resides, cannot be reached before midnight. Our men will be too exhausted to attack at dawn tomorrow and the enemy will have time to prepare for our attack. We will attack elsewhere."

A groan rose from the officers and their assistants.

"Captain Mason, we've come far to defeat the Pequots," Captain Underhill said. "The men will be disappointed if we don't attack their strongest fort and kill their leader. What should we tell them?"

"Tell them tomorrow we will destroy the Pequots' fort on the Mystic River. It will be a devastating blow and force them out of their other fort to defend their people. When they do, we will defeat their army for it will be reduced by half and too spread out to defend itself."

After some more discussion, the meeting ended, and the militia commanders returned to their units. As John walked towards Lieutenant Bull, he saw Richard Hawkes walking towards him.

"Are you ready for your first real fight?" Hawkes smirked.

"I'm ready," he answered. "What about you? The Pequots will be standing and not tied to a table."

Hawkes sprang at John. This time John was ready. He slid sideways and pushed Hawkes into the dirt with his hands. Hawkes was up in an instant but before he could charge again, Bull grabbed him around his waist, holding him back.

"Save your fury for tomorrow," Bull yelled. "I won't let you fight with us if you can't control yourself."

After Bull released him, Hawkes turned to John and announced, "I will see you on the battlefield."

As Hawkes strode away, John whispered to Bull, "He can't be trusted."

"I told Captain Mason this, but he thinks Hawkes is a 'fighter' and we will need him tomorrow."

John slept fitfully that night. The militia set up camp near a small swamp between two hills. They were too close to the Pequots' fort to light campfires, so as night fell, the men chewed dried corn and beef under a clear moonlit sky. John was posted as a sentry far outside the camp and close to the Pequots' fort. As he crouched among the trees, he heard the Pequots singing and celebrating inside the fort. *We have surprised them*, he thought.

John was unsure what kept him awake. Hawkes's threat was on his mind, but it was insignificant compared to his worry about the coming battle. But this was not what he thought of as he lay on his back looking at the moon. He thought about his parent's love and the shining face of young Henry Hayward. God created them and he wondered if His design was for them to be saved or to be damned. It seemed impossible He created them to be damned because they were pure in spirit; but Reverend Stone claimed this was not evidence of His grace. *Where will I be if I die tomorrow*, he asked God. There was no answer.

John woke with a start as the militiamen near him moved about. He fastened his bandolier over the shoulder of his buff coat and strapped his belt around his waist. He threw a piece of dried beef in his mouth, chewing it as he fastened his scabbard with his sword and knife onto his belt. Thirty yards away, he saw Lieutenant Bull, Deacon Hart and the other officers forming the men. He threw on his mulberry wide brimmed hat, slung his musket over his shoulder and grabbed the musket's rest. In moments, he was at Lieutenant Bull's side.

The militia was in a line of trees before a cornfield in front of the Pequot fort an hour later. The fort was on a steep hill, making its fifteen-foot-high palisade appear impregnable. Richard Hawkes was ahead of John. Hawkes stood straight with his chin high and stared at the fort.

John glanced at Bull who stood directly to his left and asked, "Where are the Mohegans and Narragansetts?"

"They won't attack with us," Bull answered. "They say they will stay behind in the trees and fire arrows at Pequots leaving the fort."

Captain Underhill, whose men were at the militia's rear, walked past John towards Captain Mason who stood before the formation just inside the trees. The two men spoke briefly before Mason motioned for Bull to join them. After a brief discussion, Bull returned to John's side.

"We are splitting the militia." Bull announced. "Our militia will attack the front of the fort with Captain Mason, while Captain Underhill attacks the rear with part of the Massachusetts Bay militia. Remember your training and stay on my right in the melee."

Captain Mason walked through the trees into the cornfield. He turned, faced the militia massed in the trees, and waved it forward. John fought to control his breathing as he strode out of the trees on Lieutenant Bull's right with the rest of the militia. They flowed across the cornfield and up the hill towards the fort's palisade.

"Forward men, forward," Bull whispered as he led his men up the hill.

Militiamen spread across the hill as they neared the palisade. The fort was hushed, magnifying the slightest noise. John heard a dog bark inside the fort.

"Owanux, Owanux," voices yelled from inside the fort.

John knew the words: they were Algonquin for "English, English."

"They've discovered us," Bull yelled. "Gird your loins and form a firing line before the fort. It's time to fight. Don't think . . . act."

John rushed to the line and pulled his matchlock from his shoulder. When all four companies were on the line, Lieutenant Bull yelled out the firing sequence. A few arrows flew without effect from the palisade's gaps just as Bull gave the command to fire. An ear-splitting roar rose along the firing line. Chunks of wood and bark shattered the palisade's timbers while several Pequot warriors dropped to the ground on the other side of the gaps.

Captain Mason moved to the front of the firing line as the men reloaded. Mason raised his arm and waived the men forward to the fort as he advanced towards the palisade. Chaos surrounded John as he dropped his musket and drew his sword. Ahead of him the pikemen were already charging. Bull lifted his pike and strode towards the fort following them. *Stay on his right, stay on his right*, John thought as he advanced.

In an instant they were at the fort's entrance. There they ran into a wall of militiamen. John struggled to get through the bushes and tree limbs piled there by the Pequots as a barricade. Arrows flew through the palisade's gaps, most striking the ground at their feet. Finally, John and the other men cleared enough bushes so they could work their way into the fort. He followed Bull through the narrow opening.

Inside the fort, Pequot men, women and children fled from the entrance while a few Pequot warriors ran among the fort's two dozen wigwams. Everything was a blur of movement, a cacophony of men yelling, and women and children screaming. John saw Captain Mason leave a wigwam and point towards what seemed to be the fort's main pathway. At once, Bull rushed onto the path. John sped to keep up with him. Women's screams surrounded them when John and Bull reached Mason.

"The Pequots are hiding in their wigwams," Mason yelled. "Burn them out."

Several militiamen stormed into the wigwams near John. He wanted to follow them, but Bull held his arm.

"Watch the path!" Bull yelled.

John turned towards the path. It wound through the wigwams deep into the fort. Four Pequot warriors charged towards them up the path. Three more Pequots charged from a wigwam to their right. Bull raced down the path towards the first group of Pequots with his pike pointing at them. John charged on Bull's right with his sword raised. Three other militiamen trailed them.

The two forces collided and what was once a blur became a

whirlwind of racing bodies, flashing blades and flying arrows. Lieutenant Bull was struck in the chest with a Pequot arrow just as he was about to engage three Pequots. John watched Bull parry the blow of a Pequot's hatchet with his pike before driving its point into the Pequot's chest. Bull tried to pull the arrow from his chest, but it broke, leaving part of it still there.

Bull dropped his pike and drew his sword as the second Pequot charged. He swiftly lifted the sword and brought it down on the Pequot's head, splitting it open. Bull grabbed an arrow from the third Pequot and rammed it into the Pequot's eye before drawing his hatchet and thrusting it into a fourth Pequot's neck.

The pace of the melee was beyond John's grasp and he stayed on Bull's shoulder unsure what else to do. He saw more Pequots moving to attack them. He watched Bull fight another Pequot when out of the corner of his eye he saw a hatchet's blur. He ducked, evading the lunge, and buried his shoulder in the Pequot's chest, knocking him to the ground. He dropped his sword and rolled on top of the prostrate Pequot while drawing his hatchet. Kneeling over the Pequot, he raised his hatchet to strike him. Before he could, he was driven to the ground by another Pequot who came up on his right side in the melee. He rolled with the Pequot's tackle, swiftly pinning him to the ground. He drew his knife but froze before plunging it into the Pequot's chest when he saw the Pequot was only a boy. The boy quickly freed himself from John's confused grip and fled back down the path into the maze of wigwams.

When he stood, John saw more militiamen in the fort and watched the Pequots who had attacked fleeing down the path towards the wigwams. Twenty feet to his left Lieutenant Bull stood between five fallen Pequots.

Captain Mason stood before the militiamen and yelled, "Don't follow the Pequots! Fire their wigwams and leave the fort. We will set up a firing line outside the fort to keep them from escaping."

Militiamen ran from wigwam to wigwam throwing torches on their thatched roofs. The rising sun brought with it a strong wind which caused the fire to jump from wigwam to wigwam until all the wigwams were aflame.

The fire's heat drove Pequot men, women and children into the path between the wigwams. John realized he and Bull were the last Englishmen left in the fort. Bull was still braced for a fight when John grabbed his right arm and pulled him towards the fort's entrance.

The heat was oppressive as they ran through the heavy smoke. Suddenly, Bull stopped and ran back into the smoke. *What's he doing*, John thought, as he waited for Bull. A few moments later Bull emerged from the smoke carrying an Englishman on his shoulders. John ran towards Bull to help and arrived in time to strike a Pequot down with a hatchet blow to his head. Two other Pequots attacked them but turned and fled back into the smoke when they saw John's hatchet.

Together, John and Bull carried the wounded soldier from the fort. When they reached its entrance, John heard a musket crack. Chips of wood sprayed past his face. Fifty feet ahead of him he saw militiamen forming a firing line. Richard Hawkes was in the line's center. Hawkes's musket was the only one pointing at the fort's entrance. The other men were just beginning to load.

As he and Bull passed through the firing line with the wounded man, Bull glared at Hawkes.

"Identify your target more carefully," Bull yelled.

"Yes sir," Hawkes answered.

Two militiamen stepped forward and helped carry the wounded man behind the firing line. John found his musket and its rest and rejoined the line. There were forty men on the line with him. He lit the musket's match with a burning stick being passed along the line and was setting it on its stand when twenty Pequots charged from the burning fort. A load roar rose up around him as the men on the line fired. He lifted his head in time to see several Pequots fall. The surviving Pequots charged forward.

To John's right several men on the line dropped their matchlocks and drew swords. He loaded his matchlock and placed it on its stand while these men charged towards the oncoming Pequots. The rest of the firing line held its fire as the charging militiamen slammed into the Pequots. The melee was brief and soon John saw ten Pequots lying on the ground before the line as the surviving militiamen walked back carrying the wounded.

A hush fell over the battlefield as each militiaman stared at the fort's entrance. John heard the moaning of the wounded; an occasional clank of armor; and, the conversation of men around him. But above all sounds, there was a ubiquitous roar.

"Look above the palisade," a militiaman yelled. "The whole fort is burning."

Smoke and flames rose skyward above the palisade. The wind swirled furiously, and smoke spread over the trees behind the fort. *No one can survive this*, John thought. Above the burning palisade John saw a few Pequots in the flames firing arrows on the English army while other Pequots jumped from the palisade to escape the flames.

Suddenly, a cloud of arrows flew over John's head from the woods behind him. He looked back and saw the Mohegans firing at the handful of Pequots scrambling away from the fort. Pequots not felled by the arrows were quickly cut down by militiamen's swords as they charged the firing line.

Within minutes, the battle's sounds were hushed, and John again heard the fire's roar. It was much louder this time. Lieutenant Bull appeared before the firing line, blood dripping down his face. John guessed it was from the wound he received in the fort.

"Reload," Bull yelled.

Before all the men on the line could reload dozens of Pequots charged through the fort's entrance. John aimed his matchlock at them. When they were twenty feet from the firing line, Bull yelled, "Fire."

Just before John fired, he recognized the young Pequot boy he earlier spared. He fired his matchlock. Its sound merged into a single roar with the fire of the other matchlocks. The Pequots were blasted backwards. He knew he'd killed the boy.

Except for the roar above them, it was quiet again on the battle-field. The bodies of dead Pequots lay together before them like piles of bloody rags, their individual forms an intermingled mass of torn torsos, arms and legs. Beyond the pile of mutilated bodies, the fort burned brighter. Its smoke obliterated the sun as it began rising over the trees to John's left.

A hush fell over the firing line. Every man turned to the fort's entrance. No one moved. Two Pequot women and four children emerged from the smoke and began walking towards them.

"Hold your fire!" Bull yelled.

As the small Pequot party approached, the silence was broken by a musket's explosion. One of the Pequot women collapsed onto the ground. John turned to the musket's sound and saw Richard Hawkes holding a smoking musket pointed towards where the woman fell.

Hawkes grabbed a loaded matchlock and its rest from the nearest militiaman.

"Give me your weapon," Hawkes yelled. "I'll use it if you won't."

Hawkes placed the matchlock on its rest, aimed at the Pequots and fired again. This time a small Pequot boy fell. Hawkes grabbed a loaded matchlock from another militiaman. His shot dropped the other Pequot woman.

My God, John thought. *He'll kill them all. I must stop him. But for my oath he wouldn't be here.* He turned his matchlock's stand and placed his matchlock on it, aiming it at Hawkes. He pulled the matchlock's trigger, but before its ball left its chamber, Bull pushed he and the matchlock to the ground. The matchlock's explosion drove its ball harmlessly into a tree.

"Damn it John," Bull yelled looking down at him. "Murder isn't the answer." Bull faced the firing line and yelled, "Hold your fire, hold your fire!"

Bull raced towards Hawkes as Hawkes took a loaded matchlock from another militiaman and aimed at a small Pequot girl. Before Hawkes fired Bull drove him to the ground.

"You bastard!" Bull shouted. "You're a butcher!"

Hawkes stood just as Captain Mason reached Bull's side. Mason's eyes were ablaze as he stared at Bull and screamed, "Thomas, why are your men not firing with Richard Hawkes?"

"These are defenseless women and children," Bull answered. "My men are trained to fight warriors, not women and children. They're saving their musket balls for the next Pequot charge. If you want to kill women and children, look to Richard Hawkes who seems to enjoy it."

"I have no time to argue," Mason said. "I'll have Hawkes pick ten volunteers to fire at the women and children to keep warriors from sneaking from the fort by hiding among them. Have the rest of the line ready to fire at warriors coming out en masse."

Instantly, Hawkes picked James Eastman, Edward Roach and eight other militiamen. They began by firing at a much larger group of women and children fleeing the fort. At the same time, the Mohegans began raining arrows on any Pequots trying to escape. Soon a pile of bodies lay before the fort's entrance. Gradually, fewer and fewer Pequots emerged. Soon none came from the flaming fort.

Above the roaring fire, John heard the horrific screams of the men, women and children still in the fort. Soon the fort's only sounds were the fire's popping and cracking and the thunder of the collapsing palisade.

The men around John stood silently until Hawkes and his men began cheering. A few other militiamen joined their cheering and a moment later all the men began cheering their victory. John didn't cheer. Instead, he stared at the bodies of the women and children laying before him. Bull stood next to him. John turned just in time to see Bull attempt to remove the rest of the arrow from his chest. Bull pulled off his breastplate.

"Bless me," Bull said. "The arrow stuck in a piece of cheese under my breastplate."

John nodded. They both turned back to the fort and watched the flames rise. The firing line was silent. Some of the men turned to pack their belongings but most just stared at the flames with wide eyes and open mouths.

"This was not a fight for soldiers," Bull announced.

"What could we do to stop this?" John asked.

"Nothing. Hawkes is Stone's aide and Mason is in command."

"Where is God?" John asked.

"Not here. Satan, in the guise of Richard Hawkes, rules here today."

PART THREE
1637 - 1640

Chapter 25

John Lee walked across the bridge over the Little River on a crisp October morning. It was five months after the Pequot fort's destruction and four months after the survivors were defeated while fleeing west toward the Mohawks' lands. A boy approached him from the bridge's opposite side. John's memory flashed back to the Pequot boy he first spared and then killed at the Pequot fort. He took a deep breath and passed the boy with his eyes fixed on the bridge's boards while answering the boy's greeting with a garbled grunt.

He crossed the bridge into Hartford's South Plantation. Here the town's growth was greatest as the newest settlers spread west along the Little River and to the south past the Dutch fort all the way to the village the Suckiaug moved to just before the Pequot war. He glanced back through the trees lining the river at the houses of Reverend Hooker, Reverend Stone and Elder Goodwin in the North Plantation. Behind him, George Wyllys's house rose like a cathedral. Its enormity seemed out of place in Reverend Hooker's town, but in the South Plantation it was surrounded by other huge houses, for those who lived here were among the wealthiest in town.

He turned west at Wyllys's house and was soon among more modest houses. Cornfields spread behind the houses. The corn was abundant and ready for harvest on all but one plot. That plot was where Richard Hawkes's house sat. John was not surprised since Hawkes was never home. Word was he was now in Boston.

John left the road along the Little River onto a dirt path winding through oaks, maples and pines towards a simple one-story house. As he approached the house his pulse quickened. *Today's the day*, he thought. *With God's help I will do it.* He knocked on the door three times. Lieutenant Bull opened it with a smile.

"Welcome John," Lieutenant Bull said. "So, will today be the day?"

"Perhaps," John said.

John knew better. He was certain he would beat Bull today in their weekly training match. After all, their recent matches were close, and he was faster than Bull. Though slower, Bull was stronger, especially when they went to the ground. Bull would not take him to the ground today. He would stay upright and spring at Bull only when he was confident, he could bring his stick across Bull's throat before Bull could bring him down.

Together they walked behind Bull's house. Once there, they replaced the metal knives in the sheaths on their belts with the blunt wooden knives used for training sessions and wrapped their hands with leather to keep from injuring them. Bull removed his wool doublet, leaving only his beige linen shirt as cover for his chest and arms. John elected to enter the contest wearing only his linen tunic. They faced each other with their wooden knives drawn.

"Here we go," Bull announced with a smile.

They circled each other counterclockwise. After three revolutions, Bull began to creep closer. John knew Bull was trying to close the distance between them so gradually that he would not notice until Bull charged. In their past contests, John backed away, keeping the distance between them the same. This time, John didn't. His strategy was to lull Bull into thinking he was not aware the distance between them had closed.

On the fifth revolution, when Bull was close enough, John turned sideways and kicked out his left leg striking Bull's right knee. Temporarily stunned, Bull backed away, but then closed on John and threw a punch glancing off John's forehead.

The two men continued to circle each other, both looking for a weakness in the other's defense. Suddenly, Bull lowered his shoulders and charged. John slid to his right and pushed Bull to the ground on his stomach using Bull's own momentum. Even though Bull's defensive position was weakened, John didn't try to take advantage of it by jumping onto the prostrate Bull. He made that mistake in an earlier contest and Bull used his superior strength to win the grappling that followed.

Bull rose and the two men continued to circle each another. Bull threw an overhand punch at John's head. John blocked the punch by grabbing Bull's right wrist and pushing Bull's arm down causing Bull to temporarily lose his balance. John swung at Bull with his wooden knife. Bull grabbed John's right wrist with his left hand. John pulled his wrist free by quickly dropping lower and again thrust his knife at Bull. This thrust was towards Bull's stomach, causing Bull to drop lower and forward so he could parry the thrust with his right arm. Bull was momentarily off balance due to his forward movement. John pulled Bull over his left leg to the ground on his back. Confident Bull's position was so weak he could quickly win the contest, John risked being taken to the ground by driving his knife towards the prostrate Bull's chest. With lighting quickness, Bull grabbed John's right wrist, stopping his thrust and drove his knee into John's chest pushing him away.

Again, both men were up and circling each another in crouched positions with their wooden knives in their right hands. John thrust his knife towards Bull's neck. Bull deflected the thrust with his left arm. Immediately, John dropped lower and with his left hand grabbed for Bull's throat causing Bull to back up slightly as, in turn, John swept his wooden knife at Bull, barely missing his chest.

Bull was still moving backward as John turned with his left shoulder to Bull and his back turned at a forty-five-degree angle towards Bull. He thrust his left foot into Bull's right ankle knocking him to the ground. As Bull fell forward onto the ground, John quickly jumped over him and kneeling drove his wooden knife at Bull's neck, stopping just before it struck.

Bull rolled onto his side and laughed, "Excellent, excellent. You won! I will need to work harder if I am going to win next time."

John beamed while looking at Bull who sat upright in the grass below him. He finally won a contest with Bull. He reached down and helped Bull to his feet.

"You trained me well," John said.

Bull led him to the house's porch where they sat together.

"You are nearly eighteen," Bull said. "What will you do when you leave William's house?"

"I want my own farm," John said. "But good land is disappearing in Hartford."

"Why not be a soldier?" Bull asked. "You are a skilled fighter. Connecticut will always need soldiers like you."

John hesitated. He knew Bull agreed to train him because he said he wanted to be a soldier, but after the Pequots' massacre his desire was not as strong. He would need to choose his words carefully.

"My life is here with Reverend Hooker's congregation. I want to help the congregation grow so it can better serve God. I will put what you've taught me to use as a member of our militia."

"As one of Connecticut's best soldiers you can serve more than Hartford," Bull said. "You can serve all of Connecticut. Perhaps even all New England. God gave you a gift John, think carefully before you reject it."

John lowered his eyes before lifting his head and gazing into Bull's eyes, "I will consider what you said sir,"

Chapter 26

Richard Hawkes rode his stallion west along the Little River towards Matthew Allyn's gristmill. Heavy black clouds forecast the coming rain. James Eastman rode alongside chatting aimlessly about something Hawkes was uninterested in, while Edward Roach rode in silence fifteen feet behind them.

It was September 1639, two and a half years after Deacon Hart said he wanted Hawkes to operate the gristmill. While the delay in turning the mill over to Hawkes was in part due to the Pequot War, since then, Allyn continued to resist Hart's efforts to convince him to leave the mill. Today Hawkes would do the convincing.

Financially, Hawkes didn't need control of the mill's operation. His fur trade had prospered after he made an example of Megedaqik. Some Pocumtucs wanted revenge when Megedaqik's head appeared on a pike near their village. But the tribe's sachem had felt threatened by Megedaqik and he quickly convinced the tribe Megedaqik deserved what he got for working for an Englishman. No one cared, let alone dared, to take down Megedaqik's head. This was the result Hawkes anticipated.

As he rode, Hawkes's mind turned to John Lee. It had been five years since Lee swore to keep Hawkes's theft of the chalice secret. At first, Hawkes thought Lee would reveal the secret. After all, a simple oath would not keep him from doing that if it served his purposes. But now a realization struck him. Lee was a pious Puritan who believed violating the oath would show that he had not received God's grace. For five years Hawkes was frustrated that Lee had control over him, but it was he who had control because of the oath. He would let Lee live and continue to squirm under his control. He began to laugh.

"What's so funny Richard?" Eastman asked.

"A simple thought about a simple man," Hawkes said.

He waited until Roach pulled his horse alongside them as a light rain began falling.

"Allyn operates the mill by himself," Hawkes said. "He'll be alone. Follow me into the mill. We will confront him together."

"It's about time we forced Allyn from the mill," Eastman sneered.

Hawkes turned and stared at Eastman, "I'll decide what happens today," he said. "Do what I tell you and no more. Is that clear?"

"Yes," Eastman stammered.

"I will make Allyn an offer that will get him to move without need of threats or violence," Hawkes said. "My miller will meet us at the mill so he can plan the mill's transfer when Allyn agrees."

A drenching rain was falling when they reached the mill. Water slid from the rims of their broad brimmed hats and from the hems of their black capes when they stopped their horses. A tall slender man stood under the overhanging roof near the mill's entrance. He walked towards Hawkes.

"Good day Mark," Hawkes said. "These are my men, Edward Roach and James Eastman."

Hawkes turned to Eastman and Roach, "This is Mark Scott. He just made the passage. He owned three grist mills in Dedham."

"Mills now in the hands of Anglicans," Scott spit.

"You'll make a new fortune in Connecticut working for me," Hawkes asserted.

Hawkes dismounted and handed his stallion's reins to Scott, who also took the reins of Eastman's and Roach's horses before moving back under the mill's overhang. Hawks led Eastman and Roach up the outside stairs to the mill's second floor entrance. Below them a fifteen-foot paddle wheel steadily turned in the current of the trough built to control the volume of water applied to the wheel.

Corn dust and the sound of the mill's grinding stone filled the air as they entered the grinding room. Allyn dumped a sack of corn kernels into the grain hopper above the grinding and lode stones' casement. A sweeper guided the kernels into the hole in the middle of the grinding stone dropping them onto the lode stone which ground them into cornmeal. Allyn watched the top stone carefully as it turned below him. At over two hundred pounds, he was a big boned man. Hawkes had taken only three steps towards Allyn when Allyn turned and faced him. Allyn's hair was coated with corn dust and fell unevenly to his shoulders. He removed his tight linen cap and tucked it into his apron's pocket.

"What are you doing here?" Allyn asked.

"Deacon Hart sent me," Hawkes said. "These are my men."

Allyn's broad face broke into a smile as he asked, "Why has he sent you?"

"To discuss a business proposal," Hawkes answered.

"What business proposal?" Allyn asked. "It better not be that I give up operation of my mill. Stephen has pestered me about this long enough. This is my mill and I will run it myself."

"Deacon Hart asked me to take over operation of this mill. In return you . . . ."

Allyn cut Hawkes off in mid-sentence by slapping his hands together raising a cloud of corn dust. Allyn placed his hands on his hips and with a tight-lipped stare leaned forward into Hawkes's face.

"I would not turn my mill over to God himself, let alone to you. I don't care if Stephen Hart is the majority owner of this mill. I built it and I will keep operating it."

Hawkes felt the heat of Allyn's breath on his face.

"I understand how you feel," Hawkes confided. "You built this mill without Deacon Hart's money. Only after you needed to make improvements did you ask for his help. No matter what happens this is your mill. Deacon Hart understands this."

Hawkes continued, "Your arrangement with Deacon Hart made

you wealthy. You are part owner of this mill and will soon be part owner of Deacon Hart's new mill if you leave this mill's operations to me. As you know, the town has decided to build its own mill. Others will also build mills. If Hart's new mill is built now, you and he can stay ahead of your new competition. Your skills are too great to be wasted on operating this old mill. Instead, you should focus on building any new mills Deacon Hart plans."

Allyn leaned towards Hawkes and groaned, "But I like operating my mill."

"You can help me operate this mill anytime you want," Hawkes said. "Once Deacon Hart builds enough new mills, he'll return operation of this mill to you if you like, though I suspect you will have other interests by then."

"When would I need to move?"

"I brought my miller with me," Hawkes said. "I want him to begin operating the mill by week's end. That's why I need your answer today."

Allyn dropped his eyes and sat on the stool next to the grinding stones. He wiped the cornmeal dust from his eyes with the linen cloth around his neck. He looked up and smiled wistfully, "Tell Stephen I will leave the mill under the conditions you gave. I will be ready to help build the new mill next week."

The rain was ending when Hawkes led Eastman and Roach down the stairs and along the stone path to meet Scott, who stood with their horses.

"Allyn agreed to leave within a week," Hawkes said.

"I will make arrangements to take over operation tomorrow," Scott said.

"Earlier, I asked you to be prepared to discuss how we can take cornmeal without others discovering it?" Hawkes said.

"There are several ways millers take part of milled corn for themselves," Scott answered. "We could install a larger casement around the millstones trapping more of the customers' milled corn. Alternatively, we could install a hidden chute to the underside of the millstones leading to a separate bin and use a control gate to siphon off the amount of cornmeal we want. There are other ways we could use, but these two are the most promising."

"What do you recommend," Hawkes asked.

"Using a hidden chute under the millstones. It can be put in when the stones are cleaned, and the running stone lifted. It can be removed anytime the stones are cleaned if someone becomes suspicious."

"Do it," Hawkes ordered.

Chapter 27

John Lee lay on his back staring at the attic ceiling in William Westwood's house on a February morning in 1640. The fingers of his right hand tapped the floor's wooden planks, while the fingers of his left hand scratched his scalp and pulled his hair, repeating the process again and again. The view was the same as the last four years. The same knot stared back at him from the tenth board up from the spot where the ceiling met the wall. Its crack was only a fraction of an inch larger.

"Stop it," Sam protested from his bedding. "Ya drivin' me crazy."

"Stop what?" John replied.

"Stop tappin' ya fingers, pullin' ya hair and starin' at the ceiling'. Ya been doin' it for the last month. No way for a Hartford hero to act. What's troublin' ya?"

"Nothing."

"Damn there's not."

"Don't swear. You'll go to hell."

"I'm bettin' God's given me His grace. Anyways, I think you's bored. You're near twenty and still sleepin' in William's attic. I'll be outta' here the day my indenture ends. Do what I did and find a woman like my Abigail and get out of the house. I know lots of girls who'd be good wives. I'll help you meet 'em if ya like."

"Where will I build? Hartford's best land is taken. The first settlers have fertile land along the Connecticut and the others line the Little River to the west. There are more than fifty farms south of the Little River. Where do I go?"

"Just get outta' this attic." Sam said. "Besides, I need the space until my indenture ends in June. But right now, ya better be gettin' ready for supper at Deacon Hart's house. I gotta' go back to the fields."

Bridget's voice flowed up from the main floor, "John hurry. It's time to leave."

John changed into a clean doublet and breeches before sliding down the ladder from the attic. He met William and Bridget at the porch just before they walked outside.

It was a cold gray day and William and Bridget were bundled in heavy wool cloaks. The damp cold bit into John and he regretted not wearing a cloak over his doublet. They approached Hart's house through the trees lining the path from the main road.

Hart opened the door before they knocked.

"Welcome, welcome," Hart said. "Come in."

Hart led them into the house through the interior porch where there was a warm glow from the large fire in the hall adjoining it. To their left, stairs led to the house's second floor and to their right another stairway led down to its cellar. Hart led them past the cellar stairs into the hall where his wife, Sarah, waited for them.

On each side of the hall's massive fireplace was an intricately carved oak chair. Facing the fireplace was a fine-grained English oak bench. Carved into the bench's high back were four flying birds, three looked ahead and the larger one, its head cocked slightly to the bench's front, looked directly at anyone who might approach the bench to sit in it.

"What does the oak bench's symbol mean Deacon Hart?" John asked.

"It represents our family and the responsibility I have to protect it from any person or spirit who threatens it," Hart said.

"By the looks of the largest bird, it would not pay to be an intruder in this house," John quipped.

"This is serious John," Hart said. "Satan looks for our weaknesses and exploits them. One of our congregation may be an agent of Satan and we might not know it until it's too late."

John's face blanched. Standing beside him, William and Bridget shifted nervously back and forth.

"Ahem," Sarah cleared her throat. "Supper is ready. Follow us into the parlor."

The parlor was on the other side of the fireplace. A heavy two-inch rectangular oak table dominated the room. Seven oak chairs surrounded the table. Adjacent to the fireplace was a large dresser displaying pewter plates, cups and chargers. They passed through the parlor and stepped down into a lean-to kitchen Hart had added to the house.

A young woman was at the fire preparing supper. The aroma of beef stew mixed with fresh baked bread filled the air.

Sarah and her daughter Mary placed wooden trenchers and cloth napkins on the parlor table before serving the beef stew and baked bread. John ate his stew's broth with a wooden spoon while Hart grabbed a hot piece of meat with his napkin and tore into it with his teeth. Hart washed it down with a swallow of beer from his wooden noggin, which he promptly held out for Sarah to fill for the third time.

"I have a complaint William," Hart said slurring his words.

"What is it?" William asked.

"Your committee unfairly divided the common land," Hart belched. "Why did you give Matthew Allyn more than three times the acreage I got? I should have received as much as Allyn. After all, it was I who pushed our move from Massachusetts Bay. I also disagree with the decision to award William Goodwin more acres than me."

Before William could answer, Sarah motioned for Mary to follow her to the kitchen. Bridget also excused herself and moved to the kitchen. John and Daniel Hart sat quietly while the conversation between Hart and William continued.

"The committee considered many things," William said. "The forty acres you received were as many acres as Reverend Stone received and more than given to most other first settlers. John Steele received only a few more acres than you and Lieutenant Bull received only twelve acres."

"Your committee's decision has opened my eyes to what is happening," Hart said while quaffing down more beer. "The positions of power have been set and those with greater wealth continue to get more of it."

"But Stephen you are among the town's most important men with more land than dozens of other founders. Can't you see you are within the class of men you complain of?"

"Your committee didn't treat me that way," Hart said. "You and eleven other men were given twice the acres I got. I will always be in the second tier here. That's why I am seeking other opportunities."

"What opportunities?" William asked.

Hart leaned back in his chair and smiled broadly.

"Two weeks ago, I traveled west with several other men to visit land along a river the Indians call the Tunxis," Hart answered. "They call the place Tunxis Sepus, which means bend in the river. The soil there is much richer than here. The Tunxis Indian's village lies where the river bends. I am moving there as soon as I can."

"Tell me about your land in Tunxis Sepus," William asked.

"It's on the river. The soil is rich, and my harvests will be bountiful."

Excitement flowed up John's spine. He leaned forward across the table and looked at Hart.

"Has all the land there been taken?" John asked. "I'm looking for where I can build my own house, farm the land, and raise a family.

"Most land is claimed," Hart said. "But some men with claims have no plans to build soon. Two have plots near mine."

"I can't pay for their land," John said.

After an awkward silence, William spoke, "If you find land you want, I will help pay for it. You can repay me with crops you raise in the coming years."

John was stunned. He couldn't believe William's generosity. "Thank you, William," he stammered.

Sarah, Bridget and Mary returned to the table. After everyone ate, the two women and Mary, cleared the table as the men continued talking.

While William and Hart spoke, John rose from the table and glanced through an open window at ten-year-old Mary drawing water from her family's well. She cleaned the napkins, spoons and wooden trenchers the women took outside earlier. John marveled at how she worked with Sarah and Bridget as equals while washing everything. He was captivated by her infectious smile and laughter. Suddenly, Mary turned her head to the window and looked at him. Her smile disappeared as they stared at each other. Looking into her pale blue eyes, John felt he was looking into a soul far older than her age.

"Come back to the table John," William said, "We're talking about Tunxis Sepus again."

John sat down at the table facing the two older men with Daniel at his side.

"Talk to Thomas Newell and Joseph Kellogg," Hart said. "Joseph owns the plot next to me and Thomas, the plot next to him. Combined, these two plots are as large as mine and will give you room for a house and planting fields.

"Thank you," John said. "Do you know these men William?"

"No. They're from Wethersfield. I will arrange a meeting. I think both will sell if they can make a profit."

John's heart raced. He was going to own his own house and farm. His mind spun through the things he had to do. He would need to clear the land, gather stone to build a chimney, prepare timbers to erect the frame to his house, and acquire seeds for planting.

He was still thinking of what he needed to do when Sarah, Bridget and Mary returned to the hall. He fought unsuccessfully to keep his eyes off Mary. Her enthusiasm and cheerfulness were like a magnet attracting everyone in the room who starred at her with him. The man who married her would be fortunate indeed.

At that moment, twenty-five miles northeast, Richard Hawkes, Edward Roach and James Eastman were hiding on their horses in the trees surrounding the rendezvous cave. In the clearing, were Matunaaqd and Rowtag along with the Indians they brought to trade with that day. Hassun, Achak and Aranck followed two Dutchmen into the clearing. Behind, a third Dutchman guided two oxen pulling a cart containing a wooden box. When he stopped the cart, the Dutchman pried the box's top open with his knife and pulled out a musket. He held the musket high above his head with his right hand and with fiery eyes gazed down at the Indians there to trade.

"I brought twenty new snaphaunce muskets," the Dutchman said. "Now show me your pelts."

Hawkes's heart beat furiously as he watched from the trees. His excitement was tempered by the realization that the Dutchman raising the musket was the focus of attention and not him. Hiding his identity carried a price and that price was anonymity, something Hawkes detested.

Chapter 28

Sam Pierce dreamed of this day from the moment he signed his indenture to William Westwood. He worked for this day every moment during the seven years he served William after that. It was early June 1640, and Sam's friends would soon surround him. A month earlier, William gave Sam the land for his house as a gift for completing his indenture. The plot was south of the Little River on a road running parallel to the road along the Little River and within earshot of Lieutenant Bull's farm.

Sam, John Lee, and several other men, spent a month cutting down most the oak, pine, and maple trees at the back of Sam's plot to clear for farmland. They set aside the felled trees to build Sam's house. Using broadaxes and an adz, they stripped the felled trees of bark and squared them so they could be used for the house's frame. When there was enough squared timber for the frame, they dug a six-foot-deep cellar and lined it with stone. A large stone chimney rose from the cellar's floor at the back of the house with a fireplace set level with where the house's main floor would rest. They fit a wooden sill over the stone foundation with mortises cut wherever a post for the frame would stand.

They decided the house would need only six posts, three on each side of the house, for its frame. At the foot of each post, they cut enough wood away to leave a tenon joint with a hole which would fit into its mortise in the sill. Wooden round treenails were made to join the posts' tenons to the sill.

After all posts were prepared, the men laid each post on the ground near its mortises. The upper girts were fitted into the posts and pinned. On the day before the house raising, the men placed the two assembled frames on the ground by the side of the sill where it would be raised.

John, Sam, and his new bride Abigail arrived at the site of the house raising early in the morning. A bright sun foretold a hot afternoon. John and Sam set up tables for the women to place food they brought. After John and Sam checked to make sure everything was still in place on the frames laid around the cellar the day before, they sat at a table with Abigail and waited for the others to arrive.

"I have a gift for you," John said.

John brought a large bag from William's cart. He pulled a black leather doublet from the bag and handed it to Sam.

"You're now a free man," John said. "And a free man needs a handsome doublet to wear on special occasions."

Sam's eyes opened wide as he laid the doublet on the table, spreading it out so all its details were visible.

"What a great doublet!" Sam exclaimed. "Its white hooks and points at its shoulders stand out against its black leather. Thank you."

John beamed as he watched Sam put on the doublet. Abigail's fleshy face quivered with joy as Sam grinned when he finished putting it on.

The families who would help raise Sam's house started arriving a few hours later. William and Bridget Westwood came first. Bridget placed food on the tables while William took Sam to a massive old oak tree. John watched them. He couldn't hear what they said but it was easy to guess when he saw William place his right hand on Sam's shoulder.

Joseph and Katherine Barnard arrived with John Steele and his family a few minutes later. Now in her mid-forties Katherine's once petite frame was plump. Joseph was still handsome even though his light brown hair was receding and was touched with flecks of gray. John Steele continued to serve as a Deputy to the General Court after William left it to become a Hartford Selectman. John greeted Steele and his wife Rachel while Katherine Barnard took her children to a table.

John started worrying as noon approached. The young men who helped clear Sam's land and promised to raise his house were late. He glanced at Sam, who was busy talking with Joseph Barnard, apparently unconcerned about the time of day. John promised Sam he would lead the house raising and he was not going to put worry in Sam's head. He decided to deal with the situation himself.

An hour past and still the young men weren't there. John guessed he had only five more hours of good light to raise the house. As he thought about possible solutions to his dilemma, Deacon and Sarah Hart arrived with their children.

"I thought the house would be raised by now," Hart grumbled. "Where are the men doing it?"

"They're on their way," John lied.

Finally, John realized help lay little more than a stone's throw away. He rushed down the road he took from the bridge over the Little River that morning, all the while praying the man he sought would be home. He turned onto the path leading to the third house. He held his breath after knocking.

When the door opened and Lieutenant Bull appeared, he thanked God.

"Good day John," Bull said. "I'm surprised to see you. What's the occasion?"

"I need your help," John said. "Could you get some of your neighbors to help with a house raising."

"When would you need their help."

"This afternoon."

"You are in a tight spot. I'm glad you came to me. I will find some men and bring them to the house raising. Where is it?"

"It's on Sam Pierce's land three plots west on the road."

"I know the place. He and his friends laid a fine foundation. I'll bring men within the hour."

"Thank you, sir," John exhaled.

Bull laughed heartily. When he stopped laughing, he looked at John and shouted, "Go now. It's time for action."

Lieutenant Bull arrived at the house raising with sixteen militiamen. Surprised to see his fellow militiamen, John shook his head with laughter while thanking them for coming. He led them to the house's foundation where he placed them around it and in the cellar with poles to push the house's frames into place. When the men were in position, John climbed on the chimney's ledge and looked down on the people below.

"It's time to raise Sam's house!" John shouted.

Everyone stopped talking and looked up at John. He pointed at the militiamen beneath him. "Raise the frame!" he yelled.

In response, the three men on each frame simultaneously pushed the frame as high as they could with their hands. When they could push the frames no higher by hand, they placed wooden poles on the frames' top girts and pushed each frame's tenons into the mortises prepared for them in the sill. Meanwhile, the men in the cellar used their poles to keep the frames from passing vertical.

When both the front and rear frames were in place, the men holding the chimney girt and the rear girt on their shoulders steadied themselves on the benches they stood on and guided each girt's tenons into the front and rear girts' mortises after which the two men in the cellar climbed out and drove in the treenails holding each tenon in its mortise.

The people cheered as the frames were driven into place, while John breathed a sigh of relief. He could finally enjoy himself. He took Lieutenant Bull to the table where William and Deacon Hart were seated with Bridget and Sarah.

"An impressive house raising John," Hart said. "A nice touch bringing Lieutenant Bull and the militia."

John smiled, "Surprises often lead to other surprises."

Everyone left the house raising before sunset. Sam and Abigail were temporarily living in Joseph Barnard's attic and Abigail left with the Barnards so Sam could spend time at his house. Finally alone, Sam put on his new doublet and walked around his newly framed house staring with pride at every beam, the sill, and finally the fireplace.

Suddenly, he sensed movement near the road. He turned towards the movement. In the twilight he saw Richard Hawkes staring at him on a black stallion. Hawkes touched the brim of his hat with his right hand and nodded. He ignored Hawkes and turned back to his house where he came face to face with Edward Roach. Ten feet behind Roach was James Eastman. Sam often saw these men with Hawkes, but this was the first time he was close enough to talk to them. Roach's pock marked face was no more than three feet from him. Eastman smiled broadly.

"Edward, move away from Sam so I can talk to him," Eastman said moving closer.

Eastman moved forward until he and Sam's faces were three feet apart. Roach moved to Sam's left, placing himself between Sam and his nearest path to the woods. Eastman reached out and touched the collar of Sam's new doublet, playing with it with the fingers of his right hand.

"What a fine leather doublet," Eastman smirked.

Sam looked directly into Eastman's eyes and asked, "What's ya doin' here?"

"Your house raising, of course," Eastman answered.

"Ya missed it."

"Yes, I am afraid we're late. Fortunately for you we're not too late to make you an offer."

"What offer?"

"In October your fields will be bursting with corn ready for harvest," Eastman said. "When that time comes you will need to grind your corn. Our employer, Richard Hawkes, runs two mills in Hartford. His mills are in demand. Many of your new neighbors chose to give our employer ten percent of their cornmeal. In return, their corn is ground before that of others. They're also given protection from theft while their corn grows. We will offer this service to you when your corn ripens."

Sam adjusted his doublet and glared at Eastman. "Don't come back," Sam said. "I'm not interested."

Roach strode towards Sam. Sam backed away from the taller man.

"No need for violence," Eastman laughed. "I'm sure Edward just wants to get closer so he can hear us better. Right Edward?"

Roach immediately stopped and nodded.

"There's time for you to think about our offer," Eastman said. "We will come back in the fall and give you another chance to accept it. There are some who didn't accept our service at first who now use it after they suffered unexpected hardships. We hope you will choose to avoid such hardships."

"Ya threaten' me?" Sam snapped while glaring at Eastman.

Eastman smiled, "No, just pointing out facts."

With that, Edward and James turned and disappeared into the woods.

It was nearly dark when Sam turned to walk to the road to John Barnard's house. He saw the dim figure of Richard Hawkes on his black stallion ahead of him. Hawkes touched his right hand to the brim of his hat and smiled. Sam turned away. When he turned back Hawkes was gone. Sam decided he would be better prepared for his next meeting with Hawkes and his men.

PART FOUR
1642 - 1647

Chapter 29

Two years after Sam Pierce's house raising, John Lee, Sam, and three other young men left Hartford for Tunxis Sepus. It rained heavily the night before. The rain stopped before sunrise and when they left Hartford a bright April sun was trying, with little success, to dry the muddy road they were on.

The path to Tunxis Sepus was well known for the town now consisted of over a dozen houses perched along a narrow road called the Town Path, running north and south above the Tunxis River. The finest house belonged to Deacon Hart. Today, John and his friends would start clearing John's land, which was adjacent to Deacon Hart's, for the spring planting. William negotiated the price John paid for the two plots the previous autumn and helped John pay for them.

John and Sam were on horseback. Behind them, two oxen pulled a cart over the muddy road. On its bench, were the three young men John paid to help clear his land. In the cart were the beams and planks they would use to build a small hut to shelter them during the week they would be there. Edmund Aldburgh drove the cart, slumping forward as he held the reins to the oxen with his floppy broad brimmed hat hiding his face.

John turned to Sam as they rode and asked, "How is your farm doing?"

"Poorly the first season," Sam answered. "I had no plow and thought Indian mounds would work. They didn't. After the corn started growin', the mounds were dug up by vermin and Indians."

"I've never heard of Indians damaging our crops. How do you know it was Indians?"

Sam hesitated while he stared at the ground. He couldn't tell John he suspected that Richard Hawkes's men did it. Finally, he lifted his head and looked at John, "Well, I guessed it was Indians as I couldn't figure who else coulda' did it. I got a plow now and William's lending me the oxen when we finish clearin' your land. This year's planting will be better."

"You confuse me sometimes Sam."

"Well, you're the one that's confused. Why'd it take ya so long to start preparing your own land?"

"William became ill and I needed to stay for another year to help with his fields. Also, I didn't want to build my house in Tunxis Sepus until I bought land next to Deacon Hart's house for that's where I will build my house. William helped me buy it, but I can't wait until I build my house to plant my fields."

They traveled for two hours before the road began to slide down a gradual slope.

"Hav' ya' heard from any of Richard Hawkes's customers about his offer to mill their corn before other customers for ten percent of their corn?" Sam asked.

"No. One would be a fool to give up ten percent of their labor for earlier grinding. Why do you ask?"

Sam hesitated. Their horses strode for several paces before Sam turned to John, "No particular reason. Where does William get his corn ground?"

"He takes it to Deacon Hart's new mill on the Little River."

"And no one's pressed this additional service upon William?"

"What do you mean pressed?"

For the third time, Sam hesitated while their horses forged ahead. Finally, he turned to John, "I mean did Richard Hawkes offer this service to him."

No, it's never been offered. If it was, William would refuse it for it has no value."

Soon they were out of the forest and for the first time bathed in the sun. Below them, the Tunxis River stretched from north to south where it bent to the west. They turned south on the Town Path paralleling the river a quarter mile above it. It was not a wide path, with barely enough room to accommodate their cart. Within a few minutes John pulled back on his horse's reins and pointed below with an outstretched hand.

"This is my land," he declared with a broad smile.

Below them a field spread to the trees along the river. It was dotted with oak, maple, and pine trees, as well as flowers and bushes, which increased in number near the river.

"Not as many trees to fell as our first year in Hartford, but still lots of work to do to clear this land," John said.

The men spent the morning building their shelter after which Sam took the other men to identify the trees to be felled. Deacon Hart and his teenage son Daniel arrived just after the men left.

"Welcome to Tunxis Sepus John," Hart said. "How long will you be here this time?"

"A week."

"Sarah and Mary are preparing supper for you and your men," Hart said. "Come over in the afternoon."

John's pulse quickened when he heard Mary's name. At thirteen, she was a beautiful young woman. While once his feelings towards her were like the affection of an older brother, he now felt a longing stirring deep within him. It was not lust, for he experienced it while with young women in town. This feeling was much deeper. It was like an ache for something he desperately wanted but was uncertain he could possess.

The sun was halfway to the horizon after the men cleared three trees. John led them to Hart's house which was nearly identical to the house Hart left in Hartford. Hart led John and his men to the back of the house where Sarah and Mary had placed food on a large oak table.

"Do you have many neighbors?" John asked Hart.

"A few, but most who own land here bought it as an investment and still live in Hartford.

"When will you build your house?" Hart asked.

"As soon as I can."

John heard footfalls and turned back to see Sarah Hart walking from the house towards them.

"Stephen, John, come join us for supper," Sarah called.

Sam and the rest of John's men shuffled about impatiently around the weathered table, anxious to begin eating, when John and Hart arrived. There were no chairs. They would eat standing around the table using the spoons, trenchers and napkins Sarah and Mary set out. John was disappointed when he realized Mary was not there and wondered if she would come later. He thought of asking Sarah if Mary was coming, but dismissed the idea as being too obvious in its intent.

The men fell silent when John and Hart reached the table. Hart glanced around the table at the men and said, "Welcome to my home. Bow your heads as we thank our Lord for our blessings."

When all were silent, Hart bowed, "Almighty and everlasting God, bless the food we're about to eat. May we enjoy this meal in the moderation that we must display in all things in life and never take more from the world than we need, through Jesus Christ our Lord and only savior, Amen."

John smiled to himself, for while the prayer was common, it sounded odd when it was offered by Hart whose idea of moderation so clearly differed from William Westwood's.

The men ate while the afternoon sun continued its slide toward the tree line west over the river. John was not hungry but took a piece of hot pork when Sam shoved a trencher of food in front of him and later ate a small bowl of beef stew that Sarah insisted, he eat. Most of the time, he simply watched the others, sipped on the beer in his tankard, and talked with Deacon Hart. All the while he waited for Mary to arrive.

"I just bought John Bronson's sawmill at the east of town on the Mill Brook," Hart said. "I am building a gristmill there. Richard Hawkes will run it along with my two gristmills in Hartford."

John merely nodded, for he had no desire to talk about Richard Hawkes. But he wondered just how much Hart knew of Hawkes.

"What do you know of Richard Hawkes?" John asked.

"All I need to know. My friend Robert Rose recommended him after he made a great profit for his timber business in Boston and he has done a good job running my grist mills in Connecticut."

After eating, John gathered the men for the return to his field. He felt empty for it was clear Mary was not coming. Sam led the men back up to the Town Road on their way to John's fields while John stayed behind to say goodbye to Deacon Hart and Sarah. After they entered their house, John walked up the slope towards the Town Road.

Then he saw her. She was at the front corner of Hart's house forty feet ahead of him. She looked at him as he walked up the slope towards her. Her slender frame was wrapped in a dark green embroidered skirt with a matching bodice. Her light brown hair was tied in a bun at the back of her head. As he moved closer, he was overwhelmed by her pure complexion and pale blue eyes.

"Good day Mary, it's good to see you," he said.

"Good day, she answered. "I was coming to help my mother clear the table. I thought everyone was gone."

"I'm the only one left," he said.

He turned away from her and continued up the slope. Her eyes followed him as he walked up to the Town Path. She worried she had been rude. Still, he surprised her, and since her father forbid her to come to the supper they had set for the "rough" men who would be coming, she was afraid of what her father might say if he saw her talking to him. She liked John. She liked his open smile and handsome honest face. His hazel eyes seemed to open to his soul and his pleasant voice was just as pure as the soul she saw within him. He was like an older brother, who unlike her brother Daniel, respected her. She was comfortable in his presence and never nervous. She would be nice to him at church on the Sabbath.

Chapter 30

It had been a month since John cleared his land in Tunxis Sepus. As he approached the Suckiaug village, he saw the poles to his left. They were fashioned from birch trees, seven feet tall, three inches in diameter, and stretched from the road to the river. A heavy morning mist rising from the river engulfed them. Through the mist, he saw a man's head atop the pole nearest him. A few mosquitos, gnats, and flies flew around it, but the head was too weathered and dry to provide a meal for them.

Men's scalps hung from the tops of most of the other poles. Some scalps were decorated with a feather. Most were not, for their families were far away. He knew this place. It was called Pequot Heads. It was here Sequassen, the Suckiaug's sachem, mounted his trophies from the war with the Pequots.

John wondered if the Suckiaug would welcome him. He left William's house just before sunrise on a gray May morning. He was alone and on foot. He wore the same buff coat he wore during the Pequot War. He hoped the coat would remind the Suckiaugs he once fought with them against the Pequots because now they accused the English of siding with their Mohegan enemies.

It should not have surprised anyone when the victorious tribes fought each other for the territory and power available once the Pequots were destroyed. So it was that Miantinomo, the Narragansetts' sachem, and Uncas, the Mohegans' sachem, fought over the land once filled by their mutual enemy. At the same time, Uncas pushed west against the Suckiaugs, forcing them into an alliance with the Narragansetts. So far, the conflict had been one of stealth and subterfuge. Uncas claimed Sequassen tried to kill him with poison, with sorcery and, most recently, by having his warriors fire arrows at him as he traveled down the Connecticut River in a dugout canoe. Sequassen denied this.

Efforts at mediation by the English failed and everyone knew war between the two tribes was inevitable. When war came John's friends Huritt, Chogan and Etchemin would be caught up in it. John could wait no longer for soon it would be too late.

The mist lifted as he entered the village, which spread more than three quarters of a mile along the river from the palisaded fort Sequassen built years before. The fort was fifty feet in diameter and contained just enough room within its palisade of upright trees to accommodate only one long house and three wigwams. Few villagers would reach the protection of its walls if the village was attacked without warning. Their long houses and smaller wigwams lay unprotected between the upland meadow to the west and the river to the east.

John followed the main path into the village. It led past the fort until it turned south along the river. Smoke from the fires, both within and outside the long houses and wigwams, dotted the sky. To his left were two Tunxis men hollowing out the charred remnants of a large white pine log with metal scrapers to make a dugout canoe. When the men saw him, the older one turned to John and asked menacingly in Algonquin, "Englishman, what are you doing here?"

"I'm here to see my friend Huritt," John answered in Algonquin. "Can you tell me how I can find him?"

"I doubt Huritt is your friend," the man said.

The younger man picked up an axe and both men slowly moved towards John.

"No Englishman is our friend," the older man said. "You are not welcome here."

"I'm not your enemy," John said.

"What you say is just words. The English's actions speak the truth and the truth is that you will help the Mohegans destroy us because you want our land."

"What actions do you speak of?" John asked.

"You allowed the Mohegans to take most of our land and when we asked for your help you did nothing to force them to give it back," answered the older man, his voice now trembling in anger. "When shares of the Pequots' land were given to the tribes who helped the English fight them you gave little to us. Instead, you gave most to the Mohegans, increasing their power. And, your people built farms up to our village and set your cattle and hogs to graze in the meadows where there was once deer."

John knew the man was right. It was why he came to the village to offer the Suckiaugs help. It would be useless to tell this man this, for John knew he couldn't help them stop what was happening. He needed to see Huritt, for he would understand his offer.

"I'm sorry I came to your village uninvited," John said. "I will leave and go back to the road I came on. Tell Huritt, John Lee is waiting for him there."

The older Suckiaug's expression softened and the younger Suckiaug returned to the canoe.

"I will tell Huritt," the older man said.

John returned to the road and waited. He regretted not coming to see Huritt earlier for he didn't know how bad things were for his people. Since the war with the Pequots, John, like everyone else in Hartford, ignored the Suckiaugs. Uncas and the Mohegans were Connecticut's strongest ally against the Pequots and they were the tribe favored by the English. Still, John thought of the Suckiaugs often for he felt he owed them his service. Until recently he didn't know what this service was. Now he did, and if Huritt came he would offer it.

He stopped standing after an hour and sat along the damp road on a fallen tree in the wet grass. The sun was high, and he removed his buff leather coat in the heat. Across the road he saw scores of poles of Pequot heads and scalps with their hair blowing in the light breeze rising from the river. To his right, he watched the Suckiaug village come to life. The women scurried about planting the mounds near their homes while a few men walked down to the river with spears to fish from the small birch bark canoes along the shore.

By mid-afternoon, John decided Huritt was not coming. Even so, he waited longer. His wait was rewarded within a few minutes when he saw Huritt and his son, Chogan, walking towards him.

He was surprised with how much Huritt had changed. His lean muscular body sagged at his once taught stomach and under his arms. As Huritt got closer, John saw that Huritt's black hair was now filled with streaks of gray. John stood up from the dead tree where he sat as Huritt and Chogan neared him.

"Why are you here?" Huritt grunted. "Your visit has angered my people. I called a meeting of our council when I received your message. We met all morning. Many told me I should send you away; few felt I should invite you in. Our troubles with the Mohegans are great and your people turned away from us to them, forgetting all we did for you in your first months here. In the end, the council left it to me to decide what to do about your visit. So again, I ask, what are you doing here?"

John's heart sank. He wondered what he could say to convince Huritt he could help his people? What once seemed to him to be an important mission now seemed like nothing more than a gesture lacking significance. Finally, he mustered the courage to speak.

"I can't make things better," John began. "This is beyond my control. The Suckiaugs' world has changed. I want you to prosper in this changed world and the best way to do this is to learn about the English world while still remembering your own way of life. I offer to teach your people about the English, their language, and their ways."

"There are many who want to teach us your ways," Huritt said.

"How will what we learn from you be different?"

"They demand you conform to what they teach and want you to live as Englishmen and worship our God. I will teach your people without making such demands."

"It would be better to train us to fight with English muskets," Huritt answered.

"Knowing that won't save your people from what is to happen but knowing how to live in that world may make their lives better. Will you let me teach your people how to live with the English?"

A slight smile crossed Huritt's face. He touched John's shoulder with his hand while pointing to the fallen tree John sat on earlier.

"Come sit," Huritt said. "Let us talk."

Huritt's face was haggard. His dark brown eyes were listless as he looked at John while they sat together with Chogan on the decaying pine tree's remnants.

"Look across the path at the heads and scalps of our defeated enemy," Huritt said. "Before they died, they knew the sadness my people feel now. But they never felt the hopelessness we will soon feel, for they died fighting. My people are resigned to our tribe's slow death after we fight the Mohegans. I want my people to have hope and to keep their spirit after the battle. What you offer won't change the coming battle's result, but it will offer my people hope when it ends."

The two men looked into each other's eyes for a moment. Huritt touched John's shoulder.

"You are my people's friend," Huritt said. "Your heart is pure and your offer honest. Sequassen camps in Tunxis Sepus for it is too dangerous for him here. We will go to Tunxis Sepus to see him."

"Thank you," John whispered.

Dark clouds were churning in from the west as Huritt stood before the decaying pine tree and looked up at the deteriorating sky.

"Soon there will be a battle here. We will fight to save our village but there are too many Mohegans and many of our people will be killed. There are English who help the Mohegans, including a dark Englishman. It is said he has given the Mohegans muskets. We've only a handful of muskets to fight them with. When the battle comes don't try to help us. My people will need your help when it is over. You must live so you can help them then."

A driving rain was falling when John, Huritt and Chogan reached the Tunxis village. It was just before sunset and they stood before the bark covered long house where Sequassen had stayed for the past three weeks. The guards outside the long house glanced uneasily at John as Huritt and Chogan talked to them twenty feet away. The rain slapped against John's face as he looked up the slope above him where the English built their houses. A patchwork of newly planted fields cut into the pines, oaks and maples. Each field was neatly laid out and its soil dark.

All John could see was the long house's fire when the guard pulled back the deerskin covering its entrance. Two men and a boy sat on woven mats spread over three-foot-high birch wood benches. The older man sat to the younger man's right. The boy, who appeared about ten, sat on the younger man's left.

Huritt motioned for John and Chogan to sit next to them. The older man was not handsome, but his face was strong. The younger man looked at the older man without speaking while the boy stared into the fire.

"I brought John Lee of Hartford to see you Sequassen," Huritt announced. "He wants to help our people by teaching them the English language and English ways. He asks for nothing in return. I brought him here for your decision."

Sequassen turned and stared at John. The younger man did the same. The lodge's only sound was the sizzle of rain drops falling through the hole in the roof and striking the rocks surrounding the fire.

"John Lee was with the first English to come to Suckiaug and is my friend," Huritt announced. "He's a brave warrior and was trained by the great English warrior Lieutenant Bull. He fought with us in the war against the Pequots."

Sequassen smiled. The younger man, who was slumped against the wall, sat up straight. The boy looked up from the fire at John for the first time.

"You were trained to fight by Lieutenant Bull?" Sequassen asked. "He's the greatest of all English warriors and is a friend of our people. He's also friends with the Mohegans and their sachem Uncas. What will he do when our tribes fight?"

John answered immediately, "I haven't spoken to Lieutenant Bull about this, but I know he would never turn against a friend. He'll not take sides."

"I hope you are right, but he's now a stronger friend of Uncas and the English leaders favor Uncas over us," Sequassen said. "Uncas is good at saying things gaining him favor and he'll say whatever it takes to gain the power the Pequots once had."

"I know Lieutenant Bull," John replied. "He'll not fight with the Mohegans against the Suckiaugs."

"What will you do John Lee?" Sequassen asked. "Huritt says you want to help our people. Will you fight with us against the Mohegans?"

"I fought with both the Mohegans and the Suckiaugs against the Pequots. I will take neither side."

"You offer nothing we can use now."

"What I offer the Suckiaugs and the Tunxis is knowledge that will help them deal with the English and wise like Uncas is now. Uncas is favored by the English because he has this knowledge and uses it to his advantage."

"Tell me of this knowledge my people don't know."

"It's knowledge of the English's ways. I will teach your people the English language and customs, how they trade, how they build their towns and how they make their tools. I will also teach you how the

English think. If you know how they think you will be strong like Uncas when you deal with them."

Sequassen looked closely into John's eyes. John stared back resolutely. The sound of rain drops sizzling on the fire's circle of rocks again filled the long house. Sequassen nodded towards the younger man.

"This man is Pethus," Sequassen said. "He's the Tunxis' sachem. The boy is his son Ahamo. Wait outside while I talk to Pethus."

Huritt led John from the long house. It was twilight and raining heavily. They covered their heads in the dark rain with deerskins Sequassen gave them.

"I am glad you came to our village," Chogan said. "Until you did, I believed it was a mistake for my people to help yours the first winter you were here. I felt I betrayed our people when we led Reverend Hooker's people to our land. Now I know I was wrong. I hope Sequassen accepts your offer."

"Thank you Chogan. I should not have waited so long to come to you."

The darkness was broken when a Suckiaug guard pulled back the deerskin allowing the firelight inside to spread through the raindrops to them. The guard looked at John.

"Sequassen made his decision," the guard said. "Follow me."

"What of us?" Huritt asked.

"The Englishman must come alone."

John followed the guard towards the fire while Huritt and Chogan drew back through the deerskin covered doorway into the wet darkness. He stood before Sequassen.

"You have an honest face John Lee," Sequassen said. "Huritt likes you and your offer is true. But you won't fight with us and that's what we need now. Your teaching must wait until our war with the Mohegans ends. I cannot accept your offer now."

"I will come back then," John nodded.

Chapter 31

It was dark when Chogan woke in his father's long house on a July morning two months after Sequassen rejected John Lee's offer. He lay under the deerskin blanket, more asleep than awake, watching transfixed as lights from the outside played against the woven reed wall just inside the long house's entrance. The lights danced up and down on the wall. Sometimes they lit the entire wall, other times they lit none of it. Their melodic movement, coupled with the crackling of twigs under the people's feet walking past the door, added to the dreamlike quality of his waking moments. Then he smelled smoke.

Fully awake, Chogan looked about the long house. Huritt slept near their fire's remains on a deerskin covered bench lining the wall. Kimi slept on the same bench on the fire's opposite side. As he drew a breath, Chogan was certain he smelled smoke. He flung off his deerskin and rushed through the door. The wigwams before him were dark. But above them in the distance, clouds of smoke churned in a throbbing light. The village's north half was on fire and the crackling of twigs he heard in his dreamlike state was the sound of burning wigwams and long houses. He heard the pop of musket fire as he ran back into the long house.

"Father wake," he yelled. "The Mohegans have attacked."

Huritt sprung to his feet. Wearing a leather breech clout and sandals, he picked up his bow and arrows. Chogan did the same.

Huritt grabbed Chogan's shoulder, looked into his eyes, and calmly announced, "This is the attack we feared. Uncas will destroy our village unless we stop him. Go wake the people in the wigwams and long houses to the north and order other warriors to wake those to the south. Send all the women and children to the South Meadow and then bring as many warriors as you can to the north planting field. I will meet you there after I take Kimi to the South Meadow."

Chogan raced into the fires' pulsating light. Huritt turned to Kimi, who was gathering all the valuables she could carry.

"Stop Kimi, there's no time," Huritt insisted. "Go with me to the South Meadow. When the battle is over you can come back for our things."

"But what if the Mohegans burn our long house? We will lose everything."

"We can get new things. Leave with me so I can fight the Mohegans and not worry about you."

Kimi began sobbing and threw her arms around Huritt's waist, burying her face in his bare chest. He hugged her gently, then pushed her back while holding his hands on her shoulders and staring into her eyes.

"Come with me Kimi," he said. "We've lived a long life together. You must live for our son Chogan and for the children he'll have. You must live because the story of our life together will live if you can tell it. I will be stronger tonight if I know you are alive to tell of the love between Huritt and Kimi."

Kimi stopped sobbing and pulled back from Huritt. She touched his hands with hers as the flickering lights, now brighter than ever, raced across the woven reed wall. She leaned her head against his chest. Huritt wrapped his arms around her pulling her tight, then gently pushed her away.

"We have to leave," he whispered.

He picked up his bow and slung his quiver of arrows over his shoulder. They ran together through the light spreading from the fires to the north on a small path through the village towards the South Meadow. The village's people were now awake and many were outside their wigwams. The women and children stood frightened, while the men looked about trying to decide what to do.

"Take the women and children to the South Meadow," Huritt yelled as he and Kimi ran along the path. "Then join me and Chogan at the north planting field. Bring your weapons for tonight we fight the Mohegans."

It only took a few moments for them to reach the South Meadow. Already dozens of women and children were standing together in the tall grass. All looked north where the view was unbroken by trees. The fires' flames rose high above the burning wigwams and long houses. Dark smoke billowed still higher. In the distance, the pop of muskets filled the air over the lighter pop of burning wood. The acrid smell of smoke floated over them, its intensity varying with the breeze.

Huritt turned to Kimi. She smiled gently and reached out with her hand. He squeezed her hand tightly for an instant while smiling before nodding and releasing it. Without hesitating, he turned and strode back toward the fires.

The field was bright with firelight when Huritt reached the village. The fires' dry heat mixed with the night's sweltering heat. Sweat glistened on his biceps and his bare chest as he strode toward the warriors gathered in the field waiting for him. Chogan saw him first. Soon the other men saw him. When he emerged from the smoke and into the firelight's fullness the men raised their bows and hatchets above their heads and let loose a war cry so loud it drowned out the fires' noise.

Huritt walked through the men towards the fires. Chogan and the other men fell in behind. They walked swiftly through the abandoned wigwams not yet on fire. As they moved north, the popping of muskets grew louder, the fires' heat hotter, and their sight more clouded by smoke. The pace of Huritt's stride remained constant until he reached the first burning wigwam. It was difficult to see more than thirty feet into the smoke. Huritt caught brief glimpses of Mohegan warriors throwing burning wood onto the roofs of wigwams and moving in and out of other wigwams with glowing sticks as the smoke floated in the breeze.

Huritt ordered his men closer to the fires. When they were in the smoke, he turned to Chogan and four other warriors and ordered, "Follow me. Keep low to avoid being seen by the Mohegans. Fire at them when I stop."

Huritt looked at Etchemin, "Guide the other men to the path along the river when Chogan and I are in the smoke. Keep them there until we join you. Even though they will want to, don't let the men follow us into the smoke?"

"I will," Etchemin promised.

Huritt led Chogan and the four warriors he chose into the smoke. Within twenty feet it was difficult to see behind them. Before them the burning wigwams made it possible to see only slightly better and even then, their sight existed only when the breeze off the river temporarily parted the smoke. Below their feet the uneven surface caused by the mounds in the planting field gave way to more even compacted earth. Huritt knew they were out of the planting field and among the wigwams. Vague shapes moved before them in the smoke.

"Stay low," Huritt yelled above the roar of the wigwams' burning birch frames and bark walls.

The smoke thinned and they stood on flat ground between six wigwams. Three Mohegan warriors were thirty feet ahead of them. The Mohegans were examining two wigwams they were about to torch and didn't see them. Huritt knew they had to act.

"Fire!" Huritt yelled.

Two Mohegans turned towards Huritt as the Suckiaug's arrows arrived. One was struck in his chest and thigh. He fell and gasped for air. Blood spewed from his mouth with each breath. The second Mohegan was struck in the neck just below his chin. As he reached for the arrow, a second arrow drove through his left eye. He fell to the ground screaming. The third Mohegan saw the two other Mohegan's fall. He was the target of only one arrow which fell harmlessly at his feet. He quickly fled north into the smoke.

"Retreat," Huritt ordered. "The Mohegans will soon be on us. Retreat to the planting field. We will move north on the path along the river and attack their flank."

No sooner did Huritt speak than two flashes of light appeared in the smoke ahead of them. The flashes were immediately followed by musket pops.

"Drop," Huritt yelled. But it was too late. One musket ball slammed into the left arm of the warrior next to Huritt while the second ball glanced off Huritt's head. Blood flowed down his forehead and across his nose and chin.

Huritt and the other warriors dropped to the ground as three more flashes appeared in the smoke. This time the balls missed.

"Are you alright?" Chogan yelled.

"Yes," Huritt replied. "Retreat to the planting field."

Blood poured from Huritt's scalp as he led the warriors back to the planting field. He pressed his palm against his head and by the time they reached the field the blood flow had almost stopped. They sat the warrior with the wounded arm down in the field. His shattered arm made it impossible for him to draw his bow or lift his hatchet. They placed his knife in his good hand. He faced north with a determined look, waiting for the Mohegans.

A tall broad-shouldered man entered the field from the road separating it from the South Meadow. As Huritt moved towards him, he saw three more men enter the field from the road. They followed the tall man. Then Huritt and his men recognized the tall man. It was Sequassen. "Whoop, whoop" they yelled as Sequassen approached them. Huritt went forward to meet him.

"Mohegans?" Sequassen asked.

"Yes. I'm taking these men to the river to join others already there. We will attack their flank."

"I will stay here with my men," Sequassen said. "We will draw the Mohegans to us while you and your men move up river. We can still save the southern half of our village. Now go!"

Huritt led his men towards the river. A light breeze thinned out most of the smoke as they neared it. A dozen muskets cracked behind them.

"Faster," Huritt yelled. "The Mohegans reached the planting field and are firing at Sequassen and his men. We have to outflank them before they overrun them."

"Look ahead," Chogan yelled. "There's Etchemin and our warriors."

Huritt peered through the veil of smoke and began striding rapidly towards the ghost-like figures of Etchemin and the other warriors. Chogan and the rest of the warriors trailed him.

"Follow me up the path," Huritt ordered when the two groups met.

There were now nineteen warriors with Huritt. The sound of the Mohegan's muskets grew fainter and the fires' light was now on their left as they moved north along the river. The flames of the burning wigwams swam together and rose in the sky. They saw Mohegans to their left moving south through their village between the wigwams.

"Do you see the Mohegans moving to the planting field?" Chogan asked.

"Yes, they will burn the whole village if we don't attack now," Huritt said. "Take five warriors and stay here with them to guard our retreat. I'll lead the others into the village and strike them."

"Let me go with you," Chogan said. "We should attack with all our men and not split our force in two."

"There will be wounded when we return. They will need your help when the battle is over. You can't help them if you and your men are also wounded."

Huritt turned toward the fires and motioned for Etchemin and the other warriors to follow him. As they moved toward the fires, Huritt looked back at Chogan and smiled. By the time Chogan smiled back, Huritt couldn't see him for he and his men were now in the smoke.

In the smoke they were safe. But Huritt didn't want to be safe; he wanted to kill Mohegans. He knew his attack would be a surprise, for the Mohegans were intent on attacking south and expected the river to guard their flank. Once they were discovered though, the Mohegans would attack them in a number and with a fury that would quickly destroy their small force. Huritt knew their first attack must be devastating for there would not be a second one.

The path the Mohegans followed through the wigwams was well lit and less smoky than areas closer to the wigwams. Huritt would attack from near the wigwams. Fifty yards ahead, he saw three wigwams burning along the path the Mohegans were moving on. They would attack there.

"Etchemin, take ten men across the path the Mohegans are on," Huritt ordered loud enough to be heard over the fires' pops and cracks. "Place five men near each wigwam. I will hide near the wigwam on this side of the path with the other men. We will attack the next Mohegans."

Etchemin took ten warriors across the path. He saw several Mohegans moving towards them from the north. Masked by the smoke, he was certain he and his men weren't seen by them. He and his men spread around the two wigwams, trying to find places where the heat was less.

At the same time, Huritt ordered the men with him to crouch near the burning wigwam and wait for the Mohegans. Everyone's eyes focused on the path north.

At least twenty Mohegans were within range of their arrows. The Suckiaugs' looked at Huritt, waiting for his order to attack. Huritt waited as the Mohegans moved closer. The first Mohegan was short and wiry. He was past the wigwams. The last Mohegan was much taller with a solid muscular chest. He was barely within range of the Suckiaugs' arrows. The Mohegans glistened with sweat from the fires' heat as they walked past the wigwams.

Huritt waived his right arm forward and moved from the smoke near the burning wigwam. Instantly, a dozen Suckiaug arrows flew out of the smoke of the wigwams on each side of the path towards the Mohegans. Two arrows struck the short wiry Mohegan. The first arrow flew into his right thigh. He screamed a warning to the Mohegans following him. His warning was cut short by the second arrow which struck him in his ear.

Three arrows struck a Mohegan walking six feet behind the short wiry Mohegan. One struck his right shoulder. As he reached to pull it out with his left hand, another arrow struck him in his chest. It was quickly followed by the third arrow, which hit him in the neck just below his chin. Blood gushed out of the Mohegan's neck as he grabbed the arrow with both hands before falling to the ground. Huritt fired an arrow at the tall broad-shouldered Mohegan, trailing the other Mohegans. It struck him in the arm. The Mohegan looked up and met Huritt's eyes.

"Whoop, whoop, whoop," Huritt yelled as he charged. Without hesitation, the other Suckiaugs charged with him. They hit the Mohegans like a buck deer, driving ten of them to the ground. The pairs of men pulled each other to the ground and grappled in the dirt.

Huritt charged the tall broad-shouldered Mohegan. He pulled his hatchet from his belt as he charged. The tall Mohegan braced himself. Huritt slammed into the Mohegan with his chest. Any other man would have dropped, but the Mohegan didn't. Instead, Huritt felt as if he struck an unforgiving wall. Both men were stunned they weren't on the ground from the impact. They looked at each other, momentarily frozen. Huritt charged the Mohegan again. This time he swung his hatchet grazing the Mohegan's chest. Blood began to mix with the Mohegan's sweat and roll down his chest.

The Mohegan thrust his knife at Huritt. Huritt pushed the knife away with his left hand, slicing his hand in the process. The Mohegan expected Huritt to back away from the knife and was unprepared for the blow Huritt delivered with his hatchet. The hatchet struck the Mohegan in the shoulder. It dug deep into muscle and the Mohegan gasped in agony as he dropped to the dirt. Huritt's next blow struck the Mohegan in the back of his head, killing him instantly.

The grappling continued between Huritt's men and the Mohegans. Some fought in the dirt, while others were locked together trying to push each other to the ground. The sound of yelling and the clash of hatchets and knives merged with the sound of the fires surrounding them.

The fusillade of arrows reduced the Mohegan's superiority in numbers, but they still had more warriors than the Suckiaugs. Huritt knew the Mohegans would bring more men to the fight and with them there would be muskets. They had to kill as many Mohegans as possible before then.

Huritt reached down and grabbed the long hair of a Mohegan grappling with Etchemin. Etchemin pushed the Mohegan up with his knees and Huritt swung his hatchet into the Mohegan's back. The Mohegan let out a groan as Huritt pushed him into the dirt. Etchemin drove his knife into the Mohegan's chest and his groaning stopped.

Chogan heard the noise of the fight as he and his men stood near the river. The movement of fighting appeared and disappeared in the smoke as it wafted in the light breeze off the river.

"We must help our brothers," a Suckiaug warrior yelled at Chogan.

"Yes, yes, we must go now before they're killed," yelled another warrior.

"No, no," Chogan retorted. "Huritt told us to stay here to help the wounded after the fight and save our people who fled."

"If you want to stay here you can, but I'm going to help them," shouted the first man.

Chogan knew Huritt was right. His people would need him and his men to help them after the battle. But he knew his men would enter the fight without him if he didn't give them a plan that would make them feel they were helping.

"We will move north along the river and attack the Mohegans from behind," Chogan said.

Chogan ran north along the river. Two of his men followed him immediately while the other two stayed behind. Chogan looked back at them. Both men started running after him.

Within moments, Chogan and his men were positioned north of the fight. There, through the shifting smoke, Chogan watched Huritt and his warriors wrestling with the Mohegans about forty yards away while more Mohegans flooded down the path into the fight.

Chogan looked north to where the Mohegans came from. There, at the edge of the Suckiaug village, he saw three Englishmen on horseback watching the fight. The breeze from the river was stronger and the smoke was blowing west, improving Chogan's visibility.

Chogan recognized the three Englishmen. They were the same men he, Huritt and Etchemin surprised on the trail to Suckiaug when the men challenged John Lee and his friend Sam on their journey to Suckiaug with Reverend Hooker's congregation. Their leader, who Chogan knew to be Richard Hawkes, sat erect on his black horse, seemingly oblivious to his proximity to the fight.

Chogan looked back at the fight. When the smoke cleared, he saw what was happening. He watched his father strike down two Mohegans with blows from his hatchet. Meanwhile, Etchemin took his foe to the ground. Chogan's spirit rose as it appeared his brothers might win a victory. His father swung his hatchet again. This time the blow split open the head of a thick chested Mohegan. Chogan was certain his father was invincible.

At that moment, Chogan heard musket fire. He looked north from where the sound came. There, standing in front of his black horse, was Richard Hawkes, with smoke rising from his musket's barrel pointed towards the fight in front of him. Chogan looked back and saw his father fall. His father lay motionless as more Mohegans joined the fight. Nausea swept over him as he realized his father was dead.

Their leader down and the battle lost, the surviving Suckiaugs fled towards the river. The Mohegans flooded the fight scene and Chogan knew it was impossible to retrieve the bodies of his father and the other dead Suckiaug. There was nothing to do but take the survivors with him and his men back to the South Meadow, where the tribe's women and children waited.

As they retreated, Chogan looked back and watched Hawkes walk to his father's body. Hawkes bent down over the body for a moment before standing and thrusting his left hand into the sky. Chogan saw a black tuft of hair in Hawkes's hand. Hawkes waived it above his head. Chogan collapsed to his knees. Chogan heard the Mohegan's victory cries as one of his men helped him to his feet.

There were a dozen men at the bridge over the Little River when John Lee and Lieutenant Bull reached it the morning after the battle. Nervous excitement filled the men's faces as they approached them.

"Tell us about the battle," a man asked.

"We're going there to find out," Bull answered. "A few people from the South Plantation came to the meetinghouse this morning. They said the Mohegans destroyed the Suckiaugs' village. Go to the meetinghouse and wait for us. We will report what we find."

A bright sun had climbed above the eastern horizon when John and Bull passed the Dutch fort. Wisps of smoke floated around them as they passed Pequot Heads. There they saw the first burned-out wigwams in the north end of the Suckiaug village. Some of the wigwams' bark covered roofs were burned through, leaving their bark walls intact but scorched. The bark roofs and walls of many of the wigwams were completely burned away, leaving only scorched birch wood frames standing. Some of the wigwams were burned to the ground, leaving only the scorched ground where they stood as evidence they ever existed.

Farther south, past the village's planting field, flames and smoke poured out of the nearby wigwams.

"The most serious fighting occurred around the wigwams below the planting field," Bull announced. "These wigwams were set afire after those north of us."

John stared at the burned-out wigwams. Between two of them he saw Richard Hawkes astride his black stallion. James Eastman was hunched forward on a dirty gray horse forty feet to Hawkes's right, with Edward Roach sitting atop a brown horse next to him.

"Richard Hawkes and his men are near the wigwams," John announced.

"No surprise," Bull answered. "If there's mischief Hawkes is usually there."

John and Bull walked through the planting field's mounds towards Hawkes. When they were halfway through the planting field, Hawkes ordered Eastman and Roach to join him. They wheeled their horses around and rode to Hawkes's side, waiting as John and Bull walked through the burning wigwams.

"What are you doing here?" Bull asked Hawkes.

"My friends and I arrived in the early morning darkness with Uncas," Hawkes said.

"Did you help destroy this village?" Bull asked.

"No, I came to watch the Mohegans take the village from the Suckiaugs as an advisor to Uncas. I set fire to nothing. My men and I only became involved when the Suckiaugs launched a sneak attack against the Mohegans."

John glared at Hawkes, grinding his teeth together as he struggled to keep from dragging Hawkes down from his horse. Eastman's fleshy face was filled with a self-confident smile. Roach stared coldly back at him.

John was angry, and getting angrier, when he heard the deep voice of Uncas behind them, "My friend Lieutenant Bull, it is good to see you. I assume you are here to discover what happened last night."

"Yes, tell me." Bull answered.

"The Suckiaugs refused to leave the northern part of their village over which we have a just claim. Our only option was to force them to leave. We captured their guards and pushed through the village's north, forcing the Suckiaugs out of their wigwams and to the south. We burned their wigwams after they left. There would not have been a battle if the Suckiaugs in the south didn't attack us. When they did, we pushed into the planting field and southern wigwams to eliminate risk to our warriors. Over two dozen Suckiaugs attacked us from along the river when we did."

"How many died," Bull asked.

"The Suckiaugs killed four of my men and wounded thirteen. We killed six Suckiaugs who lie near the smoldering wigwams south of us.

"I want to see the dead Suckiaugs," Bull said.

"Follow me," Uncas replied.

John and Bull followed Uncas through the burned-out wigwams. Hawkes, Eastman and Roach dismounted and trailed them on foot. The acrid smell of smoke and charred wood filled their nostrils and burned their eyes. Small flames burned at a few wigwams.

Uncas led them to the remains of three burnt wigwams near where the bodies of six Suckiaug warriors lay.

"These men died a warrior's death," Uncas said. "They will be returned to their people."

John looked at the bodies while Bull and Uncas continued talking about the battle. Hawkes watched John move from body to body. John walked past the first two bodies. One warrior's face was peaceful while the other's was contorted into a grimace. Flies hovered over each man's face and lay on their chests. The next man's face was caved in and covered in dried blood.

John fell to his knees when he saw the fourth body. He stopped breathing as he stared at Huritt's face. There was a hole in his chest where a musket ball blasted through him. He was also struck in the head with a hatchet. But the wound looked odd. It was superficial and it appeared part of Huritt's scalp had been removed in uneven strokes, not from one blow. *Where is Huritt's scalp?* He asked himself.

Hawkes walked to John's side.

"A sad sight," Hawkes said. "A sorry end for your friend Huritt."

John rose and faced Hawkes. Both men were now the same height, but Hawkes was twenty pounds heavier. Still, John knew he was better trained, and Hawkes would be no match for him. But he wanted answers: not a fight.

"Tell me about Huritt's death?" John asked. "Did you see it happen?"

"Did I see it happen?" Hawkes boasted. "Not only did I see it happen, I made it happen. It was my musket ball that blew his chest open and it was my knife that lifted his scalp. Your friend was killing my friends and I stopped him."

John's jaw began twitching. He glared into Hawkes's eyes before looking down and seeing a tuft of bloody black hair hanging from Hawkes's belt. He slammed into Hawkes, driving him to the ground. Hawkes tried to crawl away, but John grabbed Hawkes by his shoulders and flung him to the ground on his face. Just as he was about to strike Hawkes's head John was tackled to the ground. He rolled over and looked up into Lieutenant Bull's face.

"Control yourself!" Bull yelled.

John pushed against Bull's unyielding strength, desperate to tear Hawkes apart with his hands. He quit trying once it was clear he could make no progress. Still held by Bull, John looked past him and watched Uncas help Hawkes to his feet.

"Are you alright now, John?" Bull asked.

"Yes."

Bull released him and they both rose and looked at Uncas, now facing them with Hawkes. Hawkes brushed the dirt off his black breeches and buff leather coat before reaching down to pick up his black broad brimmed hat. Bull walked to Huritt's body.

"What is this about my friend?" Uncas asked.

Bull pointed to Huritt's body.

"That Suckiaug warrior is Huritt," Bull said. "He was our friend."

John pointed to Hawkes, "That man killed and scalped my friend and taunted me about doing so as I mourned his death. I am not ashamed of attacking him and will attack him again if he taunts me."

"Huritt was a great warrior," Uncas said. "Both he and Richard Hawkes fought with courage last night. Richard Hawkes killed Huritt fairly with his musket. Whatever he said to you is between the two of you. I take no sides in your fight. But I won't permit your conflict to be resolved on this land which is now my people's."

"I won't fight here today," John said. "Let me take the body of Huritt to his family?"

Uncas paused. Around them the wigwams continued to smolder but the sound of wind blowing through the wigwam's charred remains replaced the burning and popping of wood.

"I will let you take Huritt's body to Tunxis Sepus," Uncas said.

In the darkness of early morning, John dreamed of the three wolves again. Led by the large black wolf they tore through the Suckiaug village's burning wigwams, chasing men, women and children before them. John's musket was loaded, and his hatchet and knife were in his belt as he stood before the onrushing Suckiaugs. They flew past him. Now only the charging wolves were before him. He knew if he killed the black wolf, he could save the Suckiaug. He raised his musket and aimed between the wolf's coal black eyes. He pressed his finger to the trigger and froze. He couldn't pull it no matter how hard he tried. In an instant the three wolves flew past him and disappeared among the burning wigwams chasing the men, women and children who fled before them.

John snapped awake, alone in the darkness of William's attic. Drenched in sweat, he felt as if he was suffocating and sucked hard trying to draw in air. His heart pounded. Finally, fully awake, he lay still in the blankets on the attic floor. As he lay there he thought of Kimi's look when he brought Huritt's body to her in William's cart the day before. Earlier he cleaned the body and tied a red cloth around Huritt's head to hide his wound. When Kimi saw Huritt she sobbed and fell into John's arms and whispered, "Thank you John Lee, I feared I would never see him again."

Chapter 32

John's stomach churned as he approached Reverend Hooker's house. It was the mid-September 1642, two months after the Mohegans defeated the Suckiaugs, but that was not what John came to talk about. It was a personal matter and the closer he approached Hooker's house the weaker his legs felt.

He turned west before the bridge over the Little River to the South Plantation onto the road along the river's north shore. The early morning cold was swept away by a bright sun casting long shadows beneath the massive trees that climbed into a deep blue sky. The gurgling river was at his back as he stood at Hooker's door. He breathed deeply before knocking. He heard footfalls on the stairs inside the house. The door sprung open and Reverend Hooker stood before him. Hooker smiled. His white linen blouse hung loosely over his baggy brown breeches and his gray speckled black hair was tied back with a cord.

"Come in John," Hooker said. "Thank you for visiting me. I'm sorry my family is away and not here to greet you. Susanna and my son Samuel are visiting an ill member of our congregation, while my daughter Mary is with my student Roger Newton at the meetinghouse working on his sermon."

"Does Roger still want to be the first minister in Tunxis Sepus?" John asked.

"Yes, and he'll be bringing Mary with him after they wed," Hooker answered. "Are you still living with William and Bridget?"

"Yes sir," John answered. "But in the Spring, I will build my own house in Tunxis Sepus."

"I hear the soil is rich there."

"It is."

Hooker led John into the hall where they sat near the fire's hearth. The two casement windows were closed, and the room was dim as the fall sun was too low to penetrate the diamond shaped panels.

Hooker leaned towards John and asked, "What brings you today?"

John cleared his throat, "There are several things bothering me. They spin in my head during the day and haunt me at night."

"Go ahead John."

John's face was flush, and a small bead of perspiration fell down his forehead as he began, "I've listened to your sermons and studied the scriptures, but I've yet to understand how I will know God has given me His grace. Last year Richard Hawkes's application for conversion was approved. What troubles me is how a man can so easily conclude he has received God's grace when I struggle so, even with the guidance of your sermons."

Hooker leaned back in his chair, "Your question is common. I'm sorry my sermons haven't helped you answer it. I will get to your question, but first I need to be certain you understand the Covenant of Grace. Do you?"

"Yes, I believe so," John said. "Reverend Stone taught it to me."

"Reverend Stone is a fine teacher. Then you know God determined our fate long before we were born, and we must search for evidence He has selected us for salvation and eternal life. We do this by determining if He has instilled in us the faith necessary for our salvation and that we haven't acquired that faith on our own."

"This much I understand," John answered. "But how can I determine if God instilled faith in me and not that my faith was acquired by me?"

"Many believe, as I do, that only through study and prayer can they determine if the faith they have was planted in them by God and not themselves."

"But what of those like Richard Hawkes who claim God revealed His grace to them in a single bright moment without the study and prayer you speak of?"

"Some Puritans believe a single event can be enough evidence of God's grace," Hooker said. "I don't believe this. I believe only through study and prayer can we determine if God gave us our faith and His grace."

"If you believe this, why did you permit Richard Hawkes's evidence to be considered sufficient to support his conversion?" John asked.

"Because, regardless of my belief, our faith allows for evidence other than derived from study and prayer. What matters is the strength of the evidence and the belief of the one seeking to prove he has received evidence of God's grace."

Hooker paused, stood up from his chair, and poked the fire arousing a bright flame. He turned back to John, "Why have you failed to determine your faith was planted in you by God?"

"I fear my sins show I am not pure enough to have received God's grace? More importantly, I often question why God would decide we must go to Hell without giving us the chance of redemption during our lives."

"Let's discuss your sins first. What sins cause you to fear God didn't give you grace?"

"I killed many men and a boy during the war with the Pequots," John answered. "Their spirits haunt me."

"What you did was not a sin," Hooker asserted. "What you feel is natural for a pious man, but what you did many who received God's grace did before you. War is a natural condition and God uses it to test man's strength. We learn this from the psalms we read. They teach us God himself gave David the power to defeat his enemies. The Pequots were heathens who ignored God. They killed our people and God gave us strength to defeat them. You didn't commit a sin but fulfilled God's will."

"But many women and children were killed coming out of the

burning fort, while many others burned to death inside the fort."

"Remember John, the Pequots, as all tribes in New England, don't worship God, nor have they accepted Christ as their savior. Until they do, they're savages who must be removed to make room for the kingdom of God we're creating here. When they make war on us, we must fight with the vigor God gives us. The guilt you feel is nothing more than Satan's attempt to confuse you, so you are not able to understand God's message of grace. Fight this guilt so you can receive God's message. You will be able to find within yourself what you search for when your mind is clear."

"I will try," John answered.

"Now let's discuss your concern that God should not choose our fate without allowing us to redeem ourselves in life," Hooker said. "This principle is the core of our Puritan faith. God exists outside the world he created. He controls everything in that world and knows everything that has been, is now, or will ever be. This includes the fate of each one of us."

John's mind spun wildly thinking of how to respond. He questioned the point of living if God failed to allow redemption. He couldn't imagine a loving God doing this; nor could he believe God would not find evil in what they did to the Pequots; nor that God could give His grace to a man as vile as Richard Hawkes. But Hooker's convictions were strong, and John knew it would be useless to say what he believed. He nodded at Hooker without speaking.

"You still appear troubled," Hooker said. "Is there something else that concerns you?"

John knew the core of his guilt must now be discussed. He looked into the fire and swallowed. He wondered what he could say that would not reveal what he swore to conceal and still ask the question in a way that would illicit an answer helping him resolve his worry?

"Years ago, I swore an oath," John said. "Because of my oath an evil was let loose upon our people. This evil is still among us. I fear my oath was a sin and by giving the oath I am responsible for the evil I let loose among us."

"What was your oath?" Hooker asked

"I swore not to reveal something."

"Was your oath given for a good reason?"

"To save another's life."

"Then your oath was for a good reason and it isn't a sin to have taken it. You must honor the oath you made and not reveal what you swore to conceal."

Hooker leaned towards him and in a voice barely above a whisper said, "Now, tell me about the evil you have unleashed through this oath."

John sat back in his chair, shocked by Hooker's demand.

"I can't tell you as it would violate my oath," John answered. "I can tell you that but for my oath this evil would not be in our town for I would have revealed its presence long ago."

"I understand why you can't tell me more John, but you must find a way to remove this evil without violating your oath."

"How can I do this?"

"God will show you."

Chapter 33

John woke on a May morning near the small hut he built in Tunxis Sepus as a temporary shelter to be used while he, Sam Pierce, and two other young men dug the cellar and built the frames for his new house. The four of them slept outside the night before, while William and Bridget Westwood, who had come from Hartford the day before in William's cart, slept in the hut. It had been nearly a year since the Suckiaug's destruction.

Bridget had packed salted pork, stewed pumpkin, boiled onions, and cornbread in the cart to be served after John's house raising. It was now time for John to get off the ground and prepare the site of his new house for its raising.

John and the young men were at the new house in an hour. While John ensured the frames of the house's sides were laid in correct positions with the needed number of tree nails, Sam and William set up four heavy oak tables where Bridget placed her food. Several other women from Hartford brought more food. Sarah Hart promised John she would also bring food and his spirit was lifted when she told him both she and her daughter Mary would be serving it at his house raising.

Hartford's people began arriving three hours after sunrise. The first families were led by Lieutenant Bull and came from Hartford's South Plantation. Altogether there were twenty men, women and children. Among them, were Joseph Barnard, his wife Katherine, and Lieutenant Bull's new wife, Susannah. Most people were on foot, but a few rode on the two carts filled with food.

"Congratulations," announced Bull while striding towards John. "It's a sharp clear morning. Perfect for a house raising. Come see Susannah."

John glanced up the slope to the Town Path and saw Susannah effortlessly pull a heavy box of food from a cart and lug it to the tables set up between his house's foundation and the Town Path. Bull brought Susannah from Boston the year before and John liked her immediately. She was once a servant in a Boston family's home and her earthy nature and spirited temperament contrasted with the more reserved women he knew. John walked up the slope to Susannah as she set plates of squash and peas on the tables.

"Just because you are the man of the hour doesn't mean you don't have to work," Susannah said. "Make yourself useful and fetch another box from the carts."

John removed his broad brimmed hat and bowed, "As you wish madam."

"Thomas, you can also bring one of the boxes to me," Susannah said in a voice loud enough for all to hear.

John watched with amusement as Bull made his way to a cart near him.

"Susannah is in good spirits today," John announced as he and Lieutenant Bull each pulled a box from a cart.

"I believe she is," Bull laughed.

After they took the boxes to Susannah, she placed her fleshy arms around John, pulling him into her tall broad frame and said, "I'm glad you're finally building your house. Now you need a wife to share it with."

John smiled sheepishly at Susannah and said, "This will come soon enough."

Within two hours, people filled the land around the house's cellar. John's neighbors from Tunxis Sepus arrived separately over the entire two-hour period. Family by family they emerged from the pine, maple and oak trees lining the Town Path. John found his way through the crowd to greet each of them.

The last group to arrive was thirty people from Hartford's North

Plantation. Led by Reverend Hooker, they came with three carts full of hams, roasted lamb, a side of beef, corn bread, squash, radishes and peas. Reverend Stone, Governor Hopkins, Elder Goodwin and John Steele and his family were with them. As John walked up the slope to greet them, he noticed Reverend Stone slithering through the crowd toward the tables.

"Good day Reverend Hooker," John announced.

"It's a beautiful day for your house raising," Hooker stated. "What a splendid view of the river. I can see why so many of my congregation are moving here. Soon there will be more of my congregation in Tunxis Sepus than in Hartford."

Hooker stiffened, "Is Deacon Hart here?"

"Not yet, but I expect him soon."

"When he arrives ask him to see me," Hooker said. "I will bless your new house when its frame is raised."

Hooker turned away and walked down the slope through the trees to the tables where everyone was gathered. With the sun now directly overhead, John knew it likely he would need to raise his house without Deacon Hart and his family there. He hesitated, for he wanted Mary to be there when he raised the house.

After several more minutes he could wait no longer and began walking down the slope to raise the house. He had taken three steps when he heard the familiar gruff voice of Deacon Hart, "Ready to raise your house now John?"

"Almost Deacon," he answered.

He turned and looked back up the slope to the Town Path where he saw Sarah and their children Daniel and Mary. He gazed at Mary longer than the others. She caught his gaze and smiled. Excitement flowed up John's spine as he smiled back. He fought his desire to hold his eyes on her and turned back to Deacon Hart, "Reverend Hooker would like to speak to you."

"I'm not surprised," Hart answered. "He wants to talk about Elder

Goodwin's proposed change to our practice of refusing baptism to our unconverted member's children. He wants to convince me to oppose the change. I will discuss it with him later."

"Goodwin and William Westwood are with him now," Hart continued. "I'll wait until they leave him."

Hart walked down the slope towards the tables, staying as far away from Reverend Hooker, Elder Goodwin and William Westwood as possible. Sarah and their children followed behind him carrying freshly baked corn bread and pork loin she and Mary prepared that morning. Finally, when everyone was there John walked down the slope and climbed atop his house's chimney ledge. With a broad smile he looked down at the people gathered about him.

"It's time to raise my house," he said.

The crowd cheered while the men raising the house moved to their positions on each side of the house and in the cellar. John immediately began giving the orders necessary to coordinate each step of the house raising.

Within an hour the house's frame was in place, Reverend Hooker had given his blessing, and the people were eating. Exhausted from the day's excitement, John walked away from the crowd and up to the Town Path to get a better view of his newly framed house. He saw Sam Pierce approaching him when he turned back to look at his house.

"Did you reckon ya could stay away from me all day?" Sam beamed.

"Sorry," John answered. "I wasn't avoiding you."

"Stop, it's me Sam. No need to square things with me. I'm your friend."

"You're right."

They both looked down on the scene below them. Soon John's eyes fell on the people milling around the tables. It didn't take him long to find Mary. A gentle breeze flowed up from the river bringing with it a light, warm, seductive scent. Then he remembered. It was from the fields of honeysuckle just above the river. It was her scent, for whenever he saw her during the last month as he built his house, that scent was in the air.

"Ya fancy her don't ya?" Sam asked.

"I suppose," John answered wistfully.

"Too bad she's so young. Deacon Hart won't let her marry for years. Can you wait that long?"

"I don't know."

"So that's why ya built your house next to Hart's land." Sam said.

"What do you mean?"

"Ya yearned to live next to her."

"Maybe, but I can't remember thinking that," John answered.

"Well, you're here now and buildin' a two-story house. Tells me you's expectin' to have a big family. You can't wait for Mary if you want that now. Abigail's got a friend ya gotta' meet. Name's Ann Green. She's from Boston here to teach Hartford's children."

"Have you seen her?" John asked

"Not yet. Ya want Abigail to introduce ya?"

John turned away from Sam and glanced down at the table where Mary was serving food. He turned back to Sam, "How is Abigail?"

"She wants children."

"How've you been Sam?" John asked. "I know your first crop was difficult. Have you fared better since?"

"Yes. No problems with Indians since I agreed to Richard Hawkes's special milling services."

John froze. He gathered himself before replying, "Be careful. Ten percent of your corn is too much for earlier milling and corn protection. Ask me for help if you want out of the deal."

"I can take care of myself."

They both walked back to the tables. Sam grabbed John's shoulder before they had gone more than a few yards, "What about Ann Green? Come to our house for supper next week and Abigail will invite her too."

"I will let you know later."

Sam shrugged and walked away from John towards one of the tables.

John walked through the people crowded about the tables, frequently stopping to accept their congratulations. He pulled his wooden spoon out of the waist of his breeches and grabbed a wooden trencher when he reached Mary's table. Most of the people had eaten and Mary stood alone ten feet from him at the end of the table. Her moist skin glowed in the light of the late afternoon sun. She turned in his direction and smiled.

"Have you eaten John?" she asked.

"Not yet. What are you serving?"

"I have little left: some boiled pork, cabbage and a small piece of cornbread"

"Sounds good." John said with a smile.

He walked the length of the table and stopped across from Mary. She looked into his eyes as he handed her his trencher. He smiled at her when she returned the full trencher to him across the table. Their fingers touched briefly, sending a wave of excitement through him. The spell was broken by her father's powerful voice, "John, is Richard Hawkes coming today?"

"I don't know," John answered. "Richard was at the meetinghouse when Reverend Hooker announced my house raising."

"Send him to me if he comes. Reverend Stone and I want to talk to him."

Hart turned and walked back to his table and resumed his discussion with Lieutenant Bull and Reverend Stone. John turned back to Mary and watched in a daze as she picked up the wooden trenchers and spoons she and her mother brought with the food they prepared. He thought about what Sam said earlier. He knew Sam was right, Deacon Hart would not let Mary wed for years.

"John, come sit with us," Lieutenant Bull yelled from the table he

THE DARKNESS AT DAWN

shared with Hart and Stone.

"We're discussing news from Colchester," Hart said. "Seems there has been an infestation of witches."

"What happened?" John asked while sitting next to Hart.

"A man named Matthew Hopkins has rooted them out," Stone said. "They call him the Witchfinder General. He claims there are hundreds of witches in East Anglia."

Lieutenant Bull cleared his throat and asked, "How can this man tell if someone is a witch?"

"Through their confession," Stone said.

"We need a witchfinder to protect Connecticut," Hart exclaimed.

"Where would we find such a man?" Bull asked.

"You don't find such a man," Stone answered. "Witch hunting is a calling. God leads one to it. Our witchfinder will find us when the time comes."

A chill passed through John. The men stared at each other silently. He knew each of them was waiting for someone else to speak first.

Suddenly, the chatter of the people stopped. John turned towards the silence. Richard Hawkes walked towards him through the crowd. Hawkes's black eyes stared at him as he calmly moved towards him while reaching into a black bag hanging over his left shoulder. A collective gasp rose from the people as Hawkes pulled a knife from the bag with his right hand. The knife's blade glistened in the sunlight as Hawkes twisted it in his hand. At first Hawkes held the knife by its white boned handle as if planning to use it, but when he reached John, he flipped the knife around and presented it to him by its handle.

"I give you this knife in honor of your new house," Hawkes said. "You may find it better than a stick if you are ever attacked on a moonless night on the trail to Hartford."

A few people in the crowd laughed at Hawkes's reference to the two men's fight during militia training many years before. More people chuckled as word of Hawke's veiled reference spread throughout the crowd.

"Thank you for your gift," John said. "I accept it with the same respect with which you gave it."

Hawkes turned and walk back through the crowd and up the slope to the Town Path. Waiting for him on their horses were Eastman and Roach. The three men turned and headed back towards Hartford on the Town Path.

Gradually, the people began leaving. Soon everyone but Bull was gone. Bull approached John when the others were gone and announced, "Ride with me before we lose more light. Show me your town while we talk."

Both men walked together up the slope and mounted their horses. Shadows cast by the pine, maple and oak trees darkened the Town Path.

"Why don't we take a tour later when there's more light," John said.

"It's good it's dark," Bull said. "Your attention will be focused on what I say."

"If that's what you want. Why don't we just talk at my new house?"

"I think clearer when I'm moving." Bull said. "What I say should be clear."

Bull trailed John as he led them down the darkening path.

"Start when you're ready," John replied, "I will keep a slow pace."

"Much has happened since we led our congregation to Suckiaug," Bull said. "But what has happened pales compared to what is about to happen. Have you thought of what will happen to our congregation and our town when Reverend Hooker dies?"

"Why are you concerned with this?" John asked. "As far as I know he's in good health."

"Ask William or any others who came here first. They will tell you he's much weaker than before. He may live more years, but his years are fewer than all of us who are younger."

John pulled his brown gelding to a stop and turned to Bull, "Alright, I expect he'll die sooner than most of us. What are you afraid of?"

"Haven't you noticed the conflict beneath his leadership?" Bull answered. "Reverend Stone and Elder Goodwin have been at each other's throats since we came to Connecticut. Alliances have developed around them. Richard Hawkes and more than half of the converted members of our church support Reverend Stone. Your new neighbor Deacon Hart leans in their direction and will support Reverend Stone against Elder Goodwin in any fight to control the congregation after Hooker's death. Elder Goodwin's pride will never allow him to accept Stone as our leader. The two factions spoke separately at your house raising over whether the future children of the unconverted should be permitted to be baptized. Goodwin and William support Reverend Hooker's opposition to this, while Stone, Richard Hawkes and Deacon Hart want the rule against it eliminated so the church can grow in power. Our congregation will come apart when Reverend Hooker isn't here to hold it together."

The two men's horses were now close. The sun was too low to stave off the cold, and they pulled their doublets tightly about their necks.

"What will you do when that time comes?" John asked.

"I can't support Reverend Stone and dislike Elder Goodwin," Bull answered. "Still, I will choose Elder Goodwin because he hasn't given ear to Richard Hawkes's counsel. What about you John? Your neighbor is Deacon Hart and you haven't hidden your affection for his daughter Mary. What will you do when that time comes?"

"I don't know. I respect William's judgment on most things, but I now live next to Deacon Hart and I do care for Mary."

"Think carefully, for if you fail to you may find yourself slip into an uncomfortable place."

"Thank you for your advice. We should head back to my house. It will be dark soon. You can stay there tonight and return to Hartford in the morning."

"There is a full moon tonight. I'll have no trouble finding my way. I will leave from here. First, I have something else to say."

"What?"

"You know Richard Hawkes's gift of the knife was a threat?"

"I didn't take it that way. It was a strange gift though."

"A man doesn't give his foe a weapon unless he expects it to be used, "Bull stated. "And a man doesn't give a weapon while reminding others of his own defeat, as Richard Hawkes did, unless he's letting his opponent know their fight hasn't ended. While the people took his gift and his reference to his defeat as a peace offering, men like him don't offer peace. In the end, they must defeat their enemy."

Bull paused and glanced up the dark path. John sat silently on his horse staring through the darkness at Bull.

"Richard Hawkes has let you know there will come a day when you will fight again. When that time comes your will to finish the fight must be stronger than his. Your physical prowess and fighting skills won't be enough for the fight may not even be physical. Not all men are pious and honorable like you. Some men are evil. The only answer to evil is to destroy it. You must not hesitate when the time comes. Your tools may not be a weapon at all, but they must end the conflict with Richard Hawkes's death. While he lives, he'll continue the fight until you are destroyed."

John slumped forward on his gelding and looked at the dark dirt beneath him. He lifted his head and stared at the knife of Bull's dead friend hanging on his belt for a long moment before looking again at Bull. They gazed at each other briefly before Bull turned his horse and began riding into the darkness towards Hartford. Before Bull went more than a few yards, he turned back to John.

"Remember what I said tonight John." Bull said.

"How can I forget?"

Chapter 34

It was dark when John Lee woke in his house in Tunxis Sepus. Sunrise was still two hours away. It was two months since his house raising; a month and a half since Sam Pierce helped him install the summer running vertically from the chimney girt to the end girt to support the horizontal joists to which the attic floor would be nailed; and, a month since they nailed planking to the attic, both floors and the roof. The exterior of his house was complete. It would still take several months to finish the interior. *But not today*, he thought. *Today I will honor my promise to Huritt.*

He dragged himself from bed and stumbled through the parlor's darkness into the hall where he put on a gray wool doublet and breeches. Under a moonless sky, he spread corn on the dirt for his chickens. When he was finished, he looked above. Thousands of stars stared down on him. He sighed as he realized he was alone now and how he missed his quiet talks with William and the parlor's bustle as Bridget fixed supper.

The sky was gray when he finished feeding the chickens and sunlight was flowing through the oaks and maples after he fed his four hogs. He climbed atop his brown gelding and rode to his planting field. He remembered his first harvest. It was barely adequate to cover his cost to plant it. But this year he planted more of his land and the early growth was good.

Shortly before noon, he returned to the house and prepared for his Tunxis and Suckiaug students. He was placing benches under the shade of a tall maple tree when he heard a familiar reedy voice, "I'll help with the benches."

He turned and laughed when he saw Sam Pierce, "Where were

you? I needed your help earlier. The benches are already in place. Bring two chairs from the house and set them under the maple tree facing the benches."

"I need to fetch Abigail and Ann Green first."

"You brought Ann?" John groaned, shaking his head.

"She's a teacher, right? She can help teach the Suckiaugs and Tunxis. Besides, I figured you've seen her a bit since you two ate supper at our house last month and would like to see her again."

"I've seen her only at church."

"What's wrong with ya?" Sam chided, shaking his head. "She's a prize. Seemed ya two got along fine at supper. Anyways, she said ya did after ya left."

"I'm too busy with my house."

Sam shook his head again before climbing the slope to the Town Path. A few minutes later he came back down with Abigail and Ann. John smiled at the two women. Both smiled back. As they moved closer, Ann's rose-colored skirt flowed in the river's breeze and the sun's rays lit the moisture on her face, causing it to glow beneath her black hair which was tied up under a white linen cap.

"Good day John," Ann smiled.

He nodded at both Abigail and Ann and said, "Good day ladies."

"This is exciting John," Ann said. "Please show me around."

"Yes, do it." Sam said. "Abigail and I will finish settin' things up."

John turned to Ann and smiled, "I'll show you the school."

"What about your new house?" Ann asked. "Can I see it?"

"If there's time after today's lessons."

He led Ann down the slope to the benches. They stood at the first bench facing the river while behind them Sam and Abigail placed two chairs and an oak table under the maple tree facing the benches.

"This is it," he said. "Not much now, but someday I will build a school house here so I can teach when the weather is bad."

"How many students are coming?" Ann asked.

"My friend Chogan said there will be twenty."

Ann smiled and touched John's shoulder with her hand while gazing into his eyes, "It's a good start John. You should be proud."

Before he could answer, Daniel Hart's shout floated down from the Town Path, "John, come up and help us bring the food."

John looked up the slope at Daniel. He turned back to Ann and excused himself. He and Sam hiked up to the Town Path. Daniel was standing with his mother, Sarah, and sister, Mary, near a small cart pulled by a gray mare. The aroma of fresh baked corn bread and hasty pudding filled the air. John grabbed the still hot iron bake kettle's handle containing the corn bread with a cloth and pulled it from the cart while Sam picked up the pudding. When the cart was unloaded, Daniel climbed back on and reined the mare around, heading back to his father's house.

"You're not staying?" John asked as the cart moved away.

"No, my father says I have work to do." Daniel yelled back.

John and Sam led Sarah and Mary to the oak table where Ann was seated. Ann smiled at John as he neared her. He nodded at her when they reached the table and introduced her to Sarah and Mary.

After the women exchanged pleasantries, John excused himself in order to prepare his lessen for the day. He sat in the first row of benches studying his notes while the women placed the wooden bowls, spoons, bake kettle and pot on the table. As John studied his notes he listened as Ann and Mary talked. Their conversation was about life in Tunxis Sepus, Mary's family, and Ann's teaching in Hartford.

After a few minutes, the conversation ended, and John looked up from his notes. Ann was no longer there, and Mary was continuing to set the table. He stared at her as she moved about the table in a plum bodice and skirt, laying out the bowls, napkins, and spoons she and her mother brought. When Mary finished setting the table, she glanced at him. She smiled slightly and lowered her eyes to the table before he could return her smile. He caught movement in the corner of his eyes and turned to see Ann staring at him from two rows behind with a stony expression. He nodded at her. She sighed, dropped her eyes, and turned away.

"John," Sam yelled down from the Town Path. "Chogan and Kimi are here with the children."

John looked up the slope. Chogan, Kimi and four children were walking towards him with Sam. The children bantered back and forth while Kimi and Chogan smiled at John as they walked.

"Good day John," Kimi said.

Her accent was strong, but John was impressed with Kimi's attempt to speak English. He gripped her by her slender wrists and stared into her soft brown eyes.

"Kwe kwe, Kimi," he said.

John turned to Chogan and smiled, "Kimi has learned some English."

"She's learned a few words," Chogan said. "She wants to learn more."

John looked at the two boys and two girls Chogan and Kimi brought. All were between ten and fifteen. He realized he saw one of the boys before. He was Pethus's son Ahamo who was in Sequassen's long house two years before. In the two years since, Ahamo had grown several inches and his black eyes were mature for his age.

"Welcome Ahamo," John said.

He looked to Chogan to translate what he said, but Ahamo waived off Chogan with his hand.

"My father sent me to learn the English's ways and observe the lessons you teach our people," Ahamo announced.

The children were lined up next to Kimi. Chogan moved behind them and placed his hands on the first child's shoulder. He was a boy of about fourteen. His black eyes were narrow with flat straight eyebrows.

"This is Abukcheech," Chogan said. "He is Suckiaug."

Chogan stepped behind the two girls, both of whom were about ten years. "These girls are Tunxis," Chogan announced. "They are Alsoomse and Chepi."

John smiled at the girls. Chepi was a large girl with a fleshy face while Alsoomse was small and slender.

John sat the children in the first row of benches. He turned to Chogan and asked, "You said you would be bringing twenty students. Why only four?"

"I am sorry," Chogan said. "Our tribes are proud, and many people refused to send their children. More will come if you keep teaching us."

Over the next hour John taught a few simple English words by showing an object and saying its name. After he taught the children ten words, he pointed to an object he taught them and asked what it was. At first the children were nervous, but after a while they became more comfortable and began to laugh excitedly as they repeated a word or guessed the name of something he taught them. All the while Ahamo watched quietly. Suddenly, during the children's laughter, when one of them stumbled over a new word, Ahamo rose from his bench.

"You taught us English words," Ahamo said. "But many of my people say your god is the source of your power. Tell us of this god."

John was stunned by Ahamo's request. He wanted to focus on practical lessons to help the two tribes learn how to live with the English. He wondered how he could teach them about God. He was not a minister. Then he realized the answer. He learned about God through the scriptures his father read to him. He would reveal God to them the same way.

"I will teach you about God through the words God himself gave us." John said. "To do this, I need your help. Will you help Chogan translate my words?"

Ahamo nodded agreement.

John taught the children a few more words over the next half hour. Then he turned to Ahamo and said, "Ahamo asked me to teach you about our god. We will start with the Bible's first book, called Genesis. I will read it in English and Ahamo and Chogan will translate for you."

As he began to read, Mary sat on the last bench behind the children. A small smile crossed her face as she listened while staring at John as he read the story of creation. On occasion she leaned farther forward, on other occasions she ran her fingers along her cheeks, on still others she closed her eyes: but all the while the smile remained. He read until he completed the first chapter of Genesis. There was rapt silence when he was done.

The sun was barely above the trees when John finished reading. He and Sam walked Chogan, Kimi and the children up the slope to the Town Path. Chogan lingered for a moment after Kimi and the children turned and began walking towards their village.

"Are you coming next week?" John asked.

"Yes," Chogan said. "My father wanted this."

After the Tunxis and Suckiaug left, Sam turned to John and said, "I'll take Abigail and Ann back to Hartford now. Will ya see Ann again?"

"Only at church," John answered.

"That's a shame. You need to let go of your dreams of Mary."

A week later Hartford's constable came to John's house. The constable wore a black doublet, black breeches and black broad brimmed hat, which told John the visit was official. The constable shuffled back and forth at John's door. It was hot and humid and small beads of sweat gathered at his hairline just below his hat.

"Governor Hopkins sent me," the constable said. "He wants you to come to the meetinghouse for a meeting this afternoon."

"Why?" John asked.

"To discuss your teaching of the Tunxis and Suckiaugs."

John wondered what interest the Governor had in his teaching the local tribes. He said nothing but continued to stare at the constable, whose face was now streaked with sweat.

"It's a hot morning," John said. "Would you like a noggin of beer before you return to Hartford?"

"No thank you. I need to notify the others of the meeting."

"Who would they be?"

"Reverend Stone and Richard Hawkes."

"Why are they coming to the meeting?" John asked.

"I don't know. The governor just asked me to tell them the meeting's place and time."

John's pulse quickened. *This won't be pleasant*, he thought.

John's doublet was stained with sweat when he finished tying his brown gelding to the rail near the porch of Hartford's meeting-house. Richard Hawkes's black stallion was already tied to the rail. He walked up the porch's interior stairs to the chamber. As soon as he entered, he saw Reverend Stone and Richard Hawkes facing him at the chamber's heavy oak table.

"Good day," John said.

Stone and Hawkes stared at him without speaking. He walked towards them through the chamber. No one spoke again until he reached them. Stone stood with his chest thrust forward and his hands clasped together behind him. Hawkes smiled smugly with his arms crossed in front of him.

"Well, I suppose you know why this meeting has been called," Stone said.

"The constable said it was about my teaching the Tunxis and Suckiaugs," John said. "I'm surprised it warranted a command from the governor to come to a meeting."

"Your teaching bothers us," Hawkes spat.

John turned from Stone and faced Hawkes. He stared into Hawkes's black eyes as he moved closer to him. Hawkes stood impassively.

"How is it possible my teaching these Indians, who we've driven into a small plot of land along the Tunxis River, offends you?" John asked. "What would you have me do? Kill them like you did? They deserve to know our language and ways so they can live among us since soon they won't be able to live apart from us."

"Teaching our language is one thing," Stone said. "But you also taught them scripture. This is dangerous business. You have no training and may vary so much from our tenets as to engage in heresy. Only a man with extensive training should teach Indians about God."

Before John could answer, the door to the porch's stairs slammed closed. He looked back to see the tall thin angular frame of Governor Hopkins.

"Good day," Hopkins said walking towards the three men. "Thank you for coming from Tunxis Sepus on such short notice John. Everyone sit at the table."

They chose seats at one end of the table. Governor Hopkins at the end, John to the governor's right and Stone and Hawkes together on the side opposite John.

"This meeting will be short," Hopkins said. "Reverend Stone and Richard Hawkes have complained to me about your teaching the Tunxis and the Suckiaugs John. They claim you are teaching them from the scriptures even though not trained to do so and that your teaching may lead to heresy. Can you ease their concern?"

"I spoke to Reverend Stone and Mr. Hawkes about this before you arrived," John said. "I told them, as I will tell you now, I began teaching these tribes to help them adapt to the new world surrounding them. The Suckiaugs lost their land and now both they and the Tunxis are pressed together on the Tunxis's land. Their hunting grounds have shrunk, and they now depend on trade with us. They must learn English and about our ways if they're to survive. They have also asked me to teach them about our faith."

"It's true I read them the scriptures. Many of our religious leaders believe the Indians are the same as us except they're darker from their long exposure to the sun. These same leaders believe that if the Indians accept God and follow his commandments, they can join our churches. If this is true, we owe them a chance to learn about God and our savior Christ. I believe it would be unchristian to refuse their request."

Governor Hopkins' eyes lingered on John, before he turned to Stone.

"What John says is true, isn't it?" Hopkins said. "Don't we have a duty to teach the Indians? Why have you complained that he is teaching what we have a duty to teach?"

"I agree we have a duty to teach the Indians about God." Stone said. "But those who teach the Indians must be properly trained. If they aren't, they may make mistakes. John Lee hasn't been properly trained."

Governor Hopkins sighed heavily, "Well Reverend Stone, if John Lee can't teach these Indians, who will? You?"

"I have too many responsibilities and no time to do this."

"Reverend Stone is right," John said. "I lack the training he has, but he lacks the time I have. I suggest I continue teaching the Indians about God while telling Reverend Stone what I have taught. If what I teach is wrong, it can be corrected in later lessons."

"A fair approach," Hopkins said. "Do you agree with John's proposal Reverend Stone?"

"I have no time to receive reports from him." Stone answered.

"It seems only John is in a position to teach these Indians what we must," Hopkins announced. "If he missteps you may come see me again."

"But Governor . . . ," Stone protested.

"The matter is closed," Hopkins barked.

Stone and Hawkes strode from the chamber. Stone mumbled angrily as he slammed the door on the way out.

Chapter 35

Three years after John's house raising there were more than two dozen houses and farms on the slope above the Tunxis River. Both the river and the town above it were now named Farmington. At twenty-seven, John Lee was a respected town leader and a Sergeant in the militia. But John was unmarried, even though the young women of Hartford and Farmington considered him a prize. Today John would lead the people of Farmington to Hartford to celebrate the Sabbath. His first stop was Deacon Hart's house.

He sat up in his saddle when he saw Mary as he neared her father's house. She was a hundred yards ahead and his eyes feasted on her as he rode through the trees lining the path to the house. At eighteen years, Mary was a woman. To him her soul was always older than her age. Her body had finally caught up with that soul. She stood next to a wooden cart staring at the door to the house. Her slender arms rested at her sides, their elbows tucked gently into her narrow waist. She tapped her toe in the dirt.

"Daniel hurry!" she yelled. "We'll be late."

John smiled as he rode out of the trees into the sunlight.

"Having trouble with your brother?" he asked.

Before Mary could answer a disembodied voice came through the open door, "I'm coming, I'm coming."

"I think you have his attention," John laughed.

"It's not him I'm worried about. It's my father. He likes to be last. He'll only come after my brother."

As he climbed from his horse, John wished Farmington had its own meetinghouse. Still, the weekly treks to Hartford gave him the chance to see Mary every week. Daniel carried a large wooden box when he left the house. He nearly stumbled on a broken branch as he raced across the dry grass while trying to stay under the box. When he got to the cart, the box fell to the ground with a thud.

"What's in that box . . . stones?" John asked.

"Food Mary prepared for supper. There's another box in the house. It's smaller than this one. I'll fetch it."

"Are father and the children ready?" Mary asked. "We need to start soon to get the townspeople to the meetinghouse on time."

The absence of a mention of her mother in Mary's plea reminded John that Mary's mother, Sarah, was no longer living, having died of chest congestion from a disease flashing through the town the previous year.

"Would you help me put the box onto the cart John?" Mary asked.

John bent over and wrapped his arms around the box, grabbing its base with his hands. Mary grabbed the box from its other side once he lifted it off the ground.

"Your brother is right," John gasped. "This box is heavy."

They pushed the box onto the cart, but the momentum of Mary's push knocked John to the ground once the box came to rest on the cart. They tumbled to the ground with Mary landing on top of John in the dusty path. Mary laughed as they untangled. Deacon Hart and the children joined in her laughter as they stood at the house's door.

"Sorry for my clumsiness," John said as he rose to his feet while dusting the dirt from his breeches and doublet.

"It was my fault," Mary laughed.

"At least you got the box onto the cart before you fell," Deacon Hart said. "My sons will finish loading the cart."

John stepped back from the cart as Daniel and Deacon Hart's younger son, Mark, lifted the other boxes onto the cart. Hart helped Rachel and Thomas, his youngest children, onto the cart where they sat with Mary. Hart then climbed onto the cart's bench and grabbed the reins to the horse. Meanwhile, Daniel and Mark stood next to the cart ready to walk when they got underway.

John mounted his horse and spun it around towards the Town Path. He nudged it forward through the trees while Hart snapped the reins and the cart's horse pulled the cart forward with Daniel and Mark trailing behind on foot. When they reached the Town Path, they turned north onto the road taking them through the mountains, meadows and farms stretching to Hartford.

The Meetinghouse yard was filled with men, women and children when they arrived. Some of the boys stood near the jail staring at the disheveled man placed in the stocks for public drunkenness. The other people were in front of the meetinghouse near several oak tables where the women placed food for supper between the morning and afternoon services.

John walked through the crowd with Deacon Hart. Daniel and Mark walked behind them carrying a box of food they brought. Mary trailed them, holding Rachel and Thomas by their hands. As they approached the meetinghouse, John turned toward the tables. Once there, he found Sam Pierce and William Westwood. Together they brought another table from the storage shed a few yards from the meetinghouse.

John looked for Mary after he set the table in place. He found her with a group of girls setting food on one of the tables. The girls talked feverishly and laughed as they worked. His gaze focused only on Mary. Eventually, he turned away and joined the people entering the meetinghouse. He took a seat on a bench in the section reserved for the men. Daniel Hart sat next to him. William Westwood was seated four rows ahead with the town's converted leaders. Two rows behind William, John saw the black broad brimmed hat of Richard Hawkes. The congregations' buzzing stopped when the west wall's door sprang open and Reverend Hooker entered the room and climbed the pulpit's stairs.

For the next hour Hooker led the congregation through the

service starting with his reading of the Ten Commandments. After he read each commandment the congregation responded, "God grant us thy mercy."

John walked outside when the morning service was finished. He stood near a table as the women and girls filled the people's trenchers with boiled lamb, squash, peas and corn mush. Mary was three tables away. He walked towards her to get the food she was spooning to the people at her table. As he neared her table, he saw Richard Hawkes standing next to her. She was smiling, her cheeks were flushed, and her eyes lowered demurely. He listened to their conversation.

"Will you be at home tomorrow when I come meet your father?" Hawkes asked.

"Yes, but I will be outside slopping the hogs and gathering corn with my brothers all morning,"

"I will delay my visit until afternoon," Hawkes said. "It seems a waste to have such a beautiful girl slopping hogs."

John cringed as he saw Hawkes and Mary break into broad smiles. He turned away from her table and walked towards the jail at the corner of the meetinghouse yard. He stood near the jail for several minutes watching the people across the yard enjoying themselves. Their laughter passed across the yard, smothering him until he collapsed onto the grass. After a few minutes, he lifted his head, rose from the grass, and began walking back to the tables. Instantly, his right shoulder was gripped from behind. He turned and met Deacon Hart's gaze.

"Follow me," Hart commanded.

They walked towards the meetinghouse door. John was curious, but not alarmed. His curiosity became greater when Hart led him up the stairs to the upper chamber. Hart entered the chamber ahead of him, causing its ten occupants to turn towards the door away from the table they sat at. Every man at the table stared at John. Richard Hawkes and Reverend Stone were among them.

"Come to the table with me," Hart said.

As they walked to the table, Hart announced, "I brought John Lee to our meeting. He'll be helpful as we move forward."

"But he's the ward of William Westwood who supports Elder Goodwin," Richard Hawkes protested. "Keep him out."

"The baptism of the unconverted's children isn't the only issue we're discussing," Hart answered. "We're also discussing the threat of witchcraft. Besides, it's been over five years since John was William's ward. He's my neighbor in Farmington now."

John stood silently near the table as the discussion continued. Even though the discussion was about him, it went on as if he was not in the room. Finally, Reverend Stone turned to him.

"John Lee is twenty-seven and his own man." Stone said. "He was my student and I trust what he says. Let him tell us how he feels about the baptism of the unconverted's children. He can stay if we're satisfied with his answers."

"I have no idea what your meeting is about nor why Deacon Hart brought me here today," John shrugged.

"Stephen, answer John's question?" Stone directed.

"I brought John here because he's respected by our congregation and when the time comes he would be good to have on our side," Hart said. "I also believe he knows our congregation's future is in jeopardy if we don't change and allow the unconverted's children to be baptized."

"Do you understand the issue John?" Stone asked.

"I do," John answered. "Because so many in our congregation haven't been converted and because it is forbidden to baptize any child not the child of a converted member of our church, many of our children cannot be baptized. Many fear our church will be weakened if we don't change our law so these children can be baptized. Others believe, if we change our law the foundation of our church will be destroyed."

"What do you think about this?" Stone asked.

"I understand both side's position," John answered. "Tradition is important to keep order and members of our congregation should be encouraged to aspire towards conversion. But it is unfair to punish innocent children for their parent's failure to convert."

"Well said," Hart announced.

"You're not converted," Hawkes barked. "Why should your opinion matter?"

John glared at Hawkes. Meanwhile, Stone sat up higher and stared at John.

"Richard has a point," Stone said. "Why haven't you sought conversion?"

John replied confidently, "I haven't sought conversion because both you and Reverend Hooker taught me only those who are certain God has chosen them for His grace should ask our congregation to be converted. When I receive this evidence, I will ask the congregation to convert me."

"A fair answer," Stone said. "Does anyone object to John sitting with us during our discussion?"

"I do," Hawkes spit.

"Does anyone else object?" Stone asked. "If not, I will let John sit with us."

No one spoke. Hawkes glared at Stone, his face reddening as he squeezed his right hand into a fist. Then he turned and gave John a penetrating gaze. John calmly stared back at him.

When the discussion about baptizing the unconverted's children ended the men agreed they would urge the rule be changed to permit the unconverted's children to be baptized if their parents swore to continue seeking evidence permitting them to obtain their own conversion.

"We have another matter to discuss," Stone announced. "It's the threat of witchcraft."

The men leaned forward.

"Do you doubt Satan uses witches to attack God's earthly kingdom?" Stone asked.

The room was quiet except for the squeaking of chairs as the men shifted in their seats.

"Do you doubt witches are already among us?" Stone continued.

Again, there was silence.

"Then why is it in the ten years we've been in Connecticut we've only found one witch?" Stone asked, the volume of his voice rising. "The witch was Alse Youngs who was hanged in Windsor last month. We haven't found more witches in Connecticut because we haven't looked for them. That was the case in East Anglia until its towns paid Matthew Hopkins, the Witchfinder General, to ferret out the witches in their midst. Tell them what we have to do Richard."

Hawkes stood and looked down the table at the men with piercing black eyes. John and Deacon Hart stared back at him, while the other men looked at their hands.

"They're out there," Hawkes announced. "The witches are out there. They're laughing at us because we're weak. They're laughing at us because we're afraid of them. This is the lessen of the Witchfinder General. He knew these facts but was not afraid. We must also be fearless. We must find them before they destroy us."

Hawkes walked the length of the table. When he reached the end of the table, he turned and stared at the men peering up from the table at him. He looked down at them.

"Our people must be vigilant," Hawkes exclaimed. "We must show them how witches work their evil. We must give them the tools to discover these witches before they spread their evil among us. When we do this, we won't need a Witchfinder General, for the people themselves will find the witches among us."

When Hawkes finished, Stone concluded, "Richard will teach our people how to find witches. He'll show them how to identify witches by the Devil's mark they bear and to use a witch picker to raise that mark where one does not appear. He'll teach them how to bind witches to a chair and test their innocence by placing them in water to see if they rise because the water has rejected them for being in league with Satan. He'll teach them the Witchfinder General's methods for examining a witch."

"What training does Richard Hawkes have to do this?" John questioned.

"You question my decision!" Stone bellowed.

"I will answer him," Hawkes said. "I studied the Witchfinder General's book where he reveals his techniques and I have questioned witches in England and Massachusetts Bay, including Alse Youngs before she was hanged."

"Is that enough for you John?" Stone demanded.

"I'm afraid many innocent people will be hanged," John answered.

"Are there any other objections?" Stone asked the men at the table. No one answered.

"Very well, Richard Hawkes will be our Witchfinder General," Stone announced.

When Reverend Stone and Richard Hawkes were done, the other men sat silently around the table for a moment before standing and shaking Hawkes's hand. John sat alone until the others were gone. A chill ran up his spine when he rose to leave.

Chapter 36

Richard Hawkes waited for Deacon Hart in the hall of Hart's house, while thinking of ways he could use the power of Hartford's witchfinder. It was a hot June afternoon in 1647 and he and Hart had been discussing the operation of Hart's grist mills. Since Hart's wife Sarah died, Hart soothed his loss by devoting more time to his businesses. While once free of supervision, Hawkes now felt Hart's constant meddling was becoming tiresome. As he stared at the fire's embers, he heard heavy footfalls behind him.

"Here's my account books," Hart declared. "I prepare them based on the monthly production data you give me."

Hart sat with the account books in his lap. Hawkes forced a smile. *What the hell is this about*, Hawkes thought. *Does he really want to go over everything in those books?*

"The books are organized by mill," Hart said. "Let's start with Hartford's old mill."

Hawkes forced another smile. He moved his chair closer to Hart's. *This will take the whole afternoon*, he thought. *Then, let's get on with it.*

For the next hour, Hawkes and Hart talked about each gristmill and where Hart might open new mills. When they finished, Hawkes looked up from the account books at Hart and said, "Let me summarize. We will expand the new grist mill on the Little River and cut back the old mill's operation until we close it next year; we will expand the mills in Windsor and Wethersfield; and, we will open a mill in Farmington within three years."

"That's right," Hart said with a self-satisfied smile.

Hawkes nodded, stood up and announced, "I will see you next month."

"But you must stay for supper," Hart said.

Hawkes hesitated. He wanted to return to Hartford to plan his next musket trade, but he realized he would have the chance to see Hart's daughter, Mary, if he ate with them. He smiled, sat down, and said, "Thank you, I will stay."

"I'll go find Mary and find when supper will be ready," Hart announced.

Hawkes walked out the front door after Hart left the hall. The sun was nearly to the horizon and the trees climbing the hill to the Town Path cast long shadows. He felt neither the sun nor saw the shadows. He was focused on something else and she was about to serve him supper. An attractive wife who already learned to run a household after her mother's death, and her prosperous and powerful father, would be a strong combination. He walked back into the hall as Hart entered from the parlor.

"Supper will be ready soon," Hart said. "Let's sit in the hall now."

They sat silently before the fire. Hart's chin rested on his chest as he dozed. *What a waste of time*, Hawkes thought. He cleared his throat to wake Hart.

"Where have you bought land?" Hawkes asked, feigning indifference.

"Mostly north along the Farmington River. I also bought some Pequot land. But now land has less value with many of our people returning to England to challenge the King."

Hawkes nodded.

"Supper is ready," Daniel announced as he entered the hall.

They followed Daniel to the parlor where they sat at the table. Mary stood among the pots, trenchers, spoons and napkins sitting on a table in the lean-to kitchen adjoining the parlor. Hawkes smiled at her as she picked up several trenchers, spoons and napkins and walked up the stairs leading to the kitchen. She smiled before dropping her eyes to the table.

"Daniel, help your sister bring supper," Hart interjected.

Hawkes stared at Mary while she and Daniel brought the pork, corn bread and peas to the table. She sat next to her father at the opposite end of the table from Hawkes. She felt Hawkes's stare. She tried fending it off by looking at her father. She still felt Hawkes's stare. Finally, she could stand it no more. She turned and looked into Hawkes's black eyes while holding her trembling hands under the table. Her heart was beating furiously as she bowed for her father's prayer.

Mary lifted her eyes after Hart's prayer. Hawkes was still staring at her. She looked back at him with a tremulous smile while passing the food. When they finished eating Mary began clearing the table. Deacon Hart and Daniel settled back in their chairs while Mary finished.

Now is a good time to talk about it, Hawkes thought.

"It's been a month since we hanged the witch Alse Youngs," Hawkes said. "Have you thought about the plan Reverend Stone and I have to root out Connecticut's witches?"

Hart leaned forward, "I have. Alse Young's actions convinced me Satan is already at work here."

Mary stood at the table placing dirty napkins into a voider. She looked at her father and interjected, "Alse Young had three young children and a husband. It's sad her children are without a mother."

Hart glared at her from his seat and snapped, "Satan must be stopped. Once she became Satan's agent, Alse Young ceased being a mother. She chose her path and it led to the hangman's noose."

Mary dropped her eyes and quietly continued placing dirty napkins into the voider. Hawkes realized her sadness and her father's rebuke gave him a chance to ingratiate himself with her.

"Mary, Satan is a powerful foe," Hawkes said. "You are right to feel sorry for Alse Young's children and, as a Christian, it is right for you to feel sadness for her, for Satan preys on those who are weakest.

Take comfort knowing before she was hanged Alse Young confessed her sins and prayed for God's forgiveness. She left this world with the hope her confession and prayer were evidence God granted her His grace."

"Did you know this poor woman?" Mary asked.

"Yes," Hawkes answered. "I was with her when she confessed."

Mary nodded at Hawkes, causing a tear to slide off her face onto the floor before she walked to the kitchen with the voider.

"Getting a witch's confession is a nasty business Richard," Hart said. "How did you learn to do it?"

"It's not hard," Hawkes said. "You just need to remember the weakness allowing Satan to capture them is still present, and you can exploit it as Satan did. You must isolate them from others and keep them from sleeping. Then most witches will believe it when you tell them they have been tempted by Satan and must now resist him. They confess when they finally realize there's no hope for their salvation unless they confess and renounce Satan since their action in doing so is evidence of God's grace."

"How will you find more witches?" Hart asked.

"By training our people to be vigilant so they let our leaders know when they believe a witch is among us," he answered. "I will examine those suspected of being witches. If I find a person is a witch, that person will be tried and hanged."

"But what if an innocent person confesses because they've been deprived of sleep or subjected to torture," Daniel asked. "Wouldn't it be wrong to hang them?"

"Daniel, are you challenging Richard's methods?" Hart asked. "God help us. Witchcraft is a serious business. It's better to execute an innocent person than to allow a single witch to go free. God will correct the mistake later."

Daniel slid down in his chair with his head down.

"It's alright Daniel," Hawkes said. "Your question is reasonable. I make sure we don't hang innocent people."

"There Daniel," Hart said. "Are you satisfied?"

Daniel nodded without speaking.

While the men continued their discussion, Mary washed the dirty napkins and trenchers at their well. She stared blankly at the trees lining the Farmington River, occasionally closing her eyes and sighing, while gently folding each clean napkin and setting it with the others on a trencher. She was nearly finished when Daniel yelled at her through the rear window, "Our guest is leaving Mary."

She dropped the clean trencher and napkins into the dirt next to the well and rushed through the kitchen and parlor into the hall. She breathed a sigh of relief when she saw that Hawkes was still standing at the front door. He knew why she was out of breath.

"Good bye Deacon Hart," Hawkes announced. "Thank you and your daughter Mary for supper."

Deacon Hart closed the door behind him as soon as Hawkes left. Mary stood like a statue. Her mouth agape and her eyes open wide.

"Fear not Mary," Hart chuckled. "He'll be back."

Chapter 37

Three weeks later, a fever swept through Hartford like a low fog on a gray summer morning. Where it touched down it did so randomly. In some areas it didn't touch down at all. Where it did touch down it did so without reason. In some parts of town it lit upon only a handful of people. In other parts of town it struck down scores. Most of those who were stricken with the fever approached death. Their coughing and gagging worsened for days before the fever's cloud lifted. By early July, the fever began to release its grip. But it would take one more life before it was through.

Reverend Hooker began coughing the last week of June. At first, no one worried for he had been prone to illness for years. John Lee, like most others, felt Reverend Hooker's physique became emaciated due to the stresses of being the town's spiritual leader. He attributed Hooker's hollow cheeks to the normal consequences of aging. But, after two days, John knew Hooker's cough was a harbinger of unwanted change.

On the third day, John learned, with the rest of the congregation, that Reverend Hooker couldn't rise from his bed. On the fourth day, he led a procession of men, women and children from Farmington to Hartford to join a vigil for Reverend Hooker at the meetinghouse. It was sweltering when they reached the crowded meetinghouse yard. The men's doublets and shirts were stained with sweat and the women dabbed perspiration from their faces with white linen handkerchiefs. The mood was somber, and children sat quietly with their parents. John led the procession along the path to the meetinghouse through people milling about in the yard until he found enough space on the grass for them to pull their carts to a stop.

As they waited for the tragedy that was about to befall them, John saw William walking towards him. William's stride was deliberate, his back hunched forward, and his wheat colored hair hanging loosely from his black broad brimmed hat to below his ears.

"I'm glad you came," William announced. "Reverend Hooker will die tonight. I have been at his house all day. Bridget is there caring for Mrs. Hooker, who also suffers from the fever. Reverend Hooker asked me to bring you to his house."

John was stunned by William's certainty. He knew it was likely Reverend Hooker would die, but he retained hope he would somehow survive. Now, this hope was gone. William touched John's right shoulder, stared into his eyes, and said, "We must hurry."

John was numb as William led him through the crowd of people in the meetinghouse yard. Most people looked blankly at them as they passed. Here and there, William touched a few friends on their shoulders as he went by.

They walked along the narrow path from the meetinghouse to the Little River near the most prominent founders' homes. They reached Reverend Hooker's house at the Little River. The door to the house was ajar to allow circulation. Nonetheless, when John stepped into the house after William, he felt an oppressive heat. He glanced up the stairs into Reverend Hooker's study. He saw the silhouettes of three people standing where the study merged into the parlor chamber.

He followed William into the hall where six men sat silently gazing at the fire's dying embers, which provided the room's light. It was even hotter in the room than at the entry way and the pungent scent of smoke hung in the air. None of the five men appeared to notice the heat nor the odor, nor did they notice the perspiration staining their doublets.

Seated in chairs near the fireplace, were church elder William Goodwin and John Steele, who still served as Hartford's deputy to the General Court. Both men lifted their heads and glanced at John and

William. Only Steele smiled. Seated randomly around the table in the center of the room were Governor John Haynes, former Governor Edward Hopkins, Deacon Hart, and Reverend Hooker's student, Roger Newton. Neither the angular Hopkins nor the slender Haynes acknowledged their entry. Instead, they fixed their eyes on the fire's dying embers. Hart and Newton looked away from the fireplace and nodded at them. John and William sat at the other end of the table, away from the other men.

"What happened since I left?" William asked.

"The physician from Windsor arrived," Goodwin answered. "He's had success treating the fever. He's upstairs with Reverend Hooker's regular physician."

"Is Bridget still with Mrs. Hooker?" William asked.

"Yes," Goodwin answered.

The room was silent again. As hard as he tried, John couldn't keep his eyes from fixing on the fireplace's dying embers. Within a short time, the embers dimmed, further darkening the room. Elder Goodwin noticed this and rose from his chair and placed two logs on the embers. The room brightened as the fire sprung back to life. At the foot of the stairs, Hooker's physician stood staring at the fire. The creases on his face filled with shadows as the firelight fell on him.

"Windsor's physician is leaving," Hart's physician announced to no one in particular. "There's nothing he can do for Reverend Hooker."

A diminutive man walked down the stairs behind Hooker's physician. His mulberry doublet was buttoned to his neck. He nodded at the men in the room as he walked out the door.

"We have done all we can," Hooker's physician said. "Go to him if you like. He may not recognize you, but he has moments of lucidness and during one he recognized me and his son Samuel."

John looked around the room, waiting to see what the others would do. At first, no one moved. Finally, Elder Goodwin rose from his chair and walked to the stairs. He looked back at the men in the hall and asked, "Does anyone want to go with me?"

"John and I will come," William answered.

Goodwin led them up the stairs. Out of the fire's light the stairway darkened until they reached Reverend Hooker's study where the glow from the four candles placed at his bed provided a dim light. Sitting by Reverend Hooker's bed was his thirteen-year-old son, Samuel.

"My father is asleep," Samuel whispered.

The great man lay beneath them on a heavy oak bed. He was propped up on several large pillows, so his closed eyes faced forward, and his damp hair hung loosely to just beneath his ears. Samuel dabbed his father's forehead with a linen napkin. John stood next to William as Goodwin sat in a chair close to Hooker.

John wondered why they were still there after the candles burned down more than an inch. It seemed unlikely Hooker would ever be able to say anything.

"Let's return to the hall John," William said. "We can come back when he wakes."

"I will stay with him," Goodwin said.

John followed William towards the study and the stair's darkness. Before they took three steps a hallow voice spoke to their backs, "Don't leave."

John froze. Hooker's voice grasped him as if it were his hands. Before John turned, William was at the bed and Goodwin was leaning over Hooker listening for his words. Hooker's son Samuel began sobbing quietly. Soon all four of them leaned over the bed.

"We had a dream of a world where we would live with God when we came to Suckiaug," Hooker whispered.

Hooker paused and gasped for air before continuing, "Who is here with me?"

"Your friend William Goodwin. With me is William Westwood, your son Samuel, and John Lee."

"Ah, my Elder," Hooker wheezed, his eyes barely open. "Is

Reverend Stone here?"

"No, he's in Boston attending a Synod," Goodwin said. "I sent word to him several days ago and expect him to arrive soon."

"I hope I will still be here when he comes," Hooker whispered. "When I see him I will tell him what I am telling you."

"What is that sir?" Goodwin asked.

"You must save our dream for I can no longer do that work."

"I promise to keep our dream alive," Goodwin said as he continued leaning over the bed. "Don't exhaust yourself. You must rest."

Goodwin spoke unnecessarily, for Reverend Hooker was already asleep.

"He's sleeping now, and I can't be certain he will wake again before he dies," Hooker's physician said. "It would be best if some of you waited downstairs with the others and not crowd around his bed."

"John and I will move to the hall," William said.

John and William continued their vigil in the first-floor hall for the next hour with the men who had not visited Hooker, while Hooker's son Samuel, Elder Goodwin and Hooker's physician stayed by his bed. The sun had set, and the hall was dark.

There was a loud knock at the door shortly after sunset. The men in the hall looked at each other, waiting for someone to answer the knock. The knock came again. This time it was more urgent. Finally, Deacon Hart walked to the door. Before he reached the door, the knocking resumed. It was louder than before. It continued until Hart opened the door.

"It's a crypt in here," Richard Hawkes announced as he burst into the hall. "It's dark, smells of smoke and the fire has nearly burned out. Where is Reverend Stone?"

"He's not here," Goodwin said walking down the stairs towards Hawkes.

Hawkes spun towards Goodwin and asked, "Where is he?"

"Returning from Boston," Hart said before Goodwin could

answer. "He's expected any moment."

"Your knock woke Reverend Hooker," Goodwin spat.

Before Hawkes could respond, Goodwin looked at the men in the hall and announced, "Reverend Hooker is awake but feeble. Come upstairs if you like, but don't crowd around his bed. I will call you to him if he has something to say to you."

One by one the men walked up the stairs past Goodwin. Deacon Hart lead the procession. He was followed by Governor Haynes, former Governor Hopkins, John Steele and Roger Newton. John Lee and William trailed them. The stairs screamed under their combined weight. When they were all walking up the stairs, Goodwin turned to follow them.

"I'm also coming to see Reverend Hooker," Hawkes announced.

Goodwin turned to Hawkes, "No sir, stay in the hall."

"Reverend Stone would want me to be upstairs to represent him."

"Reverend Stone said nothing to me about it. Take a seat in the hall. You've created enough of a disturbance tonight."

Before Hawkes could answer, Goodwin turned and climbed the stairs. Anger filled Hawkes and for a moment he thought about climbing the stairs without Goodwin's approval. He decided to wait in the hall for Reverend Stone. When Stone arrived, they would go upstairs together and when they reached Hooker's bed, he would enjoy watching Goodwin squirm in silence for Goodwin would have no option but to keep his mouth shut.

Goodwin approached Hooker's bed. Hooker's eyes were open slightly, but Goodwin couldn't tell if Hooker recognized him. The other men stood in a semicircle formed ten feet from the bed. Everyone's eyes were fixed on Hooker. The four candles placed about the bed flickered in the room's darkness, leaving the impression there was nothing in the room but the bed and the man lying in it.

Goodwin leaned over until he was within two feet of Hooker's face and whispered, "Reverend Hooker, this is William Goodwin.

Can you hear me?"

"Yes," Hooker whispered.

"I have brought the men you asked for."

"Remind me who they are."

After Goodwin announced who the men were, Reverend Hooker asked them to come to him one by one. John Lee watched as Governor Haynes, former Governor Hopkins, John Steele, Roger Newton and Deacon Hart each approached Reverend Hooker's bed and bent over to hear his words.

As each man left Hooker, John's stomach tightened. Finally, his time arrived. He hesitated and looked at Goodwin.

"Go to him John," Goodwin said.

Even though he was now a grown man of twenty-seven years and a veteran of much bloody fighting, John felt like the young boy he was when he first saw Reverend Hooker on a pulpit in East Anglia. He leaned over Hooker as Goodwin announced, "Reverend Hooker, it is John Lee."

"Ah, John Lee," whispered Hooker. "You have done so much at such a young age. You are a bridge between those of us who built God's city in Connecticut and the generation following us. Teach them our message so our mission can continue."

"I'll do my best sir," John said.

Suddenly, more alert than he'd been the entire night, Hooker pulled himself up to John and whispered, "Remember the evil you spoke of when we met. You must root it out before its darkness destroys us. God will show you how when the time comes."

Goodwin helped Hooker back onto his pillows. Goodwin leaned forward over Hooker and whispered, "Sir, you are going to receive the reward of all your labors."

"I am going to receive God's mercy," Hooker replied as he closed his eyes for the last time.

Reverend Stone droned on for an hour and John's mind began to wander. Sweat gathered on his forehead as he sat on a bench in the crowded meetinghouse. It was two days after Reverend Hooker's death and the meetinghouse was full. A few women cried early in the memorial service but their eyes dried as Stone plowed on. Hooker's casket was at the front of the room below the pulpit where Stone was speaking. Elder Goodwin, John Steele, William Westwood, Governor Haynes and former Governor Hopkins sat in the first row. Three rows ahead of him, John saw Richard Hawkes's black doublet and hair.

When Stone finished his sermon, more than half the congregation was in a daze. Governor Haynes climbed the pulpit to deliver his eulogy. Below him the congregation shifted about on their benches, knowing once he began, they would have to remain awake and still in the sweltering meetinghouse. Mercifully, Haynes' remarks were brief.

By the time Governor Haynes finished, most in the meetinghouse were awake anticipating the next speaker for they knew he would keep their attention.

"Those of us who are here today owe everything we have to the man who lies before us," began Elder Goodwin in a powerful voice heard throughout the room. "More importantly, those of us who are here today owe him for teaching us to live a godly life and come as close to God as anyone can in this earthly existence."

As he watched Goodwin, John understood why Reverend Hooker kept Goodwin close and followed his counsel. Goodwin was not just a powerful man, he also believed strongly in Reverend Hooker's mission and in the church they both served. Goodwin recounted the many sermons Hooker delivered to the congregation and how he led them through the difficult days when they first arrived in Suckiaug.

He challenged the congregation to keep the world of God on earth Reverend Hooker created pure of corruption so future generations could feel the joy of living with God each day.

The congregation sat quietly while Goodwin climbed down from the pulpit and walked back to his seat. Goodwin then led John Lee, and the other men selected by Goodwin and Reverend Stone to carry Hooker's casket. They lifted the casket and followed Goodwin, Reverend Stone and Governor Haynes down the aisle through the meetinghouse.

The congregation followed the casket through the meetinghouse's door to the hole dug for it. John held the casket's right rear with William to his left. Across from him stood Richard Hawkes. They stared at each other without smiling while shuffling across the meetinghouse yard to the hole. John Steele and Roger Newton were at the front of the casket. Sweat poured from their faces and stained their doublets as the men set the casket down next to the hole.

As he stood at the hole, John wondered how he could fulfill Hooker's order to destroy the evil he allowed to exist in their Puritan world. He stared at the black clad Richard Hawkes while Reverend Stone prayed. John knew Hawkes did terrible things, but these acts occurred in war for which he received no punishment. While there were rumors of a dark Englishman selling muskets to Indians, there was no evidence Hawkes was this man. Reverend Hooker told John he couldn't break his oath and so he faced a conundrum, the only solution to which was to discover a crime for which he was not bound to silence. Even then he lacked the power to investigate or prosecute such a crime. Then he remembered Reverend Hooker said God would show him the way to destroy the evil. His shoulders relaxed as he felt the Holy Ghost's breath fill his body. His deadline for action was in God's hands. He would wait until God showed him how to remove the evil.

"We are here to bury our brother," Stone said. "We pray that God granted him his grace and that he is now with Him."

Nothing more was said as the men each threw a shovel of dirt into the hole, leaving it for the grave diggers to complete the task of entombing Hooker's body. The men quietly walked back towards the meetinghouse. They broke into three groups before reaching it. The governor headed to the meetinghouse's upstairs chamber to retrieve his belongings. Deacon Hart, William Westwood, John Lee, Elder Goodwin, Roger Newton and John Steele went to the meetinghouse's main chamber to greet the people still there, while Richard Hawkes and Reverend Stone walked to Stone's house.

"Have you seen Reverend Hooker's will?" Hawkes asked.

"No. Have you?" Stone answered.

"I learned what was in it from the man who transcribed it."

"Why would he tell you this?" Stone asked.

"He's indebted to me."

"What does it say?"

"It doesn't mention you," Hawkes said. "William Goodwin and Governor Hopkins are executors of his estate."

Stone stopped, turned to Hawkes and shook his head, "How could he do this? How could he do this? I served him for years and yet each time he could reward me for my service he rewarded another. When we both came to Massachusetts Bay, he told me he would appoint me to be his assistant, but when the time came, he chose Reverend Cotton. Only after Cotton refused, did he offer the position to me. And now he appoints my rival William Goodwin to administer his estate."

"Reverend Hooker is gone," Hawkes said. "His choice doesn't matter. You can take charge of our church. To do this you must assume the position of church pastor without waiting for Goodwin and the church elders to offer it to you. After assuming this position let no one remove you."

Elder Goodwin walked towards them from the meetinghouse.

Stone stiffened as Goodwin closed the gap between them.

"Remember what I said," Hawkes whispered. "Claim the position of pastor."

When he arrived, Goodwin moved between Stone and Hawkes and said, "The church's leaders haven't decided who we will recommend to the congregation to be our new pastor. Until we do so, we want you to serve as our acting pastor."

"Thank you," Stone said. "I agree to serve as acting pastor and hope our leaders will make the position permanent."

"We will consider it," Goodwin said before turning and walking back to the meetinghouse.

"You're being used again." Hawkes chided. "They will let you serve as pastor only until they find a replacement. Do all you can to keep the congregation from voting for a new pastor, or even for an assistant pastor who may threaten to assume the position. Our church needs your leadership. Do everything you can to stay its pastor. There are dark times ahead. We just hanged the witch Alse Youngs. There are more witches among us. You must lead us through the coming struggle."

"I'll not let them remove me," Stone declared. "Most of the congregation supports me and Goodwin and his followers have sworn to support the church. I will never let them breach their covenant."

"And witches?" Hawkes asked.

"Together we will purge them from Connecticut."

PART FIVE
1652 - 1657

Chapter 38

John Lee sat on an oak bench in the second of fifteen rows of benches he and the other men of Farmington's new congregation placed in Deacon Hart's backyard. It was five years since Reverend Hooker's death. John missed Hooker's steady hand as the conflict between Reverend Stone and Elder Goodwin was a festering sore. Sadder to John, was the Suckiaugs move from Tunxis Sepus to the lands of the Pocumtuc. As a result, Chogan was no longer there to help him.

Behind John, the congregation's last arrivals were finding seats. He pulled his doublet close to his neck to fight the October chill, but the sky was clear and bright, and it was warming fast. The scent of burning beef wafted across the benches from the cooking pit Mary Hart and the other women were using to cook supper to be served after the church's first service. Someday, Farmington would have its own meetinghouse, but for now, John and the others in the new congregation were satisfied having services at Hart's house.

Mary stood out among the congregation's women sitting together to John's left. As he stared at her, Mary's eyes were fixed on the congregation's new minister, Roger Newtown, the late Reverend Hooker's son-in-law. Newton stood before the congregation, waiting for everyone to take their seats. Mary glanced to her right and met John's eyes. He smiled. She smiled briefly before turning back to Newton.

Newton moved to the podium. He was a slender man of forty-three years with long black hair hanging to his shoulders. Newton started with a prayer for the new church. John listened while stealing a few glances at Mary. Deacon Hart stood behind Newton on his house's backyard porch. Reverend Stone, Governor Haynes, and

Deputy Governor Hopkins sat on the bench in front of John. Ten rows behind him, John spotted Richard Hawkes. *At least he hasn't been given a seat in front of me,* John thought. *It wasn't enough for Hawkes to come from Hartford, he also spent time talking with Mary before the service began.*

Reverend Newton was reading from the Bible, but John didn't hear a word of it, nor the psalm Deacon Hart read after that.

"Holy Communion will now be given to the converted members of our faith," Newton announced.

Newton lifted a silver gold inlayed chalice from the oak table where the podium sat. He turned back to the benches and lifted it above his head.

"Behold the blood of Christ given for you for the forgiveness of your sins," Newton declared. "Drink this in remembrance Christ died for you."

John stiffened. The chalice was the same chalice Richard Hawkes stole on the *Francis*. *What is it doing here?* he asked himself.

"Our brother Reverend Stone brought this chalice for us to use on this special day," Newton said. "I will serve you from it after giving you the bread representing the body of Christ."

One by one the converted left their seats and lined up before the table. After receiving a small piece of bread from Reverend Newton, each sipped from the chalice. As the line moved forward, John saw the back of Richard Hawkes's black doublet moving with the others. Unconverted, John couldn't take communion. He fought to restrain his rage as he watched from his bench as Hawkes slowly shuffled forward. When Hawkes took a piece of bread from Newton, he turned and smirked at John, before taking a sip from the chalice.

After the morning service, Mary and the other women set the food they brought on the wooden tables surrounding the grassy area where the benches sat. Most of the congregation talked at their seats or milled about near the tables. John sat alone watching the others talk. Behind him he heard Hawkes, Stone and Hart speaking on

Hart's backyard porch. To his left, Mary was busy giving directions to the women and children who were helping bring the food. Reverend Newton and his wife, Mary Newton, stood together beaming while one by one the new congregation's members congratulated them. All around him John heard children laughing.

"Why so deep in thought John?" Lieutenant Bull asked, while sitting on the bench next to John.

"Just tired, I guess."

Both men stared at each other for a moment. John forced a smile. Finally, Bull broke the silence, "You've been in Farmington for over six years living by yourself. By all accounts your farm is doing well. But it is doing better than you. You are my best sergeant, but there's another trade for which you are better suited."

"What would that be Thomas?" John asked.

"Farmington's Constable. You know the General Court's workings from your years assisting William, and your training as a soldier will be of value when you have to hunt down and capture criminals."

"But we already have a constable."

"For now. But Nicholas Wakeman is old and can't serve much longer. Let everyone know you are interested in the position and it will be yours."

John hesitated until he realized he would finally have power to investigate Richard Hawkes's crimes and fulfill his promise to Reverend Hooker.

"Well John?" Bull asked.

"I want the position," John answered. "Will you help me?"

"Count on it."

Shortly after noon, Mary announced supper was ready. John stayed behind while the congregation shuffled to the tables where the women handed them wooden trenchers and spoons before they moved to the tables with food. He watched Mary smile as she spooned portions of lamb and corn porridge on the trenchers placed before her.

John looked forward to the next lesson he would give to the Tunxis for she would be there to help him.

He ate supper alone and was nearly finished when Deacon Hart approached him. Hart smiled and joked with several men who greeted him as he crossed the grass on which they set up their temporary church. Hart's smile became even broader as he reached John.

"A glorious day for our town," Hart exclaimed. "At last Farmington has its own church. Come to my house. Reverend Stone is waiting."

A small fire burned in the fireplace as they passed through the parlor into the hall of Hart's house. Reverend Stone and Richard Hawkes stood at the table in the center of the room. Both stared at John without speaking. Stone's lips were drawn into a tight smile, while Hawkes's arms were folded across his chest.

"Sit down John," Stone declared.

John nodded and sat at the nearest chair. Stone sat at the table's end while Hart sat to his right. Hawkes took the seat opposite John. The only light came through the small windows at the front of the house. John peered at Stone through the dim light, while through the corner of his eyes he glimpsed Hawkes's steady gaze.

"Thank you for supporting me in my struggle with Elder Goodwin," Stone said. "It has been difficult to see our congregation so divided."

"Let me be clear sir," John replied. "I support you because I believe your position is correct. Innocent children shouldn't be punished for their parent's omissions."

"The last three years have been difficult," Stone said. "Elder Goodwin brought two ministers to me, asking the congregation be given the chance to vote on them. In both instances I refused. He and his followers have begun seeking support outside our congregation. There's even talk they might seek a meeting of the Connecticut churches to issue an opinion on the matter. The fact is I have little information about what Goodwin's side is doing and don't wish to be taken by surprise."

"You should let them leave," John declared.

Stone's face froze. He leaned back, his face now red. He leaned towards John, "I will never release these people from the covenant they entered into when they joined our congregation. I didn't have you brought to me for your advice. I had you brought here to get your help."

"What help can you possibly need from me?"

"I want you to discover Goodwin's plans."

"And, how do I do this?"

"William Westwood is Goodwin's adviser. He knows Goodwin's plans. See if you can discover those plans."

John stood and glared at Stone. "You ask too much," he said. "My support does not include betraying William Westwood's confidence. Even if I agreed to do this, William would never trust me for he knows I support you."

A deafening silence filled the room. Abruptly, Hawkes stood up and slammed his fist on the table.

"I told you he wouldn't help us," Hawkes said. "Don't waste time with him."

Stone calmly looked up at Hawkes and motioned him to his seat.

"Sit down Richard, sit down," Stone said. "You too John."

Stone looked at John with a tired smile.

"Think about it for a few days John," Stone said. "You can provide a vital service to the church. William has chosen to be the church's enemy in this matter."

John was silent until Stone and Hawkes left the hall. He turned to Hart, still sitting at the table with him, and asked, "What made them think I would do such a thing?"

"Maybe they asked because they would have no trouble doing it themselves," Hart said.

Hart walked across the wooden floor to the fireplace where he threw two logs on the fire's embers. Instantly, the room's dimness was replaced by the light of the fresh fire. He pointed to a chair near the fire's hearth.

"Sit with me John," Hart said. "We've time to talk before the afternoon service."

When John was seated, Hart asked, "How does your farm fare these days?"

"My last two harvests were good."

"Have you bought other land?"

"Yes. Some a few miles north of Wethersfield and pasture rights in common land owned by the town in the meadows on the mountain above us."

"Good. Land will always have value."

Deacon Hart's smile disappeared. In a grim voice he asked, "What do you think about the threat of witchcraft in Connecticut?"

"I'm troubled for there may be witches among us but fear we may punish innocent people. What did you learn serving on the jury convicting John and Joan Carrington?"

"I learned Satan preys upon us as a wolf preys upon a herd of sheep," Hart answered. "He picks out the weakest. The Carringtons were weak. Satan gave them the power to summon him, which they did in evil ceremonies performed in the woods outside Wethersfield. He gave them three familiars in the form of cats to do their bidding. These cats went to their victims at night while they slept, haunting them with ghastly visions. They made dolls representing their victims which they used to cast their spells on them and when their victims were weak enough, they themselves visited them as spirits."

"How could you tell this happened and that the cats weren't merely ordinary cats, that the ceremonies in the woods nothing more than frivolity, and the victims simply dreamed they were visited by the Carringtons?"

"You don't believe what I told you?" Hart spat.

John immediately regretted bringing up the subject of the trial and execution of the notorious couple from Wethersfield who were hanged in Hartford the year before.

"I'm sorry," John said, "I didn't mean to question your decision. I merely asked questions because I knew you would have the answer and remove any doubts I may have as to their guilt."

"Both their victims were young girls claiming they were visited by them on the night before they each became sick. It is impossible they could have dreamed the same dream. When Richard Hawkes confronted Joan Carrington with this fact, she immediately confessed thereby removing any cause for putting the girls through more pain by having them testify at trial."

John nodded to Deacon Hart and silently stared into the fire.

"Earlier I asked about your farm and lands." Hart said. "I did this because I have seen how you look at my daughter Mary. Do you want to be her husband?"

John's pulse quickened as he stared at Hart. He wondered why Hart asked him this question. He decided to tell the truth, "I'm fond of Mary and would like her to be my wife. But she's more attracted to Richard Hawkes."

"He might be a good husband if he stayed in one place long enough, but his businesses demand he be absent too much," Hart said. "He would not make a good husband. Of course, I have little say in this matter. Mary has a mind of her own and I intend on letting her use it."

A knock interrupted their conversation. John turned towards the front door as Hart opened it. Richard Hawkes entered with a broad smile on his face.

"I've come to take Mary to the afternoon service," Hawkes announced.

Mary rushed past John to the front door while John felt his heart stop as he watched her leave with Hawkes.

Chapter 39

A small ketch moved south on the Connecticut River past the wharf stretching from the Little Meadow into the river. It was late October 1652 and through his study's window, Richard Hawkes saw the ketch's white foresail angled forward to take advantage of the north wind which had blown in the same direction throughout the week following Farmington church's first service. Hawkes assumed the ketch was heading down river from Springfield with corn and furs from William Pynchon's fort. It would likely pass Saybrook and reach the open sea where it would turn east towards Boston.

A man to be admired, Hawkes thought. *When most merchants bunched together near Boston, Pynchon built an inland trading post and now he controls the fur trade north of Hartford.* Hawkes cut into that trade only because he traded the Indians what they wanted most, which Pynchon didn't. By using Dutch traders and Indians to trade his muskets, Hawkes ensured Pynchon would never suspect he was cutting into Pynchon's own trade. Dutch traders were ubiquitous and Hawkes's Dutch traders blended in with the others.

The ketch had disappeared down the river when he heard a knock at his front door. He continued gazing out the window until one of his servants brought James Eastman and Edward Roach to his study. He turned and nodded to the servant who closed the study's door behind him.

"Sit at the table," Hawkes commanded.

Hawkes watched the two men walk across the study to the table. Roach's expressionless pockmarked face was now heavily creased with deep lines, but Hawkes knew under his brown leather doublet Roach's muscles were just as solid as in his youth. James Eastman hadn't fared as well over the years. He walked towards the table with a limp, which he claimed was due to being thrown from a horse. When Eastman sat, his behind hung over his chair and the folds of his belly draped down between his heavy thighs. The two men sat on opposite sides of the table and waited for Hawkes to sit at the table with them. He didn't. Instead Hawkes looked down at them while standing at the window framed in silhouette by the day's gray light.

"I want to talk about my fur trade and the witches in Connecticut," Hawkes announced.

Neither Eastman nor Roach spoke. Roach stared at Hawkes vacantly, while Eastman looked down at the table, shifting uncomfortably in his chair. Hawkes placed his hands on the table's end and bent over staring at both men.

"What do you know about witches in Connecticut?" Hawkes asked.

"Not much," Eastman answered. "Enough to know I want to stay out of their way."

Hawkes glared at Eastman.

"I'm serious," Hawkes barked. "Reverend Stone wants to stop looking for witches. He claims we've less to fear because fewer witches were discovered in the last six months."

"Sorry Richard," Eastman said. "All I know is Connecticut hanged some witches."

"What about you Edward?" Hawkes asked.

"I heard of a coven of witches in East Anglia," Roach said. "They cast spells on several girls."

"Well, I know a bit more than that," Hawkes said, his voice rising in volume. "Satan is here and the people are afraid. Stone wanted me to ferret out Satan's witches, but he's losing his resolve. I need your help to brace his spine by finding more witches."

"We don't know anything about finding witches," Eastman whined. "Why waste time hunting witches? This has nothing to do with your business?"

"Leave it to me to decide what furthers my business?" Hawkes answered. "You have done well by following my directions and will do so in the future. I will teach you how to find witches and pay you a fair price for each witch you find that's hanged."

Eastman slid back in his chair while Roach stared out the window.

"Satan preys on the weak and the weak are found among the seedy sort," Hawkes continued. "Search among the seedy sort to find those who are peculiar. Look for those who live alone with cats or birds. It is through these creatures witches cast their spells. Look particularly for midwives living alone. Come to me when you find someone you think is a witch and I will finish the investigation."

"We will do what you ask," Eastman said.

Roach merely nodded.

"Good," Hawkes said.

"Now, let's talk about my fur trade," Hawkes said. "I'm uneasy about the Dutch traders I hired to deliver our muskets to Hassun and his Nipmucs. England and Holland are at war and I need to be certain of their loyalty. The rumors of a dark Englishman selling muskets to the Indians stopped when these Dutchmen started delivering my muskets and I no longer fear discovery. We just received a new shipment of muskets from Robert Rose. When you deliver them to the Dutchmen assess their loyalty. If it is strong, we will continue our relationship. If not, take my muskets to Hassun yourselves until we can find some other Dutch traders to take them to him."

Hawkes was pleased as he rode the trail to Farmington later that afternoon. With or without Eastman's help, Roach would find him witches and deal with the Dutchmen. *James can no longer pull his weight*, he thought. *He challenges me too often and is fat and slow. I will wait to see if he does better; but not much longer.*

Hawkes reached Deacon Hart's house and tied his stallion to a post before the house as the sun set. Hart answered his knock.

"Come in Richard," Hart said. "We will sit in the hall."

They sat at the Hall table. A fire blazed in the fireplace and there were five candles burning down the table's middle. Hawkes reached into his deerskin bag and removed the account books for Hart's mills in Hartford, Wethersfield and Windsor.

"Let me look at the books," Hart said.

Hart examined the books while Hawkes sat across the table watching Hart turn the pages. After several minutes Hart lifted his head and said, "While the ratio of corn delivered by the farmers to the cornmeal the mills produce is better than last month, it is still too high. What can you can do to recover more cornmeal from the corn?"

Hawkes hesitated. Until their last meeting, Hart hadn't concerned himself with such details. All he was interested in was his profit. It was easy to hide the share of cornmeal Mark Scott was siphoning off for him before his last meeting with Hart. However, at that meeting for the first time Hart compared the amount of incoming corn to the amount of cornmeal set out in the books and announced his disappointment in the ratio. He had assured Hart he would see that Scott reduced the amount of cornmeal lost in the milling process. He hoped by telling Scott to steal less cornmeal over the next month, Hart would find the ratio satisfactory and stop more detailed examinations. Now, he had to deal with the issue.

"I'll have Mark Scott find better ways to reduce cornmeal losses," Hawkes said. "I will also make certain we get a more accurate count of our incoming grist. It's likely we're not suffering as great a loss of cornmeal as it appears."

"Excellent," Hart announced. "I am pleased you are doing well."

Hart turned his attention to a discussion of operations of each of his mills. As Hart examined the records for his Wethersfield mill, the solution came to Hawkes. *It is so simple*, he thought. *I will have Scott prepare two account books.* The first will accurately document all transactions and the total incoming grist and outgoing cornmeal. The other, which would be shown to Hart, will adjust both the incoming amount of grist and outgoing cornmeal so the ratio will seem adequate.

When the two men completed their discussion, Hawkes asked, "Is Mary home?"

"Not now, but she will be soon. She and her brother are helping John Lee teach Tunxis children today. They usually finish about now."

"It's a waste to teach the Tunxis," Hawkes said. "Their numbers dwindle each year and soon, like the Suckiaug, they will be gone altogether. How will they use what John Lee teaches them when they live as savages again?"

"Mary likes to teach them. Knowing that is enough for me."

Hawkes lifted his account ledger from the table and walked through the front door to his stallion. As he hung the bag with the account books on his saddle, he heard Mary Hart's voice from behind him up the slope to the Town Path.

"Richard, my father said you were coming today. I'm glad you are still here," Mary said.

Hawkes's smiled slightly. He was glad she'd returned before he left, but didn't want to give her the impression he was.

"You can't leave yet," Mary said. "I'm about to fix supper."

Hawkes climbed onto his stallion and looked down at her.

"I have to leave now," he said. "I will have supper next time I come."

"Please stay."

"How can you say no to such an invitation?" Deacon Hart said standing at the house's front door.

Hawkes smiled at Hart, "You're right."

Mary raced into the house to finish preparing supper. She had baked corn bread and cooked pork earlier that morning. All that was left was to boil some radishes and squash. She walked to the well behind the house to draw water to boil the vegetables. A man grabbed her shoulder as she pulled the bucket attached to the well sweep down into the well.

"So, you're glad I'm still here?" Hawkes whispered in her ear, while grabbing her around her narrow waist and turning her to face him.

Mary lost her grip on the well sweep's rope, causing the counterweight at the sweep's other end to yank the bucket she lowered into the well from her hands. She stared into Hawkes's black eyes. A momentary rush of excitement flowed through her, but as Hawkes pulled her tighter into him her excitement turned to fear. She fought to push him away, but his grip tightened.

"Stop Richard," she protested.

"Quiet. Relax and show me you are glad to see me," he whispered into her ear.

He thrust his pelvis into her thigh. She felt his hardness press against her and reflexively pushed her hands against his chest to free herself.

"My father will come any moment," she gasped.

He laughed, "Relax. Your father and brother took his cart to get wood for the fireplace."

"No, no. I mean it. Stop"

She can't be serious, he thought. *They always say no until they say yes.* He pressed his pelvis harder against her and licked her neck with his tongue.

Mary drove her right knee into his groin, while digging her fingernails into his face.

"Damn it," Hawkes said. "What's wrong with you. I thought you were excited to see me."

She pulled away from him, tearing the collar of her bodice. He stepped back. She lowered the well sweep's bucket back into the well and when it was filled let the sweep's pole pull it from the well. She poured the water into the large wooden pitcher she would use to carry it inside.

"Supper will be ready soon," she said without looking at Hawkes.

"I will carry the pitcher for you," Hawkes said.

"No thank you. I can do it."

They ate supper at the kitchen table. Hawkes and Hart talked about Hart's mills while Mary served the two men and her brother Daniel their meals. When she was done, she sat at the table next to her father across from Hawkes. He watched her but her eyes stayed fixed on the food in front of her throughout the meal.

"Why so quiet Mary?" Hart asked.

"I had a busy day and I'm tired," She answered.

Hart leaned towards Mary and touched her shoulder, "Don't forget we've a guest at our table. A guest you invited. Don't you have anything to say to him."

Mary looked up from the table into her father's eyes before turning and looking across the table at Hawkes. He smiled at her. She ignored his smile and quickly turned back to her father and said, "We talked while you and Jonathan went for firewood. I said what I had to say to him then."

Richard Hawkes's ride to Hartford was long and cold. A full moon lit the path, but his mind was elsewhere as his stallion walked steadily along the path. *She's like no other woman I 've known*, he thought. *The others glowed when I showed them affection. What is it that makes her think she's special? I'm wasting my time. Still, there's something about her. She's pure and there has been little purity in my life, especially when my father was drunk. I will try courting her more gently.*

Mary was shocked when James Eastman brought her an embroidered linen bonnet. Her father and brother were in the fields when Eastman came. She spent the morning deciding what she should do the next time Hawkes came to see her father. She knew she couldn't tell her father what happened at the well. *He might think I invited his attention*, she thought. It was a woman's obligation to draw clear lines and her father saw her exuberance when she welcomed Hawkes that afternoon. The best thing to do was to avoid him. Perhaps someday he would no longer have business with her father, and she could avoid him altogether.

When she opened the door, Eastman touched the brim of his hat and held out the bonnet saying, "This bonnet is a gift from Richard Hawkes. He thanks you for yesterday's supper."

Her mouth opened as she stared at the bonnet. She looked into Eastman's fleshy face and wondered how much this disgustingly fat man knew about what Hawkes did to her. Sweat poured down Eastman's face as he stood before her with a vacant smile. How could she have been so wrong about Richard Hawkes, she asked herself. His charm was a ploy and just as vacant as the man's smile standing before her now.

"Can I have a sip of beer?" Eastman asked. "It's hot and it is a long ride back to Hartford?"

At first, she wanted to run into the house and slam the door behind her. She was alone with no intention of inviting this man in after what Richard Hawkes did to her the day before.

"Wait here," she answered.

She closed the door and walked through the parlor to the kitchen, thinking of what to do with the bonnet. *It's disgusting*, she thought. She ran back into the parlor and threw the bonnet into the fireplace's dying coals. It exploded in flames. She stared as small pieces of burning linen floated up the chimney. She sobbed while watching the bonnet disappear. Tears flowed down her cheeks as she realized there would always be a barrier between she and her father. She could never tell him what happened at the well. Only she would know.

She went back to the kitchen to get the beer. As she returned to the door, she looked down at the beer swishing about in the leather noggin. She felt clean for the first time since Richard Hawkes met her at the well the day before.

Two days later the fat man came with another gift. This time she didn't think it was a coincidence he arrived when both her father and brother were in the fields. The gift was a plum colored wool scarf. She refused to take it. He frowned and insisted she take it. When she again refused, the man shook his head. He turned and walked to his horse where he stuffed the scarf into a bag tied to its saddle. She closed the door and stood behind it, listening until she could no longer hear the hoofs of his horse on the trail leading to the Town Path.

The fat man came with gifts two more times during the next two weeks. Both times she refused to accept the gift. By their last meeting the routine was so familiar that when she opened the door the fat man merely said, "This is a gift from Richard Hawkes. Do you want it, or should I return it to him?" She smiled wanly and waved him away.

Richard Hawkes came to Farmington for its church's service on the third Sabbath after the incident at the well. It was the middle of November and the day was cold and gray with a strong north wind, so the service was held in Hart's house's hall. Mary saw Hawkes when he arrived. She seethed as she watched him talk to the congregation's men and women.

It was her responsibility to lead the women in preparing the supper to be served between the morning and afternoon services. She used it as her excuse to spend nearly all the time before the service in the kitchen to avoid Hawkes.

She waited until Hawkes sat on the benches to be used for the service. She chose a seat on the women's benches as far from him as possible. She sat only a few feet from John Lee. She smiled at him before the service began. Throughout the service she avoided looking in Hawkes's direction, but all the while she could feel his eyes on her. She worried about what he might do after the service.

She bolted from her seat for the kitchen as soon as the service ended. If he was going to confront her it would have to be in the kitchen where she would be with the other women. From the kitchen she watched John Lee get his food at the tables in the parlor. Hawkes was nowhere to be seen.

A woman helping her in the kitchen asked Mary to get more water to boil the last vegetables. The large pitcher where she stored water from the well was nearly empty. If they were going to have water to boil vegetables, she would have to go to the well to get more.

She looked at the well from the kitchen door through the gray afternoon. It seemed miles away. She pulled a black wool cape over her bodice, opened the kitchen door and walked to the well. Before going no more than ten feet her left wrist was gripped firmly by a man's hand. She spun around and stared into Richard Hawkes's black eyes. His smile was tight lipped and menacing.

"It was rude to refuse my presents," Hawkes whispered.

Mary froze. *He has been waiting here since the service ended*, she thought. She glared at him. He tightened his grip to keep her from running back into the house.

"Do you have nothing to say to me?" he said.

"No, I don't," she said. "Let go of me."

He pressed his face into hers.

"Why you little bitch," he yelled. "How dare you reject my gifts of affection."

She squirmed. He released his grip on her wrist and grabbed her by both shoulders pulling her into him. The water pitcher fell from her hand as she continued to squirm.

"Release her Richard . . . now!" John Lee yelled from outside the kitchen door.

The wind was blowing, and dead leaves flew about them as Hawkes let loose of Mary. He and John stared at each other ten feet apart on the straw used for the floor to Farmington's church just three weeks before.

"Go into the house Mary," John said calmly.

Mary slowly moved towards the door while the two men

continued to stare at each other. Hawkes was breathing heavily, his face taut and his blood boiling. *First, this woman treats me like a common laborer and now this teacher of Indians is ordering me about with impunity,* he thought. Hawkes lowered his shoulder and charged John, intent on knocking him to the ground. John anticipated his charge and slid to the side while slamming his fist into Hawkes's forehead driving him to the ground on his stomach. As he lay on the ground, Hawkes's anger ebbed. He rolled over and pulled himself into a sitting position looking up at his rival through the blood pouring down his forehead.

"This fight isn't over," Hawkes announced. "The next time you won't see me coming."

"It would be best if you returned to Hartford now," John said.

Hawkes rose to his feet and reached down to pick up his black hat. He brushed the straw off it. He smiled smugly at both John and Mary before walking around the house and up the slope to where his stallion was tied.

When he disappeared, Mary looked at John and whispered, "Thank you."

"Are you alright?"

"Yes. Just shaken."

"Let's get that water now," John declared.

Chapter 40

"Why don't you come to Boston and work for me again Richard?" Robert Rose asked.

Richard Hawkes smiled across the table at Rose without answering. It was the middle of March 1653 and he'd been in Boston for over a week. He knew Rose could use his help. After all, Rose was now in his late seventies and always wore a hat to hide his baldness. *But I owe him nothing*, Hawkes thought. *He has made a good living off his ten percent of my musket trade and will continue to do so if he keeps getting muskets for me and selling the beaver pelts I get for them.*

"Maybe in a few years," he answered.

"I can't understand why you stay in Hartford. You are unmarried and have nothing to tie you down. I enjoy your company and can afford to pay you a great deal."

"Let's talk in a few years," Hawkes said smiling.

"You can wager on it," Rose answered. "What did you do on this trip?"

"I spent time with Reverend Stone. He's been in Boston for several weeks and we discussed our church's rift."

"I know of it," Rose said. "In fact, I don't know anyone in Boston who doesn't. When will you settle this dispute with William Goodwin and his followers?"

"Not soon. The opposition is trying to remove Stone. I told him to come to Boston as much as possible. When he's here they can't push a vote on his removal. We met this week and developed a strategy for defeating Goodwin's latest candidate."

"Just release them from their covenant and the problem will go away," Rose said.

"Reverend Stone won't permit it and I agree with him," Hawkes replied. "We need their tithes. It will drain our coffers if we give them up."

"So be it," Rose laughed. "Fight on if you will."

It was sunset when Hawkes returned to the room he rented for the two weeks he was in Boston. It was in the town's center overlooking the meetinghouse. Just as during every visit he made to Boston the past two years, Phoebe Williams would be waiting for him. He entered the room at sunset. She sat on a large pillow before the fireplace. Her blond hair glowed in the fire as she turned to face him.

"Let's go to the tavern tonight," Phoebe said.

"No, I want to stay here," Hawkes answered. "Go to the tavern and get two noggins of beer."

She smiled coyly and lightly touched his lips with her finger.

"So, we're staying here tonight?" She said, running her finger down his neck.

Hawkes admired Phoebe's body as she tied her bodice and stepped into her skirt. At twenty-six years her face glowed like a child's and her skin was soft and inviting. Still, there was that missing front tooth. *Damn the bastard who struck her mouth that night*, he cursed to himself. *But I don't need perfect tonight.*

He removed his cape and doublet and lay two other pillows next to the one Phoebe placed on the floor. He was lying on a pillow in front of the fire when she returned. She smiled at him, while trying unsuccessfully to hide the gap between her teeth by placing her hand in front of her mouth. He pointed to the pillow next to him. She handed him a noggin of beer as she lie down beside him. He sat up and took a drink before undoing the ties to her bodice. He fondled her breasts while licking her neck. He removed his doublet and shirt as she lie moaning with her eyes closed. He lie back down and she untied the cord of his breeches.

After a few minutes fondling each other on the floor. he began to feel the frustration of unrealized arousal. *Damn*, he thought, *this never happens to me with her.* The harder he tried, the tenser he became, until suddenly in a peak of frustration he sat up.

"Stay there while I drink more beer," he ordered.

She slid over on her pillow, moving closer to him, and smiled before slipping her right hand between his thighs.

"You are so strong Richard," she whispered. "Come back to me. I need you tonight."

He stared down at her dispassionately. *It's the bitch Mary Hart's fault*, he thought. *She has sapped my strength. Damn her. Who is she to reject me?* His frustration turned to rage as he thought of the day at Deacon Hart's well when she and John Lee humiliated him.

Phoebe tried again. This time she slid against him and ran her right hand across his shoulders, down his back and across his stomach while gently nibbling his ear lobe.

"Enough!" he yelled, simultaneously slamming his right hand into her head, knocking her unconscious on the floor.

He drank the rest of his beer after which he drank hers. She rolled onto her side moaning in pain. He pushed his right foot into her chest.

"Wake up," he said. "It's time to leave."

Still groggy, Phoebe rolled onto her back and looked up at him.

"Why did you hit me?" she cried. "Why did you hit me?"

He sneered down at her and ordered, "Get up. It's time for you to leave. I will kill you if you tell anyone what happened tonight. Understand?"

"I won't tell," she whispered.

Hawkes knocked on Rose's door the next morning. The door opened immediately. He froze as he gazed at the young woman answering it. For a moment he thought she was Mary Hart. Her resemblance to Mary was startling. *If anything, she's even more beautiful*, he thought.

"Good day sir." the young woman said. "May I help you?"

What a soft confident voice, he thought. He stared into her pale blue eyes as she stood at the door waiting for his answer. Her tight yellow bodice revealed the shape of her breasts and her slender waist. Her light brown hair was tied up under a white linen cap worn at the center of her head and her skin was fair and pure. *This woman would not frustrate me*, he said to himself while imagining how she would look with her hair hanging loosely over her bare shoulders.

"Sir, may I help you?" she repeated, louder this time.

"Oh, yes," he said. "My name is Richard Hawkes. How is it I have never seen you when I visited Mr. Rose."

The young woman lowered her eyes and announced, "I will take you to Mr. Rose's parlor room."

He followed her through the house. When she continued walking to the parlor he stopped.

"Wait," he said. "You didn't answer my question. How is it I haven't seen you here before?"

The young woman turned back to him.

"I only started working in Mr. Rose's house two weeks ago."

"What is your name?"

"Please follow me to the parlor sir. Mr. Rose will be angry if I delay taking you to the room."

"Answer my question," he said with a smile. "I will protect you from Mr. Rose."

"My name is Elizabeth Lewis. Now please follow me."

Hawkes smiled to himself as he followed her to the parlor. She was about five foot six inches in height and quite slender. She moved gracefully, suggesting at one time she served in the house of someone important.

"Please sit at the table sir," she said pointing to the oak table in the parlor.

Hawkes sat in the same oak chair he sat in whenever he met Rose.

"Where are you from?" he asked.

She bit her lower lip and said, "Please sir, Mr. Rose will be angry if I don't get back to work."

"She's from Chelmsford," Rose laughed as he entered the room. "You are free to go Elizabeth. I will call you if we need anything."

Rose smiled at Hawkes as soon as Elizabeth left. "Fancy her, do you?" Rose asked.

Hawkes leaned back in his chair with his arms folded across his chest, "Much so. How did you find her?"

"I suppose our business can wait a while," Rose answered. "She was the chief maid's daughter in my friend's house. Her father worked as the family's stable master. My friend wrote me saying she wanted to come to Boston. I paid for her passage and she's indentured to me for five years."

"She's not the type of girl you see in Boston," Hawkes said. "Would she like to live in Connecticut?"

"Why so fast, Richard?"

"My decision isn't final, but the thought of bringing her to Connecticut as my wife is intriguing. I leave in a few days and would like to learn more about her before I do."

"Tell me when you want to see her and I'll arrange it," Rose said. "Now let's talk about the fur business."

"Of course."

"I just received payment for the pelts we shipped to England six months ago. They were high quality and we received two thousand pounds for the shipment. I have deducted my ten percent commission for arranging the sale which leaves you one thousand eight hundred pounds."

"That was a good shipment. I will keep ten pounds now. Arrange for the rest of my payment to be sent by ship as soon as possible."

"I will," Rose answered.

"And Elizabeth?" Hawkes asked.

"Come here tomorrow afternoon. She'll be waiting for you."

Richard Hawkes met Elizabeth Lewis at Rose's house each day of the last three days he was in Boston. Each visit followed the same pattern. They met in late afternoon and he took her to an inn within walking distance of Rose's house. During their dinner conversations Elizabeth asked about his family and his calling. He told half-truths, saying his family owned a large farm in Essex and he made his living farming and trading with the Indians. He asked no questions about her for he knew all he needed to. The last night they met for dinner, he asked her if she would like to live with him in Connecticut. She gasped with surprise, saying she didn't know him long enough to marry him. He promised to visit her the next time he was in Boston if she first assured him she was open to marriage when they knew each other long enough. He told her if they married he would buy her indenture. When he left Boston, he knew the next time he came she would return to Connecticut with him.

Chapter 41

The apple trees were in bloom and the oaks filled with leaves as John drove his cart up to the Town Path from his house on a bright June morning. His eyes itched from tree pollen floating in the gentle breeze flowing up from the Farmington River behind him. He'd done his morning's work and the day was now his.

He turned onto the Town Path, searching his mind for anything he may have forgotten for the picnic. He and Mary had planned the picnic with her brother Daniel and Daniel's new wife Judith. Judith thought of having the picnic and Mary agreed instantly. The two women prepared the food while Daniel found a spot on the hill across the river with a clear view of both the river and the town. John volunteered to take them in his cart.

It took John all morning to clean the cart. He now worried whether he did all the small things Mary asked him to do. Finally, he convinced himself he brought the tinderbox, flint and steel for lighting their picnic fire, the stools to sit on, and the small table to place the food on.

He recalled his surprise when Mary invited him to the picnic. Looking back, he realized he should not have been. Before he confronted Richard Hawkes at her father's well eight months ago, Mary was polite to him and she was always serious when they taught at his school. After the day at the well she changed. She started more of their conversations; she laughed when they were together; she made suggestions about how they should teach the Tunxis; and, she moved closer to him when they were alone. He saw the signs but refused to accept them. He smiled to himself as the cart rolled along.

He reined in the black gelding, pulling the cart to a stop in front of Deacon Hart's house. The front door opened as he finished tying the gelding to the post outside the house.

"Good day John. I heard your cart," Deacon Hart said. "Mary is waiting."

"Please tell her I am here."

"I will. First, I want to talk to you about this damnable mess with Elder Goodwin."

Hart led John into the hall where they sat at the table. John smelled the food for the picnic and hoped their conversation would be brief.

"The matter would settle quickly if Elder Goodwin and his followers were released from their covenant," John said. "You could start your own church."

Hart frowned and folded his arms over his chest, "That won't happen. You know as well as I that Reverend Stone won't release them from their covenant. It would look like he gave in to them. Besides, the church would suffer a huge financial loss when it lost their tithes."

"There's no answer to this conflict if that's true," John asserted.

Their conversation was interrupted by the sound of women laughing in the parlor.

"Sounds like Mary and Judith are excited about the picnic," Hart laughed.

"I will help them," John said, rising from his chair with a smile.

Both Mary and Judith stood at the table when John entered the parlor. Mary turned to him with a bright smile. Meanwhile, Judith packed a large cloth bag with trenchers, spoons and napkins. She failed to notice John and asked Mary to get more napkins from the cabinet.

"Would you like me to help you Judith?" John asked.

Judith smiled at John while Mary reached up and pulled the napkins from the cabinet. Judith packed the last napkins in the bag and handed it to John.

"Here is your reward for surprising me," Judith said. "Take this bag to the cart."

"Yes ma'am," John said with a grin.

When he returned, Daniel and the two women were packing a basket with the ham, cornbread and beans. Daniel loaded it into the cart and helped Judith aboard, before climbing in next to her. With Mary seated next to him, John whipped the reins twice and the gelding pulled them up the slope from Deacon Hart's house onto the Town Path.

The cart moved slowly down the Town Path towards the road to Hartford. Time froze as they slid in and out of the sun's rays. This cycle continued for two miles while Daniel and Judith's flirting and laughing filled John's ears and the clean smell of Mary's hair filled his nostrils.

He glanced at Mary several times as they moved through the trees. Most of the time she looked straight ahead or to the trees on her right with her eyes half closed and a relaxed smile on her face. But as they neared the road to Hartford, each time he looked at her, she was gazing at him with a faraway look in her eyes. The spell of serenity broke when they reached the road to Hartford. There the Town Path's trees were replaced by broad meadows allowing the sun's rays to fall on them. He turned the cart west towards the Farmington River.

At the river, John tied the gelding to a tree with the cart next to it before climbing into the small boat used to cross the river. Daniel moved to the front of the boat, while John sat at the back. Mary and Judith sat in the center of the boat with the basket and packages resting between them. John pulled the boat across the river by a rope stretching over the river to the other side and hooked to the boat by another rope. A large hill loomed over them on the river's other side.

It was mid-afternoon when they reached the spot Daniel picked for the picnic. It was near the hill's summit in an area with few trees, allowing them to see John's gelding, the cart, the river flowing below them, and the farms above it climbing to the trees along the Town Path. John and Daniel set up the table while Mary and Judith placed the food on it.

John said a prayer when they were seated. He lifted his head and looked at Mary when he finished. She looked back at him. A warm smile filled her face. He nodded at her and squeezed her hand after which the four of them filled their plates.

"Look, a hawk," Judith yelled looking into the sky above the river. "It's diving at the finch flying above the trees along the river."

They watched the hawk swoop down on the unsuspecting bird. It struck the finch, knocking it from the air. The hawk flapped its wings until it was high enough to circle the disabled bird as it lay on the rocks at the river's edge. It dove again, this time slower, and grabbed the finch in its talons, carrying it over the trees on the opposite side of the river.

"That poor bird," Judith moaned.

"The hawk has to eat," Daniel said. "He's only following nature's rules."

"Rules or not, I still think it's sad," Judith said.

"Not all rules are fair," Daniel answered.

"That's enough you two," Mary said. "This is a picnic and the rule for a picnic is everyone has fun."

John laughed, "That's a rule I like."

It was late afternoon when they took the boat back across the river. The trip from the river to the Town Path was uneventful until they saw Richard Hawkes, James Eastman and Edward Roach riding towards them.

"It's Hawkes and his men," John cautioned. "I'll talk to them."

Hawkes and his men were within one hundred yards of the cart when John glanced at Mary. She stared coldly at Hawkes as the two parties closed. Judith and Daniel moved forward as far they could until each of them gripped John and Mary's seat. At fifty yards, Hawkes's lips twisted into a cynical smile. Both Roach and Eastman moved their horses closer to Hawkes's black stallion. Even with the three horses closer together John knew there was not enough room to guide the cart past them.

"He's blocking us," John exclaimed.

"What will you do?" Mary asked.

"It will be alright."

"Do you need help?" Daniel asked.

"No."

John reined his horse to a stop and waited for Hawkes and his men to close the distance between them. When they were within twenty feet, Hawkes stopped his stallion.

"Good day John Lee," Hawkes said. "I am surprised to see you and your friends here today."

"What brings you to Farmington?" John asked.

"To inspect my land across the river," Hawkes announced.

Hawkes pushed back the brim of his broad hat and looked at Mary and Judith with a smug smile.

"I am also pleased to be able to inspect such fine ladies today."

Judith lowered her eyes, but Mary refused to feign modesty. Instead, she glowered at Hawkes until he laughed.

"I warn you," John said, his eyes blazing. "Your language and tone are offensive. Should I assume you intended this?"

"Draw your own conclusion," Hawkes answered while his stallion pawed at the ground.

Too clever, John thought, as he saw a chance to end the confrontation.

" I assume you had no such intent," John stated. "Now move aside and let us through."

Hawkes stared at John for a moment. He knew John and Mary would be on a picnic that afternoon. Judith had told all her friends and neighbors about it. Such gossip moved quickly between Farmington and Hartford. Hawkes planned if he subtly insulted Mary as he did, John would feel bound to defend her honor. Hawkes knew he couldn't beat John in a fair fight. That's why he brought Edward and James with him. Now his dream of humiliating John in front of Mary was dashed. He decided to take control with an announcement. He moved aside letting the cart pass.

"I'm looking forward to seeing you more often," Hawkes said. "I married Elizabeth Lewis of Boston. Her beauty will light up Connecticut."

"Congratulations," John said as he passed Hawkes and his men.

Mary looked at John and shook her head when the cart was beyond Hawkes's hearing.

"That poor woman," she said. "That poor woman."

PART SIX
1656 - 1666

Chapter 42

The Hartford meetinghouse benches were nearly full when John Lee sat next to Deacon Hart. Hart glanced at him and shrugged.

"I never thought it would come to this," Hart grumbled. "This conflict started in 1647 and has raged nine years."

"It looks like everyone is here," John said.

"And some. The meetinghouse is filled with clergy from throughout Connecticut and even a few from Massachusetts Bay."

John glanced across the aisle to his left where the supporters of Elder Goodwin were seated. Goodwin sat in the center of the first row staring at the five clergymen chosen to hear the dispute between him and Reverend Stone. William Westwood sat next to Goodwin. William's hair was gray and his face heavily lined.

John was uncomfortable sitting where he was. Except for Deacon Hart, the men he sat with weren't his friends. Stone and Hawkes sat together in the front row to Hart's left whispering back and forth.

"Everyone be seated," announced the man sitting in the middle of the clergymen. "This meeting of the Connecticut clergy will begin."

The man was Reverend John Warham of Windsor, whose reputation was that of a meticulous interpreter of Puritan doctrine. On each side of Warham sat the four other ministers chosen by the clergy of Connecticut to hear the matter.

"The General Court has requested that we recommend a solution to the two sides in the Hartford church's dispute between the followers of Reverend Samuel Stone and Elder William Goodwin. We're not judges, and our recommendation is not binding. Still, it is the General Court's hope our recommendation will provide a basis for both sides to settle their differences, so the General Court won't need to decide the matter."

Warham leaned forward and announced, "Proceed Mr. Goodwin."

Goodwin rose, looked at the five ministers in front of him, and announced, "I come before you today with respect and with the belief you will issue a just recommendation. Whatever your decision, I and my followers will accept it."

For the next two hours Goodwin and three other men explained their side's position. They complained how Reverend Stone failed to recognize the principle that members of congregational churches have the right to select their minister and to vote on changes to a church's doctrines. They complained Stone refused their request for a vote to select a minister following Reverend Hooker's death and Stone took the position the unconverted's children could be baptized without the congregation's vote. Finally, they complained Stone refused to release them from their covenant with the church, when all their efforts for redress failed.

When Goodwin and his men were finished, Warham leaned forward and looked out at the people.

"It's noon," Warham said. "We'll take a one-hour break after which we will hear Reverend Stone's argument."

They said nothing new, John thought to himself. *They will change no one's mind. Why doesn't Stone just let them leave the congregation?* He glanced across the room at William. *How has it come to this?* he thought. *"What I wouldn't give to sit with he and Bridget for supper in the warmth of their home. Things can never be as they were.*

"Why so glum John?" a familiar reedy voice asked.

He looked up from his seat into Sam Pierce's smiling face. He sprang from his seat and grabbed Sam's arms with a broad smile.

"Good to see you Sam," John said. "It's been too long."

"More than a year."

"Longer, I think," John said. "How have you been? How is Abigail?"

"Good," Sam answered.

"Come back and help me and Mary teach at my school? Bring Abigail with you."

"Ah, Mary," Sam said with a grin. "When are ya two gonna' marry?"

"Soon. Mary still feels duty bound to take care of her father and her younger brothers and sisters."

He looked carefully at Sam. Sam's once smooth ruddy red face was heavily lined and his auburn hair thin. But his blue gray eyes still sparkled, and his broad smile still gleamed.

"What are you doing here?" John asked.

"I knew you'd be here." Sam answered. "You didn't answer my question."

"What question?"

"Why were ya so glum when I saw ya?"

"Just tired of this conflict."

Sam scanned the room and announced, "Everyone's coming back to their seats. I need to greet William. I'll help you teach. Abigail will come with me."

John watched Sam cross to the other side of the meetinghouse. William's face brightened when he saw Sam approach. He grabbed Sam's shoulders and hugged him. John sighed just before Deacon Hart sat down next to him.

"Reverend Stone, you may proceed," Warham announced.

Stone rose and faced the five clergymen.

"I'll speak first about what is now called the Half-Way Covenant. After I've finished, Richard Hawkes will respond to Elder Goodwin's complaint that I've refused to allow a vote on a new minister and denied them the right to move to another church."

Stone set forth an impassioned defense of the Half-Way Covenant. While acknowledging Reverend Hooker never supported allowing children of unconverted church members to be baptized, he stressed it was because Hooker feared to do so would remove an incentive for people to convert. He argued times had changed and today Reverend Hooker would support such baptisms if the unconverted parents promised to continue to seek evidence God granted them grace, so they could convert later.

Stone closed with an impassioned plea, "Why should these children be denied the gift of baptism simply because their parents haven't yet sought conversion? Surely, God didn't establish such barriers; nor should we."

John took a deep breath when Stone finished. He wondered how different things might be if Stone hadn't come under the influence of Richard Hawkes. Stone was right on this issue, but wrong on so many others.

Hawkes rose when Stone finished.

"Now what does Elder Goodwin want?" Hawkes asked. "What he and his followers want is what they could never get if a vote was taken. They want a new minister, but if a vote had been taken, the vote would have been for Reverend Stone, for our congregation's majority has always favored him. They also want to stop baptizing the unconverted's children, but if there was a vote they would have also lost, for the majority favors the baptism of these children. So, if they couldn't get what they wanted, why have they persisted in a fight they began. There's only one reason. Their leaders seek the destruction of Reverend Stone and our church."

A gasp erupted from the people on Goodwin's side of the room. Several men jumped to their feet.

"Slander, slander," shouted a man two rows behind Goodwin.

"We would have won the vote if Stone permitted one," shouted a man sitting next to Goodwin.

"Silence, silence," Reverend Warham yelled. But the shouting continued.

Hawkes has what he wants, John thought. *It is now impossible to reach a compromise.*

"Silence, silence," Warham continued.

The shouting ebbed and stopped after several minutes of Warham's pleading. When everyone was seated, Warham looked at Hawkes and said, "You may continue Mr. Hawkes."

Hawkes nodded and began speaking in a powerful clear voice.

"How do I know what their real motive is?" Hawkes said. "It's obvious because they have slandered Reverend Stone, while trying to remove him, and they have decided to leave our church, knowing this will weaken it. If this council recommends they be allowed to leave, each church in Connecticut will be threatened. What will keep a discontented minority in any of them from objecting to the majority's position on an issue and without just cause leave their church, violating the covenants they entered. Like the Hartford church, the other churches will weaken by losing tithes needed to support them."

Hawkes sat down amidst the shouts of men on both sides. John sat quietly as the shouting continued. He glanced across the aisle and saw William seated with his head bowed.

The clergymen reached a decision late that afternoon. The benches were full, and the Meetinghouse walls lined with men waiting to receive the recommendation most hoped would end the dispute. A nervous silence filled the room as Reverend Warham read the clergymen's decision.

"After hearing both sides, the council of clergy recommends the following. First, both sides shall try one more time to resolve this dispute. Second, if differences cannot be healed, the dissenters shall seek their dismissal from the church and the church should give it to them."

Goodwin's supporters cheered and grabbed each other in joy. Across the room, where Reverend Stone's supporters sat, there was silence. When the recommendation's full consequences were clear, Stone's supporters yelled in protest. John sat still, suppressing the waves of joy he felt, for now there would be an end to the suicidal struggle within the church.

Hawkes was shocked. He grabbed Reverend Stone's arm. Stone was in a daze and stared ahead at Reverend Warham in disbelief. Hawkes shouted at Stone over the noise, "You can't let this recommendation stand. It's a victory for Elder Goodwin and it will destroy us."

"What can I do?"

"Reject the decision and refuse to follow it"

"But I agreed to this council," Stone said, shaking his head.

"Withdraw your agreement now, for if you don't, this decision will take root and you can never reject it," Hawkes raged.

"How should I do that?"

"Stand and announce you reject the decision as beyond the clerics' power and not binding."

John watched with trepidation as Hawkes and Stone talked while the crowd quieted. Stone stood when the room was silent.

"I have considered the council's decision," Stone announced. "Mr. Hawkes will announce my decision."

Elder Goodwin's supporters grumbled as Hawkes stood.

"Reverend Stone thanks the convention's ministers. Unfortunately, he rejects their recommendation for accepting it means our church's death. Only the General Court can issue a binding decision. It hasn't done so."

Protests erupted from Goodwin's supporters. They shouted at the clergy and then at Reverend Stone's cheering supporters across the aisle. Hawkes led Stone down the aisle between the warring factions as half the room jeered and the other half cheered them. Meanwhile, Reverend Warham and the other clergymen sat in silence. When it was clear there could be no further proceedings without Reverend Stone, the spectators began to funnel down the aisle towards the meetinghouse door.

John flowed with the crowd into the aisle. Suddenly, he was

face to face with William. He looked at William in stunned silence. William stared back at him with a pained expression.

"What horrible evil did you bring upon us?" William spat. "How could you choose Reverend Stone and Richard Hawkes over the people who care for you?"

Before William finished, the jostling crowd pulled him and John apart. William quickly flowed down the aisle and out the door.

Chapter 43

It was a clear April morning in 1657 as John Lee rode his horse across the Little River on the bridge leading to Hartford's North Plantation. Across the bridge, his horse's hoofs dug into the road to the meetinghouse. He smiled at the people walking on the raised wooden walkway lining the road. The first people to arrive for the weekly market day filled the best spots along the path to the meetinghouse. He rode past them on the path while they set out vegetables, handmade looms, tools, clothing, and assorted items they brought to sell.

Lieutenant Bull smiled at John from the meetinghouse porch. Bull's russet doublet was opened to just below his chest, revealing his white linen shirt.

"About time you came," Bull laughed. "Everyone is inside."

John smiled and tied his horse to a post below the porch.

"I'm not late," John said. "Why is everyone so early?"

"Hungry for supper after the ceremony I suppose. The women prepared a side of beef."

They climbed the porch stairs to the chamber. When they reached the chamber door, Bull waived his right hand at the door.

"You first John," Bull said. "Your friends are waiting."

John opened the door and stared into the chamber. He was met by four dozen smiles. Immediately, Deacon Hart grabbed his arm.

"Let's get on with it," Hart exclaimed.

Hart led John down the aisle to an oak table behind which five empty seats faced them. When they reached the first row of benches Hart pointed to two empty seats along the aisle.

"We sit here John," Hart said. "The particular court's members are coming."

John's heart beat furiously. He turned and looked at the people behind him. Two rows back were Sam Pierce and his wife, Abigail. Near them sat Lieutenant Bull and Daniel Hart. Then he saw Mary. Immediately a wide smile broke across her face. He wished they were alone and not with four dozen others.

The door behind opened with a loud bang as it hit its frame. The room silenced as the five particular court's members entered the chamber. When they were seated, the Chief Judge announced, "This particular court is in session. Our only matter today is the installation of Farmington's new constable."

The room's back door opened after the announcement. John looked back. *My God*, he thought. *They're here.* His pulse beat faster as he watched William and Bridget Westwood sit in the room's last row. His eyes met William's. William nodded. Bridget's face was creased with lines, but her smile was the same as he remembered.

"We're here to install John Lee as Constable of Farmington," the Chief Judge announced. "John Lee has served Connecticut in war and peace. A hero in the Pequot War, he later served as sergeant of our militia under Lieutenant Thomas Bull, who recommends his appointment as constable."

The Chief Judge turned and looked at John.

"John Lee, rise for the oath of office."

John faced the court. After John took the oath, the Chief Judge announced, "Congratulations Constable Lee."

John turned to the people behind him and watched the men quickly set up several tables and place the food the women prepared on them. When John turned back to the judges they were gone. He spotted Mary standing behind a table prepared to serve the people in line to receive supper. He watched her until Deacon Hart grabbed his arm.

"What will you do with your power?" Hart asked.

"Learn how to use it," John quipped.

"Well old Nicholas Wakeman seems to have skipped that step. He never learned to use his power because as far as I know he did nothing."

"Come now Stephen," Lieutenant Bull said walking into the conversation. "We've Nicholas to thank for holding the position until John filled it."

As the banter between Hart and Bull continued, John looked at Mary. She was still serving the line of people at her table. He continued to stare at her until she raised her eyes and looked at him. Immediately, her face broke into a beatific smile.

"Excuse me," John said to no one in particular.

Within seconds he was beside her.

"Congratulations John," she whispered looking into his eyes.

She lowered her right hand and gently grasped his left hand as they continued to gaze into each other's eyes.

"I thought about the question you asked," she said.

"And?" he asked.

"My answer is yes."

John's heart was about to explode. He stared at Mary in silence until she laughed.

"You have nothing to say?" she asked.

He grabbed both her hands and squeezed them as they looked at each other. He realized several friends had gathered around them. He looked at them sheepishly and smiled while Mary laughed.

"Do you have something to tell us?" Deacon Hart asked.

"Not now, but soon," he answered.

In the excitement of Mary's announcement, John realized he forgot to greet William and Bridget. He found them standing near the door to the chamber talking with Lieutenant Bull. His throat tightened as he walked towards them. *What should I say, what can I say?* he asked himself. As he reached them his fear evaporated when Bridget looked at him teary-eyed and said, "It has been too long John. I missed you so much."

He touched Bridget's hand as he said, "I missed you too. Thank you for coming."

William placed his right arm around Bridget as the two men's eyes met.

"You came to this chamber and others like it with me so many times," William said. "It is only proper I come to this chamber with you now. Congratulations John."

William clasped John's right hand with both hands. A relaxed smile filled William's face as they looked at each other.

"I know you will be a good constable; you will exercise good judgment in all you do; and, be fair in all your dealings," William said.

"How could it be any other way," John answered. "You taught me this."

William released his grip on John's hand and backed up until the two men were several feet apart.

"Bridget and I must leave," William said. "You will always be a welcome guest in our home."

John watched William and Bridget until the door to the meetinghouse chamber closed behind them. When he turned back to the chamber, Deacon Hart, Mary Hart and Sam Pierce faced him. Mary dabbed a few tears from her eyes while Hart smiled, and Sam continued looking at the closed door.

"I am glad William and Bridget came today," Hart said.

"I am too," John whispered.

A guest, John thought. *That's what I will always be now. There's too much between us for me to be anything else.*

Chapter 44

The rocks were everywhere. Wherever Sam plowed, rocks flew, and the share's cutting edge pushed them onto the moldboard from where they slid back to the ground behind the plow. They rolled over each other in the dry dirt as the plow moved through it and then, as if by some sinister design, fell together back into the furrow he just cut. He looked above at the heavy gray May sky and cursed his luck, for it was these rocks that kept him from having good harvests. Sam resigned himself to another useless day in his fields, without any hope tomorrow would prove better.

Abigail left early morning to see a sick friend living a few miles north of town and would not return until the next afternoon. Sam removed the plow's harness from the two oxen he borrowed from William Westwood. He placed the harness in his cart, then hooked the oxen to the cart. As the oxen pulled the cart across his rocky field, he thought of his impossible situation. Richard Hawkes agreed to temporarily forgo taking ten percent of Sam's corn for a year so Sam could keep enough to pay his farm's expenses. Sam was now a year behind his payments and had traded his own oxen and plow for enough corn to survive the winter just ended. He received a visit from James Eastman and Edward Roach the month before. They demanded payment of this ten percent. When Sam said he no longer had a plow nor an ox, they told him to plant corn in mounds like the Indians for Richard Hawkes would not find his excuse adequate.

It was a month since Sam watched John Lee become Farmington's constable and while he knew his old friend would help him if he asked, Sam's pride would not let him ask John for help. Instead, he went to William. William immediately loaned him two oxen, a plow, and a cart for the planting season. Even so, William's generosity was not enough, for Sam knew his problem was never a lack of equipment or manpower. His problem was always the rocks now crunching under the cart's wheels as the oxen pulled him closer to his small wooden barn where he would store the plow until tomorrow.

It was dark when Sam reached the barn. He lit a candle once inside. He placed the candle on the ladder leading to the loft ten feet above him and went outside to get the plow. The oxen were grazing before the cart when he lifted the plow from the cart's bed to take it into the barn.

He was startled when he heard the whine of James Eastman's voice behind him, "The plow looks too heavy for you to handle on your own Sam. Let me help you."

The plow hit the cart's bed with a thud as Sam dropped it back down and spun to face Eastman and Edward Roach. There was enough light for him to see Eastman's smug grin and broad flat nose. Edward Roach towered six inches above Eastman. Normally expressionless, tonight Roach smiled revealing the black gap where his front teeth had been torn out.

Sam backed away from the cart towards the barn while looking for a way to escape. Roach quickly slid behind him, cutting off any chance to reach the woods behind the barn.

"Relax Sam," Eastman announced as he moved to the cart. "Pick up the plow and I will help you carry it into the barn."

Sam walked slowly back to the cart. He lifted the plow from the cart's bed. Eastman announced, "Well, I guess you don't need my help. We will follow you into the barn."

Richard Hawkes watched the three men enter the barn while sitting on his black stallion just beyond the trees behind Sam's barn. He tied his horse to a post outside the barn. He heard Eastman's voice inside as he approached the barn's door.

"Pay us the corn you owe for last year within a week or give us your farm?" Eastman demanded.

Sam dropped the plow on the barn's floor and stared at Eastman, "I got no corn to pay for last year and, so far as I seen, Richard Hawkes has done nothin' to earn it nor any corn I harvest this year."

Roach grabbed Sam from behind, pinning his arms to his side. The black gap in Roach's mouth grew even larger as Roach's smile broadened. The scent of manure filled the air as Sam struggled to free himself. When it was clear he couldn't break Roach's grip, Sam relaxed and glared at Eastman.

Eastman slammed his right fist into Sam's face. Blood flowed from Sam's nose, but his glare remained. Eastman slammed his fist into Sam's face again. A nasty red welt appeared beneath Sam's left eye and blood poured freely from his nose.

"Enough James," Hawkes ordered as he entered the barn. "Sam is our customer and if there was any doubt, he now knows what he owes me for my services. Release him Edward. It's hard for a man to talk when the breath is being squeezed out of him."

Roach released Sam and stepped away from him. Sam took a step back and glared at Hawkes. Hawkes smiled calmly while walking to Sam.

"James shouldn't have hit you," Hawkes said. "You had a hard year and I am willing to modify our agreement's terms."

Sam wiped the blood from his nose and stared into Hawkes's black eyes, "I told 'em I got no corn to give ya and as far as I can tell I got nothin' for what I gave ya already."

"Sam, Sam," Hawkes whispered shaking his head. "We made a deal years ago, and until last year, when I loaned you what you owed me so you could keep your farm afloat, you fulfilled your promise and I fulfilled mine. Your corn was always ground earlier than those who refused my offer, and no one stole your corn. Did I promise anything more?"

"But I never got more than them that didn't pay ya extra," Sam answered. "They got their corn ground and there have been no corn thefts in years."

"A bad bargain is still a bargain," Hawkes said. "You still owe me enough corn to pay the ten percent of your last harvest. I will forgive what you owe me if you agree to pay me twenty percent of each of your future harvests."

"I don't want a new agreement," Sam shouted. "I'm endin' the one we got now."

"It's too late," Hawkes answered, his arms crossed in front of him. "Either accept the agreement I offer, or I will take your farm."

Sam glared through the flickering candlelight at Hawkes and snapped, "I won't make a new deal with you and you can't have my farm. To hell with you. Now get off my property."

Damn him, damn him, Hawkes raged inside. *I can't let him challenge me in front of my men.* Instantly, he drove his fist into Sam's face. Sam fell to the ground. *That son of a bitch*, Hawkes thought, as he jumped on Sam with his legs straddling his body. He bent over Sam, sticking his face into his.

"This is your last chance," Hawkes yelled. "Agree to my terms."

Sam spit in Hawkes's face. Hawkes felt the slimy wad of spit slide down his cheek. *God damn the bastard*, he cursed to himself.

"You better kill me now, 'cause if ya don't, I'll tell Constable Lee what you did tonight," Sam yelled.

Damn, damn him. No, no, Hawkes raged. He saw a rock near Sam's head. *Yes.* It was in his hand in an instant. *Now.* He heard a loud thud as he slammed the rock into the side of Sam's head. Silence filled the barn as Hawkes exhaled.

Roach smiled as he stood over the two men. Sam lay motionless in the dirt while Hawkes knelt over him staring into his lifeless eyes. Eastman stood farther away staring at the same scene in stunned silence. Hawkes lifted himself from the ground. *Stupid, stupid*, he thought. *Now you will get nothing from this weasel.* He looked at Eastman.

"Fix the barn so it looks like he fell from the ladder to the loft and struck his head on the rock," Hawkes ordered.

Hawkes immediately turned and left the barn.

Roach pulled the ladder down and laid it on the ground near where Sam lay. He smeared the rock with blood from Sam's face and placed the rock on the ground near his head. Eastman stood still watching Roach.

"I didn't plan to kill Sam," Eastman whispered.

"So what?" Roach answered. "We've killed lots of men before."

"I know we have," Eastman whispered with his eyes fixed on the dirt at his feet.

"Green," John Lee said as he pointed at a leaf on the tree next to him.

On the benches facing him ten Tunxis children said in unison, "green."

He broke the leaf from the tree and held it before the children, pointing to it he said, "It is green."

The children looked puzzled but still managed to repeat the phrase, "It is green."

John decided to do what he tried to avoid when he taught a new phrase or word: he would give the children their people's word for what he said in English. He pointed to the leaf again. This time he said, "ojawashkwa." The children smiled and nodded their heads as they announced, "It is green."

John nodded at the children and moved away. Daniel Hart stepped forward to continue the day's lesson. John sat on the grass beneath the trees above his house and remembered the day of his house raising years before and how Sam Pierce pulled him out of his melancholy thoughts at this very place. He wished his friend could be with him now and once again bring him out of his sadness, but that was impossible.

When John heard of Sam's death his first thought was of Sam's wife Abigail. He wondered how she was coping. It was of some comfort when William and Bridget brought Abigail to stay with them in their home while she grieved. When John visited Sam's grave, he stopped at William's house to see Abigail. He invited her to come to his school whenever she wanted to.

William brought Abigail to the school a few days later. She sat with Mary on the last row of benches behind the Tunxis children as Daniel continued his lessen. Earlier, William sat with them. John wondered where William went until he heard his voice behind him.

"I miss Sam too," William said, as if reading John's mind.

William sat in the grass next to John and continued speaking, "Abigail kept her spirits up through all of this, but without a husband it will be hard for her. I am helping her sell Sam's farm, but the rocks make it unattractive. She knows she can stay with us as long as she likes."

"What about you and Bridget?" John asked. "Are you going to leave Hartford with the rest of Elder Goodwin's supporters when they're freed from their covenant?"

"I suppose, but it won't be for some time, for Reverend Stone and Richard Hawkes fight us at every turn."

"I hear you all are planning to move to Hadley north of Springfield."

William nodded before both men fixed their eyes on the Indian students sitting below them. A few minutes later John turned back to William and said, "Thank you for coming today. There have been so many changes, it is good to sit with you as we did so often before."

William nodded with a slight smile. "There will always be change," he said. "All we can hope for in this life are quiet moments with our friends before things change again."

Chapter 45

It was the day of the Indian schoolhouse's raising and as the sun rose above the mountains behind him, John Lee sat near the schoolhouse's cellar. Daniel Hart and the men who helped construct the cellar and the frame to be raised would be there in a few hours, but the raising would have been more joyful if Sam Pierce, now dead over a year, was with him today.

John wasn't certain how many people from Farmington would come at noon, the time set for the schoolhouse's raising. When he completed all he could do by himself, John sat on a schoolhouse bench. He heard Mary's voice after sitting for a few minutes.

"John, Thomas is here."

He walked up the slope to his house. The tall sinewy figure of Lieutenant Bull stood above him next to the door to John's new lean-to kitchen.

"A fine job," Bull said. "I doubt there's a finer lean-to kitchen in Farmington."

"Funny what a man will do for his new bride," John beamed.

"Word of your schoolhouse's raising reached Hartford two days ago," Bull announced. "It didn't go over well. Word has it, Reverend Stone and Richard Hawkes plan to disrupt it."

"Reverend Stone has whined about me teaching Indians for years but has done nothing to stop me. Why would he and Hawkes make trouble for me now, especially since Farmington has its own church."

"Did Reverend Newton oppose your school when he was your church's minister?" Bull asked.

"No, he even came to my lessons and helped teach scriptures before he returned to England."

"Reverend Stone hasn't spoken against your schoolhouse, but Hawkes has," Bull said. "Since he supports Stone, I assumed Stone was behind Hawkes's threats."

"Richard Hawkes has other reasons for wanting to harm me."

Lieutenant Bull glanced at Mary before turning back to John, "I suppose it's true. Just the same, bring Deacon Hart to your schoolhouse's raising in case Stone comes with Richard and you need clerical support."

"Is Hawkes bringing men?" John asked.

"It's likely. He was waiving one of your notices during market day yesterday. He claimed it's dangerous for you to teach the Indians about God and our ways. Some of the crowd yelled the Indians would use what you teach against us."

"When will Hawkes be here?"

"Your notice said you would raise the schoolhouse at noon. He'll likely come then since you will be weakest when raising the schoolhouse's frames. I will stay to help you fight him and his men."

"This isn't your fight," John exclaimed. "I have plenty of men. Please leave. You have given me enough: a warning I can act on."

Bull glared at John and announced, "I'm staying. It's a waste of time to tell me to leave. I choose my own fights. Now let's gird our loins."

John nodded.

Daniel Hart arrived at mid-morning with the three men who helped John build the schoolhouse's cellar and frames. They cleared the ground around the cellar and set up tables for Mary to place the food she and the other women prepared. When Daniel and his men were finished, John brought them together at a table with Lieutenant Bull.

"Lieutenant Bull came with a warning," John announced. "He believes Richard Hawkes will bring men from Hartford to stop us from raising the schoolhouse. He'll stay to help if there's a fight."

"Do you really think there'll be a fight?" Daniel asked.

"Depends on Hawkes," John answered. "If your father is here it's unlikely. Pray he comes."

Over the next hour twenty men and their families from Farmington arrived. The wives helped Mary set the tables. The older children took the younger children to a grassy area where they watched them play. Meanwhile, John outlined steps the men would follow when they raised the schoolhouse's frames.

John positioned eight men around the schoolhouse's cellar at noon and gave them poles to push up the wall's frames. He stationed six other men in the cellar to guide each post's tenon into the correct mortise in the sill over the stone foundation.

As if on cue, several Tunxis emerged from the woods above John's house near noon. They were led by the twenty-six-year-old Ahamo, who since his father Pethus's death, was the Tunxis' sachem. Following them were several of John's first students. They walked down the slope followed by two of John's new students, Wematin, a Tunxis boy of eight, and Sucki, a Tunxis boy of nine. As they neared him, John saw a small Indian boy of about six holding Ahamo's hand. While the boy looked like a young child, there was something unusual about him. Instead of fidgeting and moving his eyes about, the child walked forward with his dark brown eyes fixed on John. John found the child's gaze disarming.

"Welcome friends," John announced.

"Good day John," Ahamo replied.

Ahamo pointed to the young boy holding his hand and said, "This is Nesehegan. He is your new student."

"Welcome Nesehegan," John said beaming. "I'm happy to be your teacher."

John looked into Nesehegan's eyes. They exuded serenity. Spellbound by Nesehegan's gaze, John froze as an overpowering sense of peace embraced him. He couldn't turn his eyes away, even though in the back of his mind he knew all around him people were waiting for him to turn back to Ahamo.

Ahamo finally broke Nesehegan's spell, "Thank you for building a schoolhouse for us. We brought you a gift."

Ahamo reached into the deerskin pouch on his belt. When he withdrew his hand, it was filled with a beautiful string of wampum. Ahamo held it before John, allowing part of it to slip from his hand revealing its length. The people gasped upon seeing the pearl white and purple black beads touching the ground.

"This is one of the longest strings of wampum the Narragansett have made," Ahamo said. "We hope this gift is great enough to honor you for your service to us and the schoolhouse you are building."

"It's more than enough," John answered.

The people cheered. Their roar could be heard throughout the town; and, it could be heard by Richard Hawkes, Reverend Stone, James Eastman, Edward Roach and the ten men with them as they turned off the road from Hartford onto Farmington's Town Path. They'd travelled two hours. Some, including Hawkes and Stone, were on horseback. Five men walked behind them. A tinge of excitement flowed up Hawkes's back. The roar meant a large crowd was at the schoolhouse and a crowd meant an audience.

"What was that noise?" Stone asked.

"The noise of an insidious celebration," Hawkes said as he pushed his stallion to a trot, forcing Reverend Stone to do the same to keep up.

As the riders' pace increased, the men on foot fell behind. Stone shouted at Hawkes, "He won't raise the schoolhouse if I order him not to. Even a town constable can't deny God's will and with Reverend Newton gone God speaks through me here."

As Hawkes, Stone and their men on horseback approached the school, John was positioning the men raising the schoolhouse's frame. He gave the order to start and the frames to the front, rear, and side walls rose. The people cheered once the girts were in place.

As the cheering died, John saw nine men ride out of the trees along the Town Path. His pulse quickened when he saw they were led by Richard Hawkes and Reverend Stone. He knew unless Deacon Hart arrived it would be impossible for him to defend the schoolhouse without appearing to challenge the church.

He turned to Daniel, "Bring your father here now!"

Daniel nodded before striding through the trees towards his father's farm.

The townspeople were silent while they watched Hawkes, Stone and the other men dismount, tie their horses to the trees, and walk down the slope towards them. John walked up the slope to meet them. Lieutenant Bull and two men who helped raise the frames followed John as the two groups converged.

Stone glared at John with his arms folded across his chest, while Hawke's stared down the slope at John. Behind Hawkes, Edward Roach smiled, and James Eastman gazed about nervously. Suddenly Ahamo shouted, "Nesehegan, Nesehegan come back. Come back Nesehegan."

Both groups turned and looked down the slope at the little Tunxis boy scrambling up the slope towards them while Ahamo sped to catch him. Nesehegan was at John's side before Ahamo could stop him. An instant later, Ahamo was next to them.

"Wait behind us with Nesehegan," John ordered Ahamo. "If there's a fight take him to the house."

With Lieutenant Bull at his side, John turned to Stone. Meanwhile, Hawkes stared transfixed at Nesehegan whose eyes were now locked on his. Hawkes wondered who this boy was and why he couldn't take his eyes off him. The boy's gaze was soft yet powerful; gentile but penetrating; and completely glowed with love. No one had ever looked at Hawkes this way. *Enough!* Hawkes thought, pulling himself from the boy's gaze and focusing again on the confrontation.

"Welcome Reverend Stone," John said. "I'm glad you came. Please help celebrate our schoolhouse's raising."

"I am not here to celebrate," Stone spit. "Your schoolhouse is an abomination. Tear it down now!"

"Why should I Reverend?" John asked.

"You know why. When you teach the scriptures without training it is certain some of what you teach will be heresy."

"I only read the scriptures. I don't interpret them. How is that heresy?"

"I don't need to justify my order," Stone said. "I speak for God."

"I won't tear down the schoolhouse," John said, his teeth tightly clinched. "This school is under the Farmington Church's jurisdiction, not the Hartford Church. That means Deacon Hart controls it, not you."

"Your school still needs a minister to teach the scriptures or heresy will result," Stone said. "Deacon Hart isn't here anyway. He only has jurisdiction if he exercises it."

"I taught the Tunxis here for years under authority given me by Governor Hopkins," John said. "You were there when he gave it. Your actions violate his order."

"Hopkins is dead and your authority was never in writing," Hawkes countered. "Besides, he authorized you to teach, not build a schoolhouse,"

"Reverend Stone has spoken," Hawkes said. "Tear down the school or I will do it under his authority. Stand aside and no one will be harmed."

John's greatest fear was realized. Hawkes had clerical authority behind him, and this was a clerical matter. While John was constable, he lacked clerical authority. He stepped aside as Hawkes and his men passed him on their way down the slope to the newly framed schoolhouse. Some men who raised the schoolhouse frames stepped in front of them.

"Don't stop them," John said. "We will raise the schoolhouse later after Deacon Hart approves it. It's not worth the risk of one life to try to stop these men. I will see they're punished later."

John's men stepped aside as Hawkes led his men past them to the schoolhouse's frame. As soon as they reached the frame, one of Hawkes's men handed Hawkes an axe. John's supporters yelled at Hawkes as he approached the school with the axe in hand. Hawkes turned back to the crowd and raised the axe.

"This is what happens when you teach what you don't know," Hawkes said. "This place won't be used to commit heresy."

Then, in the excitement of his triumph, Hawkes saw Nesehegan. The boy was staring at him. There was a glow on Nesehegan's face, and he smiled gently at Hawkes with love in his eyes. It was then Hawkes knew. He knew it as clearly as if the child had told him. The love in the child's eyes was for him. Momentarily confused, Hawkes lowered his axe and stared back at the small Indian child. The crowd was silent.

After a few moments, Hawkes pulled his eyes from the boy and looked back at the crowd. He walked toward the small schoolhouse's frame. When he reached the front frames' end post he thrust the axe into the post just above the wooden sill into which its tenon was placed. The crowd screamed at Hawkes in protest. Hawkes drew the axe back again and drove it into the post. This time, except for a few moans, the crowd was silent. On his third thrust the post broke free from the sill and the wooden frame's corner gave way. While the front frame stayed in place, the side frame collapsed, and its beam fell into the cellar with a thud. The crowd was silent.

Hawkes moved to the next post. When he reached it, he drove the axe into the post. But as he prepared to swing the axe again a gruff yell came from the slope above, "Stop now!"

Hawkes turned and looked up the slope. Striding towards him was Deacon Hart. When he reached Hawkes, Hart asked, "Why are you tearing this schoolhouse down?"

"Reverend Stone ordered it," Hawkes answered.

Deacon Hart turned to Stone, "Why did you order this?"

"John Lee has been teaching the Indians the scriptures," Stone answered. "He's not trained to do this. If he builds a schoolhouse, he'll draw Indians from all Connecticut. The risk of heresy is too great."

"This is my congregation," Hart barked. "You are exercising authority where you have none. Reverend Newton taught scriptures at John's school and watched John teach scriptures. Reverend Newton found no evidence of heresy. Order Richard Hawkes and his men to leave."

Reverend Stone looked about nervously. John knew what Stone did now would decide if there would be a fight, for if Stone refused to order a halt to the school's destruction, he would attack Hawkes and if he attacked so would Lieutenant Bull and the men who came to raise the schoolhouse.

Finally, Stone spoke, "If you claim responsibility for what is taught here you can have it Stephen. But if I hear heresy is taught, I will challenge not only this schoolhouse but also your congregation's authority over it."

With that, Stone motioned Hawkes to follow him up the slope. Hawkes was furious but knew there was nothing he could do but follow Stone back to Hartford. The crowd remained silent as the invaders walked up the slope. When they reached the slope's summit Hawkes looked back into the little Indian boy's loving eyes. Next to him, James Eastman also stared into the boy's eyes. Suddenly, Hawkes broke his gaze from the boy and grabbed Eastman's shoulder.

"Stop staring at the boy," Hawkes said. "It's time to leave."

"But his eyes and smile," Eastman answered. "They look like a portrait of Christ I saw in a church in East Anglia years ago."

Hawkes grabbed Eastman by the shoulder and pulled him up the slope towards their horses.

"Stop imagining things!" Hawkes yelled. "He's just a child."

Chapter 46

It was a bitter cold morning eight months after the Indian school-house was raised. Richard Hawkes rode his black stallion toward Farmington. A storm passed through Hartford the day before. During the night the sky cleared, and a full moon lit the dusting of snow muffling his stallion's hoofs.

Deacon Hart's message came the day before. It was only a sentence, "Be at my house tomorrow morning."

Even though his relationship with Hart was strained after Hawkes's attempt to tear down John Lee's schoolhouse, Hawkes still thought the message odd. Hart never requested a meeting by sending him a message and during the years he ran Hart's gristmills he always met Hart the fourth Friday of each month. This was the first Thursday in February and they had just met a few days before. He was offended by the message's tone. It didn't ask him to come; it demanded him to.

Regardless, he'd no choice but to go if he wanted to continue operating Hart's gristmills. He did well over the years. In addition to gristmills in Hartford, he now operated Hart's gristmills in Windsor and Wethersfield as well as the sawmill Hart owned in Farmington. He smiled as he remembered his warehouse in Hartford was full of cornmeal siphoned into hidden chutes by his miller, Mark Scott. Soon, he would have enough gristmills of his own so he would not have to concern himself with Hart's short notice meetings.

The sun was up when he reached the farms west of Hartford. The snow-covered fields shined from the reflected sunlight and he pulled his hat's brim close to his eyes to shield them. He wondered why Hart wanted to meet. He assumed it was about Hart's mills. Had it been two years ago, he would have thought the meeting was about Elder

Goodwin and his followers. However, after Reverend Stone released them from their covenant, they moved to Hadley, twenty-five miles north of Hartford. No, the meeting must be about Hart's gristmills.

It was still early morning when Hawkes turned off Farmington's Town Path into Deacon Hart's farm. He tied his stallion to a post in front of Hart's house and threw his bear skin across its back. Daniel Hart opened the front door before he knocked. *Odd*, he thought. *Where is Hart's servant?*

Daniel neither spoke nor smiled. Instead, he led Hawkes through the house into the hall where Hart and John Lee sat by the fire. Hart was dressed in a black serge doublet and breeches, both finer than his normal attire. Lee wore a buff deerskin coat with black leather breeches. His face was soiled, and his buff coat sprinkled with mud. *He's ridden fast and far to reach here*, Hawkes thought.

"Good day Deacon," Hawkes said. "I'm surprised you called a meeting so soon after last week's meeting. I am also surprised to see John Lee here. I assumed our meeting was about your gristmills and I didn't see his horse in front of your house."

Hart stared at him coldly before answering, "His horse is behind the house. And yes, this meeting is about my gristmills."

Hart rose and motioned for Hawkes to sit at the table in the hall. Hart sat at one end of the table while Hawkes sat to Hart's right opposite John Lee and Daniel Hart.

"I've received complaints from some of my customers," Hart said. "They claim the cornmeal they get back from my mills is far less than what they should have received. These complaints are persistent and consistent with my own concerns which I told you of sometime ago."

Hart pointed to Lee and continued, "As a result, I asked Constable Lee to investigate my mill's operations. When he finished investigating my Hartford mills, I sent a message to you asking for today's meeting. This morning Constable Lee returned from Wethersfield where he finished his investigation of my mill there."

Hart turned to Lee, "Tell Mr. Hawkes what you found John."

"My investigation of Deacon Hart's Hartford mills was straight-forward," John announced. "I went to the complaining customers and asked them to keep records of the grist they delivered to the Hartford mills. I asked them to measure the amount of cornmeal they received back. When I collected this data, I took it to a miller I know. His analysis revealed that on certain days the cornmeal returned to the customers was ten percent less than they should have received. I asked Hartford's constable to get records from the two mills there so I could compare them to our results. The mills' records revealed on days where the customers' records showed they received ten percent less cornmeal than they should have, the mill received ten percent less grist from the customers than the customers' records showed."

"What does this establish John?" Hart asked.

"It shows there was a plan to steal cornmeal by the mills' opera-tor," John answered. "This is the only explanation for why the mills' account logs on the days of customers' losses always show the incom-ing grist is ten percent less than what the customers' accounts show they sent to the mill and why the unaccounted-for loss is also ten percent."

"Tell Mr. Hawkes what you found at my Wethersfield mill yesterday."

"The same thing. Again, this is evidence of a deliberate attempt to steal cornmeal and hide it from discovery in the mill's records."

Hawkes stared across the table at Lee for a long moment. He knew Lee's case was solid and his own false records were the lynchpin of that case. He wished he hadn't ordered Mark Scott to create false records. These false records convinced him no one would be able to discover the true amount of lost cornmeal he stole from Hart's cus-tomers since comparing the amount of grist listed in the false records to the amount of cornmeal would always show an appropriate amount of lost product. He never imagined Scott would be so careless and steal the same percentage of cornmeal as the percentage of grist he deducted from the amount he listed on the log. He needed to buy time so he could shift the blame for the theft of cornmeal to Scott.

Hawkes turned to Hart and shook his head, "I can't believe someone would steal this much cornmeal from our operations. I just can't believe it. I will find out what happened. If someone has stolen from us and our customers, I will turn them over to Constable Lee."

John cocked his head and asked, "So you deny you had anything to do with this?"

"Of course not," Hawkes exclaimed. "Your investigation found no evidence I was involved and it's slanderous to accuse me. I'll conduct my own investigation and when it's finished all will know who was responsible."

Hart said nothing as Hawkes and John stared at each other across the table. Hawkes finally turned to Hart, "I promise to find the answer and report back to you by week's end."

Hart shrugged and looked back at John. Before another word was said, Hawkes rose from his seat, quickly pulled his cloak over his shoulders, and tipped his hat to Hart before leaving.

The three other men remained seated. Finally, Hart looked at Lee and asked, "Do you think he stole the missing grain?"

"Yes," John answered. "But he didn't confess as you hoped and your rush to confront him didn't give me time to speak to his miller who won't return from Boston for two more days. Richard's other millers weren't involved and know nothing. I will confront Scott when he returns."

Damn it to hell, Hawkes thought as he rode back to Hartford. He pushed his stallion at a slow walk to avoid suspicion, not picking up the pace until turning onto the road to Hartford. After the turn, he pushed his stallion harder and they were soon racing along the road at a brisk trot.

A thrill coursed through his spine. *They think they've caught me, but they haven't,* he thought. *I need to get to Mark Scott before he finds out about Lee's investigation. His latest message from Boston said he would return tomorrow, two days earlier than planned. Fortunately, he was the only one of my millers stealing cornmeal for me and he only did so on days he operated a mill. Besides him, only James and Edward know. If I move quickly, by the end of tomorrow only James and Edward will know. How was I surprised? I told James to watch Lee. If he did so, he would have learned Lee was investigating the operations of Hart's mills as soon as Hartford's constable examined the mills' records.*

Hawkes reached home at sunset. He brushed aside his servant and tossed his bear skin and cloak into her hands before racing up the stairs to his study. He lit two candles and carried them to the table near the study's window. He had to find which of Hart's mills Scott would be running the next day and to do this he had to locate Scott's latest schedule.

As he opened the chest where he kept his records, Elizabeth interrupted him, "Good evening Richard. I'm glad you're home. What are you looking for?"

"Nothing," Hawkes growled, startled by her interruption. "Now, get out of here."

Elizabeth's mouth fell open as she stared at Hawkes.

"I said leave!" he shouted while striding across the room towards her.

Before he could reach her, Elizabeth fled from the room. Just outside the door their two sons, seven-year-old Peter and six-year-old Paul, watched their mother race past them as Hawkes slammed the study's door shut in their faces.

He quickly found Mark Scott's schedule. It showed Scott would be operating the first gristmill Matthew Allyn built on the Little River. *So, his employment with me will end where it began,* Hawkes thought. He still had to find Eastman and Roach for he would need their help when he confronted Scott at the mill the next day. He knew Roach would be hard to find for he was a loner and lived by himself north along the road to Windsor. However, he knew Roach would likely not be home for he often spent time alone deep in the woods of western Connecticut. Roach never said what he did on these trips, but he usually had fresh Indian scalps on his belt after one of his western forays.

Eastman was another matter. Unlike Roach, his patterns were predictable. Tonight, as most nights, Eastman would be at Joseph Mygatt's tavern on the Little River's opposite side with his face buried in beer. Hawkes didn't relish going back into the cold, but time was short and only if he went would he be certain of reaching Mark Scott with both his men in the morning before Scott learned of Lee's investigation.

Hawkes reached the tavern half an hour later. It was little more than a roughhewn single room with a fireplace. He spotted Eastman sitting at a table at the room's far end with two middle aged men. After more than twenty-five years working for him, Eastman easily recognized the sound of Hawkes's footfalls as he strode across the creaking wooden floor towards him. Before Eastman could turn to greet him, Hawkes slapped Eastman across the back of his head. The two men at the table stiffened and began to rise from their chairs, but Eastman waved them off.

"I have business with this man," Hawkes said. "Move so we can discuss it."

The two men rocked back in their chairs and looked at Eastman. The older man leaned forward and asked, "Do you need help James?"

"No, no," answered Eastman. "Give us time alone."

The men moved to another table where they continued staring at Hawkes as he took a seat across the table from Eastman.

"I told you to watch Lee," Hawkes whispered. "You didn't and now I'm dealing with the mess you created."

"What do you mean?" Eastman asked. "I watched him. He's done nothing to threaten us."

"You didn't watch him close enough. This morning I was confronted by both Lee and Deacon Hart in Farmington. They claimed we stole cornmeal from Hart's customers. We need to reach Mark Scott first thing tomorrow morning at Matthew Allyn's old mill before Lee talks to him. Go find Edward and bring him to my house before daybreak."

"What if he's not home?"

"Find him in the woods," Hawkes yelled slamming his fist on the table. "He lives west near the main Indian trail. Don't waste time."

Eastman and Roach reached Hawkes's house before dawn. Hawkes knew they needed to hurry if they were to surprise Scott. On days he operated a mill, Scott gave the regular miller the day off and arrived at the mill at daybreak. He then siphoned off as much cornmeal as he could by noon before the local farmers brought new grist for milling.

Hawkes figured sunrise would be in an hour, so he ordered Eastman and Roach to follow him on horseback at a trot up the Little River to the old mill. They reached the mill with the sun's first streaks of light. Hawkes chose a secluded spot in the woods along the Little River to wait for his master miller. *It's a shame*, he thought. *He's a good miller and will be hard to replace.*

"What are we going to do when Mark arrives," Eastman whispered as the three men sat on their horses waiting for Scott.

"Take him into the mill and question him about the loss of cornmeal," Hawkes answered.

"But we already know what happened," Eastman whined.

"Can't you think? I told Deacon Hart I would investigate why cornmeal's missing. After today, I will be able to tell Hart Mark confessed to its theft and we killed him when he tried to escape."

"We're going to kill Mark?" Eastman asked, his eyes bulging.

"Quiet, he's coming," Roach whispered to Eastman.

The three men moved forward on foot to the forest's edge. Scott's slender frame made him easy to identify as he approached in the sunlight from the west on the road along the Little River. He was on time and casually walked down the road's center.

"Move west to inside the tree line to cut off his escape," Hawkes whispered.

Hawkes pulled his musket from the sleeve where it hung on his stallion and handed it to Eastman.

"Load and prime it," Hawkes said. "Hold it for me while I go meet Mark. Bring Edward and the musket with you to the mill a few minutes after I go in with Mark."

Hawkes stepped from the woods into the sunlight and turned to meet Scott on the road near the mill's entrance. He smiled at Scott from the wooden platform leading to the mill's door above the trough running past the mill turning the mill's paddle wheel. The wheel was still, but as soon as Scott opened the sluice gate it would start turning.

Scott picked up his pace when he saw Hawkes on the mill's platform. As he approached, Scott smiled and said, "Why are you here Richard?"

"It's a pleasant day for a walk and I need to discuss some things with you," Hawkes said. "Let's go in the mill."

Scott frowned, "Alright, but I have many orders to work through today. I hope our meeting is short."

"It will be," Hawkes said smiling broadly.

Hawkes's pulse pounded in his ears as he walked across the platform with Scott. Scott unlocked the door, pulled back the hinge, and opened the door. He motioned for Hawkes to enter. Once inside, Scott lead Hawkes to a small table where they sat near the two millstones.

"What is it?" Scott asked.

Hawkes leaned forward, "Farmington's constable discovered you stole cornmeal from Hart's customers when you milled their grist."

Scott's face turned ashen and he slid back in his chair just as the door to the mill opened and Eastman and Roach walked in. Scott jumped out of his chair, his eyes moving from Hawkes to Eastman and Roach and again back to Hawkes. Finally, Scott whispered, "What are you going to do?"

"I'm going to blame you for the theft, of course," Hawkes answered. "You don't expect me to confess, do you?"

"But you asked me to do it," Scott pleaded. "I did it for you and you gave me none of the cornmeal I stole for you."

"You have been a loyal servant. Now it's time for you to serve me in another way."

Scott looked about frantically before dashing for the stairs to the floor above. Roach tackled him on the stairs. Both men rolled on the wooden floor kicking up cornmeal dust until Roach pinned Scott to the floor.

Hawkes casually watched Scott and Roach struggle. When the struggle ended, he stepped towards them.

"Stand him against the wall Edward," Hawkes ordered.

Roach pulled Scott up and slammed him against the mill's wall near the running and load stones. Mill dust filled the air.

"James, open the sluice gate and start the running stone," Hawkes ordered.

The running stone ground away as mill dust floated in the air. The millstones' noise was deafening, making it impossible for anyone outside to hear their voices.

Hawkes bent close to Scott and yelled as the two stones ground away, "You are about to die. The only thing you need to worry about is whether you die with or without pain. Your death will be painless if you cooperate."

Scott pulled his slender body up until it was ram rod straight. He stopped trembling and calmly looked into Hawkes's eyes.

"If I deserve to die for what I have done, so do you," Scott yelled over the grinding stones' din. "Death will come to you soon enough and when it does you will reside in hell for eternity. Pray God grants you salvation. What do you offer me?"

"I pray to no God, least of all the one leading you to where you are now. Walk to the door. Edward will open it. You will be dead before the sunlight strikes your face."

Scott straightened his doublet and brushed off the dust on it. He glared at Hawkes before turning to the door. Eastman handed Hawkes his musket while Scott walked toward the door. Roach's hand was on the door's handle. Hawkes brought the musket to his shoulder and took aim at the back of Scott's head as Scott neared the door. Roach turned the door's handle. Hawkes pulled the musket's trigger. Roach pulled the door open and sunlight poured into the room just as the musket's ball blew the back of Scott's skull off. Scott fell to the floor. As Hawkes promised, he was dead before the sunlight struck his face.

Hawkes handed the musket back to Eastman.

"I need to see Deacon Hart now," Hawkes said. "I won't need my musket. Take it to my house. Leave the mill stones running until the mill's neighbors arrive. Tell them Scott stole grain from his customers and we shot him when he tried to escape."

That afternoon, Deacon Hart stared at Richard Hawkes across the table of his first-floor hall with his arms folded across his chest.

"You shot your miller in his head before he left the mill?" Hart said. "Why didn't you just chase him? There were three of you after all."

"He was about to escape from the mill and would have reached the woods before we could catch him," Hawkes answered.

Hawkes sat across the hall's table from Hart and John Lee. John frowned at Hawkes before standing up and staring down at him.

"Edward Roach is swift. I doubt your miller could have escaped," John said. "What proof do you have this man stole Deacon Hart's customers' cornmeal?"

"The proof is straightforward, and I blame myself for not being more vigilant," Hawkes answered. "My men found a chute beneath the stones. Scott opened it when he wanted to steal cornmeal. He opened the chute only on days he operated the mill alone. My records show losses were greatest at each mill on these days."

"Is that it?" John asked incredulously.

"He confessed to me and my men before he fled. Isn't that enough?"

John looked at Hart and shook his head.

"I'm sorry I trusted Scott," Hawkes said looking at Hart. "I will be more vigilant in the future."

Hart thrust his chest out and shook his head.

"There will be no need for vigilance," Hart said. "You no longer run my mills. Leave now."

Hawkes sat in his chair and stared at Hart without speaking. *That bastard*, he thought. No one spoke as Hawkes turned and left the house.

"What do you think John?" Hart asked.

"I think he murdered his miller to cover up his own crimes."

"Then arrest him."

"His men would just lie him out of jail. No, it will take more evidence than we have to convict him."

"What can we do?" Hart asked.

"I should have insisted we wait to confront him until after I talked to Mark Scott,"

John replied. "We've no witnesses and we can do nothing until we get one."

"It's my fault," Hart said. "My anger got the best of me. I should have listened to you."

"We may still find a witness. Someday Edward Roach or James Eastman may turn on him. If one does, his crime will be murder and not just theft."

"Will you talk to them now," Hart asked.

"Yes, but now they will just lie. Later one of them may tell the truth."

Chapter 47

James Eastman and Edward Roach reached Richard Hawkes's house at midmorning. It was a year since Mark Scott's murder. The murder still weighed on Eastman who, as did Edward Roach, denied neither they nor Hawkes killed Scott when questioned by John Lee. They each claimed Hawkes shot Scott when he tried to escape. A light snow fell as they tied their horses near the house's burnt red door. Eastman's leg hurt more today, and he limped on the path to the door. Roach followed him, satisfied to accommodate the pace dictated by Eastman's deteriorating leg.

A craggy faced woman servant greeted them. She led them to Hawkes's study, where they sat at an oak table facing the large square paneled window looking down on the Connecticut River. Thirty minutes later Hawkes burst into the room, "I told you not to come to my house unless I ordered you to."

Eastman grimaced in pain as he swung his legs to the right to face Hawkes, "There was no choice. We've just returned from a meeting with Matunaaqd and Rowtag. The news is bad."

Hawkes held up his hand, motioning for Eastman to stop speaking. After closing the doors to the parlor and hall chambers, Hawkes turned back to Eastman and said, "Continue."

"For the fifth straight year the northern tribes brought fewer beaver pelts to trade for our muskets," Eastman said. "Each year there are fewer beaver on the Connecticut. Even Pynchon's trading post gets fewer pelts."

Hawkes looked at Eastman for a moment and shook his head. *He brings me nothing but problems,* he thought. *Never answers.*

"What do we do?" Eastman asked.

"What should I do?" Hawkes asked, his arms crossed over his chest.

"I don't know. Trade farther west?"

"Don't be a fool, who will we trade with? The Iroquois? The Huron? They already trade with the French and Dutch. We must continue trading with the Algonquins."

"But they're in Connecticut and Massachusetts where beaver are even scarcer."

"I know. That's why I need to meet with them and find what else they can trade for our muskets. New England is a powder keg. The Wampanoag and Narragansett are squeezed into a smaller area and what they have to trade is of less value to English settlers. Soon the Nipmucs, Pocumtucs, and Paugussets will feel threatened. No, we don't have a problem. What we have is an opportunity, for the demand for our muskets is greater than ever and we still have Dutchmen to help deliver them. What we need is to find something the tribes can trade for them if they don't have enough beaver pelts."

"How do we do it?" Eastman asked.

"We go north and meet our Indian and Dutch agents. We then meet with the tribes we trade with. We will make a new arrangement with them at the meeting."

Hawkes found Elizabeth with their young servant, Ann, setting the parlor table for supper. Elizabeth reached the cabinet's top shelf next to the table for a pewter serving plate. As she reached, her cherry bodice separated from her black skirt revealing the outline of her narrow waist through her transparent chemise. Shivers of passion passed through Hawkes.

"Leave the parlor Ann," Hawkes ordered. "Close the doors to the porch and kitchen when you do."

Elizabeth almost dropped the serving plate when she heard his voice. She turned towards him and smiled.

"But Richard, we haven't finished setting the table," she said.

"It can wait."

He locked the door to the kitchen.

"Take off your bodice and chemise." He ordered

"I must prepare supper."

He raised his right hand, threatening to slap her cheek, before sweeping the pewter plates, noggins, spoons and napkins from the table onto the floor. Elizabeth backed away as he walked towards her. She backed into the cabinet causing the pewter serving dish to fall, bringing with it several clay plates all smashing to pieces when they hit the floor.

"You bitch, look what you've done," Hawkes spit.

He slapped her. She sobbed as he undid the stays holding her bodice together and pulled it from her shoulders. He inhaled the clean scent of her chemise while untying it before pulling it over her head revealing her soft shoulders and breasts. Her hair fell to just below her shoulders as he undid the pins holding it together in a tight bun.

Fully aroused, Hawkes placed Elizabeth face down across the table and slid her black skirt from her hip until it lay on the floor. He dropped his breeches and turned her over onto her back and spread her legs apart. She held her breath, lying motionless, as he pushed. She forced herself to count his thrusts. At the count of eighteen he moaned and jerked involuntarily. The door to the porch opened.

Their six-year-old son, Paul, stood at the door staring at them.

"Close the damn door Paul!" Hawkes yelled.

Paul ran away.

Hawkes pulled himself up and reached to the floor for his breeches. He looked down at Elizabeth who lay naked and still on the table staring blankly out the window.

"I'm leaving tonight," Hawkes said. "Pack me salted pork and journey cake. I will be ready for supper in an hour."

Elizabeth lay on the table until Hawkes left. After dressing, she went to the kitchen to find Ann. Supper was ready within an hour.

But when Elizabeth told Hawkes supper was ready, he shouted, "I can't eat now. Feed the boys. I will be down later."

Alone, Hawkes rose from the table and stared out the window at the Connecticut River. The clouds had broken, and the sky was changing from a dirty gray to a dark blue. Here and there the wind drove a wave against the shore in a white froth. He pondered his dilemma. *Losing Deacon Hart's mills was my first set back since I came to New England*, he thought. *Now this. My fur trade will wither away. Damn it. I won't let it happen. They need muskets but I can't just give them away. There must be something I can get for them.*

The clouds disappeared. To the east and north the land across the river spread as far as he could see. The shrubs and bushes spread along the river until merging into the forest of maples, oaks, pines and sycamores climbing up from the river until they reached the horizon. In that moment, he found the answer he was searching for.

Hawkes wanted his sons to be fighters, so, after supper, he took them to the fields behind his house. Elizabeth stood at the rear window looking down at Hawkes and the boys. Hawkes picked up his musket and looked at his oldest son, Peter.

"What type of musket is this?" Hawkes asked.

Peter looked back at him, his eyes tightly squeezed together. *Damn it to hell, Hawkes* thought. *He has no idea what type of musket this is even though I spent an hour explaining to him what type it was and how to use it.*

Peter dropped his eyes to the ground. Hawkes slapped the back of Peter's head with the palm of his hand knocking the boy's brown cap from his head. Peter fell to the ground sobbing.

"Quit crying," Hawkes yelled. "Stand and look at me."

Peter stopped sobbing and stood while his six-year-old brother, Paul, quietly watched the two of them. Above them, Elizabeth wrapped her arms about herself and gasped.

"Why did I hit you?" Hawkes asked.

"Because you were angry at me?"

"Yes, I was angry at you, but it isn't why I hit you. I hit you because you didn't pay attention to this morning's lesson."

Hawkes held the musket in front of Peter again.

"Now tell me what this musket is called."

Peter's lips trembled as he shifted his weight back and forth while staring at his father.

"I don't know," Peter sobbed.

Hawkes raised his hand as Peter cowered before him. He lowered his hand and calmly said, "I won't hit you now, but the next time you don't remember what I've taught you, I will hit you twice. Do you understand?"

"Yes."

Hawkes turned and looked at his other son, "Come here Paul."

Paul walked towards him. When he reached his father, Paul smiled and looked up at him. Hawkes held the musket in front of Paul, "Tell me what kind of musket this is Paul."

"It's a flintlock musket," Paul answered. "It's new and only a few people in New England own one."

For the next two hours Hawkes continued teaching his sons how to use a flintlock. They ran through the musket's firing sequence enough times so that both boys could repeat the sequence for him. Paul learned faster than Peter, but eventually even Peter knew the sequence. Hawkes handed the musket to Peter and told him to take it to the house. Hawkes and Paul trailed behind as Peter raced ahead up to the house with the musket.

Hawkes grabbed Paul's shoulder and pulled him towards him, "You saw me wrestling with your mother today. Do you remember?"

"Yes."

"Remember what I tell you now. Genesis teaches us it was woman's deceit that caused Adam to disobey God, causing God to cast man out of paradise. For this reason, woman must be subservient to man. Man can use woman for whatever purpose he desires and punish her whenever he feels the need. When you are a man you will have this power. I was wrestling with you mother because she's a woman and as a man I have the right to order her to do what I want. Do you understand?"

"Yes."

Hawkes slipped from his house shortly after Peter and Paul went to bed. It was frigid and he pulled his bearskin fur tightly around his neck over his cape and leaned forward on his stallion to keep the north wind from cutting through him.

A blast of snow followed him into Mygatt's tavern a half hour later. Two young men sat at a table near the fire at the room's rear. Mygatt pulled his skinny body up from a table near them.

"Good evening, Mr. Hawkes," Mygatt said. "What would you like?"

"A noggin of beer," Hawkes replied. "I'm here to meet James Eastman and Edward Roach," Hawkes said, pulling his bearskin and cape from his shoulders before sitting at a table near the door.

"I haven't seen them tonight," Mygatt answered.

"I'm early," Hawkes replied. "They will be here"

Hawkes guessed it would be at least an hour before Eastman and Roach arrived, so he decided to spend time developing the details of the plan he had earlier thought of only in general terms.

There are two keys, he thought. *First, I need a reliable source for the muskets. Rose has been my partner and will continue to get me muskets - even the new flintlocks. He'll also help me sell the pelts and other goods I get from the tribes. Second, I need more trading partners. The northern tribes are not enough. These must include the Wampanoag and Narragansett. The more tribes I trade with, the greater variety of goods they can trade for my muskets if they have fewer beaver pelts to trade. These tribes can also trade land, for land in the south is in great demand. The most important thing I can do on this trip is set up a meeting of all tribes I trade with. It will create fear that unless they act quickly to trade for my muskets the other tribes will become better armed.*

I will stay in the background. There's too much to risk. My Dutch agents will run the meeting with Matunaaqd and Rowtag.

Eastman and Roach entered the tavern as Hawkes completed his planning. Eastman grimaced as he limped towards Hawkes's table with Roach trailing him. Hawkes stood up, threw his cape over his shoulders, and reached for his bearskin coat before the two men reached him.

"Can't we have a beer before we leave?" Eastman pleaded.

"No," Hawkes said. "I came early and had one already. You could have done the same. We start now."

Hawkes's feet and hands were numb by the time they passed through Windsor. Eastman had complained about the cold for nearly an hour, but Roach seemed immune to its effects.

"Please Richard. Can we stop to warm ourselves?" Eastman pleaded over the wind's howl.

"No. We can't afford to lose more time. We need to meet Rowtag and Matunaaqd at dawn so they can tell the tribes of our meeting. Lean into your horse for warmth."

Eastman moaned and buried his head in his horse's neck. Hawks knew he couldn't show Eastman his discomfort and straightened up on his horse as his hands and feet screamed with pain. He refused to let his mind listen. Soon he no longer felt the pain for his mind was in the room his father and mother rented in Colchester when he was a boy.

He remembered trying to silence his mother's screams by burying his head in his pillow. His father and mother had yelled at each other since his father returned from work. He didn't know what triggered their fight and at half the size of his mother, Hawkes knew he couldn't do anything about it. His mother's screams were louder, and he pulled the pillow from his head for it was useless to muffle them. He curled himself on his bed and tried unsuccessfully to think of more pleasant things. He was screaming uncontrollably when his father reached his bed.

"Stop screaming Richard," his father yelled, the strong odor of beer on his breath.

He stopped screaming, rolled over, and looked up at his father. His father's face was bleeding from scratches on his chin, nose, and forehead. His linen shirt was torn and blood stained.

"There has been an accident," his father said calmly. "Your mother fell. I think she's dead."

Hawkes remembered lying in his bed while several men came to take his mother's body away. His father met them at the door to their one room apartment. Hawkes tried to hear what they said but their voices were too quiet to make out more than one word. The word was "bury" and it was his father who used it. His father never spoke about what happened to his mother. Hawkes was afraid to ask.

They reached the cave before dawn. It had been over ten years since Hawkes was at the place and more than twenty since he killed Megedaqik there. The cold was replaced by the thrill he remembered the day he killed Megedaqik. *I have power here*, he thought.

Hawkes sat with Eastman and Roach in the pine trees before the cave. Eastman's limp was worse and Hawkes knew Eastman was in no condition to find Rowtag and Matunaaqd, nor the Dutch traders who worked with them. He told Roach to find them alone. Roach nodded before riding into the woods.

Even though the wind stopped and the sun's rays streamed through the tree tops, Eastman still shivered as he sat before the cave.

"Get up James," Hawkes ordered. "Clean the cave and clear a place outside it for tomorrow's meeting."

"Please build a fire so I can warm first," Eastman pleaded. "I can't feel my face or fingertips."

Hawkes shook his head and spit on the ground as Eastman pulled himself into a ball with his arms wrapped around his knees.

"Start moving!" Hawkes shouted as he kicked Eastman in the back.

Eastman groaned and rolled onto his side. Hawkes kicked Eastman again, this time in the butt, "Get up!" he yelled. "I will keep kicking you until you do."

"Alright, alright, but give me time," Eastman pleaded.

Eastman slowly pulled himself to his feet. White chalky patches of skin spread over his nose and right cheek. Similar patches spread across his fingers.

"Clear the rocks, shrubs, and tree limbs from the front of the cave," Hawkes ordered. "I will build a fire."

For the next three hours, Hawkes sat at the fire watching Eastman shuffle about lifting dead branches, pulling out shrubs, picking up rocks, and moving them from a twenty square yard area before the cave. All the while Eastman limped on his right leg and moaned whenever he lifted a branch, pulled up a shrub, or picked up a rock with his frost nipped hands. Only when Eastman was finished did Hawkes let him sit at the fire.

"Thank you," Eastman said after sitting at the fire with Hawkes for half an hour. "When will Edward return?"

"Early afternoon," Hawkes barked. "Now you've rested, go collect wood for the fire."

Without a word, Eastman rose and disappeared into the woods.

Roach returned early that afternoon.

"I found Rowtag and Matunaaqd near their tribe's village," Roach said while sitting at the fire with Hawkes. "They will be at the cave at dawn tomorrow."

"Good," Hawkes answered. "And the Dutchmen?"

"They were twenty miles above Springfield on the Connecticut where Rowtag said they would be. They were trying to trade some

English pots, pans and utensils for beaver pelts and wampum. They said they're looking forward to meeting the one the Indians call the dark man."

"I'll try to make their visit memorable," Hawkes laughed.

The firelight lit Roach's face in the early morning darkness. It was bitterly cold again that night and Hawkes, Roach and Eastman slept as close to the fire as they could. Now, with dawn approaching, they sat around the fire eating the journey cakes they brought with them.

"They're here," Eastman whispered, pointing to the woods near the clearing he made the day before.

Eastman abruptly stood before the fire and yelled, "Rowtag, Matunaaqd, welcome."

"Good morning James," came a disembodied voice from the woods' darkness.

Instantly, three men emerged from the woods. The Indian in front was middle aged and of medium height with long hair flowing to the middle of his back. He wore a heavy black bear fur mantle over his shoulders and his deerskin leggings extended to his moccasins. The Indian behind him was at least four inches taller. His hair was entirely gray and as he neared the fire heavy creases appeared on his face. The third man was much younger. His hair was black and his face smooth and free of wrinkles. He was almost as tall as the old man. The first man strode straight to Eastman and grabbed his shoulders.

"Good to see you my friend," the man said. "Edward said the dark man would be here."

Before Eastman answered, Hawkes walked from the darkness into the firelight.

"I am here," Hawkes said. "It's been many years since I saw you Rowtag."

"I see the years have been good to you dark man," Rowtag said. "You have fewer creases on your face than I and no gray hair."

The early afternoon sun streamed through the tree tops when the two Dutchmen arrived. They were Diederik Paulis, a tall gangly man, and Karel Beringer, a stocky man of medium height. They moved quietly, carrying their muskets slung behind their shoulders. Both approached the fire where Rowtag and Matunaaqd sat with Eastman.

Beringer spoke first, "Good day Rowtag. The meeting place is more orderly than I remember."

"Much changes when a leader comes," Rowtag smiled.

"Good day James," Beringer said. "Where is our leader?"

"He'll be here soon," Eastman answered.

"Times are hard," Paulis said as he and Beringer sat by the fire. "Beaver pelts are scarce and Indians have little to trade for the muskets you bring."

"This problem was fated," Eastman answered. "We're here to deal with it."

"Your face is frost nipped," Paulis said.

"It's better today than yesterday. I only wish I could say the same about my leg."

"You've been dragging that thing around for years my friend," Beringer laughed. "Your complaints have pained me more than your leg has you."

Eastman smiled ruefully, "It didn't hurt when I was young. Perhaps the new plan will bring back the feelings of my youth."

When it was clear the conversation was only between the white men, Rowtag rose and announced, "We will go find Edward and our leader."

After the Pocumtucs left, Eastman smiled, "Did you bring gin with you?"

Beringer nodded and reached into the bag hanging from his belt and pulled out a leather tankard. He handed it to Eastman, "You will like this gin. It was made by a Dutchman living near Albany."

Over the next two hours Eastman and the Dutchmen finished both the tankard of gin Beringer carried and a larger tankard Paulis

brought. They spoke of the years they were young and worked together exchanging muskets Eastman brought to the Dutchmen for
thousands of beaver pelts the northern and western tribes brought to
the cave.

Eastman drank most of the gin. It went to his head and its smell
drifted languidly in the air when Hawkes entered the clearing with
Roach and the three Pocumtucs. Hawks glared down at Eastman.

"I smell gin," Hawkes fumed. "You're drunk James?"

"No, I'm not," Eastman said rising unsteadily until he fell back to
the ground on his butt while the two Dutchmen laughed.

"Edward, pick him up and put him in the cave where he can sleep,"
Hawkes ordered.

Hawkes turned to the Dutchmen, "So you are the Dutchmen who
minded my business all these years? Tell me your names."

"Karel Beringer," Beringer announced. "This is Diederik Paulis.
It's good to finally meet you. You're called the dark man by the
Indians. What's your English name?"

"My name is unimportant. You may call me whatever you wish.
What is important is the plan I present to you and the Pocumtucs
today."

Hawkes described his plan for the next hour. He promised to
bring them all the muskets they could trade but told them they could
only accept certain articles in return. Acceptable articles included
animal pelts, especially beaver; land, especially Wampanoag and
Narragansett land; and, wampum, to be valued at one half its normal
value.

When he was finished Hawkes announced, "Go to the tribes of
Connecticut, Massachusetts and Rhode Island and invite them to a
meeting at this place during the next full moon. Offer them muskets
and tell them what I will accept for them. Then come here twice
a month to trade with them. Edward and James will take the muskets the Indians trade to Karel and Diederik who will deliver them

to the sachems of tribes who traded for them. Edward and James will watch the meeting in hiding and come to Hartford to tell me about the trades."

"So, you won't be coming to the meeting?" Beringer asked.

"No. If things go well, you'll never see me again after today."

By the time the meeting finished, the sun was barely below the horizon and the sky was gray. Eastman emerged from the cave holding his head. Hawkes scowled at Eastman while the Dutchmen laughed, before leaving with the Pocumtucs. Hawkes ordered Eastman and Roach to sit at the fire with him. He crossed his arms and frowned at Eastman.

"You embarrassed me today," Hawkes bellowed. "If you ever drink before one of my meetings again you won't live to see the end of that day."

Chapter 48

Richard Hawkes sat in his pew in the empty meetinghouse for an hour before he heard the door open behind him. He turned and watched Reverend Stone stride down the aisle toward him.

"Quite a change since last year isn't it Richard?" Stone asked. "Now you have William Westwood's pew in the meetinghouse's first row."

"I only wish I made a profit selling his house like I did with the houses of the rest of Goodwin's flock," Hawkes responded.

"They couldn't leave for Hadley fast enough," Stone laughed.

"They probably were afraid you would rescind your release of their covenant after you made them pay an extra year's tithes to escape the church."

Stone motioned to the door at the meetinghouse's rear, "Let's talk upstairs in the chamber room."

How different things are now, Hawkes thought as they climbed the stairs to the chamber. *John Lee's investigation failed to tie me to the theft of Hart's cornmeal after Eastman and Roach told him Mark Scott confessed and I now have four mills of my own along the Connecticut. My musket trade is booming now that all the tribes fear war with the English and compete for muskets. And, the Wampanoags and Narragansetts have traded great tracks of land to me, much of which I sold to colonists making me even wealthier. If there was a God, most would say he smiles on me.*

When they were seated at the chamber's table, Stone asked, "So, what brings you to see me?"

"Our great enemy Satan," Hawkes said. "There are many strangers among us now."

"What do you mean?" Stone asked.

"Haven't you noticed?" Hawkes answered leaning towards Stone. "There are many new people and not all attend our church. Some are dangerous. I asked James Eastman and Edward Roach to investigate them. They found them spiritually weak and perfect vessels for Satan. They also saw some of them in the woods dancing around fires. We ignored this growing threat when we became focused on defeating Goodwin."

Reverend Stone leaned back in his chair and asked, "Did they find witches?"

"Dancing around fires in the night isn't normal, is it?" Hawkes asserted.

"Were they chanting?"

"Some were?"

"Chanting what?" Stone asked.

"My men didn't get close enough to hear," Hawkes said. "But do the pious chant in the woods?"

"No, they don't."

"It's been seven years since we executed a witch," Hawkes said. "Do you really think Satan stopped trying to destroy us since then?"

Stone looked down at the table before looking at Hawkes.

"You're right," Stone said. "We haven't been vigilant. What should we do?"

"Between 1647 and 1654 we hanged more than a half-dozen witches in Connecticut," Hawkes said. "We did this because we rallied our people who brought forth the evidence needed to convict them. We must rally the people again, remind them evil lurks among us, and ferret it out wherever it exists."

"I will speak of Satan and his agents more often in my sermons and you will continue your efforts to find and eliminate them from our midst."

"What do we do about old John Jennings's son Nicholas and his wife Margaret?" Hawkes asked.

"They're in the hands of a particular court," Stone said. "I have no authority to act."

"They're witches, for God's sake," Hawkes said slamming his hand on the table. "You have authority from God."

"The trial starts Monday," Stone answered. "I will attend it and lend my help when needed."

"It will be a blow to our efforts fighting Satan if they're not hanged," Hawkes said. "I will be at the trial. The pious will have a voice through me."

"Didn't Nicholas fight with you in the Pequot War?" Stone asked.

"Yes, but he froze on the firing line."

"He's both a coward and a witch then," Stone exclaimed. "You are right. It's time to search for witches again."

John Lee sat at the rear of the meetinghouse chamber. From there he could see only a few court members through the people's heads in front of him. The chamber was packed and those who couldn't get a seat were outside near the meetinghouse porch where the guards reported each development as the trial proceeded.

John raised his head above the crowd to get a better view. Nicholas Jennings was slumped in his chair. Next to him his wife, Margaret, sat up straight, her eyes fixed on the court's members as they took their seats at the front of the room.

She has a powerful presence, John thought. *Poor Nicholas. She dragged him away into God knows what. They claim the two of them killed several people with spells. I can't believe Nicholas had enough brains to learn how to do that.*

The hum of scores of individual conversations stopped and the meetinghouse chamber fell silent. John struggled to see the court's Chief Judge between the heads of the people in front of him. His view blocked, he had to look between the heads of Reverend Stone and Richard Hawkes, who sat together in the first row with James Eastman and Edward Roach.

"This particular court is called to order," announced the Chief Judge, William Allyn of Windsor. On each side of Allyn sat the court's magistrates, Samuel Wyllys of Hartford, William Phelps of Windsor and Richard Treat of Wethersfield. These men would decide all issues of law the court would address.

The jury's ten members were seated in two rows of benches facing the spectators to the right of Allyn. Deacon Hart and Lieutenant Bull were on the jury. John knew both men would do their duty, but Hart would find this duty easier to perform for he'd always been a strong opponent of witchcraft. Lieutenant Bull was less concerned about such things.

Allyn announced, "The defendants will rise and hear the indictments against them."

Both Nicholas and Margaret stood.

"You are charged with familiarity with Satan and with sorceries causing the deaths of Reynold Marvin's wife and Balthazar de Wolf's son for which, according to the law of God and the laws of this Commonwealth, you deserve to die should you be convicted."

My God, John thought. *This is really happening.* He looked at the accused witches. Margaret stared at Allyn defiantly while Nicholas began trembling as soon as Allyn began reading the indictment.

"I'm not guilty," Margaret said with a steady voice.

"You don't need to say that Goodwife Jennings," Allyn said. "Pleas of not guilty are already entered for you and your husband."

"I want to say it anyway so all will know I am innocent."

"As you wish," Allyn said. "The first witness in this case is Reynold Marvin of Saybrook."

The door to the chamber opened and a tall thin man about fifty entered the room. He ambled down the aisle toward the witness chair placed between the table Allyn and the magistrates sat at and the benches where the ten jurors sat. When Marvin reached the witness chair, he turned to Allyn and swore to testify truthfully.

"When did you first meet Nicholas Jennings," Allyn asked.

"We served together in the Pequot War," Marvin said.

"You two were neighbors on land formerly the Pequots?" Allyn asked.

"Yes."

"Did you come to regret living next to him?"

"Yes, his two boys were undisciplined rabble." Marvin answered. "They chased my pigs and cattle from their pens and stole chickens from my barn. I had enough when they cut down the saplings around my pond."

"What did you do?" Allyn asked.

"I went to their father's house and told him what his sons did."

"What did he say?"

"He didn't get a chance to say anything," Marvin answered while pointing at Margaret. "Before he could open his mouth that woman jumped between us and began yelling vile things. She ordered me from their house and slammed the door in my face."

"Why do you accuse these people of sorcery?" A magistrate asked.

"Well, after I told my wife, Mary, what happened she was concerned about the two boys' welfare. The next day she confronted Nicholas and Margaret on the road passing our house, claiming they weren't providing a proper Puritan upbringing for their boys. Margaret said it was none of her business how they raised their two boys."

"Did you do anything about the matter after that?" asked a juror.

"Yes, we did," Marvin answered. "My wife reported the matter to the New Haven constable and Nicholas and Margaret were ordered by a particular court to explain how they were raising their two sons. It was after that they murdered my wife with sorcery."

"How did they do that?" Allyn asked.

"They both came to our house and began cursing my wife for complaining to the authorities. When I ordered them to leave, Nicholas swung his fist at me. He missed and I grabbed him to keep him from hitting me. They both damned my wife for what she did and prayed she would die for it. She died of fever two days later."

Several spectators gasped. A few yelled while others raised their fists. Ahead of him, John saw Richard Hawkes, James Eastman, Edward Roach and several other men seated at the meetinghouse's front yell "witch, witch, witch."

"Silence, silence," Allyn yelled until the room was quiet.

The final two witnesses were also neighbors of Nicholas and Margaret. They were a short stocky dark-haired middle-aged man named Balthazar de Wolf and his tall thin wife, Judith. They also complained about how Nicholas and Margaret were raising their boys.

Gazing at Balthazar, Allyn asked, "Tell us how Nicholas and Margaret Jennings used sorcery to kill someone you knew."

A hush fell over the spectators.

"It happened when my wife and I went to their home. They were furious when we complained they weren't teaching their sons proper Puritan behavior. When we told them we would complain to the constable if they didn't teach their sons better manners, Margaret asked if our own son was being properly cared for. When we said he was, Margaret said this was good, for if he weren't being properly cared for, he would become sick and die. Our son became ill shortly after Margaret said this and died within the month."

Once again cries of "witch, witch, witch" rose from the spectators. Allyn looked at both defendants once he restored order.

"Do you deny you used witchcraft to kill the wife of Reynold Marvin and the son of Balthazar and Judith de Wolfe?" Allyn asked.

"We deny it!" Margaret hollered. "We're not witches."

"Do you agree with your wife Nicholas Jennings?" Allyn asked.

"I do," Nicholas answered quietly, his eyes staring at the floor.

"It is claimed you didn't raise your sons to be proper Puritans," Allyn asked. "What do you say to this?"

"We taught our sons the best we could," Margaret answered.

That was the defendants' last answer.

John watched the jury leave to deliberate. Both Deacon Hart and Lieutenant Bull stared straight ahead with grim faces. *It won't be an easy verdict*, John thought. *Two deaths and Richard Hawkes has worked the people into a frenzy.* John looked ahead at Reverend Stone who barely moved during the trial. He wondered what he was thinking.

Most people stayed close to their seats while the jury deliberated. John assumed they expected a quick guilty verdict. He left his seat and walked into the meetinghouse yard where he watched the jailor lead Nicholas and Margaret back to the jail. He walked to the bridge over the Little River. From there he could see the meadow where Lieutenant Bull set the cattle to graze the day Reverend Hooker and the congregation arrived from Newe Towne, which was now named Cambridge. The optimism of that day seemed hundreds of years ago.

After an hour, John walked back to the meetinghouse. Everyone was still there, but now more people were outside in the yard. Richard Hawkes was talking with a dozen men across the yard near the jail. *No good can come from that*, John thought, before entering the meeting-house and taking his seat.

To nearly everyone's surprise, it took the jury all afternoon to reach a verdict. As they walked down the aisle to their seats, the only sound John heard was the hammering of a woodpecker on the large oak tree just outside the chamber's window. He took a deep breath when Allyn asked if the jury had reached a verdict.

"We have," the jury foreman announced.

"What is your verdict?" Allyn asked.

"We find the accused not guilty due to our inability to reach a unanimous finding of guilty."

"The jury will be polled," Allyn announced.

One by one each juror stood and announced his decision. Conviction required a unanimous vote. The first four jurors announced they found both Nicholas and Margaret guilty. Deacon Hart then stood, looked at Nicholas and announced, "I find Nicholas Jennings guilty." He next looked at Margaret and announced, "I find Margaret Jennings not guilty."

Immediately, the chamber was filled with shouts of "no, no, no." This time all the shouts were directed at Hart. Hart calmly stared into the angry crowd.

Unlike the people screaming at Hart for finding Margaret not guilty, John focused on the other half of Hart's verdict and wondered which, if any, remaining jurors had spared Nicholas's life by finding him not guilty.

The next three jurors found both Nicholas and Margaret guilty.

Then Lieutenant Bull, who was the next to last juror, pulled his weathered body out of his seat. He stared at the spectators and announced, "I find Margaret Jennings not guilty." Silence filled the room as he prepared to announce his second verdict. He stated, "I find Nicholas Jennings not guilty."

John smiled slightly at Lieutenant Bull over the protest springing up around him. Bull nodded at John and retook his seat while the protest continued.

Instantly, Reverend Stone jumped to his feet. At once the uproar stopped. Stone stared at Allyn and sneered, "The verdict is the work of Satan. Only those who understand Satan can judge his servants. I demand in the future that both Richard Hawkes and I be assigned to investigate all cases of witchcraft."

Reverend Stone walked to the aisle with Richard Hawkes. Loud cheers followed them down the aisle and out the meetinghouse door. They were followed by the men who gathered earlier around Hawkes in the meetinghouse yard. Meanwhile, the remaining spectators continued jeering as the final juror announced he found both defendants guilty.

Ten miles away, Mary Lee sat before the fire in the upstairs parlor while the light of its flames danced across her forehead. John told Mary he expected to be home before sunset when he went to Hartford for Nicolas's trial. It was now long past that time. She put their two-year-old son, Martin, to bed over three hours earlier and was worried.

She put another log on the fire. In the fresh light she glanced across the parlor at young Martin sleeping peacefully in the small maple bed his father built for him. John insisted the bed be maple because only a maple bed would last long enough for their grandchildren to use it for their own children. He said it would be a good thing for those children, who would be born in a new century, to be able to touch something their great grandfather made. The remembrance of the moment brought tears to Mary's eyes as she thought of how wonderful her life with John was, and like all else in life, it would inevitably change. She let the tears slide off her cheeks without wiping them off.

Before she dried her eyes, Mary heard the downstairs door open. She smiled to herself when she didn't hear the door close for she knew John closed it quietly to avoid waking she and their son. She couldn't hear John's footfalls on the stairs, but each step was followed by the stairs' creaking despite his best efforts to avoid it. She smiled at him from her chair when he entered the room.

"You didn't need to stay up for me," John whispered to avoid waking their son.

"I was worried and couldn't sleep. Sit with me. You look exhausted. Is the trial over?"

He sat on the other chair at the fire and stared into the flames. He cleared his throat as the burning wood popped and cracked.

"Yes, it ended late this afternoon," he answered. "There weren't enough votes to convict Nicholas and his wife."

Mary let out a deep breath, "I'm glad for my father. He'll have fewer sleepless nights than if they were convicted."

They both stared into the fire for a few moments before Mary whispered, "We need to seek conversion in Farmington's church for the sake of our child."

John turned to Mary, a pained look on his face, "But I haven't found evidence God selected me for His grace."

"Why not?" Mary said with a sigh. "You are pure of heart. What more evidence do you need?"

"I have killed Indians, am alarmed with the way our people treat the Indians, and with their seeming blood lust to label people witches."

"Don't you believe there are witches?" Mary asked while leaning towards John.

"I did once, but now I have doubts. Those who are persecuted almost always are unpopular people singled out because they're poor and eccentric, or because their accusers want to destroy them for personal reasons."

"But the Bible demands we kill witches," Mary said as she crossed her arms. "You are Farmington's constable John. Be careful not to speak to others about not punishing witches."

John smiled softly, "I didn't say there are no witches. I only worry that the evil we find in our world be real and not imagined."

Mary sighed, "And what about conversion?"

John grasped Mary's hands while looking into her eyes, "I will seek conversion with you if you want. I still believe God would never decide our fate without first giving us a chance at atonement."

"All have doubts John," Mary answered. "Even me. Let's seek conversion this month."

"Very well," John said squeezing Mary's hands again.

While he and Mary talked, John remembered why he loved her. He found her strength in expressing her concern about conversion both pure and attractive. She moved her hands expressively but not unnecessarily, while the worry in her face showed her vulnerability and caring, playing against that strength. As their conversation continued, he heard less of what she said as he began to find his exhaustion was being replaced by the arousal he often felt when he watched

Mary assert herself in her controlled yet feminine way.

She was wearing her loose-fitting bed clothing which opened at the front revealing the moist softness of her breasts' cleavage. He smelled her scent, the same clean scent floating in the air over the years they were together. He knew he was tired, but any thought this might be the cause of his arousal ended when he felt his pulse racing and his face flushed. No longer able to resist his building desire, he looked at Mary and smiled.

Mary dropped her head and looked through the tops of her eyes with a flirtatious smile. He slowly rose from his chair and stood over her as she remained seated in her chair. He reached down and grasped each of her hands and gently pulled her out of her chair. He pulled her towards him and slipped his arms behind her, clasping his hands together at the back of her slender waist. Lost in the scent, touch and sound of each other, they closed their eyes and floated together while he ran his lips across the nape of her neck. He gently pushed her against the wall, pressing against her until she felt the hardness between his legs pushing between her thighs. He caressed her hair with his left hand, while with his right hand undoing the bun that kept most of it together. Her long silken hair cascaded down her back, its scent rushing over him. He gently undid her nightgown. Her breaths were irregular, and her sweetness smothered him as he removed her skirt and dropped it to her ankles. Her full form revealed, his only thought was how much he wanted her.

He took her right hand in his right hand and placed it on his lips. As he gently kissed it, with his left hand, he undid his breeches and dropped them to the floor. Mary lifted her head and smiled while her pale blue eyes stared directly into his. She lay on the rug on the floor on the bed's opposite side from where little Martin was sleeping and pulled John down on top of her.

In an instant, he was in her and as they rhythmically moved together, she began to moan, quietly at first and then louder with each breath she exhaled. Soon he began to feel a rising warmth coming over him in wave after wave as they moved together. The waves accelerated with each wave reaching a higher peak until suddenly a final peak struck. She let out a breathy moan as everything around them froze.

Their lovemaking over, Mary asked, "Do you remember Martin's birth two years ago?"

"I do," John answered. "It was hard. You labored for eleven hours. I feared you would die. I don't want to go through that again."

"Nor I," Mary answered. "But life has few guarantees. We may have conceived our second child tonight and will have to deal with the consequences over the next nine months."

"The future should not be allowed to control the present," John said. "Life has too many twists and turns to forecast them. If we have a second child as a result of what we did tonight only joy will result."

"Yes, there is time to worry later."

"I agree," John said as he rolled Mary onto her back while kissing her neck. "Besides, it is well known that a second child slides through its mother's womb quickly as it seeks its life."

"That doesn't mean there is no pain to the mother."

"True, but we have done this before."

Chapter 49

Richard Hawkes slammed his fist into his pillow. Someone was pounding at his front door, yet none of his servants answered it. He rolled onto his side and pulled his pillow over his head to drown out the noise, but the pounding couldn't be silenced.

"Damn it to hell," he yelled. "Someone answer the door!"

Elizabeth raced from the upstairs hall into the upstairs parlor where Hawkes's bed was. She crept forward in the dim light of the parlor's dying embers until she reached his bed. Again the sound of knocking echoed through the house. Hawkes bolted upright in bed and stared directly into Elizabeth's eyes.

"What the hell are you doing in my room?" Hawkes asked.

"Making sure you're alright."

"I'm fine. The problem is the damn knocking. Why hasn't a servant answered the door?"

"You rented our servants to the Governor for the night."

"Damn it. I'll get the door. Go back to bed."

Hawkes pulled his cape over his bed clothes, lit the candle at his bed, and walked down the stairs into the porch. He glanced into the hall and saw the fire's embers were nearly out. He threw two logs on the fire just as the knock thundered again. He turned towards the door with the knife he kept on the hall table in his right hand and the candle in his left

"Who is it?" he asked through the closed door.

"Reverend Stone."

Hawkes slid the bolt from the door and opened it. Reverend Stone stood before him in the candlelight.

"Get dressed," Stone said. "We're going to George Wyllys's mansion."

"Why?" Hawkes asked as they walked into the hall.

"To observe the possession of Ann Cole."

Hawkes turned from Stone towards the stairs. By his second step he had a broad smile on his face. It had been a year since the Jennings' trial, and this was a new opportunity to raise the specter of witchcraft.

Once upstairs, he climbed into his black breeches and brown doublet. He bounded down the stairs where he grabbed Stone by the shoulder and led him from the house.

They rang the bell to the gate of Samuel Wyllys's house just after dawn. On the hill above them loomed the largest house in Hartford. It was dark except for a lighted window on the second floor. Within a few minutes an old man arrived. He drew a key from his belt and inserted it in the gate's lock.

"Good day sirs," wheezed the old man as he opened the iron gate. "Mr. Wyllys is expecting you. I will take you to him."

The old man led them up the path to the house. The path wound through dormant gardens and orchards where withered trees and plants had drawn their life into themselves to survive the winter. As they climbed higher, Hawkes saw a large wooden barn and stables to the house's left. Down the hill behind the house acres of fields ran until they reached a small gray house.

"Samuel Wyllys asked me to come to his house to observe Ann Cole," Reverend Stone said as he and Hawkes followed the old man up the path.

The old man pointed to the small house Hawkes saw earlier at the end of Wyllys' s fields and announced, "Ann is a servant of Mr. Wyllys and lives with her father in the house at the end of the field behind his house. She's having strange fits. Her father brought her here hoping Mr. Wyllys could help her."

"Is there evidence Satan causes her fits?" Stone asked.

"You are here to find out," the old man said. "He also invited Reverend Samuel Hooker, the son of the late Reverend Thomas

Hooker, and Farmington's new minister. Mr. Wyllys knows him from their days at Harvard College."

"I asked our church's teacher Reverend Whiting to come," Stone said. "My assistant, Joseph Haynes, will come later."

When they reached the house, Hawkes grasped Stone by the arm and said, "You must lead us here; not these other men."

"Don't worry, I will," Stone answered. "I've done this before. None of the others have."

They heard the girl's screams when the old servant opened the door. The screams floated down the house's staircase until they were replaced by moaning, which, in turn, was replaced again by screams. At times the girl's screams were high pitched, while at other times they were guttural, coming from deep in her throat.

"Hurry, let's get to her before the attack ends," Stone yelled, motioning for Hawkes to follow him upstairs.

Within seconds, they were inside the room where the girl lay. She'd thrown her pillows on the floor and was writhing in pain as she screamed and moaned. The curtains to the window were tightly drawn and the only light in the darkened room came from three candles resting on a maple chest across the room from the girl's bed.

"Thank you for coming," a tall thin man with a peaked nose announced. "This latest attack started a few minutes ago. It won't last much longer."

"I will do what I can Samuel," Stone responded.

Near the bed knelt a short stocky man with deep black circles under his bloodshot eyes. He glanced back at Stone and begged, "Please help my daughter Reverend Stone. She's possessed by Satan."

Stone nodded at the man before turning back to Wyllys, "Has the girl said anything intelligible since the attack started?"

A voice from the corner's darkness behind Stone answered, "No. She has uttered nothing but nonsense when not screaming or moaning."

Hawkes and Stone turned to Reverend Whiting and Reverend Hooker sitting to the right of the three candles. Whiting rose from his chair and walked across the room to Stone. Hawkes stared at Whiting as he approached. Whiting ignored Hawkes and nodded at Stone when he reached them.

"This girl is suffering from her own mental infirmities and not from possession of Satan or his demons," Whiting said.

Hawkes stepped between Whiting and Stone and asked, "How can you say that? It's obvious this girl is possessed. Listen to her pain."

"I was speaking to Reverend Stone," Whiting said.

"I have the same question Richard has," Stone said. "Answer his question please."

Whiting glared at Hawkes before turning back to Stone, "I've been watching this girl for several hours. Not once during this time did Satan or his demons reveal themselves. If she's possessed, they would have by now."

"What do you think Reverend Hooker?" Stone asked.

Hooker, whose beardless face made him appear more youthful than Reverend Whiting, looked across the room at Stone and said, "I disagree with Reverend Whiting. It's too soon to reach his conclusion."

"Reverend Hooker is right," Hawkes said. "We must watch the girl longer before reaching a conclusion."

"I agree with Richard," Stone said. "Pull your chairs close to the bed. Richard and I will sit on the bed's opposite side. Reverend Hooker write down what the girl says until Reverend Haynes arrives. After that he will record what happens."

The girl continued to scream and moan. With each scream her body convulsed. Her arms and legs thrust out and pulled back to her body as she rolled herself into a ball. As soon as she was pulled into a ball she rolled onto her back and then onto her other side, all the while moaning in a strange raspy voice.

"Reverend Stone," Hawkes whispered. "This voice can't be her's.

It's impossible for her to make this sound on her own."

"Pain can make possible that which seems impossible," Stone said.

"Listen carefully Reverend," Hawkes said. "Even in pain this girl can't make the moaning we hear."

"Perhaps, but we can't be certain until we watch her longer."

Reverend Stone's assistant Reverend Joseph Haynes arrived within an hour. Barely twenty-one, Haynes fine light brown beard was nearly impossible to see even in daylight. The girl's seizures stopped a half hour before Haynes's arrival and except for Reverend Hooker, all the men were in the parlor next to the hall where the girl lay.

"Sit with Reverend Hooker at the girl's bed, Joseph," Stone ordered. "Keep a record of what she says. I will come soon."

Stone turned to the three men in the parlor chamber, "What do you think causes the girl's fits."

"Satan," Wyllys said. "Her father believes this too. He claims she's never made these sounds."

"I disagree," Whiting said. "Her screams simply show she's in pain. We need to find the cause. When we do, we will discover it comes from her body or her mind."

Hawkes laughed, "So you think the hellish sounds this girl makes are from a piece of moldy bread, a skinned knee, or a headache? These sounds are from Satan who is using her as his vessel. We must force him to reveal himself so we can rip him from the girl's bosom."

"What should we do Reverend Stone?" Wyllys asked.

"Steel yourself for battle Samuel. We're going back in that room and discover the demons Satan is using to torment this girl. We will then drive them from her."

They lost track of time in the dim light of the hall chamber. The girl breathed slowly in a pattern so predictable and sonorous that on occasion the men seated in two of the four chairs at her bed dozed off to its rhythm. When this happened one of the men standing at the back of the room took their place. Only Richard Hawkes and

Reverend Stone stayed awake. Sitting side by side they stared at the girl while across the bed the two chairs were alternately filled by the other four men.

Then the girl started to whisper. The whisper was like the faint sound of gently rustling leaves in the tops of trees caused by the light winds of an oncoming storm. Reverend Stone pulled his chair closer to the bed and leaned forward, placing his ear to the girl's mouth.

"I still can't understand what she's saying," Stone whispered. "It's only one word and she's whispering it rhythmically over and over again in a consistent interval."

Hawkes stole a glance at the other men in the room. They were transfixed, frozen where they sat or stood, as they stared through the dim candlelight at the girl lying on her back, her eyes closed, with Reverend Stone's ear hanging just above her mouth. *They believe*, Hawkes thought.

"Her whisper is louder," Stone said. "I can almost understand it."

He pressed his ear closer to the girl's lips while holding his left hand in the air signaling the other men to stay quiet.

"Just a little louder," Stone whispered. "Come on you can do it child, just a little louder."

"It's coming, it's coming," Stone whispered. "I am certain the word contains an "r" and an "s" slurred together at its end.

"The word is ————," Stone said before the girl rose to a sitting position and yelled, "curse, curse, curse," before falling back onto the bed.

The men exchanged startled looks before staring at the now silent girl lying on the bed. After several minutes, Stone leaned over the girl and asked softly, "Tell me about the curse Ann. Tell me about the curse."

The girl didn't answer. Instead she began to repeat the word "curse" over and over again.

Again, Stone asked, "Tell me about the curse Ann."

Again, the girl ignored the question and continued to repeat the word "curse."

Stone asked again, "Tell me about the curse Ann." This time the girl stopped repeating the word "curse." In the silence that followed, each man held his breath. The girl's eyes opened, and she stared directly at Stone, now seated two feet from her. In a young girl's voice, she said, "They placed a curse on me sir. They placed a curse on me."

Stone leaned forward and whispered, "Who placed a curse on you?"

Before the girl could answer, her arms and legs sprung straight out. She yelled, "No, no, no. Stop. Stop," while curling herself into a tight ball, as she did earlier, and began screaming. The original pattern of screams followed by moaning began anew.

Wyllys and Hooker at the back of the room, as well as Whiting and Haynes sitting in the chairs across the bed from Stone and Hawkes, fought to breathe. They knew what was happening and the horror of it pressed against their chests making it hard to. Hawkes stared ahead at the girl while repressing a smile. *It is done*, he thought.

"The girl is possessed by Satan and he won't let her answer my question," Stone said.

"What should we do?" Whiting asked.

Even Whiting believes now, Hawkes laughed to himself.

"We will free this girl from Satan's grip and find who placed the curse on her?" Stone said.

The girl screamed and moaned for the next half hour, while, like a sentinel, Stone sat next to her. Finally, exhausted, the girl stopped screaming, lay on her back and began to breathe slowly and deeply. Soon she fell asleep and the room was quiet.

"We can't allow Satan to keep the truth from us Reverend Stone," Hawkes said. "We must keep pushing for it."

"But this girl will die if we keep pushing," Whiting exclaimed.

Hawkes glared at Whiting before turning back to Stone, "Ask the girl who placed the curse on her."

"But what if Reverend Whiting is right?" Stone asked.

"So be it, for it will be God's will. Would it be better for her to endure the pain coming from being accursed? Don't wait any longer. Ask her now."

Stone nodded, turned to the girl and asked, "Who placed the curse on you Ann?"

The girl opened her eyes, looked at Stone and, in a voice so youthful and clear the men knew it must be her's, said, "There are evil women in our town. They torment me when I sleep. They threaten to afflict my body, to spoil my name by accusing me of vile acts, and to destroy my future husband's love for me. They're witches and they will kill me."

"Who are these women?" Stone asked.

"These women are Rebec. . No, no, not again. Stop, stop, please stop," the girl screamed as her arms and legs flung out from her before she rolled onto her side and began moaning as before.

"Satan controls her," Hawkes announced. "Ask the question again and keep asking it until you get an answer.

"But she can't bear the pain," Stone answered. "It would be cruel to make her suffer so."

"It is Satan who brings her pain and it will be God who ends it."

"So be it, may God give me strength," Stone answered.

Stone's face was flushed and small beads of sweat gathered on his forehead. He touched the girl's shoulder and asked, "Tell me the names of the witches who torment you."

Still tucked into a ball, the girl slowly opened her eyes. She looked across her pillow into Stone's eyes and said, "Satan and these witches won't let me. If I do, they will hurt me."

"God will protect you. When you tell me their names, they will no longer have reason to harm you. Say the names before they can stop you."

"Rebecca Greensmith," shouted the girl who immediately

screamed in pain before she tucked herself into a ball again.

As she lay moaning, Hawkes asked to no one in particular, "Who is Rebecca Greensmith?"

"She's Nathaniel Greensmith's wife," Wyllys answered from the room's rear. "He's a contentious man with little piety. He owns a small farm down the hill behind my house near John Cole's house. Goody Greensmith is a vulgar woman with an ugly face."

"I am going to ask the girl for the other names," Stone said. "Hold her down if she has fits."

The other men moved to the bed prepared to restrain the girl.

Reverend Stone leaned over the girl and calmly said, "Ann, I'm going to ask you the names of the other witches who torment you. Give me their names even if you are in pain. Keep going until you give me all their names. Only then will the pain stop because Satan and his familiars will no longer have reason to hurt you to keep you from giving me the names. Do you understand? Will you forget the pain and give me the names?"

The girl opened her eyes, peered into Stone's eyes and nodded.

"No matter what happens, don't take your eyes from mine," Stone said. "Tell me the witches' names."

Immediately, the girl's legs and arms flew straight out from her body. She lay on the bed as if pinned to it. She flailed about like a rag doll being shaken. Hawkes grabbed her left leg and pinned it to the bed while Hooker did the same with her right. At the top of the bed Wyllys and Whiting held her arms, while above her Stone peered into her eyes.

"Don't scream Ann," Stone urged. "Instead, when the pain is so great you feel you must scream, yell out the witches' names."

"It hurts, it hurts," the girl yelled repeatedly as she tried to squirm free from the grasps of the surrounding men. "Make the pain stop, please make it stop."

"Ann, I promise you it will stop if you give me the names," Stone urged.

The girl's eyes were wet with tears and the veins in the faces of the men holding her bulged when she screamed, "Elizabeth Seager is one. Mary Barnes is another."

"Are there more?" Stone asked.

"One more," screamed the girl.

"Name her."

Suddenly, the girl stopped fighting against the men's grasps. As Stone watched, her eyes rolled back under her eyelids and she began to breathe in the same deep rhythmic pattern she had earlier. Then she started to speak. At first, the men didn't recognize it as speech but soon they recognized the language to be English, but English so tarnished with an accent it was barely recognizable.

"What is that accent?" Hooker asked.

"Dutch," Stone said. "Goodman Cole, how did your daughter learn to speak this way?"

"She's never spoken like this before."

"Satan must be confounding her speech to keep us from learning the last witch's name," Stone said.

"Press on Reverend," Hawkes growled.

Stone turned back to the girl, leaned over her, and asked, "Tell me the witch's name."

In a voice so heavily dominated by a Dutch accent it was nearly impossible to understand, the girl began to speak.

"There was a girl who lived near a Dutch family years ago," she said. "The girl was tormented by a band of witches. They haunted her at night, pinching her arms until she screamed from the pain. These are the same witches attacking me. They come as vapors in the night and pinch my arms until I scream from the pain. Even now they're confusing my speech to stop me from saying the last name."

"Give me the last name," Stone demanded. "I can understand you. Satan hasn't made your speech so unclear I can't."

"Judith Varlet," the girl declared. She, Rebecca Greensmith, Elizabeth Seager and Mary Barnes are in league with Satan. They plan to terrorize the people of Hartford. On Christmas they're meeting Satan to assign their souls to him for the power to work his will."

Exhausted, the girl lapsed into sleep. The men holding her down released her.

"An amazing story," Whiting said. "These women may be witches, but her evidence is only spectral. Unless there's more evidence we cannot convict them."

"I disagree," Hawkes said. "The evidence isn't just spectral. This girl spoke with a strong Dutch accent, an accent she never had before. Coupled with the spectral evidence this girl told us of, her accent proves these women are guilty."

"I agree, there's enough evidence to charge these women with witchcraft," Stone said.

Rebecca Greensmith was a great deal uglier than her reputation when John Lee first saw her on a December morning in 1662, a month after Ann Cole's revelations. In fact, she was repulsive. Try as he might, John couldn't stop thinking about her prune-like face, scraggly hair, and leather skin, while the Chief Magistrate of the particular court conducting her pre-trial hearing read the charges against her.

Rebecca stood before the six magistrates and twelve jurors while the Chief Magistrate read the charges, "Rebecca Greensmith, you've been charged with engaging in preternatural acts and familiarity with Satan."

John knew conviction of either charge would be enough to order her hanging; conviction of both would assure it.

The Chief Magistrate stroked his beard as he turned to Rebecca Greensmith, "How do you plead to these charges?"

"I am innocent."

The Chief Magistrate looked at Reverend Stone sitting in the chamber's first row and announced, "Reverend Stone, you may present your report regarding Ann Cole's accusations against this woman."

"My assistant, Reverend Haynes took notes of what Ann Cole said that night," Stone said. "He will read them to the court."

For the next twenty minutes, Reverend Haynes described the events occurring at Samuel Wyllys' mansion. At times the spectators were frozen in their seats, all eyes glued to the young minister. At other times, a groan, or gasp rose from the spectators. When Haynes was finished most in the chamber were convinced Rebecca Greensmith was a witch.

Hawkes fixed his eyes on Rebecca and kept them there until Haynes finished his testimony. When Haynes began, Rebecca's face was confident, defiantly so. As Haynes told of Ann's ravings Rebecca's confidence disappeared. When Haynes told of Ann's unexplainable Dutch accent, Rebecca's eyes dropped to the floor. Finally, when Haynes said Ann Cole accused her of being a witch, Rebecca's lips began quivering.

After Reverend Haynes was done, the Chief Magistrate turned to Rebecca, "Having heard Reverend Haynes' testimony, do you wish to change your plea?"

Rebecca's eyes stared at the floor while she mumbled to herself incoherently. Finally, without lifting her eyes from the floor, she whispered, "No."

"Your plea is accepted," the Chief Magistrate announced. "We will now recess for supper."

Immediately, Richard Hawkes grabbed Reverend Stone's wrist, "Let me talk to her. I can make her confess."

The meetinghouse's chamber cleared as the spectators left for supper. Before the Chief Magistrate left, he was approached by Stone and Hawkes.

"Sir," Stone announced. "Richard Hawkes knows the art of examining witches. Let him question Goodwife Greensmith during this break. She weakened when she heard Reverend Haynes's testimony. I believe Richard can obtain her confession."

Hawkes smiled, "I'm certain of it."

The Chief Magistrate stared carefully at Hawkes before announcing, "I will permit Mr. Hawkes to examine her but only during the time allotted for supper."

Hawkes waited for the accused witch across the meetinghouse yard at a table in the town's jail. Outside the jail, a beefy man's arms and legs were strung through the holes of a stock used to punish minor offenses. The man's sign said, "Drunkard." The man would be set free when the sun set. As he sat in the jailhouse, Hawkes knew when he was finished with Rebecca, she would be set free only at the end of a rope.

The jailors brought Rebecca across the yard through the crowd gathered in front of the meetinghouse sharing supper. Her unkempt hair looked like a bird's nest when they sat her down before Hawkes and left the room. Her head was down, and she was trembling. "Look at me, Rebecca," Hawkes ordered.

She kept her eyes fixed on the table.

"Look at me Rebecca. I won't hurt you. You're safe with me."

Still trembling, she slowly raised her eyes to meet his. Her ravaged pockmarked face relaxed as soon as her eyes met his eyes. He leaned across the table and grasped her trembling hands.

"You should be afraid," Hawkes said calmly. "I would be too."

She dropped her head.

"Trust me," he said. "What I say now will save you so you can live to see your two daughters marry."

She lifted her head and looked into his eyes, "How can you save me?"

"Your life will be spared if the court believes you are repentant.

The court will believe this only if you confess and identify other witches. One of the witches you name must be your husband, for the court will only believe you are repentant if you name someone close to you."

"How can I be sure this will happen if I do what you say?"

"Because I am telling you. Do you have any other choice? You will be hanged unless you do what I say."

"While I did the things I am accused of, I haven't entered into a covenant with Satan."

"Tell this to the court when you confess," he said. "It will ensure your freedom. If you do, I will testify you are repentant and shouldn't be hanged."

She stared at the wall for nearly a minute. Finally, she turned toward him. Her face was relaxed when she said, "I will do what you say."

Hawkes returned to the meetinghouse chamber after the supper break. He nodded at Reverend Stone as he sat next to him. Rebecca Greensmith was already sitting on a bench at the front of the chamber. Her husband, Nathaniel, sat behind her.

Hawkes stood as soon as the Chief Magistrate called the court to order and announced, "Rebecca Greensmith desires to change her plea."

"Is this true Goodwife Greensmith?" the Chief Magistrate asked.

"It is," Rebecca answered. "I am guilty and wish to give my confession."

"Move to the witness chair," the Chief Magistrate ordered.

The chamber was quiet as Rebecca Greensmith began. After the Chief Magistrate administered her oath, he asked, "How did you first meet Satan?"

"Two years ago, I was alone in the woods west of town gathering berries. Suddenly a fawn appeared. It stared at me for several minutes and ran around me before stopping before me and speaking. It spoke of my life and of Satan and how he loved me."

"Was the fawn a familiar of Satan?"

"No sir," said Rebecca. "The fawn was Satan"

Gasps came from several people in the audience, but they were quickly silenced by the rapt stillness of everyone else in the room. No one moved and everyone's eyes were on Rebecca as her testimony continued.

"How did you know it was Satan?" the Chief Magistrate asked.

"Because it changed to Satan before me."

"What did Satan look like?"

"He was tan, almost red, and his eyes burned like candles. That's all I remember. I was too frightened to look at him longer."

"What did Satan do next?"

"He removed my fear. In his presence I felt helpless to stop him from making sexual use of my body."

There were gasps from some in the audience.

"Did you see Satan again"

"Yes, many times."

"Did you worship Satan?"

"Yes."

"Did you worship him with others?"

"Yes."

"Who were they?"

"I worshiped Satan with a band of witches. We met in the woods at night and one time we met on the green near my house."

"What did you do when you worshiped Satan with these other witches?"

"We danced around a maypole and drank beer. Sometimes the other witches would come to worship in the form of cats, black crows or other creatures."

"Who are these witches?"

"They are Judith Varlett, Elizabeth Seager and Mary Barnes."

The room erupted. People gasped, groaned, yelled and jeered. Some were simply shocked; others were angry; and, still others shook their heads in disbelief. When the chamber was quiet again the Chief Magistrate asked, "Rebecca Greensmith, have you and these other women ever signed a covenant giving your souls to Satan?"

"Not yet. We were going to do this during Christmas two weeks ago, but our arrests kept us from doing so. Satan promised to come to us in the woods while we were worshiping him, and we were going to sign the covenant together."

"This was truly Satan's plan," Reverend Stone yelled jumping from his seat. "Christmas is a pagan holiday and Satan uses it as a time to take advantage of the weak."

"Thank you, Reverend Stone," the Chief Magistrate said. He turned back to Rebecca and asked, "Did you and the other women cast a spell on Ann Cole?"

"We did. She saw us in the woods, and we were afraid she would say we were witches. We tried to keep her from doing so."

The Chief Magistrate paused briefly and glanced around the chamber at the people in the audience. After a minute passed, he looked back at Rebecca and asked, "You've admitted you are a witch and have had familiarity with Satan. Are you sorry for what you did, and do you ask for God's forgiveness?"

"Yes, I am sorry for what I did and beg God to forgive me."

"How can we know you truly seek redemption?"

"You can know this by what I am now doing. God, as well as my love for my husband, who must open his heart to the truth, compels me to tell you that he too is a witch who has had familiarity with Satan."

"How do you know your husband is a witch?" the Chief Magistrate asked.

"I know this because I saw him talk to strange red creatures and black dogs in the woods when he didn't know I was watching him.

When I asked what he did in the woods, he lied, saying he was hunting foxes. I also saw him uproot trees with his bare hands. Such strength could only have been given to him by Satan."

Rebecca Greensmith's husband slumped in his seat. Throughout the chamber the spectators gasped. Immediately, Nathaniel Greensmith was grabbed by the court's guards and whisked away to the jail to await further proceedings. John knew immediately in the end there would be a hanging. Ahead of John, Richard Hawkes fought to keep from smiling as he sat in his seat.

When the room was silent, the Chief Magistrate announced, "Trial will be held one week from today. In the meantime, we will hold a pretrial hearing for Nathaniel Greensmith, Elizabeth Seager, Judith Varlett and Mary Barnes. Each of them indicted at the pretrial hearing shall be tried with Rebecca Greensmith."

Chapter 50

John Lee arrived at the trial earlier than to Rebecca Greensmith's pretrial hearing the week before. This time his seat was in the middle of the spectators' benches. Mary thought about coming but felt it too painful to watch her neighbor Mary Barnes tried for witchcraft along with Elizabeth Seager, Judith Varlett and Nathaniel and Rebecca Greensmith, who had each been indicted at pretrial hearings.

The scene was the same. Except for two new jurors, the same Chief Magistrate, magistrates and jury conducting the pretrial hearings spread out before him against the meetinghouse chamber's front wall. Once again, Reverend Stone and Richard Hawkes sat in the first row of benches directly facing the Chief Magistrate. Deacon Hart sat in the front row on the room's other side.

Like most in the town, John heard the rumor that Nathaniel Greensmith begged his wife not to testify against him when he spoke to her at the jail earlier in the week. The rumor was that in exchange, he promised to care for her two teenage daughters. John was waiting to see if Rebecca did what Nathaniel asked. Richard Hawkes didn't wonder. He spoke with Rebecca three more times that week and knew exactly what she would say.

Gradually, the din of the many nervous conversations died in expectation of the defendants' arrival. The room was hushed when the door to the chamber swung open and the first of the jailor's assistants entered. The people froze when the second assistant entered, knowing the accused witches would follow. An attractive woman entered the room. Most spectators strained their necks to look back at her as she followed the jailers down the aisle. Some men stood for a better view, for Judith Varlett, a member of the small Dutch community that stayed behind after the Dutch left their fort years before, was un-known to nearly everyone in the room. She was a woman of medium height but seemed taller because of her slender frame. Her dark brown hair was clean and pulled up under a small linen cap. She walked with an aristocratic gait and looked directly at the Chief Magistrate.

A short plump woman dressed in a faded tan bodice and a slight-ly torn, but serviceable wool skirt, entered the room after Judith. Everyone knew Elizabeth Seager, but few liked her, for her reputation was soiled by years of association with women of ill repute and intem-perance. This was not the first time she was accused of being a witch and, if she avoided the hangman today, most believed she would meet him again later. Her face was flushed, and her eyes darted about while she walked down the aisle. The two women took seats on a bench left of and facing the Chief Magistrate and the rest of the court. Mary Barnes, the next of the accused, entered the room. Her shoulder leaned against the tall jailer walking with her, making her look even more fragile than she was. He guided her down the aisle while her eyes stared at her feet. John's stomach turned and his pulse quickened as he watched the jailer guide her to a seat next to Elizabeth Seager.

Nathaniel and Rebecca Greensmith entered the room last. Rebecca walked a few feet ahead of Nathaniel with her head held high. Nathaniel followed her looking down the aisle avoiding the glares of people staring at them from both sides of the aisle. Rebecca's dishev-eled dirty brown hair was streaked with gray and matched her coarse wool skirt and bodice. Nathaniel sat at the bench next to Mary Barnes who trembled with her head bowed. Rebecca stood, staring at the Chief Magistrate and then at each of the twelve jurors. Finally, she turned her eyes to her right and looked directly at Richard Hawkes. As Hawkes returned her gaze, John noticed a slight smile at the cor-ners of his mouth. Rebecca nodded at Hawkes before she sat next to her husband.

For the first hour the trial followed the same script as the pretrial hearing. As before, Reverend Stone introduced Reverend Haynes who testified as to Ann Cole's ranting, contortions and accusations. The Chief Magistrate looked at Rebecca Greensmith and said, "Rebecca Greensmith, you've pled guilty to the charges of witchcraft and familiarity with Satan. Richard Hawkes has interviewed you and he told the court you will testify today. Are you ready to do so?"

"I am."

"Move to the witness chair."

Rebecca testified as she did during her pretrial confession, implicating each woman tried with her. She turned to her husband who was shaking uncontrollably and announced, "My husband Nathaniel is also a witch." As in her confession, Rebecca described the things her husband did to support her conclusion.

During the rest of the morning the other accused testified to their innocence. Judith Varlett spoke in a thick Dutch accent as she denied ever meeting with Rebecca or the other women in the woods. Elizabeth Seager was far less respectful. She accused the court of allowing into evidence the unreliable rants of Ann Cole and the accusations of a guilty woman bent only on saving her life. She denied she was a witch and claimed she was neither a friend of Rebecca Greensmith nor Mary Barnes.

Mary Barnes didn't move when it was her turn to testify. The Chief Magistrate repeatedly urged her to move to the witness chair. Finally, when it was clear she would not, the Chief Magistrate asked if she wanted to testify from where she sat. She nodded without speaking. Finally, the Chief Magistrate crossed the room, stood directly in front of her, and asked, "Mary Barnes, do you deny the charges you are accused of?"

"I do," Mary whispered, her voice only loud enough for the Chief Magistrate and the accused sitting with her to hear.

"She says she's not guilty," the Chief Magistrate said loud enough for everyone in the chamber to hear. "Do you deny you met in the woods and on the green with Rebecca Greensmith, Judith Varlett and Elizabeth Seager to cavort with Satan as testified to by Rebecca Greensmith?"

"I deny it," Mary whispered.

"She says she didn't do these things," yelled the Chief Magistrate. "Do you have anything else to say?"

Mary sobbed softly. She looked at her husband sitting ten feet away from her in the front row of spectators. When their eyes met her face filled with pain. She began to rock back and forth on the bench while speaking quietly to herself. Finally, she whispered through her sobs in a voice loud enough for most in the room to hear, "I am not a witch. What will become of my children without their mother? What will happen to them? What will happen to them?"

For the first time that day John Lee felt the pangs of desperation. Could God really permit this woman to be hanged? Around him he could hear sniffling and the sound of several people blowing their noses.

The Chief Magistrate dismissed the jurors to deliberate. John glanced ahead to the chamber's first row as the jurors filed past him. He scanned the row until his eyes found Richard Hawkes. Hawkes was smiling broadly at Reverend Stone while the two men talked with a few other men at the chamber's front bench. Hawkes turned towards John and their eyes met. Instantly, Hawke's broad smile disappeared. It was replaced by a nod and a smirk.

The jury returned to the chamber at mid-afternoon. As they filed past John, he looked for any sign of what their verdict was. There was none. The chamber silenced as soon as the jurors were seated. Each juror stared at the Chief Magistrate.

"Has the jury reached a verdict?" the Chief Magistrate asked.

"We have," answered the man chosen by the jury to lead them.

"Announce it."

"We find Nathaniel and Rebecca Greensmith guilty of the charges.

We find Judith Varlett and Mary Barnes guilty of the charges. We're not able to find Elizabeth Seager guilty of the charges as only six of the jurors voted to convict her. The other six jurors believe the evidence against her, while strong, isn't enough to convict her."

John's heart sank. *How could the jury convict Mary Barnes?* he asked himself. He bowed his head and prayed for her, her husband and their children. When he lifted his head, the room was filled with the buzz of scores of individual conversations. At the chamber's front, the magistrates remained seated waiting to determine the sentences to be given to the convicted. The Chief Magistrate raised his hand, silencing the room, "Does anyone wish to speak for any of the convicted before the magistrates decide their sentence?"

John and five other men raised their hands. Richard Hawkes was not one. John glanced at Rebecca Greensmith. She stared at Hawkes with her head tilted to the side and her eyes open wide. John turned to Hawkes. He was staring at Rebecca impassively. Suddenly, Rebecca's mouth fell open. *Hawkes did promise her*, John thought. *He has betrayed her.* Hawkes turned away from Rebecca with a slight smile on his face.

Of the six people who raised their hands, all but one of them spoke for Mary Barnes. Along with the other witnesses John praised Mary's devotion to her family and her church and stated he didn't believe she was a witch. He closed by asking the court to spare her life.

The sixth witness was an old man from the Dutch settlement where Judith Varlett lived. He spoke of her education and good character, promising he would bring a letter to the court from Peter Stuyvesant, the governor of New Amsterdam, vouching for her character and seeking her release.

The magistrates gathered together to decide upon sentences for the convicted soon after the final witness testified. It took them only fifteen minutes to reach their decision.

"The magistrates are ready to announce the sentences of the accused found guilty," the Chief Magistrate announced.

John's heart raced as he and everyone else in the room leaned forward to hear the sentences.

"The following are the court's sentences: Nicholas and Rebecca Greensmith, having been convicted of engaging in preternatural acts and familiarity with Satan, this court sentences you to death by hanging. Judith Varlett, you've been found guilty of engaging in preternatural acts and familiarity with Satan. However, this decision is subject to change depending on the testimony promised by the Governor of New Amsterdam. Until such time as this testimony is received you shall be kept in Hartford's jail. Mary Barnes, having been convicted of engaging in preternatural acts and familiarity with Satan, this court sentences you to death by hanging."

Mournful wailing erupted at the front of the chamber. John looked ahead where he saw Mary Barnes's husband sobbing uncontrollably. Several people rushed to the man's side trying to console him, but it was obvious his pain was too great, and he began rolling about on the floor.

Rebecca Greensmith glared at Richard Hawkes as she was led from the room by her jailors. She fought against their restraint like a caged animal.

"Liar, liar," she yelled. "Richard Hawkes is a liar. He said I would not hang if I accused my husband."

"Silence," the Chief Magistrate yelled. "This court made you no promises."

Hawkes said nothing in response to Rebecca's claim. He simply stared at her impassively before turning away. Rebecca screamed until the guards restrained her and forced her from the chamber.

The spectators buzzed about the room in scores of conversations after the convicted witches left. John remained seated. *It is my fault,* he thought with his head down. *Richard Hawkes would never have been able to convince Rebecca Greensmith to testify against the others if I didn't take the oath. He would not even be here. He would have had no future in New*

England at all.

"Why so glum John," Deacon Hart asked as he placed his arm on John's shoulder.

John looked into the older man's eyes for a moment while thinking of what to say. Finally, he answered, "I can't believe Mary Barnes is to be hanged based on that troubled woman's accusation."

"It's God's will John," Hart said. "If she's innocent God will embrace her. If she's guilty her torment will be eternal. I hope for her sake she's innocent."

Chapter 51

The message reached John at noon on a hot July Saturday. It came after he finished helping Nesehegan nail fresh clapboard along the west wall of the Indian schoolhouse he built five years earlier in 1658. The message was addressed to him and was sealed with the mark of Hartford's church. John didn't know why Reverend Stone sent him a message. It was six months since he last spoke with Stone during the witchcraft trial of the Greensmiths and Mary Barnes. Their conversation was little more than an awkward greeting. He put the unopened message in the waist of his pants and went back to work.

He worked on repairs to the schoolhouse all morning. Daniel Hart and two students, Wematin and Sucki, replaced several support beams and removed rotting clapboards while John and Nesehegan nailed new clapboards where the rotted ones were removed.

Wematin and Sucki were eight when they first came to the school. They were now in their teens. Both spoke English, understood arithmetic, and were skilled in hunting with the new flintlock musket, now the preferred weapon of most Connecticut tribes. They also knew the Bible's stories; but neither knew these stories as well as their friend Nesehegan. It seemed to them Nesehegan memorized every book, chapter and verse.

At thirteen, Nesehegan was already a skilled carpenter. He sawed and trimmed the deteriorated clapboard and hammered the nails for the new clapboards. It was sweltering when the message came and even though sweat poured down Nesehegan's bare back, he smiled the entire time he and John worked together.

John was surprised when Nesehegan asked, "Why do you think Reverend Stone wants to see you teacher?"

John frowned and asked, "How did you know the message was from Reverend Stone?"

"I recognized the seal."

"How do you know his seal?"

"I don't know," Nesehegan answered. "I just do. I must have seen it before."

"Even I don't know what the message says," John said. "What makes you think Reverend Stone wants to see me?"

"I just know."

John shrugged, "I suppose we will when I open the message after Mary brings supper this afternoon. We've lots of work to do first."

Nesehegan nodded and began hammering nails into the clapboard John held against the school's frame. Before they finished John heard a cart's squeaking wheels. The cart was driven by Christopher Smith, the husband of Sam Pierce's widow, Abigail. Mary and Abigail sat on the cart next to Christopher. Walking behind the cart was a boy of about thirteen. He held his head high and walked briskly.

"John, have everyone sit at the table outside the school," Mary said as the cart neared him. "Supper is ready."

John gathered the others and they unloaded the corn bread, peas, and pork roast Mary prepared and gathered around the table. The boy held back, staring at John while the others sat at the table eating. John caught the boy's gaze and smiled. He turned to Christopher.

"Introduce us Christopher," John said.

"Oh . . . sure John," Christopher said as he was about to pick up a piece of pork with his napkin. "This is Joseph Henry, my late brother's son. He died last year, and I paid for Joseph's passage. He's from Colchester and lives with me and Abigail."

"Welcome Joseph, I am sorry you lost your father," John said. "I lost my father when I was about your age. Sit and eat with us."

The men and boys sat around the table while Mary and Abigail served the food. They ate for a few minutes as John gazed at Joseph sitting across the table from him.

"You are from Colchester, Joseph," John said. "I am too."

"I know."

The others stopped talking and listened.

"I left Colchester in 1634 when I was thirteen," John said. "How old are you Joseph?"

"Almost fourteen sir."

"We've much in common," John said.

"I hope so sir."

"Why do you say that?" John asked.

"I heard about you from the boys in Hartford." Joseph answered

"I can't believe they know about me," John said. "What do they talk about?"

"Who hasn't heard of John Lee, the constable of Farmington?" Joseph answered excitedly. They say you were a great soldier who fought with Lieutenant Bull when you were young. When they were younger, the boys pretended to be you in their make-believe battles. They say you now help those you fought."

"Legends have a way of growing," John smiled.

John pointed to the Indians at the table, "These men are from the Tunxis tribe. I never fought them. I've taught them for years. During that time, I learned more from them than they from me. After supper I will show you the schoolhouse and, if you like, you can help repair its roof."

"I would like to," Joseph said.

After supper, the men and boys went back to work while Abigail and Mary cleaned the table and, with Christopher's help, loaded the cart. After they left, Joseph stayed with John to repair the school-house roof. Before John could ask, Joseph was atop the roof smiling down at him.

"What do you plan on doing up there?" John laughed.

"Should I come down?" Joseph asked with a broad smile.

PAMELA ROBERTS LEE

"No, Nesehegan and I will hand you boards to replace the damaged ones," John said. "Place them on the roof and we will come up to replace the old boards with the new ones. We will then place shingles over them."

John, Nesehegan and Joseph worked the afternoon on the roof while the other Tunxis replaced clapboard on the school's east wall. As they worked, John quickly discovered Nesehegan and Joseph didn't need his help. Nesehegan's carpentry skills and Joseph's strength were enough.

Nesehegan smiled at John when they were done, "You haven't opened Reverend Stone's message yet."

John pulled the message from his doublet and broke its seal.

"What does it say?" Nesehegan asked.

"The message says, 'John come see me immediately. Reverend Samuel Stone.'"

"Will you see him?" Nesehegan asked.

"You don't know the answer already?"

"I do. You are going to see him tomorrow."

"You are a remarkable young man Nesehegan," John said before turning to walk to his house.

As he walked, John thought of how exceptional Nesehegan was. He always had a serene smile, knew each Bible verse and was kind to everyone. While he could handle a bow and musket as well as anyone, unlike the other boys, Nesehegan was only casually interested in talking about them. What Nesehegan wanted to talk about were the feelings and concerns of the people he knew and of how God's message of love could help them live better lives. At first this was disconcerting to some, but soon Nesehegan had a small following of friends who sought his guidance on such matters.

Waves of moist hot air blew across John's face. It was noon on the Sabbath, but he knew Reverend Stone was not at the meetinghouse. He would be bedridden at home on the Little River south of the meetinghouse.

Reverend Stone's house faced the Little River not far from the meetinghouse. The final bell rang announcing the start of the Sabbath's first service as he reached the weathered door just past the front yard's weed infested garden. He imagined the garden's deterioration tracked the course of Stone's illness, which began shortly after the Greensmiths' and Mary Barnes's hangings.

Stone's wife Rachael opened the door when John knocked. She was Stone's second wife and much younger than her husband. Her eyes were red with heavy dark bags as she announced, "Welcome John. Reverend Stone hoped you would come. Please wait in the hall. I will tell him you are here."

Stone's hall was empty, but John knew after the Sabbath service it would be full of Stone's family and visitors from the congregation. A malodorous odor filled the hall. He tried to ignore it. Despite his best efforts to avoid doing so, he began to speculate as to its cause. It was so strong that at times he felt he could taste it. He rose from his chair to look for its source when he could stand the smell no longer. It took only a few minutes for him to find it. It was a medium sized rat that died behind the hall's maple cabinet. He was about to remove the rat when Mrs. Stone entered the room.

"What are you doing on the floor?" she asked.

"There's a dead rat under the cabinet. I was about to remove it before you returned."

"I'm sorry John. Since Reverend Stone became sick, he hasn't been able to do things he used to. Please remove it."

John gripped the rat with the iron tongs used to move logs in the fireplace and dropped it into the woods behind Stone's house. Mrs. Stone was waiting when he returned.

"Reverend Stone will see you now," she said. "He's lying in bed in the parlor chamber just past his study at the top of the stairs."

John noticed a few open books resting on Stone's desk in his study. Like the desk, they were dust covered. The parlor was dark and smelled of aged clothing. Stone was propped up on several pillows on a large bed resting against the wall with his eyes closed. The room was lit by a single candle next to the bed.

"Sit in the chair at my bed," Stone said in a raspy voice.

John sat in the chair and looked at Stone. The old man's frame was more emaciated than John remembered; his cheeks were so hollow his head looked like a skull; and, his night clothes were wet and clung to the bones of his arms. His breathing was labored, and he wheezed as his chest heaved up and down.

"I thought a great deal as I lay in this bed for the last few months," Stone wheezed. "I asked you here to share these thoughts before I die. I suppose you could say you will be my confessor."

"Why are you telling me these things?" John asked.

"Because I trust you and because you are close to God."

"What makes you think that?"

"I've known you since you were a boy. You were my brightest student. Your questions about faith frustrated me because I couldn't answer them. I now believe God gave you those questions not just for you but also for me for we must always be certain what we do is His will and not ours"

Stone paused and gasped for air. He coughed for a minute before he laughed, "God brings all of us to our knees in the end, doesn't he John?"

"I suppose that's true sir."

Stone continued, "The hardest thing about getting old is losing friends. I guess I helped that process along, didn't I John?"

John smiled and said, "I imagine some might say that."

"How is my old friend William Westwood?"

"He's well. He built a house in Hadley and he and Bridget are converted members of their church."

"When you see him tell him I thought of him." Stone said.

"I will."

"I am pleased you and Mary converted in Farmington's church."

"Thank you." John replied. "It was finally time for me. Mary has been ready since she was a child."

"Do you really believe God selected you for His grace?" Stone asked.

"No man knows this for sure."

"You are honest." Stone said. "It's why I admire you. Truth is, I don't know if God has selected me either. I will learn today."

Stone coughed again for a few minutes. When he was done, he took a deep breath before turning back to John, "How do you think God will judge me?"

John paused before answering, "It's not for me to say Reverend. No one can know God's mind."

"How do you judge me?"

"You are a man who did what he believed right but also a man who made many mistakes."

Stone laughed and wheezed, "I knew you would tell me how you felt, but you are not right about one thing. I didn't always believe what I was doing was right; often I knew it was wrong. I blessed the Pequots' massacre to gain power for myself, not because it was right. I fought against your Indian school so only I would have the authority to decide what would . . .."

Before he could finish his sentence, Stone began to cough and wheeze again. This time the attack lasted longer. When it finally stopped Stone took a deep breath and continued, "Where did I finish John?"

"You were speaking of my Indian school."

"Oh yes, I fought against your Indian school so only I would have the power to decide how we teach the Indians. Then there's our church's schism. I fought against the withdrawers to feed my own ego, not for the glory of God. Then there were the witches. Do you believe there are witches?"

"The bible teaches that," John answered. "Because of that I believed this once but now I believe that it is our fear that leads us to persecute the weak and eccentric. Satan does not need the witches we create in our minds."

"I hope you are wrong John, but fear you are right," Stone said.

Stone coughed for a minute before saying, "The reason I searched for witches had little to do with whether they existed. I searched for them because it increased my power. Many were wrongfully hanged because of my pride."

John said nothing and the parlor chamber remained quiet for several minutes as Stone's chest wheezed while rising and falling with each breath.

"Why don't you like Richard Hawkes?" Stone asked.

"He can't be trusted because he cares only for himself."

"What happened on the *Francis* that made you enemies?"

"I can't tell you," John answered. "All I can say is I've seen him do terrible things and watched fearfully as he became close to you and Deacon Hart. He's clever and uses people as his tools."

"So, you think he used me for his own purposes?"

Before John could respond, Stone wheezed again before leaning over and spitting out blood and phlegm into an iron pan on the table next to his bed. After he fell back onto his pillows, he took several deep breaths.

"He didn't use me, even though he may think he did," Stone said. "He gave me advice, but I decided whether to follow his advice or not. He didn't deceive me. This is my confession: if he was Satan, I would have followed his advice for the same reason I followed Richard's advice. I would have followed it if I felt it would benefit me. This is the reason I now beg for God's forgiveness."

John said nothing. He simply stared at the dying man lying before him. He knew Stone would never have imagined doing what Hawkes suggested and it was Hawkes's implanting of each idea in Stone's head that triggered his actions. Even so, it was a revelation to know Stone often followed Richard's recommendations for his own reasons. After several minutes, when it was clear Stone was sleeping, John left the room.

John was with Stone for nearly two hours and the Sabbath's first service was finished when he walked into the hall. There, sitting in all the seats and standing against the walls, were Reverend Whiting and twenty members of Stone's congregation. Richard Hawkes leaned against the wall farthest from John. John and Hawkes stared at each as Hawkes walked towards him.

"Good day, John," Hawkes stated imperiously. "Why did you come from Farmington to talk to a dying man?"

"Because he asked me to," John grunted.

"What did you talk about?"

"He said it was his confession."

Hawkes's smile disappeared and his faced reddened. He leaned toward John and ranted, "Don't mock me. Tell me what he said."

"What he said was for me, not you. You can ask him, but I doubt he'll tell you either."

Before Hawkes responded, John turned and walked outside into the sunlight.

Heavy thunderstorms tore through Hartford the day they buried Reverend Stone. Inside the meetinghouse, the congregation and dignitaries from surrounding communities were gathered. Reverend Whiting gave the eulogy under black clouds heavy with rain. Most people sitting in the room were wet. Small pools of water dotted the floor and the musty scent of wet wool floated on the invisible currents of air flowing through the room.

Richard Hawkes sat in a bench in the first row. His only goal was to make certain he would sit in the same row the next time he sat in the meetinghouse. John and Mary Lee sat together at the back of the room in a section reserved for people from other congregations.

Reverend Whiting's eulogy was unremarkable. The meetinghouse was still dim as the people filed out after the service. Hawkes waited until Whiting was done speaking to the last of the congregation before he approached him. It was important that what he said to him be done without others present. When the meetinghouse was empty, Whiting walked to the meetinghouse's front to collect his belongings. Hawkes met Whiting beneath the pulpit.

"An excellent eulogy Reverend," Hawkes said.

"Thank you," Whiting grunted while gathering his belongings.

Whiting wound his way up the pulpit's stairs. Hawkes waited until Whiting came down to make his offer. He moved to the base of the pulpit's stairs. Hawkes stood between Whiting and the aisle to the meetinghouse door, forcing Whiting to stop in front of him.

"As you know, I served as Reverend Stone's advisor for many years," Hawkes said. "As our congregation's minister you will need an advisor who knows our congregation and has learned how politics and commerce can affect it. I would be pleased to serve you in the same capacity I served Reverend Stone."

Whiting stared impassively at Hawkes, "Thank you for your offer," Whiting answered. "But I don't need an advisor. Even if I did, I would not choose you after the conflicts we had over the revelations of Ann Cole last year?"

With that, Whiting walked around Hawkes and strode to the front door. Hawkes watched Whiting until he was gone. He sat in the bench he sat in for the years he assisted Reverend Stone and stared at the floor beneath him. After several minutes he raised his head and stood up. His spirits lifted as he confidently walked down the aisle. By the time he opened the door he knew he would overcome this new challenge as he had all others before it.

Chapter 52

After two years, Richard Hawkes was certain Reverend Whiting did him a favor. He questioned why he ever felt the need to rise on the backs of others. Inevitably, they would look out for their own interests. When those interests clashed with his they would abandon him. After all, that's what he would do. Without the need to depend on the good will of others he was at last free to concentrate on the pieces of his own business and now those pieces fit together like a seamless web.

He stared out his study's window. The fall harvest ended three weeks before and most leaves lay in the dirt near the bare oak, maple and birch trees dotting the view before him. Two pinnaces were anchored fifty yards off shore in the river's channel. Several shallops scurried back and forth between the pinnaces and the landing, offloading chests of fabric, clothing, houseware, ironware and furniture from Boston, and loading sacks of ground corn, beaver pelts, lumber and dried beef. He was amused by the scene's irony, for aside from the beaver pelts (most of which were his), there was little of value being returned to Boston.

"What do you say?" James Eastman said. "Can you meet with Karel Beringer and Derrick Paulis today?"

Hawkes turned from the window and back to the table where Eastman sat. Edward Roach sat next to Eastman staring vacantly at the sunlight streaming through the window.

"Bring my horse to the meetinghouse after the first service." Hawkes said. "I will meet them here between the morning and afternoon services. Also, I want you two to come to my house tonight to meet with my master miller."

"Why are you meeting him?" Eastman asked, slouched in his chair with his fat thighs spread widely apart.

Hawkes ignored the question and pointed to the study's door.

"Leave now," he said. "I need to go to the meetinghouse."

Hawkes turned back to the window and thought about John Lee. Early in their meeting Eastman reported Lee was busy. The good news was that Lee had ceased his efforts to tie him to the theft of cornmeal at Deacon Hart's mills due to Mark Scott's "confession." However, Hawkes was concerned because Eastman discovered Lee's investigations now included his land transactions in New England. Throughout the years he had fraudulently acquired land throughout Connecticut, particularly in the area once owned by the Pequots. Much of his wealth was derived from selling land near Plymouth Colony which was in demand. According to Eastman, Lee was working with Farmington's new town clerk, William Lewis, by checking the authenticity of deeds Hawkes filed for land he claimed to have purchased in Farmington. While alarming, the greatest threat was, with Lewis's help, Lee had contacted clerks throughout Connecticut and Daniel Hart, along with a young man named Joseph Henry, both working with Lee, examined Hawkes's deeds in several of their towns.

I have little to fear, Hawkes thought. *I filed deeds that can't be contested by the land's owner: either because it was abandoned by executed witches or accused witches who fled before their trials; the land was the Pequots that was parceled out after the war and was now abandoned by its owners; or, the land was of other Indian tribes who moved due to nearby English settlements. Still, Lee's investigation is an annoyance I can't ignore.*

Eastman also mentioned that a Tunxis student of Lee's named Nesehegan was asking Lee's Pocumtuc students about the long dead Pocumtuc Megedaqik. None remembered Megedaqik and those who heard of him said it was rumored he once ran a trading post for an Englishman the Indians called the dark man. Hawkes smiled when he heard his old nickname. He decided to make certain Lee's investigation discovered nothing more about his musket trading.

A servant knocked on his study's door and announced breakfast was ready. Elizabeth stood at the door between the parlor and the kitchen waiting to tell the servants to begin serving. Peter and Paul stood at the table behind their chairs. Even though a year younger than his brother, Paul was nearly two inches taller and ten pounds heavier. The differences between the boys didn't end there. Like his mother, Peter's hair was light and his frame slender. On the other hand, Paul's hair was black like his father's and his shoulders broad.

Hawkes nodded at the boys and took his seat at the table. Elizabeth motioned the servants to begin serving. When he finished breakfast, Hawkes rose from the table as his family continued eating. Looking at no one in particular, he said, "I'm ready to go to the meetinghouse. I will be in the study reviewing reports on my grist mills."

His family was in the hall waiting for him when Hawkes came down the stairs later. A servant brought his wagon to the door. He refused the servant's offer to drive, insisting he would hold the reins himself. He grabbed the reins as his sons climbed onto the benches at the back of the wagon. A servant helped Elizabeth onto the seat next to him.

Hawkes's family moved smartly towards the meetinghouse along the road Hartford's first settlers carved out thirty years earlier. A few two wheeled carts moved with them, but everyone else was on foot. The meetinghouse's drum was sounded, alerting all the morning service was beginning. Men and women walking on the raised wooden walkway glanced at him. When they recognized him, they lowered their eyes or looked away.

They were the last family to reach the meetinghouse. Hawkes pulled the wagon to the space he always used. It was no more than twenty paces from the meetinghouse's door. Reverend Whiting greeted them at the door. He walked forward to his seat in the front row facing the pulpit, while Elizabeth moved to the women's section and the boys climbed the stairs to the gallery where the children sat. As soon as Hawkes was seated, Reverend Whiting climbed the pulpit..

Like most men, Whiting learned not to cross Hawkes. From the moment Whiting rejected Hawkes's offer to assist him after Reverend Stone's funeral, Hawkes had two goals: to triple his wealth and to use that wealth to buy him power. He achieved both goals in little more than a year. He didn't care that most of his wealth came from the expansion of his musket trade and the sale of land he received in trade for his muskets or acquired through fraudulent deeds, for he no longer sought to be an upstanding merchant. He found he could achieve what he wanted without being accepted into the inner circle of Hartford's merchant class. Wealth alone was enough to give him the power he desired. Now, as the church's greatest benefactor, he'd regained his front row seat and Whiting listened to what he said.

When the service was over, he walked down the aisle with the Deputy Governor and the other men seated in the front row as the rest of the congregation stood at their seats watching them leave.

James Eastman and Edward Roach were waiting for Hawkes in the meetinghouse yard with his black stallion. Hawkes mounted the stallion, leaving Elizabeth and his sons behind to take part in the congregation's midday supper. The two Dutchmen waited in front of his house. Hawkes led them up the porch's stairs and into his study where they sat at the table.

"James said you want to talk about our trade on the Upper River," Hawkes said.

"Yes, things have changed," Karel Beringer said. "When the English took New Amsterdam and ordered the Dutch to stop trading muskets with the Mohawks, we expanded our trade into the Upper Hudson River near Fort Orange."

"Yes, and we thank the English for doing so," Hawkes said. "We've become wealthy trading our muskets to the Mohawks for beaver pelts since then."

"That's why we're here," Paulis said. "The Dutch traders only hid their musket trade from the English. They never stopped it. The English lifted the prohibition when they decided to ally with the Mohawks against the Hurons and French. Boston traders now compete with us."

"Do the Mohawks still have beaver pelts to trade?" Hawkes asked.

"Only pelts from tribes along the Great Lakes." Paulis answered.

"This well is about dry then."

"It will be unless the Mohawks defeat the Huron who control the fur trade along the Great Lakes." Beringer replied.

"I want us to get as many pelts as possible before the beaver disappear. The fur trade is moving west as beaver are trapped out in the east. Take all my muskets to the Mohawks. Accept only beaver pelts in return. What we don't trade to the Mohawks I will trade to the Wampanoags for land."

"What about the other traders near Albany?" Beringer asked.

"Trade my muskets before they trade theirs. Have our Mohawk allies dress as Hurons and run off or kill the Dutch traders. If you find English traders, do the same using the Dutch working for you. The English will think rogue Dutch traders attacked them and the Dutch traders will think they were attacked by Hurons."

"What about the Wampanoags?"

"Leave them to me. Now get going. You've a long trip."

The Dutchmen left, leaving Hawkes alone with Eastman and Roach.

"Does this mean we're no longer trading on the upper Hudson?" Eastman asked.

"No. It's just temporary," Hawkes answered. "I will trade there again when it's certain the Mohawks can get beaver pelts from the Great Lakes tribes. To do that, they must defeat the Huron. They will need my muskets to do that and they'll trade all of their pelts to us for muskets now."

"Take our Pocumtuc allies and visit the Wampanoags we trade with. Tell them we will soon have new flintlocks for them. Now go, I have to get back to the meetinghouse."

As soon as Hawkes returned to his house from the afternoon service, he gave the wagon's reins to a servant and strode into the house ahead of Elizabeth and their sons.

Eastman and Roach were waiting with his master miller, Thomas Aleworth. Aleworth was a robust man with a hearty laugh Hawkes found annoying. He helped Hawkes build his own gristmills. Seven in all, Hawkes's mills stretched along the Connecticut River. Aleworth was discreet. He'd been a miller most of his life and knew the milling business and how to skim off part of a farmer's cornmeal for himself. He immediately agreed to do the same for Hawkes - if he received fifteen percent of the cornmeal stolen.

As soon as the four men reached his study, Hawkes latched the door and turned to Aleworth, "Sit down, open your books, and let's talk about my profits."

Aleworth laughed, "Profits you have, profits you have. This past year's harvest was good, and your mills have been busy. Even though we skimmed off a smaller percentage of cornmeal than last year, the total amount we took is greater. My problem is where to store everything."

"Get another warehouse in Hartford," Hawkes answered. "Leave your account books here. I will review them tomorrow. We will discuss them when you pick up the books."

Hawkes looked across the table at Eastman and Roach, "Do you two have anything to say?"

Eastman shook his head while Roach stared at him vacantly.

Chapter 53

Daniel Hart and Joseph Henry walked along Farmington's Town Path on a frigid December morning in 1665. The ground was frozen and covered with crusty snow. They stopped when they reached Captain Edmund Lewis' house. It was two stories and like most houses in town, but with a unique difference. Captain Lewis, who became town clerk when John Steele died, added a one-story room, giving his house the space needed to store the town's official records. Daniel and Joseph set to work as soon as Captain Lewis let them in the room.

They started examining Farmington's land records several weeks before but stopped when John Lee asked them to review records in several other towns and to travel to Saybrook to review the records relating to the former Pequot lands. Now they were completing their review of Farmington's records. They sat at a heavy oak table where Captain Lewis placed the town's land records and deeds, they asked for. John Lee reminded Daniel earlier in the week that Richard Hawkes bragged years before of his land west of Farmington when he confronted them and their wives as they returned from a picnic. Today they would pour through the deeds filed for that land.

It was tedious work because the cross index of plots by name was lost and Captain Lewis hadn't created a new index. As a result, they reviewed the deeds by plot and not by the grantor's or grantee's name. They started with plots closest to the center of town and worked west. Captain Lewis said before his death that John Steele told him he accepted deeds to land up to four miles west of Farmington.

In the morning they examined deeds for land east of the Farmington River. Richard Hawkes' name was not on any of them. They continued digging through the deeds before them. Occasionally, Joseph turned or poked the logs, keeping the fire alive in the room's small fireplace. He was now a lanky seventeen-year-old with a maturing voice, but he still had a boy's exuberance. Several times Daniel ordered Joseph to sit still for he was distracted by his frequent humming, whistling and moving about. Each time Joseph smiled and promised to be still, only to have to be reminded later by Daniel. It was noon when Daniel lifted his head from the pile of deeds and brushed his dark brown hair off his forehead. He looked across the table at Joseph.

"We've been at this for hours and haven't found a single deed with Hawkes's name on it," Daniel announced. "Let's quit wasting time with the deeds near the town's center and move to deeds farther west."

"Why?" Joseph asked.

"It's simple. What land would you choose if you were going to file fraudulent deeds? Not land where people lived. You would file deeds where there are few people. Those lands are farthest west."

Within half an hour, they were ready to review the western deeds Joseph placed on the table. Immediately, Joseph announced, "I've found Hawkes's name on a deed."

Daniel jumped from his chair and rushed to Joseph's side. He stared at the deed.

"Look at the grantor's name," Daniel exclaimed.

"I don't know the name or the sign the grantor used," Joseph answered.

"The name is Sequassen," Daniel said. "He was the Suckiaug's sachem. This deed shows he sold land to Richard Hawkes four miles west of here."

"Look at the plot description," Joseph said. "It's huge."

"It says the north boundary starts at the Farmington River three and a half miles northwest of its bend near the Tunxis Village and goes southwest two- and three-quarter miles until just outside the swamp where it turns east three miles to the Tunxis Village and then northwest along the Farmington river until it reaches the originating point," Daniel said.

"That means Richard Hawkes has owned nearly all the land west of Farmington since this deed was executed twenty years ago."

"That can't be true," Daniel replied. "There are at least eighty more deeds for this area left on the table we haven't looked at."

Joseph grabbed several other deeds.

"This deed is for a parcel within the land covered by the first deed," Joseph said. "It transfers ten acres of land, south of the Tunxis Village to a man named William Smith of Wethersfield. The grantor is listed as Richard Hawkes."

"What is the deed's date?" Daniel asked.

"1650, two years after Hawkes received his original deed from Sequassen."

"So, Hawkes was dividing the large parcel and reselling parts of it right after he filed the deed for it."

"What do you mean Hawkes filed the deed?" Joseph asked.

"He had to file the deed with Sequassen because by 1648 Sequassen and the Suckiaug were living with the Mettabesic tribe south of us," Daniel explained. "Deeds can be filed by either the grantor or grantee. In the absence of Sequassen, only Hawkes could file it."

"Let's look at the other deeds on the table," Joseph said.

They examined the remaining deeds for the next two hours. Their review confirmed that almost the entire parcel covered in the original deed with Sequassen had been divided into smaller parcels and sold by Hawkes to English settlers. They compared the sales price for the original deed from Sequassen, which was one hundred hatchets and twenty feet of Narragansett wampum, to the total amount in corn, English pounds or wampum, paid to Richard Hawkes by the English settlers.

"Unbelievable," Daniel exclaimed. "He made a profit more than two hundred times what he paid Sequassen for the land."

They sat at the table as the reality of what they found sunk in.

Finally, Joseph looked across the table at Daniel and asked, "Do you really think Sequassen would have sold this much land for so little?"

"Perhaps, it was common for tribes to sell land for less in those days," Daniel said.

"How do we know Sequassen even owned the land?" Joseph asked.

"We must find the Suckiaug's descendants and ask those who remain," Daniel answered. "Sequassen is dead and now the tribe lives with the Pocumtucs north of here."

"I doubt the Suckiaugs ever owned this land," Joseph said. "Remember in Saybrook we found that for the deeds Hawkes filed for the Pequots' lands he claimed, both the signature for his grantors and his signature were similar."

"Even so, unless we find a grantor to challenge one of these deeds it doesn't matter for they're presumed valid unless they're challenged," Daniel cautioned.

They reviewed all the deeds for land conveyed to Richard Hawkes by late afternoon. Most of the names were of people from Wethersfield, Springfield and Windsor who they assumed to be speculators. Only a few plots were deeded to men from Hartford and none were deeded to men from Farmington.

When they were done, they gathered up their notes, which documented each deed and grantee name. They agreed Daniel would keep the notes at his house.

The Town Path was muddy after the sun melted the snow and they skirted along the path in the grass lining it as they walked in twilight to Daniel's house. While Joseph usually stayed at John's house when he helped at the Indian school, he and John's family had stayed at Daniel's house the night before so workmen could replace the roof on John and Mary Lee's house.

Daniel stopped and placed his hands on Joseph's shoulders and announced, "I will tell John what we found. Hawkes's tentacles are wrapped around Connecticut, but those tentacles will be his undoing.

We will spend tonight together, and tomorrow you will go back to Abigail and Christopher in Hartford. Next week we will begin searching for the Suckiaugs and the other grantors on the deeds Richard Hawkes claimed property under."

While Daniel and Joseph were discussing his deeds, Richard Hawkes was ten miles away in his study with James Eastman and Edward Roach. The sun had set and the view from the study's window was black. Richard Hawkes paced at the window as Eastman recounted recent events associated with John Lee's investigations. As he listened, Hawkes became concerned.

"Where is Lee now?" he asked as he spun from the window and stared angrily at Eastman sitting across the table.

"He and his family are staying at Daniel Hart's house in Farmington. The roof of Lee's house leaked, and he decided to replace it. It will take several more days to finish the work."

"What about the deeds Lee is examining?" Hawkes asked.

"Daniel Hart made arrangements to view Farmington's records again today."

"I thought Lee already had someone go through those records," Hawkes said.

"Perhaps he wanted to get the records. Daniel Hart has collected records from other towns, and it is rumored he's temporarily storing Farmington's records at his house.

Hawkes couldn't believe his good fortune. Not only were the records that might destroy him in Daniel Hart's house, but John Lee and his bitch of a wife were staying there as well.

"Listen carefully," Hawkes said. "Meet me on the Town Path above Daniel Hart's house at midnight tomorrow. Wear moccasins and bring axes, hammers, wooden planks, unlit torches and tender boxes. Tomorrow night the sky will glow above Farmington."

The cold spell snapped and by the time Daniel and Joseph returned from Captain Lewis's house, ice melted even in shaded areas behind Daniel's house. The next afternoon was even warmer and John stood behind Daniel's house watching the children play before supper.

"Do you feel like playing with them sometimes?" Deacon Hart asked John as he walked out the back door to John's side.

"Often"

"I do too," Hart said. "Soon they'll be standing as we are and wish the same for themselves."

"I suppose that will be true."

"What do you think the world will be like then?" Hart asked.

"Like it is today, I guess."

"I hope you are right," Hart said. "I fear times will be more difficult."

"Why do you say that?"

"Just look around. Our people are changing and the bond we once had is threatened by new immigrants with different beliefs and by our young who never had to endure what we did. The Wampanoags and Narragansetts are frustrated with the loss of their land and are arming with the help of Dutch traders. New England is a powder keg which will explode with the slightest spark."

Just then, Daniel Hart came from the house. He smiled at his father before looking at John, "I see my father is predicting our doom again. Let's resume this discussion tomorrow and leave this sunny day to happier talk."

Deacon Hart smiled back at his son, "You're right Daniel."

Meanwhile, in the yard the children's game ended when Daniel's thirteen-year-old daughter Lydia called the children to come into the house and help set the table for supper. John liked Lydia. She was always smiling and took to responsibility easily. She was big boned but had a softness about her like her mother. She would be a good wife and mother. Daniel's two sons were also good children. His oldest son Mark was serious and studious, while his younger son, Stephen, was fun loving and mischievous.

Supper would be ready soon and the three men moved into the house while trying to stay out of the women's way as they hustled about the kitchen and brought food into the parlor. The children washed and stood behind their chairs when John, Daniel and Deacon Hart took their seats. The women placed the corn bread, boiled onions and roasted wild turkey on the table and sat at their seats. Deacon Hart said a short prayer, and everyone passed their trenchers to Mary Lee who portioned out their meals. When the adults were served, Deacon Hart motioned the children to take their seats.

"We will miss having your family with us tonight John," Daniel said between bites of turkey. "With Joseph having left for Hartford this morning, our house will seem empty. Especially since our son Stephen is leaving with his uncle later today and will be staying with him for a few days."

"Brother, we only live just on the other side of father's lot," Mary laughed. "I promise we will stay with you and Judith as soon as we get used to our new roof. It's not our fault the workmen finished two days early."

After supper the three men moved into the hall where they sat around the fireplace. After a few minutes staring into the fire John asked, "Did you find any useful information at Captain Lewis's house yesterday?"

"Yes," Daniel said. "Richard Hawkes filed a deed nearly twenty years ago. It purports to transfer Suckiaug land to him. The land is almost all the land from Farmington to four miles to the west."

"One deed?" John asked. "Who signed it for the Suckiaugs?"

"Sequassen's sign was used."

"That's impossible," Deacon Hart said. "Sequassen couldn't have placed his sign on the deed. He and the Suckiaugs that didn't stay with the Tunxis were living south with the Mettabesics before that."

"Does Hawkes still claim this land?" John asked.

"No, there are nearly eighty deeds showing he sold almost all of it a few years after he filed the deed. Joseph and I will continue our investigation next week by finding any surviving Suckiaugs who may know whether the deed is valid."

"Be careful Daniel," John said. "Some think you have actual sales records and deeds at your house."

Daniel laughed, "All I have are a bunch of notes."

"You have no records?" John asked. "I heard you gathered original records during your investigation?"

"No, I only have notes."

"Be careful just the same Daniel."

It was a moonless night. Richard Hawkes stood on Farmington's Town Path above Daniel Hart's house. Overhead the winter sky was ablaze with stars. They appeared so close it seemed as if they were watching him. He laughed to himself and said quietly under his breath, "Enjoy the show."

Hawkes turned to Eastman and Roach and whispered, "James and I will move to the house's front while Edward goes to the rear. Signal us when you are ready Edward.

Roach nodded before moving down the slope towards the house's rear carrying an unlit torch, axe, hammer, nails, wooden planks, lamp oil and a tender box. Hawkes watched him until Roach disappeared behind Daniel's house.

Hawkes turned to Eastman and exclaimed, "Let's light the sky."

Eastman smiled vacantly.

Hawkes looked down at the house. Its windows were dark. In the distance he could hear a wolf howl. Two hundred yards to his right, he saw Deacon Hart's house. Its windows were also dark. Another two hundred yards beyond, was John's house. He knew it would be dark as well because Eastman said both John and Mary Lee were sleeping at Daniel's house tonight.

"There's Edward," Eastman whispered. "Look to the house's right."

Below, through the darkness, Edward Roach waived his arm.

"That's the signal, get to the door," Hawkes whispered.

Hawkes raced down the slope with Eastman limping behind him. When Hawkes reached the door, he propped the wooden plank between the door's right and left frame, jamming the door so it couldn't be opened from inside. He did the same to the first-floor window panes.

By the time Eastman reached the house, Hawkes had secured all escape points on the first floor of the front of the house. He looked at Eastman and whispered, "Spread the lamp oil on the door and windows and light both torches with a spark from the tender box."

Eastman tripped and fell into the door as he spread the oil over it, making a dull thud. In the distance the high-pitched bark of a small dog answered the sound. Hawkes glared at Eastman. When the dog stopped barking, Eastman crawled to his feet by bracing himself against the door. Once upright, Eastman began to spread the oil over the door and the shutters on the first-floor windows.

"Light the torches," Hawkes ordered.

As Hawkes watched, Eastman set the tender box on the ground and began striking the flint over the oiled torches. While sparks flew, they were directed away from the torch and had no effect. Hawkes grabbed the flint from Eastman and within seconds lit the first torch. He touched it to the second torch which instantly was aflame. He gave the second torch to Eastman, ordering him to light the windows, while taking the first torch to the door. As soon as he touched the torch to the bottom of the door a streak of fire erupted up the door's frame. Soon the entire door was aflame.

Roach joined them with a lighted torch in his hand.

"Light the house," Hawkes ordered.

Roach touched the torch to the house where oil had spread. In an instant the house itself began to burn.

"Is the back of the house burning?" Hawkes asked.

"Yes, more than here," Roach answered.

"Throw your torch against the door," Hawkes said. "Go south away from town. James and I will ride north on the Town Path."

Roach was gone in an instant. Hawkes turned back to Eastman and yelled, "Follow me to our horses."

Hawkes felt the fire's heat on his back as he climbed the slope. He heard screams of children over the fire's roar. He looked back. Eastman was slowly limping up the slope towards him. *Damn him, he'll not make it to the Town Path before Hart and the other neighbors reach the house*, Hawkes cursed to himself. He ran to their horses and after mounting his stallion pulled Eastman's horse down the slope to him. When he reached Eastman, he pushed him up onto his horse and dragged him and his horse behind him up the slope. As they rode north on the Town Path, he seethed with anger as he thought of how useless Eastman was that night.

Daniel felt the heat as he gagged on the smoke. Judith was sleeping next to him. He shook her but her eyes stayed shut. The smoke in the upstairs parlor where they slept was thick and growing thicker each second. It blew through the door to the porch's stairs and filled the room from floor to ceiling. Flames poured out of the room's two windows.

"Quick Judith, we must save the children," Daniel yelled.

Judith was still. He yelled at her again, "Wake up Judith, wake up."

He grabbed her shoulders and shook her until she coughed. He dragged her from the bed and laid her on the floor where the smoke was not as great. He decided to wake the children first and come back to get Judith after the children were safe.

Both his daughter Lydia and son Mark were sleeping in the up-stairs hall chamber. He crawled along the floor feeling his way with his hands until he felt the frame to the hall chamber. The smoke was now so thick he couldn't see anything higher than three feet off the floor, but he could see light through the smoke. As he crawled closer, he realized the light was from fires burning at the hall's windows.

"Lydia, Mark, we need to leave the house!" he yelled through the smoke.

"Father, we're on the floor near the bed. Hurry, help us!" Lydia screamed.

"I'm coming."

Daniel reached Lydia and Mark just as a flaming window shutter fell into the room. It landed with a thud and spread its fire across the floor. There was little time to escape the house. He fought back his fear. *God help me save them*, he prayed.

"Grab my ankle and crawl behind me. Mark grab Lydia's ankle and follow her."

As soon as he felt Lydia grip his ankle, Daniel slithered towards the hall chamber's door towards the stairs to the first floor. Smoke poured up the stairs like a chimney. He had to choose. *Should I take the children down the stairs first or get Judith*, he asked himself. *She'll die if I don't get her now.*

"Lydia, you and Mark crawl down the stairs," Daniel yelled above the sound of the fire. "Leave the house any way you can."

He squeezed his children's hands tightly before crawling back to the parlor. He moved only a few feet when a wall of flames appeared before him. Through the flames he saw Judith lying where he left her. He crawled through the flames towards her. It was too hot and smoky for him to move more than a few feet. He stopped and tried to get a breath of air but now there was no air to breathe. As he began to cough, he heard a heavy grinding sound above him. He looked up in time to see a flaming section of the house's roof falling towards him. As he lay in the fiery rubble resting on top of him, the last sound Daniel heard was his children's screams.

They didn't put out the fire's remnants until two days later. It burned the house to its foundation, leaving no evidence of what started it. The only evidence were the tracks of Indian moccasins, convincing the townspeople Indians were responsible. When the Tunxis denied responsibility and no evidence of their involvement was found, the matter remained a tragedy without an answer.

The first thing the people did the morning after the fire was quenched was remove the charred remains of Daniel, his wife Judith and their children. They wrapped their remains in linen, placed them in a simple casket and buried them in the town's little cemetery along the Town Path. Deacon Hart's grief was overwhelming when he watched the dirt shoveled on top of each grave. He held his grief inside though for what happened was God's will and he trusted in that will. Mary and John offered to take care of Daniel's son Stephen, but Deacon Hart refused. He would raise his grandson himself.

At first, Hawkes was elated when news reached Hartford of the tragedy. But when he heard John Lee was not in the house when it burned to the ground, he raged at James Eastman. He had enough with James's obesity and bad leg. James's failure to ensure Lee was in the house when they started the fire was the tipping point. As soon as his master miller Thomas Aleworth accepted his offer to take James's position, Hawkes dismissed him. A few days later Eastman disappeared.

Joseph Henry was disappointed when John Lee told him he was stopping the investigation of Richard Hawkes's land transactions since all their notes from the investigation were destroyed in the fire. Joseph pleaded with John, but John insisted he doubted their effort would produce enough evidence to convict Hawkes of fraud since only a single deed from Sequassen, now dead, tied Hawkes to the land involved. It would be nearly impossible to locate each person who bought Sequassen's land from Hawkes. Even if they found some of them, it would be impossible to prove Hawkes committed a fraud. Joseph saw the weariness in John's face when he told him this. He knew someday John would be ready to reopen the investigation and he promised he would help him when he was.

The morning after John told Joseph he was halting the investigation, he woke from an early morning dream bathed in sweat. In the dream he was staring from his upstairs window at the river below his house. A full moon glistened in the water. As he stared at the moonlight in the water, he felt eyes staring at him. He dropped his gaze from the river to the field of grass below him. In the moonlight stood a single black wolf staring at him. John's heart beat furiously when he woke. He breathed deeply for a few moments as he realized he hadn't dreamed of the wolf since he started his investigation of Richard Hawkes. He was certain the dream would come more often now that the investigation had stopped.

PART SEVEN
1675 - 1676

Chapter 54

After seventeen years of service, John Lee's Indian school's roof needed replacing. During the years he ran the school, John taught hundreds of Indians from over a dozen tribes. They learned the English language and ways, as well as reading, math, and scripture. John was so committed to this calling that when his latest term as constable ended, he didn't seek another; allowing Deacon Hart to become constable.

He picked early April to do the work and spread word to his students, his former students, and the people who supported the school. It would be cold but there might be a few warmer days when he could conduct lessons outside and avoid disrupting Mary and their five children. As the date for the project approached, he began to consider who would be able to help. He started by considering those who helped build the school. He sighed as he remembered that Chogan and Daniel Hart, who led the effort, couldn't help repair the roof. Chogan had moved north with his tribe and Daniel had died ten years before when his house burned to the ground. John decided his young protégés, Nesehegan and Joseph Henry, would oversee the roof's replacement. Both were fully grown and Nesehegan was an excellent carpenter. Wematin and Sucki, two of his former students, would also help. Both his son Martin, now sixteen, and his daughter Susan, now eleven, who helped teach at the school, volunteered to help. John would have Martin work with the men and Susan help her mother prepare food for each day's supper.

John and his son, Martin, reached the school before dawn on the day the roof was to be replaced. Together they set out the replacement boards and shingles. As they worked, John recalled the star filled nights decades earlier when he worked with William Westwood and

Sam Pierce in William's fields.

William died in Hadley ten years earlier. John went to the funeral with many others from Hartford and Farmington. Bridget welcomed him with a warm smile. The years took their toll and at sixty-seven, Bridget looked her age. During the funeral he helped her to her seat and stayed for two days after the funeral to make a few repairs to her house. He'd been back to see her several times since and he promised himself he would visit her again soon.

They worked in silence for nearly an hour before Martin asked, "Why did you pick both Nesehegan and Joseph to lead the work and not just Joseph?"

"Because Nesehegan is the best carpenter in Farmington," John answered.

"But Joseph is older. Wouldn't it be better if he led us alone?"

"Joseph and Nesehegan are friends. They'll work well together."

"Isn't it better for a leader to be firm?" Martin asked.

"Sometimes."

"Well, Nesehegan is too nice to be a leader. I've never seen him angry. Have you?"

John thought for a moment. His son was right. In all the years he knew Nesehegan, Nesehegan was never angry, "No, I haven't. But anger isn't the mark of leadership. Don't you like Nesehegan?"

"I like him, but he asks questions I can't answer."

"What questions?" John asked.

"Well, for one, after I taught our new students about the Covenant of Grace, he told me it was inconsistent with Christ's message."

"Did he say why?" John asked.

"He said Christ gave us God's new covenant which replaced His covenant Adam violated. He claimed Christ's new covenant requires only that we believe in Him to gain everlasting life."

"Our Puritan religion doesn't teach this," John asserted. "I will talk to him."

The other men arrived at sunrise. It was agreed Joseph would lead while they removed the old roof and Nesehegan would lead when they built the new roof. John backed away as Joseph climbed onto the old roof and marked its weakest sections. These would be removed first. They would next strip away the remaining sections' shingles and clapboard and assess the strength of the beams.

When he marked the roof's weakest sections, Joseph asked Wematin, Sucki and Martin to climb onto the roof to remove the shingles. Meanwhile, John and Nesehegan sorted out the strongest beams, clapboard and shingles for the new roof.

Mary arrived with their four other children at noon. She spread a blanket under an oak tree for their two youngest children: Thomas, age four, and David, age two. Meanwhile, six-year-old Stephen watched his father and Nesehegan sort the beams, clapboard, and shingles.

John turned to Nesehegan after Stephen began playing with the other children, "My son Martin told me you challenged our church's belief in the Covenant of Grace," he said. "Why did you do that?"

Nesehegan lay down the board he was holding and asked, "Can we sit to discuss this?"

John nodded and the two men sat in the grass.

"I know the Puritan faith believes God selects those who will enter His eternal kingdom before they're born and a person can do nothing during their lives to change the result," Nesehegan said. "This is why Puritans seek evidence of what God chose for them during their lives."

"Yes, I taught you this many years ago."

"You did teach me this," Nesehegan said. "Why didn't you believe in this covenant when you heard of it?"

"How do you know I didn't believe in it?" John asked.

"I just know. I also know you don't believe in it now."

"How can you say that?"

"Because I know your heart and because we've talked together about Christ's teachings, Nesehegan answered. "Was not Christ's message one of love?"

"Yes, but how is this different from our belief that God elects who will receive His grace?"

"Look at your son Steven," Nesehegan stated. "Do you love him?"

"Yes, of course," John said.

"Would you ever tell him he couldn't change his fortune in life?"

"No, I wouldn't."

"So why would a loving God choose to do this to His creation?" Nesehegan asked. "Why would He punish his creation with such uncertainty and hopelessness?

John was dumbfounded. Nesehegan had crystallized his own feelings about the Covenant of Grace in a few sentences. He looked across the grass at Nesehegan and smiled.

"Perhaps you are right Nesehegan," John said. "Perhaps I don't believe in the Covenant of Grace. But Reverend Hooker told me it is what we Puritans believe and I am a Puritan. It gives us order and for those who believe they've been given God's grace, it gives them the promise of eternal life."

"What does it give those who can't find evidence God gave them His grace?"

John didn't answer.

After a minute of silence, Nesehegan continued, "Don't be confused. Christ's message is clear. John's Gospel teaches Christ came into the world with a new covenant from God. This covenant gives eternal live to those who believe in and follow Christ."

Finally, John smiled, "You cite scripture well, but what you teach is heresy."

"Well, at least you have my explanation."

They removed nearly all the boards and shingles by early afternoon when Mary announced it was time for supper. The sky was clear and the air warm when they sat to eat. John announced it was his son

Thomas's fourth birthday. Thomas's face lit up when he heard the announcement and the freckles on his cheeks bounced as he smiled.

John watched Mary hug Thomas every time she passed by him while serving the men seated at the table. Now forty-six, her once slender waist had expanded a little with each childbirth. All the same, John still liked to grab her by the waist and lift her. He found it harder now, but he knew this was not due to her moderate weight gain but to his aging. But he was still strong and trained with Farmington's militia as often as he could.

By the time John finished supper all the men were working except Nesehegan and Joseph. They sat at a table deep in conversation. When he heard Joseph utter "Richard Hawkes" he was torn between staying where he was or moving to where they were seated.

Over the years, John tried forcing Richard Hawkes from his mind. For the most part he succeeded. Deacon Hart was now the town's constable, allowing John to focus on his family, farm and school. He felt guilty at first, but when Hart agreed there was not enough evidence to pursue charges of filing fraudulent deeds against Hawkes, John's guilt subsided.

Still, he continued dreaming of the black wolf. Over the years, he came to accept that he would be visited by the dream two or three times a week. On many occasions, while he lay in bed drenched in sweat at dawn, Mary asked what was wrong. He gave the same answer each time, "There's nothing wrong." But there was something wrong and he knew it. When Joseph said "Richard Hawkes" a second time, John sat with them.

"What are you talking about," John asked.

"Nesehegan is telling stories circulating among the Pocumtucs and the other northern tribes," Joseph said.

John turned to Nesehegan, "What stories?"

"People in these tribes tell stories of how the English stole their land. Some say they have signed agreements not knowing they were giving up rights to land far greater than what they were told. Others say Englishmen filed false deeds purporting to transfer their land to the English."

"Yes, I know," John said. "The Wampanoags are angered by the amount of land they've had to trade for English goods now they have fewer beaver pelts to trade."

"What Nesehegan speaks of is different," Joseph said.

"How so?" John asked.

"It's different because the lands Nesehegan speaks of are being stolen by the English and one Englishman rumored to be involved they call the dark man. I told Nesehegan it reminded me of our investigation of Richard Hawkes years ago."

John leaned across the table and asked, "Joseph, did I tell you the Indian rumor that a Pocumtuc warrior named Megedaqik was tortured and killed by an Englishman they called the dark man?"

"No," Joseph answered. "The first I heard of this dark man was today from Nesehegan."

"I'll talk to Constable Hart about reopening our investigation of Richard Hawkes," John said. "The dark man who stole Indian land may be the same dark man who sold the Indians muskets and killed the Pocumtuc warrior Megedaqik. If so, we may find Richard Hawkes is the dark man the Indian's speak of. Come with me Nesehegan."

Nesehegan smiled, "I have more to tell you first."

"What?"

"Metacom, sachem of the Wampanoags, who the English call King Phillip, is preparing for war against the Plymouth Pilgrims. He's asking other tribes to join him. The dark man has been selling muskets to the tribes, including the newest flintlocks, not the old matchlocks or snaphaunces many English militia still use."

"The dark man himself has come to these tribes?" John asked.

"Yes."

"In that case, it may be easier to identify who the dark man is than

I thought?" John said.

"Find out when the Wampanoags expect the dark man to visit them next."

"Should I be there when he comes?" Nesehegan asked.

"Yes."

Richard Hawkes sat on a heavy oak chair behind his house. It was sunny at the end of what had been a dark week of clouds and he wanted to breathe the pure air from the river below him. He was comforted by his aloneness but knew it would soon be interrupted by another meeting. This meeting would be with Thomas Aleworth, now his principle assistant. But it would be an hour before Aleworth and Edward Roach arrived.

The sun's rays struck Hawkes's face. He moved his chair to a large maple tree's shade to escape them. He thought about his next meeting with the eastern Indians. He would go within three weeks. Not because it was demanded by anybody he personally go, but because he missed the excitement he felt the first time he went to the Indians with muskets after decades of letting others go in his place. He thought it ironic that by keeping his identity secret by not going, he lost that identity. Now, at fifty-nine years, he felt reborn. Once again, he stood before excited crowds; once again he knew the thrill of the uncertainty that comes from doing something with both great reward and great risk; and, once again he felt alive.

He spent several more minutes sitting alone before he was interrupted by his son Paul. Paul, now twenty, was nearly as tall as Hawkes.

"Do you still want me to come to the meeting?" Paul asked.

"Yes, both you and Peter," he answered. "It's part of your training. I've taught you how to fight. Now it's time to learn how to run a business. Bring Peter to the study."

Hawkes was in his study in a few minutes. Both Paul and Peter were standing by the window when he entered. He looked at Peter first. At twenty-one he still looked more like his mother than him. He was handsome but lacked the strength of his brother.

"Today your preparation will begin by meeting my master miller, Thomas Aleworth, and my assistant, Edward Roach," Hawkes announced. "These men have served me well over the years. Even so, I watch them carefully for you can trust no man, especially a man who works for you, for every man puts his interests first. You must learn what drives the men working for you and take advantage of that knowledge by convincing them their desires can best be served by working for you."

"What are these men's desires?" Paul asked.

"Thomas wants to run gristmills and make a fair pay. If he can get wealthy, all the better, but wealth does not drive him. Edward needs a mission and someone to give it to him. Working for me, they each get what they want."

Within half an hour a servant came to the study's door and announced Hawkes's guests had arrived.

"Bring them here," Hawkes ordered.

Thomas Aleworth smiled broadly as he entered the room. Roach followed him. At sixty-years, Roach's face appeared inhuman. His pock marks were larger than ever and were joined by a bulbous nose and deep creases from his long days in the sun.

"Sit at the table," Hawkes directed.

The two men sat opposite from Hawkes and his sons.

"Let's discuss my mills first," Hawkes announced. "How will business be this year Thomas?"

"There was a good spring planting all along the Connecticut and we should do much better than last year," Aleworth answered.

"What about our Dutch friends?" Hawkes asked. "How is our trade in the west and along the Hudson near Albany?"

"Trading is good in the west," Aleworth said. "The Pocumtucs,

Paugussets and Mettabesics want the new flintlocks. Things are not good on the Hudson. Diederik Paulis trades fewer muskets now that Boston merchants have reopened their trade with the Mohawks."

"It was a good business while it lasted," Hawkes said. "Tell Paulis to trade what he can. What about our trade with the Wampanoags and the other eastern tribes?"

"You know more about this than me since you were there three weeks ago."

"Yes, I was, wasn't I," Hawkes laughed. "I traded every musket I took. I am going again in three weeks with more muskets. Edward, Diederik and Karel will go with me. If the English hear of our trade, they'll think we were Dutch."

"Isn't this risk unnecessary?" Aleworth asked. "You may be recognized."

"I will let the Dutchmen do the talking and stay in the background."

"You shouldn't go at all," Aleworth protested.

"Don't you know what's happening?" Hawkes spat while rising from the table. "There's going to be a war. Not just a simple war, but a war engulfing all New England. This may be our last musket trade until the war ends. I won't miss this moment."

"There's still risk," Aleworth insisted.

"Enough!" Hawkes yelled. "I'm going."

John Lee and Nesehegan arrived at Thomas Bull's house at noon. As he stood at the front door, John looked to his right through the trees at the small house one hundred yards to the west. It was in good repair; much better than when Sam Pierce owned it. A tinge of sadness filled him before Bull's door opened.

"Good to see you John," Bull said.

Bull's six-foot two-inch frame rose above John. His forearms were accented with sinewy muscles, while his face was more weathered and lined. His eyes were as penetrating as ever.

"Who's with you?" Bull asked, looking at Nesehegan.

"This is Nesehegan. You met him years ago when he was one of my students."

"Good day Nesehegan," Bull said. "What brings you here John?"

"Nesehegan has discovered the Wampanoags latest moves," John announced. "Tell Captain Bull what you learned?"

"King Phillip sent emissaries to all New England tribes asking them to join in a war against the English. He claims, if they're unified, they can drive the English from their land. An Englishman, the tribes call the dark man, delivered flintlocks to the Wampanoag three weeks ago. He promised to return with more at the end of this month.

I believe this dark man is Richard Hawkes," John said.

"What's your evidence?" Bull asked.

"Nesehegan is going to Metacom's camp at Mount Hope to watch the trade," John said. "That will be the evidence."

"But trading muskets to the Indians is a crime rarely enforced these days and even when it is, the punishment is light," Bull said.

"I believe Richard Hawkes committed many more crimes. Knowing he's the dark man will help prove this."

Bull turned to Nesehegan, "The militia needs Indian scouts. Will you scout for us?"

"Many Englishmen died protecting my people from the Pequots," Nesehegan said. "Our people fought together and have been allies since. If there's a war and our people decide to fight with you, I will be a scout."

They left Bull's house early the next morning. John had one more stop. It was Deacon Hart's house. Hart had been Farmington's constable for nearly eight years. If Richard Hawkes were to be investigated, he would need to authorize it. It was midmorning when they reached Hart's house. Hart knew Hawkes couldn't be trusted because years ago he and John caught Hawkes stealing cornmeal from Hart's mills. John was confident Hart would find the information they were giving him interesting but wasn't sure if Hart would agree to open an investigation upon it.

Hart smiled when he saw John and invited he and Nesehegan into his house. They sat together at the hall fireplace. Hart was much older and heavier now, but still had strong hands and a tight mind.

"Why are you here so early?" Hart asked.

"To tell you what Nesehegan knows about Richard Hawkes," John answered.

"Go ahead," Hart said.

"An Englishman the Indians call the dark man, has been selling muskets to New England tribes, including the Wampanoags. In three weeks, this Englishman will be meeting the Wampanoags again, this time at Mount Hope, their village protruding into Rhode Island's Narragansett Bay."

"Selling muskets again?" Hart asked.

"Yes," John said. "But there's more. Do you remember when we were investigating Hawkes for filing fraudulent deeds ten years ago?"

"I do."

"Nesehegan has also heard rumors that an Englishman the Indians call the dark man filed false deeds in Farmington and Hartford for large tracks of Indian lands. We know Richard Hawkes filed a deed, purportedly signed by Sequassen, for a large tract of land west of Farmington. I believe that we have the chance to show that Richard Hawkes is this dark man."

"Where does that get us?" Hart asked. "Didn't we agree years ago it would be nearly impossible to prove Hawkes's deed was false? Who would testify to the fraud? Besides, Hawkes sold the land."

"I think if we investigate, we will find Richard Hawkes killed a Pocumtuc named Megedaqik. There's a rumor among the Pocumtucs this dark man used Megedaqik to trade his muskets and later killed him."

"How does this help us?"

"Once we find Hawkes is the dark man, we will be able to convict him of selling muskets to the Indians and of Megedaqik's murder. We can also link him to the fraudulent transfer of Indian lands by finding Indians who claim their land was stolen by this dark man."

"I don't know John. I want to see Richard Hawkes punished as much as you, but after so many years who will be a witness to these crimes?"

" If we can find him, there's one person who could be."

"Who is it?"

"Richard Hawkes's former assistant, James Eastman."

"That slobbering fat man," Hart said. "He disappeared years ago. He's probably dead."

"Perhaps. But he worked for Hawkes for decades. If any man knows of Hawkes's crimes, it would be him."

"How will you find him?"

"He must be in hiding, for Hawkes would kill him if he thought he was going to tell the stories he knew," John answered. "He's likely living near a Pocumtuc or Paugussett village. If so, Nesehegan will find him."

"Alright, let's investigate this dark man and if he's Richard Hawkes see that he's punished for his crimes."

The sun was going down as James Eastman limped into his small bark covered wigwam. The woman would be back from the village with food before it was dark. She promised to stay with him that night and take care of the wound on his leg from the fall he took on rocks at the creek not far from his wigwam. A few wolves howled in the distance, but the woman was resourceful, and he didn't fear for her safety. It would be cold tonight, so he put a log on the wigwam's fire.

The small Pocumtuc party he stayed with for the past two years was camped upstream along the creek less than a mile from him.

They camped there after the winter storms and would stay there until the fall after they harvested the corn, squash and beans the tribe's women planted in the fertile soil above the creek. They permitted him to stay with them because he let them use the metal pots and pans he carried with him.

Eastman's leg throbbed with pain as he lay on a grass mat the woman gave him. The pain was so great he forgot the pain in his other leg which he'd lived with for the past twenty years. He often wished Edward Roach would find him and end his misery. But he didn't want to go to hell and the crimes he committed with Richard Hawkes surely established that God hadn't chosen him for His grace. The fresh log brightened the fire and his stomach turned as he imagined the pain he would feel if he were the log as the fire's flames licked across it.

Chapter 55

The three Tunxis men came from the west on a cool May morning in 1675. They had hiked continuously for two and a half days. They ate as they walked, stopping long enough to wet the nokehick, made from pounded dry Indian corn, they carried in hollow leather belts around their waists. Once the nokehick was softened, they began hiking again, eating it as they moved east along an intertwined maze of Indian trails.

They wound around the English town of Swansea and the farms dotting the countryside before turning south ten miles north of their destination and moving inland on a peninsula protruding into the bay. They walked among large trees as they crossed the peninsula to its east coast where they followed the shoreline south towards Mount Hope.

They would need an excuse for visiting the Wampanoag's village. Their excuse would be trade. Each of them carried a basket filled with Tunxis jewelry, pottery, axes, knives and hatchets. While the demand for Indian ware had nearly disappeared and Indians now only wanted English tools and weapons, the men didn't care if they made a single trade. The Wampanoags would be suspicious of them, for all the tribes of southern New England knew the Tunxis had allied with the English against the Pequots and would likely ally with them again. They would tell the Wampanoags they were Suckiaugs. The Suckiaugs had lost most of their land to the Mohegans and had been forced to live first with the Mettabesics and now with the Pocumtucs. Nesehegan doubted anyone would suspect that a member of such a dispersed and dispirited tribe would fight for the English.

They reached Mount Hope at mid-afternoon. It lay on a promontory rising more than two hundred feet above the water. Below them were the deep blue waters of Mount Hope Bay. It stretched three and a half miles to the north, where it met the mainland and the Taunton River, and three miles to the south, where it washed against Aquidneck Island, the largest island in Narragansett Bay.

The Wampanoag village was in a frenzy, driven by the rhythmic sound of beating drums. They pushed their way through the Wampanoag warriors milling about. The Wampanoag's faces were painted with red and black war paint and their bodies covered in bear fat which was also in their hair to make it glisten. Many warriors had covered their long black hair with soot mixed with the bear fat to make it even blacker.

"Who are you?" a teenage Wampanoag yelled at Nesehegan.

"We're Suckiaugs here to trade," Nesehegan answered.

"Trade what?" another Wampanoag sneered.

"Many things."

"Muskets?" the first Wampanoag asked, more politely this time.

"No."

The Wampanoag looked at his friend and laughed.

"Don't expect to trade here," the Wampanoag exclaimed. "Tonight, we continue the war dance. We need muskets, not pots and pans, for soon we will be killing English."

The place set aside for traders was in a large clearing near a giant pile of rocks shaped like a chair. Indians from various tribes had laid out their wares near the rocks. There were English knives, hatchets and axes; Dutch metal pots and pans; and gunpowder and shot. Wematin found a place for them to display their wares between two Narragansetts who were trading English knives and hatchets. They displayed the Tunxis hatchets, blankets, axes and beaded necklaces they brought and sat on the ground next to them smiling at the people who walked by. They were ignored.

The village was fully alive by dark. Many warriors who slept during the day joined the fury of dancing that would last until dawn. They danced around fires: some beating their chests; others waiving tomahawks; all shouting war cries against their English enemy and its traitorous Indian allies. The three Tunxis watched warily while lying on blankets they placed on the ground near their wares.

"Will they suspect us if we don't dance?" Wematin asked.

"We should join them," Sucki said.

Nesehegan laughed, "Sucki, even with your hair cut short and brushed up down the middle of your head, you could never convince the Wampanoags of the truth of your dance. It's better we lay on our blankets like the other traders and stare at the stars until we fall asleep."

The village was quiet when Nesehegan woke. The silence was ominous for today the dark man was coming. Throughout the morning here and there the Wampanoags began to rise. First, it was the women and children. They brought the fires back to life and soon the smell of boiling corn filled the air. Later in the morning, while Nesehegan, Wematin and Sucki sat together next to their trade wares, the men began to emerge from their wigwams and lodges. By noon all but the most stalwart war dancers were up.

Richard Hawkes moved through the trees towards Mount Hope that morning. The night before he heard the distant drums as he and his men lay on their blankets. His blood grew hotter with each beat.

He and his men approached Mount Hope from the north on the trail the Tunxis followed the day before. He placed Diederik Paulis and Karel Beringer at the head of their party on horseback. They led them into the village on their horses at midday. Aranck, his old Nipmuc ally, and Aranck's son, Sowheag, walked alongside the Dutchmen's horses. Aranck was now an old man nearing sixty but still fit enough to fight. His son Sowheag was not yet thirty, confident and broad shouldered. Edward Roach held the reins of the large wagon trailing them. Six large wooden chests rested on the wagon's bed. Each chest was more than seven feet long. Hawkes rode on his black stallion behind the wagon.

The wagon creaked through the wigwams, lodges and past the warriors still sleeping on the ground. Some Wampanoags recognized Hawkes from his last visit several weeks before. One young warrior began whooping when he recognized Hawkes. Others joined him and soon the sound of "whoop, whoop, whoop" filled the air, waking still more warriors. Over a hundred Wampanoag men, women and children walked with the wagon as it made its way through the village.

Excitement coursed through Hawkes's veins as he followed the wagon past the last of the wigwams into the open field before the chair of stones where the traders were. Hawkes smiled down at the men, women and children who walked beside him.

Nesehegan heard the whooping ten minutes before he saw the wagon. He knew at once the dark man was on his way to where he, Wematin and Sucki laid out their wares. He rose to his feet and motioned for Wematin and Sucki to do the same. They moved towards the rolling wave of Wampanoags surrounding the wagon.

Nesehegan's heart dropped when he saw the two Dutchmen above the crowd on their horses, for neither was the dark man. But he soon realized the Wampanoags weren't cheering for the Dutchmen heading the procession. They weren't even cheering for the wagon trailing them. They were cheering for the man who followed the wagon.

He couldn't see the man through the crowds surrounding him because the man was bent over accepting the tribe's accolades. The man rose up in his horse and glanced away from where Nesehegan was standing. He lifted his right hand up in front of him with its palm opened to the sky. When he did the Wampanoags let loose a deafening roar. The man turned on his horse while still holding his hand up, almost as if he were blessing the crowd beneath him. Suddenly, the man looked in Nesehegan's direction. When he did, Nesehegan recognized Richard Hawkes's face.

Hawkes continued gazing at the crowd after the wagon stopped in the field. All around him were the excited faces of Wampanoag men, women and children. He knew their excitement was aroused not by him, but by what lay in the wooden boxes he brought to them; but it didn't matter. What mattered to Hawkes was only that they were cheering and that he was the cause of the cheering. He drew out the cheering as long as he could by slowly turning his head as he sat on his horse, taking in the entire vista before him. Everyone he saw was smiling, laughing and cheering.

Then Hawkes saw an unsmiling face at the back of the crowd. The face was that of a young Indian and the face looked familiar. He struggled to remember where he saw this Indian before, but before he could remember, a Wampanoag warrior grabbed his arm and yelled "muskets, muskets" while pointing at the wooden boxes piled on the wagon. Hawkes took his eyes off the unsmiling Indian and looked down at the Wampanoags. By the time he looked up again, the unsmiling Indian was gone.

Hawkes dismounted and walked to the wooden boxes laying in the wagon's bed. He yelled to Roach over the cheering crowd, "Hand me the hatchet." Roach held up the hatchet to the crowd's roar. He handed it to Hawkes who raised it above his head driving the Wampanoags into a frenzy. He climbed onto the wagon bed and with a swift thrust drove the hatchet into the top of a wooden box. He pried away the wooden top and reached into the box and lifted a musket high above his head.

"I bring you muskets," he yelled above the Wampanoags cheers. "I bring you muskets."

As soon as Nesehegan knew Hawkes saw him he turned his back and ducked behind the crowd of Wampanoags in front of him. Nesehegan didn't know whether Hawkes recognized him but was unwilling to risk that he hadn't for he had what he came for.

"We leave now," he said to Wematin and Sucki.

The three Tunxis men quickly made their way from the field and back through the Wampanoag village. The Wampanoags' cheers echoed in their ears. Nesehegan knew they needed to move fast for as soon as the celebration was over Hawkes might remember him. Walking towards them on their way to the field were scores of Wampanoags who had just awakened. As a group of them passed him, Nesehegan heard one of them yell excitedly in Algonquin, "The dark man is here, the dark man is here."

They reached Farmington two days later. Nesehegan found John Lee at Deacon Hart's house with Joseph Henry. He reported that Hawkes sold muskets to the Wampanoags.

"I knew he was a thief," Hart said. "Now we know he's also a traitor. I will report this to the Governor. Hawkes must be brought to trial immediately."

"I want to see Hawkes punished for his crimes as much as you do Stephen," John said. "When he's tried though it must be for crimes meriting hanging. You pointed out that selling muskets to the Indians is only a minor crime. Now that we know he's the dark man let's use that knowledge to prove he has committed greater crimes."

"How do we do this?" Hart asked.

"Nesehegan will take Wematin and Sucki with him to the Pocumtuc villages to find witnesses to the murder of Megedaqik and to the dark man's theft of their lands."

"He won't be hanged even if we prove he committed those crimes," Hart said.

"You're right. That's why we must find James Eastman. If he's alive, he's likely staying with an Indian tribe. Nesehegan, can you find him?"

"Yes. There can't be more than one fat sixty-year-old Englishman living among the tribes of Connecticut and Massachusetts. I will spread the word I am looking for such a man. With luck we will soon learn which tribe he's with."

A heavy fog rose from the river obscuring the view through the window in Richard Hawkes's study. It was two days since he returned from Mount Hope and Hawkes was meeting with Aranck and his son Sowheag.

Before he left Mount Hope, he searched his memory again for the name of the unsmiling Indian watching him among the Wampanoags. It wasn't until they started north after trading every flintlock musket they brought that he remembered. He ordered Edward Roach to stop the wagon just before the fork Aranck and Sowheag would need to take to reach their tribe's village. Hawkes called to Aranck and Sowheag to come to him. They looked up at him as he sat on his stallion.

"A Tunxis named Nesehegan who works with John Lee saw me at Mount Hope," Hawkes said. "I've seen him with John Lee several times when they were in Hartford together. Go to Farmington and find out if any Tunxis warriors were at Mount Hope when we were there. Come to my house two nights after we arrive in Hartford with the information you find."

Aranck and Sowheag asked no questions. They immediately disappeared ahead of Hawkes along the path taking them across Connecticut to Hartford. He estimated they would arrive in Hartford at least a day ahead of him, giving them three days to get him the answer he sought.

Three days later Hawkes was about to get his answer.

"Let them in the house," Hawkes said to his servant.

He sat at his study's table facing the door. Within a few minutes the servant was back with Aranck and Sowheag.

He looked carefully at the two Nipmuc warriors. Aranck had worked for him for decades and he could see that each year was edged in his craggy face. Aranck's son, Sowheag, was young and strong and reminded him of what he and Aranck must have looked like years before.

"What did you find," he asked.

"Three Tunxis were at Mount Hope," Aranck said. "They're all young and former students of John Lee."

"Their names?" Hawkes asked.

"As you suspected, their leader is Nesehegan." Aranck answered. "He has a large following."

"Who were the others?"

"Wematin and Sucki. They follow Nesehegan."

Hawkes thought briefly. As he thought, the germ of a plan began to emerge.

Aranck interrupted his thoughts, "Is there anything else you want us to do?"

"Not now."

He sat alone for several minutes after the Nipmucs left. *They circle me like sharks*, he thought. *They all want a piece of me. It seems John Lee wants the whole. Nesehegan has likely already told him I took muskets to the Wampanoags. There will be one less witness if I have Nesehegan killed. Too risky . . . Jonathan Hart . . . of course, the people of Farmington still think his house was burned by Indians. No one has ever pointed a finger in my direction; not even Lee.*

He yelled loud enough so everyone in the house could hear him, "Paul, come to the study."

Chapter 56

It was a beautiful July morning and a light breeze brought the scent of goldenrod up the slope from the Farmington River. John Lee was teaching his students in the shade of an oak tree near his schoolhouse. Joseph Henry set up four benches earlier that morning and the six Tunxis children sat facing John as he read from the Bible.

John's students enjoyed the Bible's most fantastic stories and this morning John entranced them with the story of Noah and the great flood. He read of God's anger with man and how man's wickedness lead God to destroy man; of how God told Noah to build an ark; of how it rained for forty days and forty nights, killing all living things but the plants and animals God commanded Noah to bring onto his ark; and, of how after the flood abated God told Noah to leave the ark with his family and the animals and plants he brought with him and to be fruitful and multiply.

John was bombarded with questions when he finished.

"What is sin?" a wide-eyed Tunxis boy asked.

"Why did God not make the people do good things and not bad things?" another boy asked. "Then he would not have needed to kill them?"

"Why was Noah good and the other people bad?" yet another boy asked.

Nesehegan arrived just as John finished reading Noah's story. He stood behind John with a bemused smile as the children pummeled John with questions.

John laughed when the questions stopped, "I promise to answer your questions next time. Now go back to your village."

The children walked up the slope to the Town Path on their way to their village. Nesehegan walked down the slope past the children. Just before he reached John, Nesehegan announced, "The war has started. The Wampanoags attacked Swansea. They killed eleven English. Two days later the Plymouth and Massachusetts Bay militia drove Phillip and his people out of Mount Hope. They fled into western Massachusetts where Phillip is urging the Nipmucs to fight with him."

"It was only a matter of time," John exclaimed.

The two men sat together on a bench used by the students.

"Will other tribes join Phillip?" John asked.

"Yes," Nesehegan said. "The tribes' young warriors believe this is their last chance to drive the English from their land. Their sachems cannot stop them from joining Phillip. When the young warriors fight, they'll pull their entire tribe into the war."

"Which tribes will join the Wampanoags?"

"The Nipmucs will be the largest tribe. Smaller tribes from Rhode Island will also join. The Sakonnets and the Pocassets already have. If the English are clumsy, they'll also drive the Narragansetts into the war."

"If both the Nipmucs and Narragansetts join the Wampanoags the war will cover all of New England. What about your tribe and the Mohegans?"

"Both will fight with the English," Nesehegan answered.

John looked carefully into Nesehegan's eyes and asked, "What do you think about this war?"

"I am Tunxis. My tribe lost its old ways and will soon disappear forever. When I heard Philip started this war my blood was hot for I thought we might defeat the English and reclaim our lands. But that's impossible. Even if we win, there will be another war, and more English will come until they win the final war. In the end it does not matter, for everything changes except God. When I am with Him, I will be at peace."

John dropped his eyes to the ground. Neither man spoke for several moments. Finally, John raised his head and asked, "Have you ever felt a conflict between loyalty to your people and your loyalty to Christ?"

"Yes," Nesehegan answered. "The conflict was great at first. I didn't know what to do until an old man in our tribe, who had been a captive of the Onondagas when he was young, told me his story to help me resolve the conflict."

"During his captivity, the old man studied with the Jesuits at their mission of Sainte Marie far to the west," Nesehegan said. "He asked the Jesuit priest how he could resolve the conflict between his requirement of loyalty to Christ and to his adopted tribe, the Onondaga. The priest taught him the way to resolve the conflict based on the teachings of Gratian who the Priest called a great Christian scholar. The old man told me Gratian taught that when you must choose between greater and lesser sins or evils, the lesser must be chosen. Paul accepted this course for it was the lesser sin. So it was, that Gratian said when we're torn between two bad choices, we must submit to the lesser evil, for we sin by committing the greater. Thus, it was, that the old man chose loyalty to Christ over loyalty to the Onondaga for this choice was the lesser evil."

John smiled broadly, "Your knowledge of scripture far exceeds mine. How have you applied this teaching to resolve your own conflict?"

Nesehegan smiled, "So far, I have avoided the conflict."

"Your choice to avoid the conflict is a good choice when it is available," John laughed. "Unfortunately, this isn't always the case."

Joseph had just put a bench back in the school house and was about to retrieve another when he saw John and Nesehegan sitting together in conversation. Joining them, Joseph asked, "What are you talking about?"

"King Philip started the war," John said. "He attacked Swansea and has been forced into Massachusetts by the militia."

"They should have kept him in Mount Hope," Joseph declared. "There he was pinned in by water on three sides. Now he's free to roam. When will our militia be called up?"

"Soon," John said. "It's the Narragansetts who worry me. They fought with us against the Pequots but may side with Philip now."

"At best, we have a month to finish our investigation of Richard Hawkes before you will be called up," John said. "Can you help me find evidence we can use against him?"

"Yes," Joseph answered while Nesehegan nodded.

"Tell us what to do," Nesehegan asked.

"Take Wematin and Sucki and go to the western and northern tribes," John answered. "Talk to people in each village, particularly the old ones. Find men or women who can give witness to the dark man's theft of their land and the murder of Megedaqik. Above all, find James Eastman."

"We will leave tomorrow," Nesehegan said.

John turned to Joseph, "You examined deeds in Farmington and Hartford. Before that you looked at the records for the sale and transfer of Pequot lands in Saybrook and New Haven. Look at the Pequot land records again. Search for deeds involving Richard Hawkes. He likely filed fraudulent deeds for former Pequot lands."

The midday sky was cloudy when the three men rose from the bench.

"God be with you," John said.

Joseph nodded, his lips pressed tightly together.

Nesehegan smiled and announced, "He will be."

Nesehegan, Wematin and Sucki entered the Pocumtuc village near the English town of Deerfield. Their journey up the Connecticut River from the Agawam village took all night, but Nesehegan knew they had to move quickly because an old man in that village told him it was rumored Megedaqik was killed by an Englishman they called the dark man and this dark man traded muskets at their village two days earlier and was on his way to the Pocumtuc village.

They passed several Pocumtuc women preparing breakfast at a fire burning outside a wigwam. Near a small stream they came upon two men carving out a twenty-foot dugout canoe from a large pine tree. The two men fired the area they were carving out and the older man poured water along the edge of what was carved to keep the flames from spreading from it. When he finished pouring the water the man looked at Nesehegan and asked, "Why are you here?"

"I am Nesehegan of the Tunxis," he answered. "This is Wematin and Sucki. We're here because an old warrior in the Agawam village told us your people may be able to answer our questions."

"You are welcome here," the man said as he wiped the sweat from his forehead with the back of his hand. "I will answer your questions if I can."

"The Agawam man said an Englishman just left his village for your village. He was trading muskets. Has he reached your village yet?"

"No, but earlier this morning two of our warriors passed two Englishmen and an Algonquin with a cart on the path from Agawam heading north. They should be here in the afternoon."

"We're searching for old warriors who know of the murder of a Pocumtuc named Megedaqik many springs ago. Are there old men in the village who can help us?"

"My grandfather knows about the murder," the man said. "He told me about it when I was a boy. He's in the first long house down the path. I will take you to him."

Nesehegan's pulse quickened. He'd nearly given up hope, resigning himself to a series of unsuccessful interviews with the village's old warriors. The man led them to the long house. A wisp of smoke rose from the center of its bark covered roof, giving evidence it was occupied.

"Wait outside," the man said. "I will tell my grandfather you are here."

The man returned a few minutes later, "He will talk to you. Go inside."

The long house's interior was dark and Nesehegan's eyes had not adjusted to it when he heard the old Pocumtuc's voice, "Sit next to me."

Nesehegan turned towards the voice and gradually the old Pocumtuc came into view. He was sitting against a woven reed mat lining the long house's interior. His face was creased, and his skin hung loosely from his arms. Nesehegan sat beside him. The old Pocumtuc continued to stare ahead.

"I've been expecting you," the old Pocumtuc said. "Word passes quickly among those of us who were young when Megedaqik was murdered by the dark man. We never spoke to our children about it because we were ashamed we did nothing to punish the dark man for what he did. Why do you care about what the dark man did to Megedaqik?"

"Because he committed crimes against both his own people and ours. I am searching for evidence to use to punish him for these crimes. Are there Pocumtucs still living who saw the dark man kill Megedaqik?"

"No. Only two Pocumtucs saw it happen. They were Matunaaqd and Rowtag. They followed Megedaqik. When he was dying, Rowtag asked for our tribe's forgiveness. I sat with three of our elders to consider his plea. He told how the dark man tortured Megedaqik and besides himself and Matunaaqd, there were three Nipmuc warriors and two Englishmen with the dark man who saw it happen."

"Did Rowtag say who the Nipmucs were?"

"No."

"Did he describe the two Englishmen?"

"Yes. He said one was fat and the other's face was scarred."

"I believe this fat man is living with the Pocumtucs or Mettabesics," Nesehegan said. "Have you heard of a fat Englishman living with these tribes?"

"I heard of such a man many years ago. It was said he lived near a small Pocumtuc village to the southwest. They were last camped along a river ten miles west of the English town of Hadley."

Nesehegan heard excited voices outside the long house. The old Pocumtuc turned to the long house's entrance. "Three men are coming into the village. Two are riding a large wagon and the other is walking."

As he spoke, the old man continued to stare ahead. For the first time, Nesehegan realized he was blind.

"How do you know?" Nesehegan asked.

"When you are blind you learn to listen."

While Nesehegan wanted to rush from the long house to see what was happening, the old man deserved respect. He would stay a little longer.

"Your voice is soothing, not like a warrior's," The old man said. "Your spirit is pure."

Nesehegan clasped the old man's hands. The old man shuddered.

"I feel your spirit," the old man said. "I wish I could see your face."

Nesehegan gripped the old man's hands tighter and stared into his dead eyes.

"I see your face ... I see it!" The old man gasped.

The old man sat back, his dead eyes again facing the fire.

"You have a kind face," The old man exclaimed. "Too kind for what is ahead of you. You know your destiny, don't you?"

"Yes," Nesehegan answered. "My course was set at birth. I must leave now."

"I know," the old man whispered.

Wematin and Sucki were standing outside the long house when Nesehegan broke into the sunlight. Men, women and children moved south along the village's main path towards its entrance. In the distance, he heard the creaking of a slow-moving wagon. He decided to wait near the long house for Hawkes. He led Wematin and Sucki to a place where a wall to the long house blocked Hawkes from seeing them.

Nesehegan saw the wagon within minutes. He was standing at the long house's corner where only his face was visible from the wagon. Sitting on the wagon was Edward Roach. Hawkes sat on Roach's right wearing a buff coat and a black broad brimmed hat. A flintlock rested on his black breeches.

A crowd flowed around the wagon, bringing it to a stop in the center of the village thirty yards from where Nesehegan stood. The crowd yelled its approval. Hawkes stood up in the wagon and stared into the crowd. As he leaned forward his eyes seemed to pierce each man, woman and child. Now hushed, the crowd waited.

"I bring you muskets!" Hawkes shouted.

As the crowd cheered, Nesehegan motioned for Wematin and Sucki to follow him. They moved through the crowd until they reached the path to Connecticut. Once out of the village the three men leaned forward and plunged nonstop towards Hartford, where they would turn west to Farmington. They expected to reach Farmington the next afternoon.

Nesehegan was disappointed that he had no time to talk to anyone about the theft of their land by the dark man or to find James Eastman. In several short conversations, village men told him of two Pocumtuc men who claimed the dark man filed fraudulent deeds for their land. Nesehegan knew God's destiny would not bring him back to this village. John Lee would send someone else after the war ended to talk to these men and to find James Eastman. In the meantime, he needed to report for duty with the militia.

Unknown to Nesehegan, he and his companions were watched by Hawkes's Nipmuc follower Sowheag, son of Aranck. Sowheag trailed Hawkes's wagon until it reached the Pocumtuc village. There he moved away from the wagon into the crowd of Pocumtucs in order to discover any threats to his leader. When the wagon stopped near the old man's long house, he noticed three young men watching the wagon from against the long house's wall. They didn't push forward toward the wagon like the others.

Sowheag watched the three men while Hawkes stared at the crowd. Unlike the others, the three men didn't cheer when Hawkes declared he brought them muskets. Instead, they moved quickly south along the village's main path. Sowheag followed them until they reached the edge of the village where they surged forward picking up their pace on their way south. Sowheag recognized their leader.

By the time Sowheag returned to the village, Hawkes had traded every musket he brought. A few villagers were still talking with him, but most left when the excitement ended. When Hawkes finished talking with the villagers, Sowheag approached him.

"There were three Tunxis here today," Sowheag said. "They were led by Nesehegan who watched you at Mt. Hope. They watched you arrive and went south before you traded your muskets."

"Can you catch them?"

"No one can catch them. They're young and walking fast."

Richard Hawkes knew Sowheag was right. By tomorrow, John Lee would know he traded muskets to both the Wampanoags and the Pocumtucs.

Chapter 57

Richard Hawkes sat at his study's table contemplating the news brought to him by his servant. It was September 1675 and his pulse was racing. The Nipmucs had killed eight Massachusetts militiamen and laid siege to Brookfield, only a day's journey up the Connecticut River. No longer was the threat just from the Wampanoags. Now the militias of both Hartford and Farmington would be mustered. *It has finally happened*, he thought. *All New England will be ablaze by winter and my muskets will be in more demand.* He roared, "Peter, Paul, come to my study . . . now!"

Twenty-one-year-old Paul was behind the house practicing with his flintlock and didn't hear his father's order. Twenty-two-year-old Peter was cutting up a hog he killed earlier. Elizabeth looked out the kitchen door and shouted: "Paul, your father wants you and Peter in his study."

Peter glanced at his mother before turning back to the cutting board. She looked at him and shook her head, "Peter, go to your father now."

Paul burst through the kitchen door and stopped when he saw Peter, "Come Peter, father wants us."

Peter sighed before trudging through the downstairs hall and upstairs to his father's study. Paul and his father were sitting at the study's table when he entered.

"It's about time," Hawkes bellowed. "Sit down."

Hawkes glared at Peter before announcing, "Tomorrow you will be ordered to muster with the militia. You will be sent north to defend Massachusetts Bay's western towns. A Tunxis Indian named Nesehegan scouts for the Connecticut militia and an Englishman named Joseph Henry will be in the militia. These men are our enemies. Kill them; but make certain it looks like an accident. Do you understand?"

"Yes father," Paul said.

"How will we know these men?" Peter asked.

"Don't be stupid. You will learn who they are soon enough."

Nesehegan, Wematin and Sucki had been militia scouts for four days. They were fifteen miles ahead of Major Robert Treat's force of one hundred Connecticut militiamen. It was a sweltering summer day as they scouted ahead of Treat's force. The militia had marched north along the Connecticut River for three days. The first day it reached Hadley. Today it would reach Deerfield, which had been attacked by Nipmucs and Wampanoags two days earlier. Nesehegan's scouts were in the woods three hundred yards off the main path and five miles above Deerfield when they stopped at a brook for water.

"The Nipmucs and Wampanoags are still ahead of us," Nesehegan announced.

"Their tracks are everywhere," Wematin declared. "They're moving fast and not even trying to hide them. Should I go back and warn Major Treat?"

"Not yet," Nesehegan said. "They may be setting a trap. Major Treat sent the Mohegan scouts west and east when he sent us north. We must be certain the enemy does not double back to surprise the militia. I will go north. Wematin go northwest and Sucki northeast. Between us we should find them. Meet me at Deerfield at sunset. The militia should be there by then."

Nesehegan watched Wematin and Sucki disappear into the woods before he turned and hiked north. The late morning sun angled through the tree tops striking the ground in front of him. The attacker's tracks were easy to follow. They led north and told him they passed this way two days earlier.

He knew the war would be like this. *I would do the same*, he thought. *Attack where they're weak; hit fast; kill as many as you can; burn their crops; and move to the next village. Play on their fears and break their spirit.* The Nipmucs, now allied with the Wampanoags, had done this after their siege of Brookfield was lifted. They retreated swiftly, reorganized and attacked Deerfield thirty-five miles northwest of Brookfield in less than a month. But this time, the Wampanoags were with them. The war, which started near Mt. Hope against the Wampanoags, was now being fought nearly one hundred miles away against tribes along the Connecticut River. Now these tribes were going to attack farther up the river. *That means they'll attack Squakeag*, Nesehegan thought.

Nesehegan pushed farther up the river valley following the attacker's tracks until, instead of being spread evenly, the tracks were closely gathered together in a small clearing. *They stopped here,* he thought. *But why?* He worked around the clearing's edge until he found the reason. From the west through the trees the tracks of another large band of Indians entered the clearing. *So, they met,* he thought. *Who are they?* He spent the next half hour viewing the tracks until he knew what happened. When he was certain, he turned south and hiked towards Deerfield to meet the militia. He moved fast. His news was important.

Ten miles behind Nesehegan, Joseph Henry plodded north with the militia. Earlier he wore his buff coat, but now the sun was high, and the coat hung at his belt. Ahead of him, a young man glared at him. He hadn't known the young man's name before they mustered four days earlier. His name was Paul Hawkes and it took Joseph no time to learn he and his brother Peter would not be his friends on the march. Peter walked beside Paul but, unlike his brother, he barely glanced at Joseph and when their eyes met Peter looked away.

By late afternoon the militia reached Deerfield. The sun was below the trees and the temperature quickly dropping as the men gathered together around the small fires they built. Joseph was exhausted. He thought about brushing the dust off his linen tunic but decided it was not worth the effort. He would be marching through the dust again within the hour.

He watched Major Treat across the camp sitting near a fire talking with two of his captains. Treat's weathered face stared at the captains as he spoke. The men nodded at him. Treat had led the militia since Connecticut entered the war and always seemed to anticipate the enemies' next move, instilling confidence in him among the militiamen.

Nesehegan and Wematin emerged from the woods and walked towards Treat and his captains. Treat motioned for them to sit at the fire. Joseph watched them talk. On his knees, Nesehegan pointed at the ground with his right hand and drew a circle in the dirt. Treat and his captains watched as Nesehegan raised his arm and pointed east and moved his arm until it was pointed north. Treat nodded at Nesehegan, who stood and walked towards Joseph with Wematin.

"Good day Joseph," Nesehegan said as he and Wematin sat at Joseph's fire "No surprise here. We arrive and they run away."

"Where did they go?" Joseph asked.

"We found tracks of more than one hundred Wampanoags and Nipmucs. The tracks head north towards Squakeag. I followed the tracks until they met the tracks of another large group of Indians. The two groups merged just before the Wampanoags and Nipmucs turned east."

"And the others?" Joseph asked.

"They turned north towards Squakeag."

"Could you tell who they were?"

"Not by the tracks," Nesehegan said. "The Squakeags, Nashaways and Quabogs have been raiding together. It may be them."

"Where is Sucki?" Joseph asked.

"I sent him north to keep watch tonight."

"Major Treat said we will be moving again after supper," Joseph said.

"He told us the same. He wants to reach Squakeag by nightfall. Captain Beers's militia should be there already."

"From Watertowne?"

"Yes. He and his men were sent to evacuate the town."

Joseph felt they were being watched as he talked. He glanced to his right and saw Paul and Peter Hawkes staring at them. Paul pointed at Nesehegan but dropped his arm as soon as he saw Joseph watching them.

"Be careful of those two," Joseph said. "They're Richard Hawkes's sons and have watched me since we left Hartford."

After sharing Joseph's porridge, Nesehegan nodded to Wematin and they stood up.

"We go north," Nesehegan said. "When we find Sucki we will hike to Squakeag. Major Treat will meet us outside the town tonight. I will see you then."

Joseph woke two hours before dawn. The militia had camped south of Squakeag the night before. He was worried because Nesehegan didn't meet them. The other militiamen were still sleeping but were starting to stir. Joseph rose and stuffed his blanket into the pack he wore around his waist. The militia headed north at sunrise.

Joseph was in front of the column behind Major Treat. Coal black smoke rose above the trees ahead of them. Treat ordered the column to halt and called for Joseph.

"Take three men and move ahead," Treat ordered. "There has been no word from the Tunxis scouts I sent here yesterday. We need eyes ahead to avoid a trap."

Joseph led three militiamen forward on the path to Squakeag. They moved off the path into the trees after one hundred yards and hiked parallel to the path inside the tree line for a mile. Joseph sent one militiaman thirty-five yards ahead and positioned another twenty-five yards behind them.

They had travelled north for an hour when they saw a small hill two hundred yards ahead. As they moved closer to the hill, Joseph saw a dozen narrow poles planted in the ground along the path below the hill. Beaver pelts appeared to be mounted on each pole. They moved back onto the path and continued walking towards the hill. Suddenly, the lead militiaman dropped to his knees. Joseph ordered the other men forward, thinking the militiaman had been attacked by Indians.

As Joseph raced forward with his men, a man trailing him screamed, "My God, look."

Joseph stopped and turned to his right. Twenty feet away a mutilated head was mounted atop a pole just off the path. It was the head of an Englishman. Long black hair hung behind the head. He realized it was the hair that made the head appear to be a beaver pelt from a distance. He forced his eyes away from the mutilated head and looked up the road. There were six more poles, each mounted with an Englishman's head. His stomach turned as he looked across the road where there were six more poles, each also mounted with the head of an Englishman.

"Look," yelled a militiaman pointing at a large oak tree. "Look up the tree."

Joseph looked up. A dead Englishman hung from a metal hook stuck through his chin. A young militiaman immediately bent over and began to retch uncontrollably. The older militiamen froze.

"Help me take him down," Joseph ordered two older militiamen.

Joseph and the militiamen climbed the tree until they reached the dead man's corpse. They pushed the corpse up until its chin was freed from the hook.

"Throw me a rope," Joseph yelled to the militiamen below.

The militiamen quickly threw him a rope which he and the other militiamen in the tree tied under the dead man's shoulders and strung over the branch above them. Then they lowered the corpse to the militiamen below.

The young militiaman ceased retching by the time Joseph reached the ground.

"Go to Major Treat," Joseph ordered the militiaman. "Tell him what we found."

The young militiaman sprinted south. Joseph turned to the remaining militiamen and announced, "They must be Captain Beer's men. We will bury them later. Let's climb the hill to get a better look at what's around us."

On the hill, they found another gruesome sight. Laid out across the hill were the bodies of twenty-one Englishmen. Half the bodies were headless. All the bodies were mutilated. In some cases, there was no blood, indicating the mutilation was done after the men were dead. In other cases, dried blood was all over the body, evidence the men were tortured. There was no sign of the Indians who killed them.

Major Treat and his militiamen were taking down the last heads when Joseph and his men returned to the pole lined path a half hour later. Treat left thirty men behind to bury the dead and ordered the other men to form a column. They moved at double time towards Squakeag, which was now just two miles ahead of them.

Joseph was at the head of the column when they reached the small village. The meetinghouse and cabins were only charred remains. The biting smell of smoke hung low like a heavy mist as they moved along the rutted road passing between the burned-out cabins.

Nesehegan, Wematin and Sucki led a few villagers from the stockade and walked towards them as they approached. Nesehegan's mantle was torn and Sucki's head was covered with a blood-stained bandage. Joseph waived at Nesehegan but Nesehegan walked straight to Major Treat. Nesehegan and Treat spoke for several minutes after which Treat turned to talk to the townspeople. As Treat did so, Nesehegan, Wematin and Sucki finally walked towards Joseph.

"What happened here?" Joseph asked.

"Captain Beers and his men were attacked by the Squakeags, Nashaways and Quabogs," Nesehegan said. "We heard the musket fire as we approached the town last night. When it was clear the people were safe in the stockade we moved south. We reached the battle as it ended. Captain Beers and most of his men were already dead. We helped a few of Beers's men get away but were set upon by more enemy warriors before we reached the stockade. One Englishmen was killed, but we were able to get the others into the stockade."

"They offered Beers's men no quarter," Joseph said. "They were butchered like hogs." After pausing for a moment, Joseph added, "I hear the Pocumtucs have joined with the Wampanoags and Nipmucs."

"Yes. It surprises me," Nesehegan answered. "They gave no sign they would when I was in their village two months ago. This will be a long war."

"Our leaders know this now," Joseph said. "Everyone in western Massachusetts is retreating to Hadley."

"Without towns to attack in the west, the war may shift to the east again," Nesehegan said.

"Especially if the Narragansetts join the fight," Joseph said.

"Let's hope those rumors are false."

Chapter 58

A heavy snow fell from an unforgiving gray sky onto the frozen ground. It was December and Joseph Henry shivered in the snow-covered field near a burnt-out stockade where fifteen dead militiamen and an English trader lay frozen with their wounds carved into their half naked bodies. Three hundred Connecticut militiamen shared the cold with Joseph.

Joseph shielded himself from the howling wind. He sat with his back to the wind, remembering how shocked he was when the Connecticut General Court decided to join with the colonies of Massachusetts Bay and Plymouth in attacking the Narragansett. Virtually all western Massachusetts was now in the hands of the Nipmucs, Wampanoags, Pocumtucs and the other western tribes and it made no sense to Joseph to take on a much larger enemy on a totally different front.

But when Lieutenant Bull explained the strategy behind the attack, Joseph appreciated it. All the frontier towns were nearly abandoned, and the men, women and children of these towns herded into Hadley and Springfield where they could be fed and defended. Massachusetts Bay did the same with the people in its frontier towns by moving them back east to Massachusetts Bay's larger towns. With the English fields empty, the Indians would find little food for their warriors during the winter. With the English settlers safe, the militias of Connecticut, Massachusetts Bay and Plymouth were free to attack without fear the Indians would attack their undefended settlements as they did before.

Still, the attack's scope worried Joseph. There were more than one thousand militiamen involved - three hundred alone from

Connecticut under Major Treat. He knew coordinating such a large force was fraught with risks. *That's why we sit here in the cold in front of a burnt-out fort*, he thought. *This fort was to be the rendezvous point. It took us two days to get here after hiking from New London. Now the fort's trader, Jireh Bull, lies stretched out like a carp along with the fifteen militiamen assigned to protect him. We will soon lie with them if the Massachusetts Bay and Plymouth militias don't arrive soon.*

Through the howling snow Joseph saw a handful of men gathered together in the distance. He peered through the snow trying to determine who they were. One man was shorter than the others and was talking the most, while the tallest man loomed at least eight inches over the shorter man. Finally, he realized the short man was Major Treat and the tall man was Thomas Watts, his company's captain. When he recognized another company commander, it was clear Treat was meeting with his five company commanders.

No one was able to start a fire with the damp wood laying in the snow. The cold was too unbearable to sit and so, Joseph walked to the burnt-out stockade hoping to find dry wood among its charred remains. Several other men were digging in the piles of charred wood when he reached the stockade.

"There's no dry wood here," a familiar voice announced.

Joseph turned to the voice and looked into Nesehegan's eyes. Wematin and Sucki were standing next to him.

"We already searched here," Nesehegan said.

"I'm glad you're here," Joseph said. "Come sit with me."

They sat together in the snow. Joseph no longer felt the wind on his back and began chewing some dry corn from the leather bag on his belt.

"Where are the other militia?" he asked.

"On their way south from Wickford." Nesehegan said. "They should be here soon."

"What do you know about the Narragansetts' fort?"

"Little. But the Mohegans captured a Narragansett warrior who will take us to it. What about Richard Hawkes's sons?"

"Paul watches me constantly," Joseph answered.

Just before sunset seven hundred militiamen from Massachusetts Bay and Plymouth arrived from the north. The Plymouth men came first. They camped around the stockade with the Connecticut men, forcing the Massachusetts Bay men to camp farther from the stockade where the snow was deeper.

Joseph was colder than he'd ever been as he lay in the snow trying to get to sleep that night. Other men tried to fight off the cold by pacing about the camp. The company captains ordered their men to lie down and sleep because they would need rest for the next day's battle. Joseph knew they were right. He stared up at the falling snow hoping to take his mind off the cold long enough to fall asleep.

Joseph's right foot was stuck when he woke. He shook it, trying to break it free before he realized the leg was only asleep from being pinned under his left leg. After more shaking, the pins and needles in his foot disappeared. He snapped awake when he remembered where he was. He lifted his head and looked around. Nearly all the militiamen were lying in the snow. It was still snowing, and a heavy cover of snow lay on his blanket. He shook the snow off his blanket and pulled his flintlock away from the warmth of his body where he kept it while he slept.

Like dead men rising from their graves, a thousand men rose from the snow. Some hit their hands against their thighs or kicked their feet on the ground, trying to drive life back into them. Most were successful, but a few complained of frostbite. They had no choice but to move forward as best they could with the militia.

Within an hour the eastern sky began to lighten, but unless they looked back, none of the men knew it for they were trudging west into a still black sky through heavily falling snow. The Massachusetts Bay militia led, with Joseph Henry and the Connecticut militia trailing Plymouth's militia at the formation's rear. Joseph didn't see Nesehegan that morning, but word was he, Wematin and Sucki were ahead of the column with more than a dozen Mohegans and the captured Narragansett warrior.

By mid-morning, the heavy black clouds of morning's darkness were slate gray, giving hope the snow might stop. But still the snow continued, now heavier than when their march began. A strong wind piled the snow into drifts, further impeding their progress. Several men near Joseph complained their hands were so frostbitten they couldn't move their fingers. There was nothing that could be done for them until the battle ended and with only one day of food left for everyone, Joseph knew the battle must be fought and won soon if they were to survive.

Shortly after noon, word filtered back through the column that two companies of Massachusetts Bay's militia were engaged with a small Narragansett force on the edge of a large swamp where the entire Narragansett tribe was entrenched in a massive palisaded fort. Joseph pushed ahead with the rest of Captain Watts's company as the drudgery of wading through the snow was replaced by the anticipation of a coming battle. He glanced around at the men on either side of him as they raced forward. He saw Paul Hawkes to his right. Hawkes was staring directly at him, while his brother Peter pushed forward behind Paul staring straight ahead. Joseph turned ahead, unwilling to worry about Richard Hawkes's sons' intentions until the battle was over.

Soon the combined militias were in the middle of a frozen swamp. Their feet crunched through the ice covering the swamp as they strode briskly toward the scattered pop of musket fire. Through the swamp's barren trees Joseph saw a huge palisade on a rise three hundred yards ahead of him. Major Treat ordered his five companies to spread out along the palisade to the left of the Plymouth and Massachusetts Bay militias. Within fifteen minutes all one thousand men lay in the snow before the fort's palisade.

Joseph had never seen a palisade so high. In addition to its palisade, there was a thick hedge all along the fort's base. *God be with us*, he thought. *We'll need to get through the hedge before we reach the palisade.*

"Impressive, isn't it?" Nesehegan surprised him.

Joseph turned to Nesehegan who said, "Our scouting party went around the palisade. There are at least three thousand Narragansett men, women and children and five hundred wigwams within its walls. It has one weakness."

Nesehegan pointed to a corner of the palisade to their left and announced, "The palisade isn't complete there. There's only a pile of logs filling the gap. We will climb over them."

Joseph looked at the gap and asked, "Is that a blockhouse near the gap?"

"Yes, when we attack, the Narragansetts will have a clear line of fire. Many will die, as it's the only way into the fort."

"Why aren't you with the scouts?" Joseph asked.

"All scouts were ordered to attack with the militia. I attack with you."

"I'm glad we'll be together," Joseph nodded.

Captain Watts stood before their company with his back to the fort. A hush fell over the company's men as they waited to hear his orders.

"Massachusetts Bay attacks first," Watts yelled. "When they do, fire into the fort to cover their charge."

Puffs of smoke appeared along the firing line as the primer powder of muskets exploded, each pop immediately followed by a musket's blast. Soon the individual explosions merged into one continuous roar.

As he reloaded his flintlock, Joseph watched as the first two Massachusetts Bay companies advanced through the snow-covered swamp toward the fort. Excitement coursed through Joseph's veins as he marveled at their charge's speed. It seemed nothing could stop them. But, when they reached the logs, the charge ended as each man began climbing over them through a withering fire from the blockhouse.

Still, Massachusetts Bay's men advanced. He could see their two captains urging them forward. But in an instant Joseph's excitement was replaced by horror as he saw first one and then the other captain fall into the logs. The men in their companies paused when they saw their captains fall before they dropped into the logs for cover and began firing at the blockhouse.

Joseph watched as two more companies of Massachusetts's militia left the firing line. They rushed headlong towards the gap. "Go, go, go," Joseph yelled with the other men on the firing line while he reloaded his flintlock.

The second wave of Massachusetts men hit the gap on the run. Several of them jumped from log to log, trying to get into the fort before being cut down from fire from the blockhouse. Like the first two companies, these companies were also pinned down among the logs by fire from the blockhouse. All the while, Joseph and the rest of the firing line continued firing into the fort to provide cover for the companies advancing into the pile of logs.

Joseph knew every man's blood was up, having watched their friends fall. It was for him and the other militiamen to avenge their deaths. They continued to fire into the fort and when the last two Massachusetts Bay companies charged, they cheered so loud even the weakest of them felt his spine shiver. This time the companies were organized into a column. When the first column hit the fallen timbers, its men began falling. Immediately, those trailing took their place. Joseph marveled at the efficiency with which the column pushed through the companies charging first. Soon the fire from the blockhouse stopped. One militiaman waived back to the firing line. Immediately, a cheer erupted along the line. Joseph and Nesehegan cheered with the others, certain the fort would soon fall.

Captain Watts ran along their company's firing line. Watts stood before the men with his back to the fort. He raised his hands above his black broad brimmed hat and the men became silent.

"All of Connecticut attacks now," Watts announced. "We will take the fort with our charge. Some of you must stay here to give covering fire. Are there volunteers?"

Immediately, Paul Hawkes raised his hand, "I volunteer."

"Good." Watts said. "Are there others?"

Two more men raised their hands.

Paul Hawkes slapped his brother Peter's back, "Raise your hand."

Peter reflexively raised his hand.

Everything was a blur as Joseph reloaded his musket and formed up with the rest of his company. Nesehegan was next to him when Captain Watts ordered them forward with the other Connecticut companies. A loud cheer rose from the firing line, and from the men pinned down by fire in the gaps between the logs, as the five companies of Connecticut's militia advanced through the firing line. Joseph's heart beat furiously as he moved forward with Nesehegan on his right.

At first, the Connecticut companies marched together line abreast, but as they reached the fort Major Treat ordered one and then another company into the gap until all five companies were engaged. Joseph's company entered third. He and Nesehegan climbed over the pile of logs while staying low to avoid the lead shot flying over them from inside the fort. There were many dead and wounded, including the two Massachusetts Bay captains, within the logs as they pressed forward. Joseph dropped behind a log to fire and reload his musket, but quickly realized he needed to enter the fort with the rest of Connecticut's companies as soon as possible.

Nesehegan was ahead of Joseph. Joseph watched Nesehegan glide effortless over the logs as he fought to keep up with him. Lead shot filled the air and Joseph bent forward into it with his head down as if walking into a pouring rain. He was now almost over the logs and all around him he heard the slap and crack of lead shot striking the logs near him.

"Faster Joseph," Nesehegan yelled back at him as Nesehegan climbed yet another log. "There's cover inside the fort. We've taken the blockhouse near the gap, but there's another blockhouse across from the entrance. We have to get over the logs to escape its fire."

As Nesehegan spoke, two militiamen next to them were struck by lead balls. One was struck through the head causing blood and portions of his skull to splash onto their faces. The other was struck in the stomach. The man rolled about in agony until he lapsed into shock.

Joseph was over the last log. He rolled onto the ground inside the fort. He stood up briefly until Nesehegan pushed him back onto the ground as a lead ball splintered the log behind Joseph.

"It is ahead of us," Nesehegan yelled while pointing to a blockhouse sixty feet ahead as they crouched on the frozen dirt. "Move to the left where there's cover behind the blockhouse we just took."

Militiamen were streaming into the fort over the logs as Joseph and Nesehegan crouched low to the ground making their way to the captured blockhouse. When they reached the blockhouse, they began to fire from its corner at the blockhouse still held by the Narragansetts. Soon they witnessed a slaughter as militiamen dropped to their knees, fell forward on their faces, or collapsed in a heap, as they crossed over the last of the logs under fire from the blockhouse.

There was now a pile of bodies under the logs just inside the fort. Still the men came. Joseph watched Connecticut's captains, Gallop and Mason, try to rally their men. Gallop was struck in the head and dropped dead to the ground; while Mason was struck in the chest and flew backwards into the logs. Captains Marshall and Seeley moved towards the blockhouse with more than a dozen militiamen. Just as they reached the blockhouse, Captain Marshall's head was shattered by a lead ball and Captain Seeley was shot through the throat and dropped to the ground holding it as blood spurted through his fingers.

"That fire was not from the blockhouse," Nesehegan yelled." They were too close to it and below its firing gaps. It came from behind us."

Both Nesehegan and Joseph looked back at the firing line behind them. Heavy smoke enveloped it, but through the smoke they could see the bright flashes of musket fire. Two balls slapped into the captured blockhouse just above their heads.

On the firing line Paul Hawkes yelled, "Damn it Peter, lower your aim."

"You missed too," Peter screamed.

"Quit firing," Paul ordered. "Load for me and I will shoot Joseph Henry and Nesehegan. Father said to make it look like an accident and with everyone on the firing line aiming at the fort it will look like they were accidentally shot by their own men."

Meanwhile, all along the firing line militiamen cheered as their shots struck home. Yells of "I got one," and "take that savage," rose above the firing.

Joseph and Nesehegan turned back to the fight. More than three hundred militiamen of Massachusetts Bay and Connecticut raced towards the remaining blockhouse. Joseph waived his arm forward as both he and Nesehegan joined them. Suddenly, Joseph felt a searing pain in his left leg. Immediately, his leg collapsed beneath him and he fell to the ground with blood pouring out of his wound. As he lay in the dirt, he watched the blood pool around his leg.

Nesehegan raced to his side. He tore the left leg of Joseph's breeches away. The wound was deep enough to cause a severe loss of blood. He quickly tied the torn breeches around the leg cutting off the flow of blood. He looked at Joseph and asked, "Can you hear me?"

"Yes." Joseph whispered weakly.

"I stopped the bleeding. Our own men fired on us again. I need to stop them. Stay here until I return."

Nesehegan stood up and raced back towards the fort's entrance.

He faced the English firing line and stretched his arms above him with his palms forward as a signal to the men on the line to cease firing. Paul Hawkes couldn't believe his luck. Nesehegan had made himself a perfect target. He aimed his musket at Nesehegan's chest and pulled its trigger.

Nesehegan saw the flash of Paul Hawkes's flintlock an instant before the lead ball shattered his heart. The ball's force drove him onto his back with both his arms and legs outstretched. As he took his final breath the last thing he saw was a bright flash of light fill the sky.

A Plymouth militiaman watched the Hawkes brothers from ten feet to their right. He could only hear bits and pieces of their conversation but the names "Joseph Henry and Nesehegan" merged with the words "shoot" and "father said to make it look like an accident," as one loaded two muskets while the other fired first one and then the other musket at the fort. Suddenly, both men jumped up and cheered, while the one firing yelled, "I shot them both."

The Plymouth militiaman turned back to the fort and fired one more ball before he stood up to charge with the rest of his militia.

Joseph Henry didn't see the battle's end. He spent the next two days in and out of consciousness as the surviving militiamen carried him, along with more than two hundred dead and wounded militiamen, north to Wickford through the snow. He didn't celebrate when he was told the English won the battle and destroyed the Narragansetts' fort, killing hundreds of Narragansett men, women and children. He wept softly when he was told his friend Nesehegan died in the battle.

Chapter 59

Joseph Henry woke. His head was stuffy, and his eyes burned. As he lay on his back, he heard a fire popping. Gradually, his eyes moistened, and he opened them. Above was a heavy dark oak beam. It was set in a white clapboard ceiling along with several similar beams. He lifted his head until he could see the fireplace's hearth. The fire was roaring. *Someone just placed a log on it*, he thought. He felt the sun on the back of his head. He turned to face it and looked through the diamond glass windowpanes into a bright blue sky framed by snow on the window sill. He remembered the freezing cold and the bright scarlet blood pooling all around him in the fresh white snow. Then he remembered his friend Nesehegan was dead.

"You're awake," came a soothing feminine voice from across the room. "I will tell John. Don't try to get up. You've been sleeping for two days."

Joseph tried to answer but his lips and throat were too parched to form the words. Frustrated, he lay back on the pillow and closed his eyes. Flashing through his head were ill defined images of people he didn't know hovering over him; of a woman's hands spooning broth into his mouth; and, of children's high-pitched laughter. He remembered the worry on John Lee's face looking down at him while he was carried up a staircase. His last memory of the battle was Nesehegan tying his torn breeches around his leg as he lay in the snow inside the Narragansett's fort. Suddenly, his pulse quickened, and his stomach turned as fear gripped him. He quickly pulled himself up and reached for his leg.

"Your leg is still there," John said with a smile. "We were lucky to have you in the house with a physician available when your fever struck."

"My throat is dry," Joseph whispered.

"Drink this," Mary said as she entered the room with a noggin of beer.

After he swallowed some beer, Joseph asked, "How long have I been here?"

"Two weeks," John said. "You've been in and out of sleep since then."

A young child screamed with joy outside the room, "Joseph's awake! Joseph's awake!"

"Quiet Thomas, quiet," an older boy's voice ordered.

"What happened during the battle?" Joseph asked. "I was told we won and Nesehegan was killed."

Mary touched Joseph's shoulder, "I made stew. I will get you some while you talk to John."

John waited until Mary left before he answered, "Our casualties were heavy. Connecticut's were greatest. Four of our five captains were killed. Eighty of our soldiers were killed or wounded. The Narragansetts fled into Massachusetts Bay and joined the Nipmucs and Wampanoags. The fort and its wigwams were burned to the ground. Hundreds of Narragansett men, women and children were killed."

"How did Nesehegan die?" Joseph asked.

"He was shot through the heart with a musket ball."

"The last I remember was him turning toward our firing line after I was shot to stop our men from firing into us. Was he shot by our own men?"

"It seems so. Many men entering the fort were killed by men on our firing line."

"Where is his body?"

"He's buried in the Tunxis village."

"I want to see him."

"I will take you to his grave when you are stronger."

The two men stopped talking and stared into the fire. Its flames had burned away the fresh wood and it was now burning half as bright as when Joseph woke.

"A soldier from Plymouth came to see you last week," John said. "He said he would come back next week."

"Did he say why he came?"

"No."

The cold spell that had gripped New England for a month lifted the following week. The frozen ground was replaced by mud, making the Town Path above John's house nearly impassable. During the day a vibrant sun swam through a bright blue sky and at night thousands of stars blazed in the coal black heavens.

Four-year-old Thomas came to Joseph's room the day he woke and every day after that during the week. On the first six days Joseph was too weak to move from bed. But on the seventh day Joseph stood up and sat by the fire while Thomas and his six-year-old brother, Stephen, played together on the floor. Joseph felt he had to move and sat up and announced, "Let's go outside boys."

Both boys grabbed Joseph's hands and led him down the stairs, through the parlor, and into the kitchen where Mary was preparing supper.

"Don't fall!" Mary exclaimed.

"The boys are taking me for a walk," Joseph answered. "Can I sit in the yard above the river?"

Mary braced Joseph by placing her shoulder under his while the two boys continued holding his hands. They sat him in a chair under a barren maple tree. Below him the Farmington River flowed freely for the first time in weeks, pulling the remaining patches of ice along with it.

Joseph looked down the slope and watched John Lee and his son Martin pitching hay to feed his cattle. Abruptly, the door to the house sprang open. He looked back to see little Thomas racing down the slope towards him.

"Joseph, a man is here to see you," Thomas yelled.

Mary emerged from the house. Behind her was a tall thin man of about twenty. The man wore a buff coat. His face was tense; his boots muddy; and his musket clean.

"This is Josiah Churchill," Mary said. "He's from Plymouth."

Joseph tried unsuccessfully to stand, "I'm sorry but my leg is uncooperative."

"That's alright," Churchill said.

"Sit next to me," Joseph said.

Churchill sat in one of the three other chairs grouped together beneath the tree.

"You look like a militiamen sir," Joseph said. "Am I right?"

"You are. We were together at the Great Swamp Fight."

"So, the battle has a name now," Joseph said with a slight smile. "What brings you to see me?"

"During the battle I saw something unusual that bothers me. I hope you can make sense of it."

"I'll try."

"You charged the fort before us with the Connecticut Militia."

"I did."

"Some of your men stayed behind to man the firing line. Two of those men were right next to me. Their conversation was odd. I had the impression they were brothers. They spoke your name as they re-loaded. They also spoke the name "Nesehegan." Who is Nesehegan?"

"He was my friend. He was killed in the battle."

"I'm sorry," Churchill said. "I think these men fired at both of you."

"Why do think that?"

"When they spoke of you and your friend, they used the words 'killing' and 'father said to make it look like an accident.' To me it meant they intended to kill both of you."

Joseph stared at Churchill for several moments without speaking.

Inside he was raging. *Control yourself*, he thought. *You don't know this man.*

"Did you hear what I said?" Churchill asked.

"I did," Joseph answered. "Did you see anything else?"

"Yes. After one of them fired his musket at the fort he yelled, 'I shot both of them.' Then they both cheered."

"Thank you," Joseph said. "I will discuss this with others."

Churchill rose from his chair. He nodded as he looked down at Joseph and whispered, "Good luck Joseph Henry."

"Where are you going?" Joseph asked.

"Back to Plymouth. Our militia has little to do now that the Narragansetts are in Massachusetts Bay. The fighting will now be done by Connecticut and Massachusetts Bay."

"Well just the same, good luck to you as well Josiah Churchill," Joseph said.

Joseph stared at the river for several minutes after Churchill left. He wasn't surprised by Churchill's news. Nesehegan warned him. He couldn't even get angry at himself for not stopping what happened. *Neither of us could do anything*, he thought. *We had a duty and our duty was to charge the fort. I fulfilled that duty. Now I have another. I will avenge my friend.*

Chapter 60

John Lee's jaw tightened and his teeth ground together. He stared across his parlor table at Joseph Henry who had just told him about Josiah Churchill's visit earlier that day. John's eyes blazed, "Richard Hawkes ordered his sons to kill you and Nesehegan. They had no reason to do it on their own."

Joseph leaned across the table and answered, "They'll pay for it."

"Yes, they will!" John fumed.

"I have a plan," Joseph said calmly. "Give me permission to get one of his sons to confess. Peter is the weakest."

"Do it," John boomed. "Use whatever means you need to get a confession we can use at his father's trial."

"I will."

"We also need to finish our earlier investigation of Hawkes," John announced. "All his crimes must be tried together. Ask Wematin and Sucki to find any Pocumtuc whose land was stolen by him and, above all, find James Eastman. Nesehegan said there was a rumor of a fat Englishman living near a small Pocumtuc camp in the west. Look there first."

Wematin and Sucki surprised Peter Hawkes while he walked alone in the dark along the Little River. They had tracked him since he left his father's house that morning. There appeared little order to Peter's movements. First, he walked to the north towards Hartford's old cow pasture. He continued west until he reached the barren hill where the town had erected its gallows twenty years earlier. When he got to the summit he stared up at the weathered platform where the condemned stood on a ladder before plummeting to their deaths. As he stared at the platform, he held his arms around himself and began rocking back and forth.

Peter turned back towards the town. He walked on the road to the Little River until entering the meetinghouse. After more than an hour, Peter emerged and continued his journey towards the Little River. He turned west at the river and walked more than a mile before crossing the river's west bridge and entered the city's South Plantation.

By now, both Wematin and Sucki concluded there was no logic to Peter's travels — that was, until he entered Joseph Mygatt's tavern at mid-afternoon.

Wematin turned to Sucki and said, "First gallows, next a church and now a tavern. This is a journey of a troubled man. Bring Joseph Henry. Peter Hawkes will be in the tavern until nightfall. We will capture him when he leaves alone in the dark."

Joseph and Sucki met Wematin in the woods near the tavern at sunset. Their plan depended on Peter walking home from the tavern alone, so it was important to know who was in the tavern and to be certain no one left the tavern with him.

"I'll go in the tavern and chase him out," Joseph said. "Capture him when it's safe to do so. I will meet you at the old gristmill."

It was a moonless night when Joseph entered Mygatt's tavern. Inside, three young men were gathered at one end of a large table in the room's center. Peter was eight feet away from them seated at the table's other end near the fireplace staring blankly at the flames licking the fresh logs Mygatt fed to the fire.

"Good evening," Mygatt said when Joseph entered.

Joseph nodded at the short stocky man, "A noggin of beer."

"I'll get it. Where will you sit?"

"With the men at that table," Joseph said pointing to the table where Peter Hawkes and the three other men were seated.

The tavern keeper nodded and walked to a barrel to draw a beer for Joseph. Joseph strode to the table with his eyes fixed on Peter, who was still staring into the fire, oblivious to Joseph's presence. The three other men glanced at Joseph before resuming their conversation.

Joseph sat at the table facing Peter, whose head was bobbing up and down. Joseph realized Peter was about to pass out. It was the last thing he wanted. He leaned forward and slammed his fist on the table and yelled, "Peter Hawkes. Do you remember me?"

Immediately the tavern was brought to life. The three men at the table turned to Joseph while across the room Mygatt spilled the beer he was bringing to him. Only Peter Hawkes seemed oblivious to what happened. He raised his head and glanced at Joseph with glazed eyes before dropping his chin back to his chest.

Joseph slammed his fist on the table again and shouted, "Look at me when I talk to you."

Peter raised his head and stared at Joseph. Peter's face turned ashen and he pulled back from the table. Mygatt stood frozen ten feet away. The three other men turned and stared at Joseph.

"Don't you remember me Peter?" Joseph barked.

Peter's hands trembled as he grabbed his noggin of beer and brought it to his lips. He took a swallow and wiped his lips with the back of his hand.

"I do," Peter stammered.

"What is my name?"

"I don't remember."

"Damn it, you do. Say it."

"I don't."

Joseph stood up, leaned across the table and grabbed Peter by the neck of his tunic. "Say it," he yelled.

"Joseph . . . Henry," Peter stammered.

"Where is your brother Paul" Joseph demanded.

"He's on a trip with my father."

"Where are they?"

"I don't know." Peter stammered.

"When will they be back?"

"In two or three days"

Joseph paused and stared into Peter's bloodshot eyes. He leaned forward and asked, "Why did you shoot me in the swamp?"

Peter slouched back into his chair with his arms pulled tightly across his chest. He looked pleadingly at the three men at the table. They coldly stared back at him.

Joseph knew he had to drive Peter from the tavern. He flung himself across the table at Peter pushing him from his chair onto the floor. The other men watched transfixed as Joseph grabbed Peter's throat. Peter struggled to free himself by grabbing Joseph's hands, but Joseph knew Peter lacked the strength to break his grip. He loosened his grip so Peter could break free. He lay on the floor just long enough to give Peter time to run for the door. Joseph chased Peter out the door into the cold night air. He chased Peter for a quarter mile down to the Little River where Peter turned east along the river. Joseph stopped at the river. *That should make him think he has escaped*, Joseph thought. *Wematin and Sucki will catch him before he gets away.*

Peter stopped running when he was certain he was no longer being chased. Wematin had watched the chase. He and Sucki moved along the river just off the road until they were one hundred feet ahead of Peter as he approached them. The darkness prevented them from seeing Peter, but they were confident he would reach them in a few moments.

When he didn't reach them by then, they walked up the road to find him. Then, in the darkness, they heard water striking the frozen ground along the road. At first, they didn't know what caused the sound. Finally, Wematin recognized its cause and ran towards it. He closed on the silhouette of a man's back. Wematin drove his shoulder into the man knocking him to the ground just as the man had nearly finished emptying his bladder. Piss flew as Peter twisted onto his back. Sucki jumped on Peter, pinning him to the ground, while Wematin tied a deerskin strap over his eyes.

There was nothing to stop Peter from screaming. Soon dogs from the houses lining the road began barking. Joseph sprang from the road's darkness and wrapped a linen cloth across Peter's mouth, stopping his screams. The three men lifted Peter off the frozen dirt and carried him across the river over the bridge into the old mill's basement.

The old mill hadn't operated in ten years. Deacon Hart removed the mill's wheel and grinding stones and the mill was now little more than a decayed wooden frame upstairs, where the grinding stones had been, with a weathered clapboard covered room below, where the ground corn had been stored.

They tied Peter's hands behind him and set him down in the corner farthest from the basement's entrance. Outside, the barking stopped. Inside, Sucki started a small fire.

"Sit still and shut up," Joseph yelled. "I have more questions."

Peter mumbled through the cloth over his mouth.

"I will take off the cloth if you agree not to yell," Joseph said.

The small fire burned behind Joseph as he stared at Peter. Peter's head was moving up and down as he mumbled through the cloth.

"Does that mean you won't yell?" Joseph asked.

Peter nodded his head and Joseph removed the cloth.

"You don't need to keep my eyes covered," Peter said. "I already know who you are Joseph Henry."

Joseph removed the strap and asked, "Why did you shoot me?"

"I didn't shoot you," Peter protested.

"Who did?" Joseph asked.

"I can't tell you."

"Why not?" Joseph yelled.

"I'm not going to answer any more questions."

Joseph rose and looked down at Peter. Peter stared up at him.

Without warning, Joseph slapped Peter across the face driving him onto his side.

"Do you want to hang?" Joseph yelled. "You will if you don't say who shot me."

Peter sobbed. He raised himself back to a sitting position and looked up at Joseph with tears sliding across his cheeks, "I didn't want to shoot anyone that day, not even the Narragansetts."

"Then who shot me?" Joseph barked.

"I can't tell you."

Joseph slapped Peter again. This time Peter didn't rise.

"Alright, let's try another question," Joseph sneered. "Who shot my friend Nesehegan that day?"

Peter turned his head and looked up at Joseph, "I didn't shoot your friend."

"Did you shoot anyone that day?"

"No."

"And yet you refuse to tell who did," Joseph yelled. "You are as guilty as they are. Do you want to be hanged just to protect the person who did it?"

Peter ignored the question. Instead, he pulled his legs up to his chest in a fetal position and closed his eyes, rocking back and forth while sitting in the basement's dirt.

Joseph looked at Wematin and pointed to where the mill's wheel once turned, "Take him to the wheel stream. I'll follow."

The gate to the wheel stream had stayed open since Deacon Hart removed the wheel. The Little River's water flowed freely through it. Wematin and Sucki lifted Joseph and dragged him to the stream.

"Push his head underwater," Joseph ordered.

Wematin pushed Peter's head into the stream while Sucki held him down. Joseph stood above them while Peter thrashed about, trying to get his head above water.

"Pull him up," Joseph said

Peter coughed and gagged as the Tunxis men lay him on the ground next to the stream. Joseph stared down at Peter until he stopped coughing, "Tell me who shot me and Nesehegan."

Peter looked up at him for a moment and shook his head.

"Put him under again," Joseph ordered.

Wematin and Sucki thrust Peter's head under water. This time they kept him under longer. Peter would still not answer. It took two more thrusts into the stream before Peter finally could take no more. When he spat out the last water he inhaled, Joseph gave him a blanket and sat him before the small fire.

"Now, answer my question," Joseph said calmly. "If you don't, we will put you under the water four more times before I ask you again."

Peter shivered under the blanket. His eyes were bloodshot and his hands shaking as he looked back at Joseph, "My brother Paul fired the musket balls that struck you and Nesehegan."

"Did your father order you and your brother to shoot us?"

"Yes," Peter answered, his head bowed.

Joseph had heard enough for now. Any more questions could be asked later.

He turned to Wematin, "Keep him here until I come back from John Lee's house tomorrow. We will decide what to do with him then."

Joseph left the old mill and began hiking to John's house.

At that moment, ten miles away in Farmington, John Lee was awaked by knocking at his door. When the knock came again, he rose and dressed before walking down the darkened staircase. The knock came again when he threw a log on the hall fireplace's embers. The fire came to life, casting light about the room. The knock came again just before he opened the door and peered into the darkness. Before him, was the heavily lined face of a short thin Indian woman. Behind her was a small cart and a sway back horse.

"My name is Sokanon," the woman said. "I am Pocumtuc. We

traveled far to see you."

John pushed the door open further. Standing next to the woman was a fat faced old Englishman. He looked familiar, but it was only after the fat faced man spoke that he recognized him.

"It has been a long time since I watched you dig through the pile of bags on the *Francis* John Lee," the fat faced man mused.

John stared into the fat faced man's eyes and answered, "Yes it has James Eastman."

"Are you going to invite us in?" Eastman said. "It's cold out here."

John motioned to Eastman and the woman to take seats near the fire. Eastman limped across the floor braced against the woman. They sat at the fire while John leaned his right arm against the fireplace mantle looking down at them.

"Why are you here?" John asked.

"I had to come," Eastman answered.

"What do you want?" John asked.

"I want you to help me save my soul," Eastman answered.

John studied Eastman's eyes carefully before turning and poking the fire. He then turned back to Eastman.

"How can I do that?" John asked.

"By hearing my story." Eastman answered.

"How will this save your soul?"

"Because of my dream."

John pulled up another chair and sat across the hearth from Eastman and the woman and said, "Then tell me your story."

Eastman looked at him with a weary smile and said, "I am sick, and death is staring me in the face. Still, I don't expect to die soon. I guess you could say I've been given time to try to make amends for what I've done."

"Alright," John said, his pulse racing.

"I must now pay for what I did during the years I spent with Richard Hawkes. Still, I would like the payment to end in this life and not continue into the next."

"Nothing is ever guaranteed," John said. "The truth is I've been looking for you."

"I know. A few months ago, word spread among the Pocumtucs that a young Tunxis man was asking about an Englishman living near their tribe. Then there was my dream."

"What dream?" John asked.

"I had it first in late December," Eastman said. "In the dream a young Tunxis man came to me. He told me I was dying, and my soul could only be saved if I confessed my sins to you. The dream came every night until Sokanon and I began our journey."

"What did this Indian look like?"

"He was as tall as you, but thinner. His eyes were soft and dark brown. I felt his love when he looked at me. I can't tell you more about how he looked because I couldn't look away from his eyes. They were like the little Indian boy's eyes at your school raising many years ago. What was the little boy's name?"

"Nesehegan."

"What became of him?" Eastman asked.

"He was killed at the Great Swamp Fight in December," John answered.

"That's why my dream didn't start until late December."

"What do you mean?"

"He's a spirit now and can go where he wants," Eastman said. "He wanted to see me."

"Go ahead," John said. "Tell me about the sins of you and Richard Hawkes."

Eastman told of the day he first met Hawkes, "He was the most powerful man I ever met, it was the day in Ipswich when we boarded the *Francis*. His black eyes were so deep it seemed I could swim in them. He told me he would become wealthy and powerful in New England and I knew he would. My heart swelled with pride when he asked me to join him in his quest, for I knew I would do things with him I could never do on my own."

"When Robert Rose asked him to run his lumber business, I knew I made the right decision," Eastman continued. "He always knew how far he could go before getting caught and he knew exactly how much timber he could steal from Rose without raising suspicion."

"Early on, you were his greatest worry," Eastman stated. "He was certain you would break your oath not to tell of his theft of the chalice. For the first few years he was so obsessed with this he tried to kill you."

"When was this?" John asked.

"One time was when you and your horse fell in the pit of stakes on the journey to Suckiaug. Eventually he said you would never break the oath because you were weak."

"What about the Pocumtuc named Megedaqik?" John interrupted. "Did he kill him?"

"He caused his death in a most vile way."

For the next hour Eastman told of Hawkes's illegal musket trade, Hawkes's efforts to control Reverend Stone, and the thrill Hawkes experienced from killing in battle and torturing others. All of this was news to John. News which both angered and increased the guilt he felt in giving his oath to Hawkes on the *Francis*. But when Eastman told him Hawkes courted Mary to get closer to Deacon Hart, from whom he was stealing grain, John's anger turned to rage, and he rose from his chair and stared down at the fire.

"Sit down John, sit down," Eastman said. "I've more to tell you."

Eastman told John of how Hawkes used the witchcraft trials to increase his power. John asked no questions for he'd concluded this already.

Eastman paused and took a deep breath, "You will want to kill me for what I am about to tell you." John closed his eyes. He reopened them and stared at Eastman.

"Sam Pierce's death was not an accident," Eastman said. "He was killed by Richard and I saw it happen."

John sat up in his chair, stared at Eastman, and asked, "How can it be? I saw the rock Sam fell on and the ladder he fell from. Why would he kill him?"

"I placed the ladder and the rock where they were to make Sam's death appear to be an accident," Eastman answered. "Richard struck him with the rock when Sam refused to give him his farm for the corn Sam owed him."

John remembered his warning to Sam about agreeing to Hawkes's ten percent service fee and how prideful and obstinate Sam could be. Eastman's story made sense. He stood up and stared down into Eastman's eyes, "Did you help kill Sam?"

"No."

"Did you help Hawkes kill anyone?"

"Yes."

"Who?"

"Edward Roach and I helped Richard burn down Daniel Hart's house."

"What?" John asked, jerking his head back.

"I helped Richard kill Daniel Hart and his family by burning down his house."

Heat poured through John's body. *Why that bastard*, he raged. *That damn bastard*. He wanted to slam his fist through something but knew he had to control himself. *Hawkes will pay for this but only if I have this fat man's testimony.* He sat back down in his chair and looked at Eastman.

"Why in God's name did you do it?" John asked. "Why would Hawks want to kill Daniel and his family?"

"Because he thought you and your wife were staying at Daniel's house while your roof was repaired. He believed you would be there that night and he could kill you and stop your investigation of him."

John turned away from Eastman and looked into the fire. Images of Daniel's burning house flashed through his head. The guilt he felt for binding himself to secrecy by his oath to Richard Hawkes was now overwhelming. It was as if he himself lit the fire killing Daniel, Judith and their children. Without a word, he stood up and walked past Eastman and Sokanon into the parlor where he sat at the table where he and Mary often talked. He looked at the chair she sat in during those moments. Immediately his emptiness was replaced by resolve. He would finish hearing Eastman's story. Then he would see Eastman testify so Richard Hawkes would be hanged. He stood up and walked back to the fireplace where Eastman waited.

"Go on," John said as he took his seat. "Who else did he kill?"

"Richard shot his chief miller Mark Scott in the head so he could blame the theft of Deacon Hart's grain on him. I watched him do it. His brain splashed against the door to the mill."

Who else did he kill?" John asked.

"Probably more, but no one I know of. After he dismissed me, I went into hiding. I knew he would send Edward Roach to kill me to keep me from telling of his crimes."

The two men had spoken for nearly two hours and it was almost midnight. John leaned forward across the hearth and looked into Eastman's eyes. Strangely, John felt sorry for him. He doubted Eastman had the heart of a killer, but in the law's eyes he was one. Maybe God would save him from the fires of hell if he testified against Hawkes. Of course, Puritan teaching said it didn't matter since God's decision was made long before Eastman was born. Perhaps his testimony would be evidence Eastman was given God's grace.

"You know you will be hanged for what you did?" John asked calmly.

"Probably, but there's a chance I might not if I testify against him. Even so, I can only be hanged once in this life. It's my punishment in the next life that worries me."

A sudden knock echoed through the hall as Eastman finished. It came again and again; louder each time.

Eastman's face turned ashen and he began to shake, "Edward Roach," he yelled in a shrill voice. "He found me."

John rose from his chair and walked to the door, "I don't think so James. Roach would not announce himself if he was about to kill you."

As soon as John opened the door, Joseph Henry burst into the house. He was breathing heavily, and his face was red from the cold night air. He stopped just inside the door before entering the hall to catch his breath. When his heavy breathing stopped Joseph looked at John with a broad smile and announced, "Peter Hawkes . . .."

Before Joseph could finish, John raised his hand. "Stop, I have company."

He motioned for Joseph to enter the hall. Eastman and Sokanon stared at Joseph as he and John entered the hall. He pointed at Eastman and announced, "Joseph Henry, meet James Eastman."

Joseph stiffened and stared at the fat faced man for a moment before saying, "Good evening."

"James has been telling me of his life with Richard Hawkes and will testify to Hawkes's crimes," John Lee said. "Right James?"

"Yes," Eastman said.

"Stay here James," John said. "I need to talk with my friend."

"Where would I go?" Eastman groaned.

John picked up a candle and led Joseph through the parlor into the kitchen. He placed the candle on the kitchen table and the two men sat down.

"Why the rush to see me?" John asked.

"I can't believe James Eastman is here," Joseph said.

"It was a shock when he appeared at my door."

"Is he really going to testify against Richard Hawkes?"

"I'll make sure he does."

"What will he say?"

"I'll tell you later," John answered. "Now, tell me why you are here."

"Peter Hawkes admitted he helped his brother, Paul, kill Nesehegan. Wematin and Sucki are holding him at the old mill."

"Will he testify?" John asked.

"I'll get him to," Joseph said.

"What a night," John said. "We now have a case worth presenting to Constable Hart. Go to his house and bring him here. I will stay with Eastman."

"Now? At this late hour?"

"Just tell him when he hears what we've to say, he'll be glad you woke him," John beamed.

As soon as Joseph was gone, John's smile evaporated. He returned to the hall and glared at Eastman.

"Stay here tonight," he said. "I will find a safe place for you tomorrow. You will stay there until you are placed in the Hartford jail. Remember this though, you are not my friend. Even now your motive is selfish. If I were God, after you are hanged, I would send you to hell."

"I understand," Eastman smiled. "Thank goodness you're not God."

Deacon Hart was wide awake when he arrived at John Lee's house with Joseph Henry. Joseph had already told Hart that Eastman was at the house and Hart rushed past John into the hall when he arrived.

"So, you came to us before we found you?" Hart said glaring down at Eastman.

"Yes Deacon, I have," Eastman sighed.

"So, tonight you told John about the crimes you committed with Richard Hawkes," Hart continued, taking the seat John sat in earlier. "Now you will tell me about these crimes."

For the next hour Eastman retold the story he told John about his early days with Richard Hawkes. During most of that time Hart stared at him from across the hearth. Later, when Eastman told of Hawkes's theft of his corn, Hart looked at John and said, "This is no surprise." The story of Sam Pierce's murder invoked only a simple "poor Sam" from Hart.

Eastman sat up and cleared his throat, "What I am about to tell you will be hard to hear. When you hear it remember Richard Hawkes ordered me to do what I did."

Hart frowned and stared at Eastman under his heavily lined brow, "Enough, just tell me what you did."

Eastman exhaled and looked at John who pursed his lips and nodded. Beads of sweat glowed on Eastman's upper lip in the firelight. He swept his hand across his forehead, removing the sweat gathering there as well.

"Alright," Eastman said. "I helped Richard Hawkes set fire to your son Daniel's house."

Hart peered at Eastman. Joseph leaned forward in his chair, his eyes bulging. Suddenly, like a cat, the old man sprang from his chair and drove Eastman onto his back. Before either John or Joseph could react, Hart gripped Eastman's throat with his hands pressing his thumbs into his Adam's Apple.

"Damn you to hell; damn you to hell," Hart yelled as he tried to squeeze the life out of Eastman.

John flung himself at Hart and grabbed him around his shoulders trying to pry him off Eastman. But Hart would not let go. Eastman's face was beet red and his eyes appeared about to pop from his head. Joseph raced around John and pushed up on Hart's chest with his shoulder while prying the old man's hands away from Eastman's throat. Finally, the two men wrestled Hart to the floor.

"Get out of here James. Go to the kitchen," John yelled at Eastman while he and Joseph pinned Hart to the floor.

Sokanon helped Eastman from the floor. The two of them limped through the parlor into the kitchen.

Gradually Hart ceased his effort to free himself and the three men sat together on the floor before the fire. Now exhausted, Hart exclaimed, "I could see that devil Hawkes as I squeezed the life out of that fat man. Both will hang."

"I will tell you the rest of James's story tomorrow," John said. "I think we should all go to sleep now. Tomorrow we will see the Deputy Governor about a trial for Richard Hawkes, James Eastman and Edward Roach. Joseph also has charges to press against Paul and Peter Hawkes for wounding him and killing Nesehegan on their father's orders. It will be a busy day."

Chapter 61

Deputy Governor Leete was in a dour mood. He touched his expansive forehead with his fingers and pulled them through his thin gray hair. The war hadn't gone well and now the Narragansetts were united with the Nipmucs and Wampanoags. Sitting in front of him in his study was Deacon Stephen Hart, a legendary founder of Connecticut and still a powerful presence at seventy-three years of age. Hart had just asked him and Major John Talcott, a senior member of the Court of Assistants, to bring one of the most wealthy and powerful men in Connecticut to trial for crimes of murder, illegal musket trading and theft. Leete couldn't wait for Governor Winthrop, the son of Massachusetts Bay's founder, to return from Boston where he and the other New England leaders were planning how to fight the war. Until Winthrop returned it was Leete's responsibility to govern Connecticut and he didn't like being told he must bring Richard Hawkes to trial.

"Your evidence is weak since it relies on one man's testimony," Leete said peering at Hart. "We must move cautiously. What happens if we stir up a hornet's nest only to see James Eastman recant?"

"He will not recant," John Lee said. "He believes that only by testifying will he confirm that he has received God's grace."

"But what of the war?" Leete asked. "Trying Richard Hawkes will distract us from fighting it. It will also create controversy. Remember, Richard Hawkes paid for most of the improvements to this meeting-house and to many other town buildings. He's also a hero to many who followed him during the witchcraft trials and is still remembered for his heroism at the Pequots' fort."

"He's no hero," John proclaimed. "All he did was kill women and children."

"You overreach, Mr. Lee," Leete said, his hands clenched into fists on the desk in front of him. "Many think he's a hero because he stood firm and fired his musket while others didn't."

John replied, "This trial won't be divisive. Joseph Henry fought in the Great Swamp Fight. He'll tell you what he learned from Richard Hawkes's son Peter. It will change your mind about the trial's impact."

Joseph, who was seated behind John, stood and faced Leete, "Sir, Peter Hawkes and his brother Paul served with our militia at the Great Swamp Fight. When our militia charged the Narragansetts' fort both brothers stayed behind to provide covering fire. During the battle, I was shot in the leg and my Tunxis friend Nesehegan was killed by a shot to the heart. Both shots were fired from behind us. Last night Peter Hawkes confessed he and his brother were ordered to fire on us by their father and his brother Paul fired the musket balls that struck us."

Leete sat back in his chair, then moved forward, leaning again on his desk and asked, "Why would he order his sons to kill you?"

John interrupted, "Because Joseph and Nesehegan were helping me investigate Richard Hawkes's crimes."

"What makes you think his son is telling the truth and, if he is, that he'll testify against both his brother and father?" Leete asked.

"Because he's afraid of them," Joseph said. "He knows they'll kill him if they learn what he told me."

Major Talcott, who had said nothing during the meeting, peered at Joseph and said, "Some men on our firing line accidentally fired into our men while they charged. It's just as likely one of these men wounded you and killed Nesehegan."

"That's right," Leete said. "What makes you sure you and the Tunxis were shot by Hawkes's sons?"

"Because I was there," Joseph answered. "Paul Hawkes glared at me throughout our march; Josiah Churchill, a Plymouth militiaman, saw them fire their flintlocks and heard Paul Hawkes use both my name and Nesehegan's; and, Peter Hawkes has confessed."

"Deputy Governor, you must bring this case to trial," John pleaded. "The testimony of two men support it and you need to let a jury hear it."

Deacon Hart watched quietly as the discussion among the other men took place. He could take it no longer. He rose from his chair and stared at Leete.

"Bring this case or I will see the people know you didn't, even though the evidence is strong," Hart said. "I'm still Farmington's constable."

Leete glared at Hart, "Don't threaten me sir. I will bring these charges, but only if you and John Lee agree to run the prosecution and bring the witnesses to court. I won't waste the Court of Assistants' time by asking them to do so. They'll only ask questions at the trial."

"We will prosecute the case," John proclaimed. "Where will the accused be kept before trial?"

"Richard Hawkes will remain free," Leete answered. "The other accused will stay in Hartford's jail."

"Two Tunxis warriors are guarding Peter Hawkes at the old mill," Joseph said. "We will move him to the jail."

"James Eastman and Hawkes's other assistant, Edward Roach, should also be held in the jail," John said. "Roach will be hard to find as he frequents the western woods."

"Alright," Leete answered. "Major Talcott, have the Hartford constable apprehend Roach, if possible, and keep him and these men in the jail."

"That's not enough," Deacon Hart said. "Richard Hawkes should also be put in the jail."

Hart's statement cast a pall over the room. John realized the enormity of what they were about to do. It was one thing to talk of bringing Richard Hawkes to trial, it was another to drag him from his house and family and throw him in jail.

Leete glared at Hart before announcing, "I won't order Richard Hawkes to be jailed. He's admired by too many who believe he has given much to Connecticut."

Hart raised his right hand and pointed his index finger at Leete, but before he could speak John grabbed Hart's hand and pulled it down.

"Deacon Hart and I will begin preparing for trial immediately," John said.

Hart frowned before sighing and sitting back in his chair.

For the next few minutes the men discussed the trial's logistics. It was agreed it would be held in the meetinghouse since only it could seat the large audience expected. Deputy Governor Leete would preside at the trial with the Court of Assistants' members serving with him to rule on legal issues. The trial would be held within two weeks of the Grand Jury's approval of the charges.

As they left the Deputy Governor's study, John looked at Deacon Hart and Joseph Henry, "It's begun." John announced. "I don't know how it will end, but one thing is certain: Richard Hawkes will fight us until he stops kicking at the end of a hangman's rope."

Chapter 62

Richard Hawkes stood in disbelief at the door of his house. How could Deputy Governor Leete, to whom he donated tons of corn to pay for improvements to the Governor's mansion and the meeting-house, have authorized such charges. After he glanced at the charges, he handed them back to Leete, who stood with Hartford's constable at the door.

Leete immediately handed the charges back to Hawkes and said, "Richard, this paper is for you. Keep it. You will need it to answer the charges."

Hawkes looked at Leete and smiled, "As you wish, but these charges will be dropped long before I face a jury."

"I hope so Richard," Leete said. "If the grand jury dismisses the charges the matter will end. But your son Peter and your former assistant, James Eastman, made serious allegations against you and it's possible your assistant, Edward Roach, who we have yet to find, will make similar allegations. Therefore, I've no other choice but to refer the charges to the grand jury."

Hawkes glared at Leete, who stood facing him awkwardly, shifting from foot to foot.

"Is your son Paul here?" Leete asked in a halting voice.

"Why do you ask?"

"I've ordered him to be held in jail before trial," Leete said. "His brother's allegations were too serious for me to resist the demand of Deacon Hart and John Lee that he be held there until the trial."

"That's preposterous," Hawkes said. "What are the charges?"

"Murder of a Tunxis Indian named Nesehegan and wounding of a Connecticut soldier named Joseph Henry. Will you bring him to me, or will the constable have to get him?"

Hawkes turned to his servant and ordered him to bring Paul to him.

Leete dropped his eyes and said, "Your other son Peter is already in jail. He faces the same charges as Paul."

Hawkes took a step back before speaking, "Have you gone mad? Since when does a Deputy Governor obey a constable and a teacher of Indians from Farmington?"

"I'm sorry Richard," Leete whispered.

"If there must be a trial, you can at least show me the courtesy of presiding over it."

"I've already decided to do that. I've also told Deacon Hart and John Lee they'll have to prepare the case and bring witnesses to court for the Assistants to examine."

Paul reached them while the two men were talking. He looked calmly at his father and asked, "What is this about?"

"Just a misunderstanding. It will be cleared up tomorrow. In the meantime, go with the Deputy Governor and don't answer any questions until I see you in the morning."

Hawkes stood at the door and watched the Deputy Governor, constable and a guard lead Paul to the small horse drawn cart they arrived in. The guard placed Paul in the cart. Hawkes watched the cart until it disappeared into the trees.

Hawkes felt a chill when he reentered the house. He decided to go upstairs to his study to read the charges. Before he moved, he saw Elizabeth walking down the stairs towards him.

"What's happening?" Elizabeth asked. "Why did they take Paul?"

"Just a misunderstanding. Go back to your work."

Elizabeth's eyes darted about the room and her hands trembled as she spoke, "How can you say that? Our son was taken to jail by the constable. People only go to jail if they're accused of a crime."

She dropped her head and began weeping.

"Shut up woman," Hawkes yelled. "If you really want to weep about something know this: both your sons are now in the Hartford jail."

Elizabeth dropped to the floor in a weeping heap. Hawkes strode past her and up the stairs to his study.

Hawkes sat at the table in his study with the charges lying before him. He knew he needed to examine them, but his rage was too great for that now. He'd not felt such rage since the day his father beat him for the last time. There was no apparent reason for the beating. There was never a reason before. The pattern was always the same. His father would come home drunk and angry while cursing his life as a mediocre carpenter who was usually out of work. At first, his father's rage would be directed against the well to do and the middling class who he claimed kept him down. But as his father's rage continued it would be directed at him.

He returned from work as a carpenter's apprentice late in the afternoon. He and his father lived in a single room above a bakery in the poorest part of Colchester. When he entered the room, his father was sitting on the room's only chair staring at the door. The smell of beer hit his nose like a hammer. He wanted to run but his legs were cast in place.

"What are you doing here so early you greasy egg shell?" his father slurred. "I expected you to be out with your filthy friends up to mischief until late tonight."

He said nothing. Experience taught him it would only make matters worse.

His father raised himself from his slumped position in the chair, leaned toward him and continued, "The haughty fat snipes forced me from my work on the house today. They said my carpentry was inferior and I smelled of beer. Well it's them that's inferior."

With that, his father threw the noggin of beer at him, spraying beer on his face as it flew by before crashing against the wall behind him. In an instant his father was upon him. The full weight of his father's massive body slammed him to the floor.

His father struck his face with his fist as he yelled, "You hideous knave! It's because of you my life has been miserable. You and your damn mother!"

The beating went on until his father's rage was quenched. Then his father stumbled from the room drunk and exhausted.

He knew his father would be at the Horse Head Tavern when night fell. It was only a few hundred yards away if one cut through an alley through a large block of buildings. His father took this alley going to and returning from the tavern. He always stayed at the tavern until just before midnight. Hawkes smiled as he remembered the power he felt when he decided he would end his father's beatings in the alley that night.

By eleven, he and the three thieves he'd stolen with for two years were outside the tavern. He'd cleaned his bloodied face as best as he could, but the wounds were too fresh and the cuts too deep to go out without bandages. He remembered the taste of blood sliding into his mouth mixed with the mist settling on his face while watching his father through the tavern's open door.

He stationed the thieves so his father would be trapped by the four of them in the alley. His father stumbled from the tavern just before midnight, almost tripping as he took the porch's last step onto the muddy road. He cursed under his breath as he shuffled towards the entrance to the alley.

It hadn't been easy for the four of them to take his father down. It was only after he and one of the thieves each buried a knife in his father's back that the big man fell. The three thieves were holding his father down when he approached him. Even then, his father might have saved himself. But when he knelt over his father bleeding in the dirt, his father smiled smugly and said, "Ah, Richard, I see you and your friends are having some fun tonight. Well, to hell with you!" His father spit in his face. He answered his father with a knife. Even now he could hear his father's curses as he drove it through his rib cage.

I will stand up to the abuse I face now just as I did to my father's, he promised himself. As his resolve grew, it became clear that this new challenge would be his greatest and, in the end, be his supreme triumph. He leaned back in his chair and began formulating a strategy to destroy his enemies.

He lifted the list of charges from the table and laughed to himself when he read the first charge. It alleged he fraudulently stole land from the Suckiaug and Pocumtuc Indians. *Who would testify to this,* he wondered. He sold most of the land years ago and the land records would not show that any transfers were fraudulent. It would be impossible to prove this charge without witnesses and he doubted any could be found to testify to events so long ago.

The same could be said for the second and third charges, alleging he illegally sold muskets to the Indians and murdered Megedaqik. Only James Eastman could testify to this alleged crime. Both Matunaaqd and Rowtag were dead and the only other witness to the sale of muskets and to the murder of Megedaqik was Edward Roach. Even if apprehended, Edward would never testify against him. With Nesehegan's death, the only possible witnesses to his flintlock trading with the Wampanoags and Pocumtucs were Edward, Aranck and Sowheag. None of them would testify against him.

He quickly glanced at the next three charges: the murder of Sam Pierce; the murder of Mark Scott; and, the murder of Daniel Hart and his family. So far, only James Eastman had agreed to testify to these charges. *So what,* he thought. *I will destroy him when he does.*

The last two charges: the murder of Nesehegan; and, the wounding of Joseph Henry, would present him with a more difficult task. Only his sons, Peter and Paul were involved, and Peter had apparently confessed. It would be almost impossible to discredit Peter's testimony. He would need to find a way to keep Peter from testifying.

Done with his analysis, Hawkes handed two sealed notes to a servant. One was addressed to James Langdon, the Boston lawyer who advised him on business matters, and the other to Edward Roach. He instructed his servant to see that the note to Langdon was sent by courier to Boston and that the note to Edward was placed in the tree where Edward normally picked up his messages. Edward's assistance would be needed now; Langdon's would be needed in three weeks when the grand jury met.

Chapter 63

The Grand Jury had met for two hours in the meetinghouse's up-stairs chamber and John was worried. Most of its time was spent reviewing the deeds which Joseph Henry said showed the transfer of thousands of acres of Indian land to Richard Hawkes. Joseph attempt-ed to show that the similarities between the grantor's handwriting and Richard Hawkes's handwriting were enough to establish the deeds were part of Hawkes's plan to fraudulently obtain the land. Even John was bored by the process, but there was no other option, for neither Joseph Henry, Wematin nor Sucki was able to find Indian witnesses to testify to the theft of the land. While he knew it would be hard to prove Hawkes stole the land without such witnesses, John had not an-ticipated how tedious a process reviewing the deeds would be.

John was present as part of the prosecution team which was seated on the chamber's right side in the first row of benches facing the grand jury. Deacon Hart and Hartford's constable sat to his right. John now regretted their decision to address the charges against Hawkes and the other defendants in the order in which they were listed. Thankfully, the Grand Jury was nearly finished reviewing the deeds Joseph presented.

Earlier that morning, Hawkes appeared before the Grand Jury and denied the facts set forth in the charges against him. His son Paul did the same while Peter said he and Paul fired at Nesehegan and Joseph on their father's orders.

After reviewing the deeds, the Grand Jury turned to the second charge: the illegal sale of muskets to Indians. John announced that two witnesses would testify to Hawkes's trading of muskets to the Wampanoags and Pocumtucs immediately before the current war's outbreak.

Joseph lead Wematin and Sucki to the front of the chamber. The two Tunxis testified for only a few minutes, during which they recounted how Hawkes brought wooden boxes containing flintlock muskets to each tribe. After Wematin and Sucki left the chamber John announced, "The next witness will testify about the remaining musket sales and all murder charges except the final one pertaining to the Tunxis Indian Nesehegan's death and the wounding of Joseph Henry."

"I will get the witness from the jail," the constable announced.

In a few minutes the constable and two guards returned with James Eastman. Eastman moved slowly, using a cane to pull his corpulent body down the aisle. His testimony took nearly an hour. Eastman testified as to each charge and how Hawkes built his fur trading empire.

When Eastman's testimony was through, the constable and guards returned him to the jail. After which, John announced, "Our last witnesses will testify regarding the Tunxis Indian Nesehegan's alleged murder and Joseph Henry's wounding. Constable, bring Peter Hawkes and Paul Hawkes to the chamber."

The constable was gone for only a few minutes when the chamber's silence was shattered by men yelling in the meetinghouse yard. John looked back at the chamber door. No one moved until they heard the clanging of metal striking metal. John knew at once what caused the clanging and raced to the door intent on swiftly getting to the meetinghouse yard. Joseph ran after him. When they reached the meetinghouse porch they strained to see into the dusk's darkness.

John charged blindly towards the sound. At first, he saw only darkness as he charged toward the unmistakable sound of a sword fight. Two men lay on the ground as he approached the sound. Within five more strides he saw they were the two guards who went with the constable to get Hawkes's sons. One guard rolled over on the ground screaming in agony, while the other lay motionless. Further ahead he heard swords clanging.

John was upon them in an instant. One man was the constable. He was bleeding from a slash across his forehead and defending himself as best he could through eyes blinded by blood. John couldn't see the other man's face as he was turned away from him while the two men circled each other; the constable looking for a way to escape and the other man for a way to kill.

The other man was a good four inches taller than the constable with much broader shoulders. John closed cautiously for he only carried a knife and the man was obviously a formidable swordsman.

In the distance, John heard Joseph yell, "Stop, stop, stop," just as two horsemen flew past him on his right along the path out of the meetinghouse yard.

When John turned back to the fight, the light from the meetinghouse fell on the man's face and for the first time John recognized the pock marked face of Edward Roach. He sprinted past the constable and rammed his shoulder into Roach's chest, driving him to the ground. He quickly drew his knife as he sat on Roach's prostrate body. But before he could use the knife Roach knocked it out of his hand and thrust his palm into John's neck pushing him off. Immediately, John plowed back into Roach and soon they were rolling on the ground.

Roach was a rock, not giving an inch when John pushed against him or tried to pull him down on his back by gripping his arms around his neck. Grappling would not work. John broke free from Roach and jumped to his feet. He saw Roach's sword lying where it fell when he first tackled him. He had two choices: to use it or to put it where Roach couldn't. He chose the latter and heaved the sword as far as he could into the darkness.

Roach was also on his feet and the two men circled each other, with only John holding a weapon — his knife. While Roach's advantage was strength, only John knew the trick that would end the fight.

He lunged at Roach with his knife, knowing Roach would try to grab his wrist and pull him down. When Roach did, John dropped the knife, grabbed Roach's wrist and pulled him to the ground on his stomach. As they fell, he swept the knife from the ground with his left hand and held it across Roach's neck as he lay on top of him.

"I'll slit your throat if you don't yield," John yelled.

Roach ignored him and tried to free himself. Before John could slit Roach's throat, Joseph knocked Roach unconscious by striking Roach's head with the flat edge of Roach's sword.

As John and Joseph sat on the ground looking at Roach's unconscious body, Joseph announced, "Peter and Paul have escaped. One guard is dead and the other mortally wounded."

John pointed into the darkness, "The constable is lying over there. His head has been slashed but he'll live."

"What do we do about this one?" Joseph asked, pointing to Roach.

"Tie him up and throw him in jail," John said. "The court will now have all three main defendants in its custody."

"But Peter and Paul Hawkes have escaped, and we have no witness for the murder of Nesehegan."

"We still have Josiah Churchill," John answered.

Chapter 64

John watched scores of people walking towards him across the yard as he stood on the meetinghouse porch. Their heavy boots crunched in the icy snow. Bundled in mulberry, brown, tan and dark green coats, their colors contrasted with the pure white snow.

The escape of Hawkes's sons was a severe blow to John's prosecution of Richard Hawkes for killing Nesehegan and wounding Joseph Henry. Deputy Governor Leete still ordered the trial to start as scheduled with Edward Roach added as a defendant, along with Hawkes and Eastman. The Grand Jury quickly approved charges against Roach arising from the alleged crimes he committed with Hawkes, while Leete reserved charges against Roach for killing the two guards and wounding the constable while freeing Hawkes's sons from jail for a separate trial later, if necessary.

The meetinghouse was half full when John entered. Directly beneath the pulpit sat a heavy maple table. Deputy Governor Leete sat at the table's center with the Court of Assistants, three on each side of him. Samuel Wyllys, an assistant from Hartford, was assigned the task of examining the witnesses. The jury was assigned two rows, each of six chairs, to the table's left. The witness chair faced the jury.

John looked above as he walked to his seat in the spectator section's first row and spotted Mary seated in the balcony's women's section. They exchanged nods as he continued down the aisle. Both Joseph Henry and Deacon Hart were waiting for John when he reached his seat.

"A beautiful day for a trial," Hart said. "Richard Hawkes has only a few more days of sunlight to enjoy. That's too bad. He deserves nothing but dank dark final days."

John nodded at Hart and turned to Joseph, "Are all witnesses ready?"

"Yes, but nervous."

John looked to his left across the meetinghouse's center aisle where the three defendants were seated. Hawkes was twenty feet from him in front of his wife Elizabeth, who was seated a row behind him. Hawkes was talking to James Langdon.

Alone, and in groups of two or three, several men stopped and gave Hawkes encouragement. A jailor guarded Edward Roach who was shackled and staring ahead impassively with a white linen bandage wrapped around his head. Sitting alone, four feet past Roach, staring straight ahead, was James Eastman.

Scores of people crowded through the meetinghouse's door, bunching up until they were through the door, then spreading to take their seats in the two sections of seats on the main floor or climbing the stairs to the balconies hanging along each side of the meetinghouse. John gave a tight-lipped smile to Lieutenant Bull who sat three rows behind him.

Richard Hawkes turned and looked about the room. *All of Hartford's great families are here*, he thought. *They're here because of me and when I defeat John Lee my reputation will be greater than ever.*

Hawkes took his seat just as Deputy Governor Leete and the six assistants walked down the aisle to their seats. Following them were the twelve jurors.

"Quiet. Quiet," Leete announced. "This court is called to order."

When the room was silent, Leete announced that the Grand Jury approved all charges accept those relating to the filing of fraudulent deeds. This was fine with John since the case's core was the murder charges.

After reading the charges, Leete turned to Samuel Wyllys and said, "You may call the first witness."

"Josiah Churchill, come forward to testify," Wyllys announced.

The spectators turned to the back of the room. A tall thin framed man in his early twenties wearing a buff coat and dark brown breeches walked down the aisle towards the witness chair. His blue eyes stared straight ahead as he strode down the aisle. After he was sworn in, Churchill sat in the witness chair with his back straight and his hands resting on his knees staring at the Deputy Governor until Leete announced that Wyllys could ask him questions.

Wyllys faced Churchill while brushing his gray hair off his forehead, "Sergeant Churchill, do you know any accused in this case?"

"Not personally sir," Churchill answered. "I did serve with Mr. Hawkes's two sons, Peter and Paul, at the Great Swamp Fight."

"You are here to testify about the alleged murder of a Tunxis Indian named Nesehegan and the attempted murder of Joseph Henry," Wyllys said. "Tell me what you saw related to these alleged crimes."

"I was waiting to attack the Narragansett fort with Plymouth's militia when we were ordered to fire into the fort to protect the militiamen from Massachusetts and Connecticut who attacked ahead of us," Churchill said. "The militiamen near me yelled and cheered as they shot the Narragansett warriors. Next to me were two men from the Connecticut militia who stayed behind to cover the attack. I knew them to be Peter and Paul Hawkes. They fired into the fort several times. Then Peter started loading for Paul, who did the firing. I saw Paul fire twice. After he fired the second time, they both cheered. I heard Paul say, "I will shoot Nesehegan and Joseph Henry." He also said, "father said to make it look like an accident." They both jumped and cheered when Paul said, 'I shot them both.' "

"What did you conclude from this?"

"I concluded they killed the men in the fort named Nesehegan and Joseph Henry." Churchill said. "I also concluded their father told them to do it and to make it look like an accident."

"No further questions Deputy Governor," Wyllys said.

Richard Hawkes stood and looked at Deputy Governor Leete,

"Mr. Langdon is here with me today because I thought I might have him examine the witnesses in my case. But I now realize I have done things for myself my whole life and don't need someone to defend me today. I can defend myself without anyone's help."

At first the spectators met Hawkes's words with silence; but it was a silence like a simmering volcano. Even John Lee could feel the power of the moment Hawkes created. Suddenly, a man cheered from the back of the room. He was soon joined by the cheers of scores of people on the meetinghouse floor and in the galleries above. John looked about the room as the cheering continued. He knew Hawkes was supported by many people in the town, particularly in its lower class, who despised the established order, but he never imagined so many would come to support him today. They cheered for several minutes, while John and the other spectators sat frozen in their seats.

Deputy Governor Leete let the cheering continue until it died its own death. When it did, he looked squarely at Hawkes and announced, "You may question the witness Richard."

Hawkes stood before the jurors before turning to the rows of spectators sitting on the meetinghouse's benches. Directly in front of him sat Josiah Churchill on a chair isolated from all other chairs in the room.

"You are a member of Plymouth's militia?" Hawkes asked calmly.

"Yes sir."

"I was also a militiaman when I was your age. I was trained to fight and drilled with others. Were you trained to fight?"

"Yes sir," Churchill answered.

"Were you trained to load a musket?"

"Yes sir.

"Were you trained to fire a musket?"

"Yes sir."

"Were you trained to identify your target before you fired your musket?" Hawkes asked.

"Yes sir."

"When you were trained to identify your target, were you told if you were uncertain you shouldn't fire until you were certain?"

"Yes sir."

"And were you told the reason you needed to be certain was so you would not kill one of your own men?"

"Yes sir."

"You didn't know the two men you claim to be my sons before the battle, did you?"

"No, I didn't know them before the battle, but I knew who they were."

"You didn't actually see anyone fall from the shots you claim these two men fired, did you?" Hawkes asked.

"No, I didn't."

"Now, remember your training. Isn't it true what you saw was not enough to establish with the certainty needed to shoot someone in battle, that Paul and Peter shot Nesehegan and Joseph Henry?"

Churchill dropped his eyes and remained silent for several seconds. Then he raised them and glared at Hawkes.

"I know what I believe," he said.

"So, you are not even certain they shot anyone, are you?"

"They cheered after firing and Paul said, 'I shot both of them.' " Churchill answered.

"That could be because he shot the enemy, couldn't it?"

"That's not what they said."

"But you didn't see Nesehegan or Joseph Henry fall from their shots, did you?" Hawkes asked.

"No. I didn't see them fall."

"Couldn't they have been accidently shot by someone else on the firing line? Hawkes pressed.

"It's possible I suppose." Churchill whispered.

"I have no further questions," Hawkes said before resuming his seat.

"The next witness is the Tunxis Indian Wematin," Wyllys announced.

The door to the meetinghouse slammed shut. With that, Wematin strode down the aisle towards the witness chair.

"I will tell the truth," Wematin answered when asked if he agreed to do so by the Deputy Governor.

"Are you Wematin of the Tunxis tribe camped near Farmington?" Wyllys asked.

"Yes."

"Richard Hawkes and Edward Roach are charged with selling flintlocks to the Wampanoags and Pocumtucs just before the current war started. Tell us what you know of this."

"I saw them do it," Wematin said matter-of-factly.

"How many times did you see them do it?" Wyllys asked.

"Two times."

"When was the first time?"

"I first saw them do it at Metacom's camp at Mount Hope in June last year."

"Is this Metacom the man also called King Phillip?" Wyllys asked.

"Yes. Some English call him that."

"Is he the same King Phillip fighting the English now?"

"Yes."

"Why were you there?"

"I was there with Nesehegan and Sucki of my tribe," Wematin said. "Nesehegan was going there to witness the sale of guns by a person many call the dark man. Nesehegan asked me and Sucki to go with him."

"What did you see?"

"Four men came with a large wagon carrying large wooden boxes. Two men were Nipmucs. The other two were English. One's hair was black; the other's face was scarred. The black-haired man opened a box and held a musket above his head."

"Are these Englishmen in the meetinghouse now?"

"Yes," Wematin answered. He pointed to Hawkes, "The black-haired Englishman is sitting there." He pointed at Roach, "The scar faced man is sitting there."

"Did you see these men sell flintlocks to the Wampanoags that day?"

"I didn't because we feared being discovered and left before the sale, but I did hear Richard Hawkes say he brought them muskets."

"When was the second time you saw these two men sell flintlocks to these tribes."

"It was in July last year at the Pocumtuc camp near the English town of Deerfield."

"What happened?"

"The same two men brought a wagon with a wooden box full of flintlocks to the camp."

"Did you see them sell flintlocks to the Pocumtucs?"

"No, but I heard the voice of Richard Hawkes say they had brought the Pocumtuc muskets."

"Why didn't you see the actual sale?"

"Because we were afraid of being discovered and left as soon as they arrived."

John Lee was satisfied with Wematin's testimony for it was the best he could do. He would have brought a man from the Pocumtucs to testify to the actual sale, but it was impossible now they were at war.

"You can ask questions now Richard," Deputy Governor Leete announced.

Hawkes rose from his seat, looked behind at the spectators and turned to Wematin with a confident smile.

"You are a member of the Tunxis tribe?" Hawkes asked.

"Yes."

"And so was Nesehegan?"

"Yes."

"And so is Sucki, who will testify next in this case?

"Yes."

"Both of them were your friends?"

"Yes."

Hawkes pointed to John Lee and asked, "John Lee is your friend?"

"Yes."

"And, Joseph Henry, seated next to John Lee, is also your friend?"

"Yes."

"You know John Lee and Joseph Henry, along with Deacon Stephen Hart, are behind the prosecution of this case?"

"Yes."

"You want them to win this case, don't you?"

Wematin hesitated briefly before saying, "I do, but it would also be a just result."

"Well, let's talk about your contribution to their efforts to win this case, which you say you support," Hawkes said while crossing his arms across his chest. "You never saw me before the events you described that occurred at Mount Hope, did you?"

"I never saw you before that."

"How far were you away from this dark-haired man at Mount Hope when you saw him?"

"About fifty feet"

"That would be about the distance from where I am to the meetinghouse door?" Hawkes asked.

Everyone in the room looked down the aisle at the meetinghouse door.

"Yes, about that distance."

"How long did you see this black-haired man from fifty feet away before you and your friends Nesehegan and Sucki fled from Mount Hope?"

"I can't say for sure?" Wematin answered.

"Was it less than the time it takes for you to shoot a deer with your musket?"

"No, it was more than that?"

"Not much more time though was it?

"Not much more time." Wematin answered.

"Was your view of this dark-haired man obstructed at any time during this period?

"Nesehegan was standing in front of me for a while."

"This made it more difficult for you to see the dark-haired man didn't it?"

"Sometimes, but I looked around Nesehegan."

"But this was not much more time than it takes you to shoot a deer, so there was even less time than that for you to observe this dark-haired man?"

"Probably less, yes."

"You never saw this dark-haired man actually sell muskets to the Wampanoag at Mount Hope, did you?"

"I heard him say he brought them muskets."

"That's not what I asked. Deputy Governor please tell this man he must answer the question I asked."

Deputy Governor Leete had been leaning forward. He shot up in his chair and announced, "The question was whether you saw the dark-haired man actually sell muskets to the Wampanoag at Mount Hope. Answer it."

"I didn't see him actually sell muskets."

John froze in his seat as Hawkes asked the same series of questions to Wematin about the sale of muskets to the Pocumtuc a month later. The answers were virtually the same. He tried not to reveal his concern and stared only at Wematin until Hawkes asked his final questions.

"Would you agree it has now been more than six months since you saw this dark-haired man at Mount Hope and at the Pocumtuc Village from more than fifty feet and for less time than it takes you to shoot a deer with your flintlock?"

"Yes."

"And your identification of me as this man is based solely on these short observations?"

"Yes."

"And you kept these images in your head for these six months and it is based on these long-held images you identified me as that man here today?"

"Yes."

"Have you ever seen someone from a distance who you thought to be a friend to only find them to be a stranger when you got closer?"

Wematin paused for several moments before he said, "Yes."

"I have no more questions Deputy Governor," Hawkes said.

John Lee winced when Samuel Wyllys announced, "The next witness is the Tunxis named Sucki."

Sucki's testimony was identical to Wematin's and like he did with Wematin, Hawkes poked holes in it during his cross-examination. When he was done with Sucki, Hawkes strode back to his seat with a satisfied smile. He and Langdon then whispered to each other, smiling frequently as they did.

Neither John Lee nor Joseph Henry ate supper during the court's afternoon break. It was obvious to both the case against Richard Hawkes would rise or fall on James Eastman's testimony.

"We know things about Richard Hawkes neither the jury nor the others in this room do," John said. "They'll not view what Eastman says the same way we will. While we believe what he says is true, many won't because they think Richard Hawkes is a good man. Before the jury can convict him, they must trust Eastman and distrust Hawkes."

The afternoon break ended with Samuel Wyllys's powerful voice, "The next witness is James Eastman."

Every eye in the meetinghouse watched as Eastman pulled his

obese body from his seat and limped twenty feet to the witness chair. His eyes were barely visible through the folds of loose skin hanging over them. His buttocks and thighs hung over the chair, making its seat appear to have been swallowed by his body.

"Tell us when you first met Richard Hawkes and Edward Roach?" Wyllys asked.

For the next fifteen minutes Eastman told of how he met both Hawkes and Roach on their trip from Ipswich to Boston in 1634; how they became friends; and, how Hawkes was always their leader because he was clever and knew how to say things in ways they didn't.

"How long did you work for Mr. Hawkes?" Wyllys asked.

"For more than thirty-two years."

"Why did you stop working for him?" Wyllys asked.

"He dismissed me."

"Why did he dismiss you?"

"He never told me." Eastman answered. "I guess he was unhappy with my work."

"Did Edward Roach keep working for Mr. Hawkes after you were dismissed?"

"As far as I know."

"You, Mr. Hawkes and Edward Roach are charged with selling muskets to the Indians, and of the murders of the Pocumtuc Megedaqik, as well as Sam Pierce and Mark Scott of Hartford, and Daniel Hart and his family of Farmington. I hold your confession in my hands. Let's go through it."

Eastman sat up as straight as he could and looked at Wyllys. The slits below his forehead, where his eyes were buried, opened slightly as he answered each question Wyllys pulled from his confession. He told of the web of Indians and Dutchmen Hawkes wove to support his fur trade that depended on trading the best muskets available to the Indians and how he and Edward Roach delivered those muskets for years; he told of how Hawkes blew off both of Megedaqik's kneecaps with musket balls and sliced his foot off with his sword before allowing Achak to slit his throat; he told of how Hawkes smashed Sam Pierce's head open with a rock because Sam would not give him his farm; he told of how Mark Scott's skull blew open when Hawkes shot him with a musket as he walked to the old mill's door; and, he told of how the three of them set Daniel Hart's home ablaze and the sound of his children's screaming as they left.

John didn't watch Eastman testify. Instead, he focused on the jurors. All but three of them knew Richard Hawkes. Four of them were members of Hawkes's church. None of them knew Eastman. They all were slouched in their chairs when Eastman's testimony started. The three jurors who didn't know Hawkes leaned forward slightly when Eastman told of Megedaqik's murder. The nine others remained slouched. Two more jurors leaned forward when Eastman told of Sam Pierce's killing. The remaining seven jurors remained slouched. By the time Eastman finished telling of the burning of Daniel Hart's home all but the three jurors from Hawkes's church were leaning forward.

When the hour was finished, John knew most jurors considered Eastman's testimony might be true. He had no idea whether it was enough to create the trust in Eastman and distrust in Hawkes needed for them to convict Hawkes.

As soon as Wyllys sat down, the Deputy Governor announced, "You may question the witness Richard."

Hawkes glared at Eastman as he rose from his seat. He continued to stare at Eastman without speaking until he was standing before the jurors facing Eastman. Then, in a voice loud enough to be heard in the meetinghouse's farthest corner, he asked, "So, you worked for me for over thirty years?"

"I did."

"And during those thirty years, you claim I did all the vile things you described?"

"Yes"

"And yet, in spite of all the vile things you said I did, you never quit working for me?"

"I didn't."

"In fact, didn't you keep working with me right up until the day I dismissed you?"

"Yes," Eastman said, his eyes lowered.

All twelve jurors were now leaning forward in their seats with their eyes shifting from Hawkes to Eastman and back again as the questions came in rapid succession.

"You were surprised when I dismissed you, weren't you?" Hawkes asked.

"Yes."

"You never found another job?"

"No, but I never looked for one either."

"In fact, your job with me was the only job you ever held in New England?"

"Yes."

"Was it difficult for you to live without the income you received from me?"

"Sometimes."

"Is it true you've been living with the Pocumtucs for the past seven years?"

"Yes."

Hawkes pointed to Sokanon, who was sitting in the gallery's highest row and asked, "Is it true the Pocumtuc woman I am pointing to is your companion?"

"She is."

"You didn't marry her in a Christian church?"

"No."

"The Pocumtucs attacked the settlers at Deerfield when you lived with them didn't they?"

"Probably, but I don't know for sure."

"You knew the Pocumtucs were going to fight against the English with King Phillip before it happened, didn't you?"

Eastman dropped his eyes again. He said nothing. Several jurors who knew Hawkes were again slouched back in their seats, two of them with their arms crossed before them. The remaining jurors leaned forward with their eyes fastened on Eastman.

Eastman answered in a halting voice, "There was talk among the Pocumtucs along those lines."

"So, you did know about it?" Hawkes asked, his arms folded across his chest.

"Well … I think I may have."

Deputy Governor Leete moved forward in his seat and glared at James, "Did you or did you not know the Pocumtucs were going to join King Phillip?" Leete asked.

"Yes, I knew this," Eastman grimaced.

"You never told the English the Pocumtucs were going to attack, did you?" Hawkes asked.

"No," Eastman whispered after a long pause.

Now even two of the jurors who didn't know Hawkes were slouched back in their chairs with their arms crossed.

Hawkes glared at Eastman again. This time his coal black eyes were blazing, "You disgust me. Don't you feel any guilt for the lives lost when the Pocumtucs attacked Deerfield?"

"There was nothing I could do."

"But you didn't even try to warn the people of Deerfield or Connecticut, did you?"

Eastman lowered his head without answering, but everyone in the room knew the answer and Hawkes decided to move to the next question. "I am told you are dying. Is it true?"

"Yes. They tell me my lungs are diseased."

"When did you learn this?"

"About six months ago."

"Did you tell anyone in authority the stories about me you told today before you learned you were dying?"

"No, I didn't."

"So, the first time you told these stories was when you told them to John Lee seated over there?" Hawkes asked while pointing at John.

"Yes."

"Did you tell him you were dying?"

"I did."

"So, whether you hang or not you expect to die within a few months?"

"That's what I've been told."

"You claim I participated in the killing of a Pocumtuc named Megedaqik almost forty years ago and yet right up until today the Pocumtucs haven't sought vengeance for this alleged murder, have they?"

"As far as I know they haven't."

"You claim I murdered my miller Mark Scott," Hawkes continued. "Isn't it a fact you gave a sworn statement to then Constable John Lee that Scott confessed to stealing corn from Deacon Hart and he was trying to escape when I shot him with a musket?"

"I did tell him that."

"You said I killed Sam Pierce with a rock. But Hartford's constable found he was killed when he fell from a ladder, didn't he?"

"He did, but only because you made me make it look like an accident."

"So you say, but that's what the constable determined didn't he?

"Yes."

"And, of the tragic deaths of Daniel Hart and his family; isn't it common knowledge that their house was burned by Indians?"

"People believe this because you planned for it to look like Indians started the fire by having Edward and I wear moccasins."

"So you say."

Hawkes paused with his eyes fixed on Eastman. He walked up to Eastman's chair, leaned over, and glared down at him. Barely above a whisper he asked, "You know you will be hanged because of your confession?"

"Yes, probably."

"Would you rather not be hanged?"

"Of course," Eastman said. "I think it would be painful."

A few spectators laughed, while others shook their heads and smiled. All jurors but the two who didn't know Hawkes glared at Eastman.

"Would you like for this court to spare your life as a reward for testifying against me?"

"I doubt the court will, but, yes, I would like for that to happen."

Hawkes turned back to the Deputy Governor and announced, "I have no more questions of this man."

"John Lee has given me no more witnesses but has handed me some questions for the witness," Samuel Wyllys said.

"Did you confess only to save your life or was there another reason as well," Wyllys asked.

"As I told John Lee, I confessed to give me a chance to save my soul."

"Do you think your soul will be saved because you confessed?" Wyllys asked.

"It might be if my confession is evidence God granted me His grace at birth."

"I have no more questions," Wyllys announced.

Half of the jurors were slouched back in their chairs. The other half were sitting upright looking at the floor before them. Joseph Henry was breathing unevenly next to John as he stared vacantly at Wyllys. Twenty feet to his left, Richard Hawkes tried unsuccessfully to repress a smile.

"Richard, do you have any witnesses?" Deputy Governor Leete asked.

"I have one witness." Hawkes answered.

"Who is it?"

"Myself," Hawkes said. "I will testify to remove any doubt about my guilt."

"Edward Roach, do you have witnesses?" Leete asked.

Roach stared ahead impassively without any sign he heard the question. Deputy Governor Leete asked him two more times before stating it was clear Roach had no intention of calling witnesses. Eastman announced he was not calling any witnesses either.

The Deputy Governor turned to Hawkes. "You may take a seat in the witness chair now Richard."

Hawkes walked briskly to the chair and quickly said "I do," when asked by the Deputy Governor if he swore to tell the truth. He held his hands together as if he were about to give a sermon and turned to the jury.

"You are all my friends, even those of you who don't know me," he began. "You are my friends because we share a common dream. A dream to make a world of God in a place free from the depraved world we left. I have struggled with you to make our new world pure and to strengthen our church. The last thing I would ever do is taint what I've worked so hard for."

Hawkes pointed at John Lee.

"John Lee brought this case against me for reasons I don't know. He has called a Plymouth militiaman and two Tunxis Indians, witnesses who drew faulty conclusions in situations where they had far too little information or vantage point to draw them. This would be bad enough, but he also brought forward James Eastman, a man who has disowned all of us and chosen to live with the heathens from whom we've captured this new world for God."

"I am innocent of the crimes I've been charged with by John Lee. I did none of the things James Eastman alleges. While well intended, Josiah Churchill and the Tunxis, Wematin and Sucki, simply drew conclusions far beyond what they should have under the circumstances. The conclusion I traded muskets to the Wampanoags and the Pocumtucs made by the two Tunxis warriors was wrong because I did no such thing. The conclusion made by Josiah Churchill that I ordered my sons to kill the Tunxis Nesehegan and Joseph Henry is outlandish. I never did that, nor would I ever do that."

Hawkes pointed to John Lee and said, "I've no doubt John Lee convinced these men to say what they did."

"James Eastman is another story. He's a traitor to his people who has decided to get back at me for dismissing him from his position by telling lies, and he is a man who never voluntarily left my employment, despite the things he says I did. In fact, his staying with me is further evidence I didn't commit the crimes he accuses me of. Even now he holds out hope, that because of his testimony against me, he might avoid the hangman's noose. What a pitiful man he is."

"I didn't commit the crimes James Eastman accuses me of. Ironically, James Eastman is also not guilty of these same crimes. What James Eastman is guilty of is inventing these crimes in his head and accusing me of committing them. He has smeared my reputation. A reputation I've earned over many years of service to our town and its people. You my friends of the jury can help me restore my reputation. I ask you to do so today."

John Lee looked about the meetinghouse when Hawkes finished speaking. Each spectator watched Hawkes as he walked back to his seat. Some with their lips parted; some with newly moist eyes; and others breathing slowly as if in a trance. The jurors were now all leaning forward. Their heads turned as one as they followed Hawkes until he sat in his chair. John wanted to scream the truth to the people but knew it would do no good.

After a few moments Deputy Governor Leete broke the spell, "Mr. Wyllys, I assume you have no questions for Mr. Hawkes."

"I have no questions." Wyllys responded.

John knew Wyllys' decision was correct. Cross examining Hawkes would only give him another chance to tell his lies and bolster the conviction of most in the meetinghouse he was innocent.

"Richard, unless you changed your mind and want to call another witness, I will ask the jury to deliberate." Leete announced.

Hawkes felt triumphant: admiring looks came from those around him; James Eastman was sitting to Hawkes's left with his head bowed; James Langdon whispered to him, "You have won;" and, twenty feet to his right, John Lee stared at the floor. Hawkes didn't want the feeling of triumph to end, but his pulse was slowing, and he knew the feeling would end soon. Suddenly, Langdon brought him out of his euphoria, "The Deputy Governor asked if you want to call another witness."

Hawkes stood up. He was about to say he had no more witnesses, when inexplicably a plan came to him. The plan was fully formed, clear and inspired. If he carried it out, his triumph would be even greater. His pulse quickened again and the excitement of this vision of ultimate triumph drove him forward. He thrust his chest out and looked around the meetinghouse before looking at the Deputy Governor, "I've one more witness."

"Who is that?" the Deputy Governor asked.

"I call John Lee of Farmington."

There was a gasp from the spectators. Langdon grabbed Hawke's arm. Hawkes looked down at Langdon. Langdon whispered, "No, don't do this. You have won. You have won."

Hawkes smiled at Langdon and whispered, "Don't worry. I know what I am doing."

Within minutes John was in the witness chair. He stared into Hawkes's coal black eyes. Hawkes stared back at him with a confident smile. The meetinghouse was silent with every juror, spectator, and Court member watching the two men. To the two men it didn't matter what the spectators or jurors were doing, for in that moment the only thing John Lee and Richard Hawkes saw was each other.

"I have only a few questions," Hawkes said. "You brought this case against me, didn't you?"

"Yes, Deacon Stephen Hart and I did," John said matter-of-factly.

"Do you remember when we both came to New England on the same ship?"

"Yes, I do. The ship was the *Francis.* It was over forty years ago."

"You were a ward of William Westwood, weren't you?"

John smiled as he remembered his early days with William, "I was. I was, indeed."

"During this trial my good character has been slandered by many. I would like for you to help me reclaim it. Do you remember the beautiful silver and gold chalice William Westwood brought with him onto the *Francis*?"

"I do."

"He was bringing the chalice to Reverend Hooker's new church in Newe Towne, which we now call Cambridge, wasn't he?"

"Yes, he was."

Hawkes pointed to a small table resting beneath the pulpit near the larger table where the Deputy Governor and Assistants were sitting, "In fact, that chalice is the one I am pointing to sitting on the church's table, isn't it?"

"Yes, that's the chalice William Westwood was carrying."

Hawkes's heart was racing. For over forty years John Lee kept his oath of silence for he believed to break it would mean his eternal damnation. Now Hawkes would use that oath to force Lee to restore Hawkes's reputation and make his victory over him final.

"During the voyage did William Westwood claim the chalice was lost?" Hawkes asked, his hands trembling.

"He did."

"And did I find and return the chalice to William Westwood?"

John hesitated for a moment. *What is he up to*, he wondered.

"I can't say whether you found the chalice," John answered. "You did say you found it when you returned it to William."

I have him now, Hawkes thought. *I have him now.*

"So, when I was given the chance to steal this valuable chalice on the *Francis,* I didn't, but instead returned it to its rightful custodian?"

John slid back in his chair surprised by the question and the quandary it left him in. For the first time he understood Hawkes's plan. *He wants me to lie under oath for him because to do otherwise would violate the oath I swore on the Francis,* John thought. He stared at Hawkes as he thought about how best to answer the question. There seemed no way to avoid answering it. Hawkes was smiling broadly. Suddenly, John heard a voice in his head whisper "Gratian." The voice was soft, like a gentle caress. He knew it was Nesehegan's voice. *Of course,* John thought. *Where two choices are a sin, chose the lesser evil. The lesser evil here is clear.*

John sat up, leaned forward in his chair and stared at Hawkes with a slight smile and answered, "It would be a lie if I said you didn't steal the chalice," John said. "I won't lie. You did steal the chalice."

At first Hawkes didn't understand what John said. Then it struck him like a thunderbolt. *The damn bastard has broken his oath,* Hawkes thought. *He has accused me of stealing the chalice.* Everything around Hawkes turned black except a tunnel of light leading to John Lee. The spectators, the jury, the Deputy Governor, the Assistants all disappeared. Before him sat the same impudent boy he jumped down on from his black stallion to beat with his fists in Newe Towne. Now the same impudent boy had destroyed his triumph. *Damn it, he'll not get away with this,* Hawkes raged as John Lee continued.

"You were nineteen and I thirteen when I saw you steal the chalice on the *Francis.*" John continued. "It was on the 'tween deck during the darkness of a storm and I was not certain of your theft until the next day when you confessed your crime to me and threatened to kill William Westwood's other ward, Grace Newell, unless I swore an oath to never tell anyone you stole the chalice. I agreed to swear to keep this secret if you agreed not to harm Grace and to return the chalice to William. You returned the chalice that day and became a hero when you lied that you found it. Since that day I've carried the burden of knowing I allowed a thief and liar to live among us undetected. Over the years I've learned you committed greater crimes and brought this case to see you are punished for them. Telling a lie today would be a greater evil than breaking my oath."

"You bastard, you bastard," Hawkes yelled, spit flying from his mouth. "You swore never to tell that I stole the chalice. How could you violate your oath to never tell this? God damn you, God damn you."

Then, Hawkes realized the enormity of his mistake for the tunnel between him and John Lee disappeared and all around him Connecticut's people were staring at him. He straightened his coat, brushed his breeches, and looked at the Deputy Governor.

"I . . . umm . . . have no more questions," Hawkes stammered while looking at the meetinghouse's floor.

"Then take your seat Mr. Hawkes," the Deputy Governor said sternly. "You are excused John. The jury will begin deliberations."

The twelve men gathered together briefly at the front of the meetinghouse below the pulpit. John watched them as they whispered among themselves. The jurors were back in their seats within thirty minutes.

"Have you reached a verdict?" Deputy Governor Leete asked.

"We have," the jury foreman answered.

"Announce your verdict."

The eyes of everyone were on the jury foreman as he stood up. "We find Richard Hawkes, James Eastman and Edward Roach guilty of the murders of the Pocumtuc Megedaqik, Sam Pierce, Mark Scott, and of Daniel Hart and his family. We also find Richard Hawkes guilty of ordering the murder of the Tunxis Indian Nesehegan and of the attempted murder of Joseph Henry. Finally, we find Richard Hawkes, James Eastman and Edward Roach guilty of selling muskets to the Indians of the western tribes for more than thirty years and we find Richard Hawkes and Edward Roach guilty of selling muskets to the Pocumtucs and Wampanoags during the past two years."

Within minutes, Deputy Governor Leete announced that for their crimes each of the three men was sentenced to be hanged.

John slumped into his seat but was quickly pulled to his feet by Joseph Henry who smiled and yelled, "You did it John, you did it."

John was too stunned to answer. Instead, he looked away from Joseph towards the Meetinghouse's aisle as three guards led Richard Hawkes, James Eastman and Edward Roach out of the meetinghouse to the city's jail. John glanced up into the women's section of the overhead gallery where Mary sat during the trial. She smiled and nodded at him. John knew this was no time to celebrate, for death, even one well earned, was always tragic. They would share their joy when they were home.

Chapter 65

John considered not going to the hangings, but he realized he owed it to those who were yet born to be able to tell the story of Richard Hawkes's death.

It was dawn when John reached the gallows. He looked above at its platform. Three nooses swung gently against a backdrop of heavy black clouds. The nooses were spaced evenly on a horizontal beam fifteen feet above the platform. This beam was attached to vertical beams at each end which rose from the ground and through the platform. Seventeen-foot ladders rested against the horizontal beam at each noose. A few people stood about in the cold, but none spoke. To most Puritans a hanging was a time for contemplation and taking stock of the condition of one's own relationship with God. It was not a time for celebration.

Fifty people were milling around the gallows within an hour. There were a few quiet conversations, but most people silently listened for the sound of the carts' wheels bringing the condemned men. Soon, John heard the creaking of the carts' wheels. He looked down the path leading to Hartford. Three carts were working their way up the hill along the path through the barren trees.

"It won't be long before the fires of hell are feasting on Richard Hawkes's soul," Deacon Hart growled.

John nodded while they both stared at the oncoming carts. In the lead cart, James Eastman sat slightly hunched over on his coffin holding his hands together between his knees. In the second cart, Richard Hawkes held his head high, looking as if he was surveying some newly purchased land. When his cart reached the crowd, he began looking into the eyes of the people lining the path. Each person dropped their eyes when his gaze fell on them. In the last cart, Edward Roach's eyes darted about like a caged animal looking for a place to flee.

When the carts were within the crowd, a hand gripped John's shoulder. He looked back into the heavily creased face of Lieutenant Bull. Bull leaned on the cane he now carried and proclaimed, "Fine job John. Fine job."

John nodded at Bull.

There were a few women in the crowd. Elizabeth Hawkes was not among them. Word spread she was leaving Hartford for Boston with Hawkes's wealth. John hoped she would find some measure of happiness there. He doubted she would mourn the loss of her husband, but she was likely worried about the fate of her two missing sons who were rumored to be hiding in Maine's forests.

The carts were even with John when he heard Joseph Henry's voice. "Did you think I would not come to Richard Hawkes's hanging?" Joseph said with a broad smile.

"You're late," John declared.

"No, I'm on time. When this is done you will have been freezing for nearly two hours while I will only have been for a few minutes."

Joseph looked at the carts' arrangement, "It looks like Richard Hawkes will get the position of honor in the middle when they're hanged."

The guards unloaded the condemned men one by one starting with Eastman. Eastman's face was vacant as a jailer led him up the platform's stairs. Richard Hawkes waived off the jailers assigned to him and strode straight up the stairs without their assistance. The normally stoic Edward Roach was anything but stoic when three jailers tried to take him down from his cart. He struggled until the jailers lifted him off his feet and carried him up the stairs. Hawkes turned back to the crowd below him just as the sun broke through the clouds. He sneered down at the people huddled before him and laughed. Gasps rose from the crowd as he began to speak, his coal black eyes flashing in the rising sun's rays.

"You are all fools. You are slaves to a god existing only in your minds. You believe this imaginary god may have already condemned you to a place which you call hell; a place that's also imaginary. So, each day of your lives you seek to achieve the impossible. You seek to discover if this imaginary god has selected you to go to an imaginary place you call heaven. But after all of your efforts you can never know whether you've been granted your god's grace."

The people around John were in a trance. Even Deputy Governor Leete stood transfixed.

"I will die today," Hawkes continued. "But I've done something none of you will ever do before I die. I have lived! I have done what I wanted to do without any imaginary restrictions on how I lived. I pity you and your smallness. But most of all I pity you for your fear. You are afraid of everything, especially death. I don't fear death for I know it is nothing more than the end of existence and in that there's no pain, no punishment, and no reward. I will feel pain today at the end of a rope, but that pain will end when I die. Your pain will go on."

"Someone stop him," Deacon Hart shouted.

Immediately, John bounded up the gallows stairs and pushed Hawkes into the arms of one of the guards while ordering, "Bind and gag him."

Now silenced, Hawkes could only watch John continue.

"You have done enough to harm these people," John yelled at Hawkes. "Your last words have been spoken and you can do no more harm."

John turned to the townspeople looking up at him and continued, "Soon Richard Hawkes will learn the truth and that truth is that what he said to you is a lie; a lie as vile as his crimes; a lie as vile as the life he lived; and, a lie as vile as the thoughts filling his mind even now. Forget what he said. It was said only to feed his ego and meaningless even to him. We have created a godly world in land given to us by God for that purpose. A world free of the evil of the old world. A world where we can teach our new neighbors of Christ's promise. We must keep it that way. Richard Hawkes and his ilk seek to tear at the love that binds us. Ignore them for they are sent by Satan.

John turned to the hangman and guards and ordered, "Now, do your duty."

John walked down the gallows' stairs as the guards forced Roach, Hawkes and Eastman up the ladders to the nooses, silently fixing them around their necks. Reverend Whiting moved in front of the three men and said a brief prayer.

Several people turned away as the three men were pushed from their ladders and the snap of their nooses broke the silence. Eastman's fall instantly broke his neck and his body hung motionless while Hawkes and Roach thrashed about as they slowly strangled. Hawkes died last.

"It is finished," John whispered to himself.

Chapter 66

Nesehegan smiled at John with his arms stretched down at his sides and his palms opened to him. Nesehegan didn't speak but simply continued looking at John with a beatific smile. John wanted to get up from bed and go to him, but he couldn't move. He was both frustrated and afraid because he'd never been unable to move before. He smiled back at Nesehegan before Nesehegan faded before his eyes. He was unable to move until Nesehegan completely disappeared.

The sun shined through the window of John's upstairs parlor when he opened his eyes. He couldn't remember the last time he slept until the sun was up. To him dawn had always been dark. He looked to his left and saw Mary lying next to him in their bed. Her hair was now touched with gray and her face had fine lines on her forehead and around her eyes and lips. Even so, she was more beautiful than ever. He continued staring at her as the sun's rays worked their way across her face, highlighting each line she'd earned.

Then John remembered seeing Nesehegan. At first, he thought it was a dream, but Nesehegan was so clear it felt as if he could touch him. He remembered how he struggled unsuccessfully to get up so he could do that. Even if it was only a dream, he was certain in the dream Nesehegan reached out to him to let him know his task was complete.

John rolled onto his back and stared at the dark stained beams above him supporting the ceiling that was replaced when he and Mary stayed with her brother Daniel's family. How senseless it was for Richard Hawkes to kill them. He thought about what Hawkes said the day of his hanging. He wondered if Hawkes might be right that only he'd lived and that everyone else hadn't. He thought of what a sad world this would be if it were true. Yet, he himself had trouble accepting some of the things his faith taught. Even now, he disagreed with the idea of the Covenant of Grace and from time to time he questioned whether God could hear his prayers.

Then the answer came. It didn't matter whether Hawkes was right. It didn't even matter what his neighbors believed. The only thing that mattered was what he wanted to believe in and what he wanted to believe in was the God Christ spoke of, who was the same God his father taught him of, and the same God Nesehegan showed him. True or not, he wanted to believe in a God of love and forgiveness, not retribution and arbitrariness.

As he played with these thoughts, it dawned on John that evidence of the God Christ spoke of lay in the loving people he'd known. He thought of his mother and father who led him to God and then to Reverend Hooker. He thought of William and Bridget who cared for him when care was needed. He thought of Thomas Bull who taught him how to be a warrior before he learned that he was not one. He thought of Sam who helped him in the early years and remained his friend until the end. He thought of Stephen Hart, whose rigidness overlay an unwavering faith which taught him to follow his convictions. He thought of Mary, who showed him the beauty in everyday things and the joy of life every time he looked into her eyes. He thought of Huritt and Chogan who had generously shared corn with him and the others in the early days. And, he thought of Nesehegan who gave him the answer to his conflict with Richard Hawkes.

As he lay thinking, out of the corner of his eye he saw movement near the parlor's fireplace. He turned and saw his young son Thomas.

"When are you getting up?" Thomas asked. "Martin is waiting for you to help him clear the trees at the edge of the woods that fell on our fields during last week's storm. Should he wait for you or start without you?"

John smiled at Thomas and pulled himself up from his bed.

"Wait for me," he said. "I am ready to get to work."

CPSIA information can be obtained
at www.ICGtesting.com
Printed in the USA
BVHW070731180121
598042BV00001B/26

9 781977 212856